Asleep in
a novel by Sonny Valentine

the Skies

...part of the Detective Theo & Doctor Valentico Series

with foreword by writer and creator Shaun Vain

ISBN: 978-1-953818-00-3
Library of Congress Control Number: 2020921588

Publisher's Cataloging-in-Publication Data

Vain, Shaun 1988–

Asleep in the Skies: a novel by Sonny Valentine/ Detective Theo & Doctor Valentico Series, created by Shaun Vain.

308 p.
ISBN 978-1-953818-00-3

1. Fiction—Detective and mystery stories. 2. Fiction—Novels. I. Vain, Shaun. II. Title.III. Series name.

PS3622.A.36 D.484 2020
810.54 ddc   LCCN: 2020921588

10 9 8 7 6 FPS e 4 3 2 1
10 18 24 23 22 21 20
First edition.

This book is a work of fiction. All characters, including its author, are a creation of S. Vain. Any similarities to persons living, dead, or imaginary are coincidental.

Detective Theo & Doctor Valentico Series logo designed by Mary Parrish.

THIS IS A FUTURE PUBLISHING HOUSE PUBLICATION
BALTIMORE, MARYLAND

Foreword
by Shaun Vain

I've studied character. Alongside the finest individuals, and I say walk around enough. The streets of any city you'll find people who are discipline in the study and deep understanding of some of the finest… subjects.

In all his finest moments, Sonny is the journalist that I want to read. Because the moment you think he's rambling or on a tangent, you're wrong, oh boy, are you wrong. Because something is lurking that will return one day, later in the story. Something so great will come back when you least expect it to.

He isn't just a true crime writer. He's a journalist and an semi-professional science writer at times. The book I present to you could aptly be titled *The Science Writer Studies People* and it is fitting for the time at which it is published because our world is equally in the midst of struggles, socially and environmentally.

The Procurements of Sonny Valentine is a testament to the time which we are living, a time in our planet's history where our story as a race of beings takes places. It's told today. In Sonny's story it started in the middle of the last century, a time when industry caught up with technology, and to imagine people saving themselves from their own devastation is a dream of any naturalist.

Asleep in the Skies is a continuation of one of Sonny's stories.

Until more words,

S. V

Prologue
by Sonny Valentine

In an attempt to show exactly what it is like for the Oriel Family during the events that lead up to the treacherous actions that were meant to divert the delivery of processes that were engineered to keep Earth prosperous . . .

We begin this case with a tale told by the oldest Oriel. It's a conversation which takes place within his lab prior to the abduction. Truly, the lab was filled with the most illustrious and discrete mechanisms for recording the human voice. In order to appreciate this case, the reader must understand the importance of the Oriel Family.

Why did Captain Larry Stegner feel compelled to break the sacraments of the institution he held dear by giving his orders for Theo & Valentico to monitor the family? Below is an excerpt from *The Procurements of Sonny Valentine: All Kinds of Stories*. The following is a recorded testament from Captain Stegner regarding his instructions:

I came in after briefing the press about what happened at the convention.

"You lied to them, right Stegner?" asked Theo.

"I told them what they needed to hear," I said.

"Which was a lie," said Theo.

"If anyone is after the old man at the convention, they should think he's dead," I said.

"Exactly," said Theo, "you lied to them. Good job, Captain."

"Where is he now?" asked Cynthia.

"He left on the balloon," I replied.

"That man needs some boundaries," said Cynthia.

"They went back home to Never York. They're the people who are going to fix this mess with the tides. I got to tell you both something, but it's not my jurisdiction."

"What?" asked Theo.

"My . . . I have no say in it . . . . But if we let something get in the way . . . . The Oriel Family are very important to the . . . our survival. They're restarting the tides."

"They're restarting the tides?" asked Theo.

"Yes," I said. "The tides have slowed down without much notice to most people, but something to do with the moon and its gravitational pull. I don't know the specifics just yet, but the old man has a strange crystal to fix it all."

"They're restarting the tides?" asked Cynthia.

"They're restarting the tides!" shouted Theo.

"Elixiumbrium!" I declared. "That's what it is, the crystal the old man has, I mean."

"I see," said Theo.

"Do whatever it takes, you two," I advised them. "Go to the ends of the Earth to make it so."

"You're serious!" shouted Cynthia in disbelief.

"Take what you want from here," I said. "The cameras are off for Theo and Valentico." I held out a key. I even handed it to Theo who put it in his wallet to be used when the time was right, when the world would need the husband and wife duo to spring into action.

x

Even though Theo & Valentico appear sparse and seldom in the opening chapters of the case, the reader should assume the detective and doctor had been well-informed by my reporting on the case to them (when I took over *The Crusader* for instance, I renamed it *The North American Crusader*). It should come as no surprise, since the couple have already publicly admitted to spying on the Oriel Family, as exhibited in Chapter One. Again, Stegner delicately pulls Theo and Valentico aside to talk to them privately about the Oriel family:

> While they are together they check in on where the Oriel Family is staying to make sure that the high profile family are safe in their rooms, but there is a police detail there.
>
> "Just the old man and his grandson," says Windhurst. "Everyone else had better things to do."
>
> "We've got it covered here," says Stegner. When Windhurst steps away, Stegner gets close to Cynthia and Theo. He says, "You too keep an eye out for Inspector Cary Oriel. He's coming to town later. Everything goes smoothly, the old man thinks he can restart the tides."
>
> "Do you think he's right?" asks Theo.
>
> "Does he seem in his right mind?" asks Cynthia.
>
> "Well," says Stegner. "He has some stories. He has his memories. And I'll be at the presentation to see, so we'll see."
>
> "I hope so," says Theo before he walks his wife to catch her train and return to her private office in the city.

Finally, it is my hope and purpose of being to show through investigative reporting that human nature does prevail. Invention and ingenuity are among other positive attributes for the reader to find, which are exhibited by the people in *Asleep in the Skies*. Understanding the Oriel Family will unlock the basic truths of what it means to be alive and well on this planet today.

Sincerely,

Your Sonny Valentine

Introduction

ON a transmission trained on a private line, the doctor and detective find monitoring the Oriel Family to be more difficult than they had planned. Cary Oriel is an inspector who spends much of his time in a public building with security, and the Oriel Estates has carefully equipped tactical surveillance counter measures.

Yet, here they are coming in clear as a ringing church bell, coming in clear on Theo's transmitter as Valentico takes notes:

It's a solemn afternoon going from their warehouse to the city and back to spend time with Adeline, so the old man, Oriel, decides to wake his grandson with a story he has been telling Henry Edwards, a story he claims to be true. He says:

"From one end of the Earth to the other, I have been around on hot air balloons and had close contact with political officials during my explorations as a form of community outreach.

1

But I would not have made it off the ground if not for the help of a few individuals—"

"Like the man who built the museum, and the guy who fixed the balloon's sail when it ripped last," asks Henry Edwards.

"No, Henry," replies Oriel. "They're very good in their own way, but I'm talking about some people you've never met before."

"Oh," says Henry Edwards.

"I'll tell you all about it," says Oriel, "and most of it is the truth. I swear."

"Oh," says Henry Edwards. "Sure."

"Don't listen to your father, kid," says Oriel. "I'm telling you true. I swear."

Henry Edwards nods, so Oriel continues where he left off: "There was my brother-in-law who was a true iconoclast; Chet started as a private detective, but he ended up trying everything he could to get away from carrying a badge. And for a valid reason… Do you want to hear the whole story?" The boy says nothing, but his eyes talk for him.

Oriel chuckles and says, "I mean to say, Henry, do you want to hear the gory details?" Henry Edwards nods and says, "Sure."

"Well, I suppose you're old enough now," says Oriel, "but the less your father knows I'm telling you . . . the better." He scratches the scruff on his chin and says, "We were at a bar together when he told me he wouldn't be working as a detective any longer . . ."

Chet was telling Oriel what it was he hated about working on the police force; he knew he could trust him, and he had a couple of drinks in him already, so he spared not a single detail. He told about the cover-ups…

Chet's voice rang through that bar like the roar of a cannon: "When you go into a place where you know damn well who's place it is, and when you find something that was once living but, isn't . . . any longer. I'm told to keep quiet." He couldn't hold onto the information on his own any longer. That's for certain.

"What did he see, grandpa?" asks Henry Edwards.

"Well," says Oriel, "hang tight. Let me just say that I didn't want to see him hurt himself, so I tried to come up with something for him to do. I was worried about the guy. He was like my family. I knew him since I was a boy, and seeing him like that was scary to see. His eyes were red from drinking and he was getting mad about it, like I couldn't keep up with, Henry.

"But I had a solution: I said, 'Go to the press with it . . . . I know a guy to talk to from my division.' I was in the Air Force still, and I made some reliable connections before Big-Brother and I parted ways—which reminds me," Oriel turns up the radio, and he switches it to a modern country channel.

"You never know who is listening," says Oriel. Henry Edwards laughs to which Oriel says, "What's so funny? I'm not kidding you. I'm connected, kid. One of my connections happened to be a top reporter that talked with my division about our efforts on a weekly basis. The reporter promised to deliver a news piece that glorified our pilots if we fed him some very confidential information. His name was Jackie Danzel, and he never let us down with his reports. I was certain Danzel would be interested in hearing what Chet had to say about police corruption. His ears will bleed when he hears what Chet has to say, I thought.

"When there's a story this juicy for the papers they'll come running to us, we thought, and we were right too. The receiver wasn't in the air for longer than it took for Jackie Danzel to hear the tone of my voice before he was convinced he had to move on it or risk having competition. We could have certainly had our own reports drummed up by any vulture that writes copy. We could have spread reports about corruption across the nation to anyone who wanted the story, and he knew we were capable of it too, so he leapt with joy into his red speedster and bolted to the Louisville Airport, where he lived, to get to us.

"The reporter showed up ready for the story. "We met with Danzel at a ballgame because . . . it was a loud place, Danzel figured."

He told Oriel the plan on the phone, "We'll go to a home game with a lot of pride, so they'll be making so much noise in the stands that nobody will be able to hear what you boys tell me—hell, I might not hear it either if the game's as good as I think it's going to be." At that time Danzel was well-known for his sports writing, especially baseball and hockey.

Not long into the meeting with Danzel, into the second and third inning of the game, Chet was telling Danzel the truth about his department and the cover-ups their fraternal order had committed. The entire thing was done with such haste. Oriel kept looking around, over his shoulder since they were sitting low on the bleachers, and he was sure that anyone in the row behind them could hear what Chet was telling the reporter.

"Chet talked about the bodies in the cellar of a well-known senator's estate," says Oriel.

"Wait," interjects Henry Edwards.

"Yes?" asks Oriel.

"What did you say?" asks Henry Edwards. "He saw bodies buried under ground? Like in a graveyard."

"No," says Oriel. "Chet claimed there were strange rooms, many of them locked from the outside, but some were filled with trinkets and clothing from the people that must have been buried away by the public official, who was on vacation when Chet's unit showed up to the estate to respond to an alarm. The loud honking must have prompted Chet to look into the cellar . . . ."

"Anyway, Chet got to telling Danzel about the part where he confronted the members of his own department about the department's involvement in the cover-up."

The agitated Oriel spins around on his barstool and gets to his cane. With knees bent, he spills coffee on his way to the album of black and white photographs. He removes one of two men working in overalls, Chet and Oriel as a young man. In the photo, they're busy putting together a strange machine of profound capabilities. They're on the deck of a steamship, out at sea.

"We went to meet the reporter, and, well, that's when we were approached by a man in a purple suit who was eating popcorn by the fistful . . ."

Kernels fell from the bag of popcorn the man in purple dumped out in front of their ground-level bench, and he wiped his oily hands on a napkin that hung from his coat pocket. He asked who was winning the baseball game, but neither Chet nor Oriel had been paying attention. Danzel, who had an empirical sense for the game, said, "Bottom of the Third, two bases, no outs, tie-game."

Oriel told him to keep an eye on the scoreboard and out of their business.

The man picked at his teeth with a toothpick. He heard them talking and was listening closely to hear what Chet was saying. He possessed impeccable hearing for such an effort of eaves-dropping. He made no efforts, however, in the concealment of his newly acquired knowledge for he asked Chet without hesitation, "Do you really feel like wasting time on that bag of dead meat?"

They were shocked, and Danzel stopped writing in his legal pad to listen to the man explain: "This senator isn't going to live much longer, and his policies have saved a few hundred lives, perhaps. And then there's the matter of how his administration stopped an international tragedy when he put the ban on nuclear testing in his district. Your timing is off, for a scandal like that will blow up in your face, son."

The inventor, as most learned to call him, swelled up with pride and released all hesitation. He looked Chet and Oriel directly in the eyes as he said, "Why not make something good for the World when you're working so hard to sell a story to bury someone?"

"It didn't take us too long into working with Mr. Hollindais to see just how impactful his inventions were," says Oriel, "but that he needed us to keep them safe and present them to world leaders . . . it became clear . . ."

"World leaders," says Henry Edwards, "like the president?"

Oriel thinks to himself before saying, "The president did send people. And other people from around the world . . . . But I'll tell you about them later . . . .

"On top of his warm invitation to be a part of his operations, Hollindais promised Jackie Danzel would have better stories for his paper publications along the way . . . . Jackie Danzel was writing on his pad of paper when I stood up on the foot rail of our bleacher seat over the funny looking man that came from out of nowhere to interject his own opinions into our discussions, a matter that could get any one of us put in a box underground if we weren't careful. My message was received clearly by our opinionated passerby when he turned away to watch the game over the fence.

"We couldn't keep talking freely after what just happened, so Chet came up to the fence and stood next to him. Leaning on the iron railing, he whispered, 'I don't know who you are or who you think you are, mister. And I don't know if you're working for the man or what—'

"The strange man with a French accent said, 'I'm not working for that scoundrel. I assure you, sir," Oriel says in his best imitation. He continues, "And Chet said, 'Well, the dead bodies piled up in the cellars—that's too much to live with—'

"Hollindais said, 'If you're living now—pfft—you won't be when you burst that great big bubble . . . . Trust me, sir, I've seen a few things that lead me to believe that biding your time and waiting for the right moment is preferred in place and instead of rushing in when the bases clear.'

"Just then, we watched one of the players get tagged out for trying to steal second base. It seemed like we were saved that day. Chet told everything to the reporter anyway, and Jackie Danzel agreed to work up a story, but he wouldn't pass his story along to any publications until Chet gave the word. The man who convinced Chet to slow down releasing that information changed our lives forever that day.

"When we worked with Mr. Hollandais, the work paid well, and it was always meaningful. We got along with the inventor, except he wanted to be called Monsieur Hollandais, and neither of us spoke a lick of French, so we ended up calling him Mr. Hollandays, and he kept on correcting us until we said it right."

"Mr. Hollandays," said Oriel with a clipped flat-top covering his head then from being in the Air Force. His head could have fallen off the top of his body; he looked like someone leaned a mop upside-down against a wet wall. He started working with Hollindais before he got a chance to build any real muscle in the service, and Hollindais helped keep him out of the cockpit of a fighter plane and safe on the ground. Although nothing in life comes that easy, since he needed Oriel to risk his neck for other causes.

"I suppose," Oriel reminisces, "it's fair to say when you're born you're meant for a certain amount of troubles. Don't you worry, Henry. You'll get yours too."

"I don't want to have any troubles in life," says Henry Edwards.

"Not real trouble, kid," says Oriel, as he nearly misses a turn to get off the highway. "I'm talking adventure. I ducked out of the Air Force early by faking an injury to take part in Mr. Hollandais' experiments. I learned that trouble had its way of tracking down its victim when it needed to feed. And, like a sharp-toothed bloodhound sinking its fangs into my soft skin, trouble would find me still."

Mr. Hollindais was the type of man that rarely said what was on his mind, even after he got to know people. The things he said were the same to everyone, no matter if he knew the person well or not, so he sometimes came off as eccentric or odd to new people. Complete strangers would often react with laughter or humiliation when he would spout the things he felt were appropriate. The man had no filter around strangers, no common decency, Oriel thought, and he went on thinking that until he got to know him. He started to realize that this might have been a diagnosable disease that went untreated throughout his lifetime.

Be it as it may, as a result of saying eccentric things to strangers, Mr. Hollindais was left to seem less interesting to the people around him that actually cared. The man hardly told a joke. Even anecdotes were hard to find when listening to him speak. His odd behaviors were more than enough to make up for his lack of storytelling. The people closest to him got few words from him but were witnesses to him working on *strange* tasks at hand.

Mr. Hollandais has focused on his assignments all the time. Yet, he would get off of the tasks at hand as readily as he possibly could when an opportunity presented itself. He called them 'field experiments' or research he was doing to understand a certain subject.

An example of his field research is the weeks he spent learning to build cabinets when the shop was already furnished with finely-made Dutch cabinetry, but he made claims that the field experiment was helping him conceptualize the prototype of his first rocket capsule, which was indeed a success. Oriel still has too many cabinets around his estate, so many that he loses his belongings often. For, having too many cabinets gives one too many places for things to get stowed away. One could suppose the number of times one leaves a car key, or an important document, in a mysterious cabinet far outweighs the neglect of leaving those things scattered around tables and counter spaces.

The inventor was fascinated by other things, too, that seemed to hardly relate to his business, like elastic bands, right angles, and mice. He thought the mouse was different, unlike anything else; the inventor did marvel over small helpless creatures. He felt their pains so much so that he decided to issue a forbiddance of the natural predator of the mouse: the owl.

In such learning pursuits, the inventor was close to discovering how the owls spoke to each other. Right away he developed a technique based on his observations of movements and inspired by some of Charles Darwin's work. The inventor discovered a method for communicating with the owl, but it was not yet effective. For he would make the sound on his own with his hands (and he developed mechanisms for this as well), and they worked on the owls in the field, but they had no effect on the barn owls that insisted on bothering the mice at the warehouse. Strangely enough, the owls in the field would flutter away sometimes or give a hoot, but the farmhouse owls acted differently.

"The procedures he developed for speaking to the owls were quite impressive, rather I was impressed when he first mentioned them to me," Oriel says. "I was sitting in my car listening to a talk from a professor about the war efforts being pointless and how we should waste less money on war. I knew full well this professor was funding experiments like ours. And the funny thing was we had no idea how close we were to proving his dream, but he, like the rest of academia, cursed us before he knew about us.

"Some people are so poisoned by what our family's legacy stands for," says Oriel, "that they refuse to believe that hiding our agency from the public is in the best interest of all living things."

As the inventor developed bird calls to speak to owls out in the field, he started testing them and became puzzled as to why they weren't working on the owls at the estate. He started looking closely at the owls. He noticed the splotches of white on the backs of their necks. He noticed the red in their eyes and their dull movements. He was sure these birds were wicked in some way.

He told Oriel, "I will pierce their eyes if they should come near us."

The owls stayed at bay, far from the ground. They remained perched, necks rotating, eyes piercing every inch of the world, every crevice. They were far from the property when Oriel saw the inventor on his own perch; Hollindais sat on a tree branch with his suit tails draped over it, and he held onto the trunk for safety from falling.

"Truthfully, to be fair—he wasn't more than eight feet off the ground," says Oriel to Henry, "but when I saw him get that high . . . . Well I have been up there myself. I would build tree houses and rope swings as a boy, not now, of course. I climbed a tree once to prove to a girl how brave I was, in fact. I was used to heights; the altitude makes my blood warmer than ever, I say. But the inventor was stuck to the nearest gravitational pull. I used to joke with him that he must have gotten lead stuck to his pants that melted into his legs and holds him down. He would say, 'I don't need to be up high. That's your job.' So seeing him up there, calling to owls in the middle of the woods, was rare."

Oriel felt safe leaving the unattended balloon with its basket anchored by rope, pin and rock on a small island off the coast, not more than 40 miles from where it was kept at the farmhouse. Without warning the balloon could pick up with the heat still collected underneath the vinyl, which is why Oriel made sure to use the right knot on strong, new rope, and he tied it off to a rock that looked like it would never leave the Earth as long as gravity remained constant. He shot off a firework—a bottle rocket— that would be seen along the coast, something he still deems unsafe to do in the air, because of the combustible fuels. He tried it once before that day and nearly blew up midair. So he moved away from the hot air balloon before holding out his empty root-beer bottle, a glass launching platform suitable for his tiny bottle rockets. He shot a pair of them. One at a time they exploded and rained down like shooting stars for anyone along the coast to wish upon.

He waited there. He thought of how the coast looked clearer than ever; it was once a bustling stretch of ocean when the ports were exporting furs and bringing out more shipments from logging companies. Oriel tried to remember the times when it was hard to see the ocean's edge with all the masts and billowing sails creating a premature horizon that shifted with the wind. The motorboats and large barges replaced the need for small commercial vessels. Instead, any given point along the coast was home to, at most, a dozen vessels on any given day. This meant the ocean and coast were becoming more remote, more peaceful, and more enjoyable to visit—

He sat perched on the tie-down rock with the hot air balloon still lifted but only hovering. It sank closer to the ground at a rate of about one inch per minute, until it no longer hovered. He looked out to the coast and listened for his sign. He knew he was close to where his brother-in-law, Chet, would anchor his steamer.

From behind a large brown stone of Earth and mineral rocks, emerged a shadowy figure dressed in dark colors. Even though Oriel was cautious when engaging in mysterious habits, this shadowy individual was spry enough to obscure their presence. The mica glistening from the rock created a harsh glare so that Oriel needed to put his aviator-style sunglasses on (the white and black stripes on the temple leading to the earpiece of the glasses crossed perpendicular to his gray hair and dark shadows created on his scalp). And to their great fortune, the shadowy figure had enough time to duck along the outline of the rock-ridden dirt and grass outline of the cliff; the figure managed to get out of the way before the balloon pilot neared the glaring rock formation.

Without delay, the return signal appeared. In moments Oriel loaded the basket with the deflated balloon. And he worried not about the balloon or basket being safe from thieves—what, with the coast hardly ever being traveled by anyone apart from sailors, and the tiny islands were far too high above the tide for even the most observant seamen to get a visual of the land above water. "What business do sailors have using a hot air balloon anyway?" he asked himself as he prepared for the dive to follow. He tossed a rope down and jumped flippers first without hesitation. He would kick while swimming on his back to take a final look at the island and found the rope twisted around the craterous island rock; it clung-on magnificently so, he thought.

As Oriel swam farther than the outermost jagged rocks of the island before reaching the sea—rocks that would have been his death if they were in way of his dive—the shadowy figure emerged to peer in the distance at the secret meeting.

While Oriel, the aviator, was swimming out to a secret meeting aboard the steam ship, the man who invented the ships to travel and pluck from space the rare crystals to aid the planet—The same man who falsely claimed to discover said crystal, called Elixiumbrium, (including the discovery of the magnetic field production qualities the crystal carries), Monsieur Hollindais was around a captive audience in the way that nature often does provide to people when they busy themselves with scientific discoveries.

Strangely, the inventor spoke to the animals in his shop. The mice in their little homes had all the convenience that life could offer a small furry rodent, including artificial sunlight, healthy foods, and entertainment. There was a crack in the farmhouse where actual sunlight came in through the wall, and sometimes the mice would huddle there to gain all the warmth they wished to acquire that day.

"Please," said the inventor, "will you let me be? No? You must. Take the bread from my beard," he said. He shook crumbs from his coat and beard left from a muffin he had earlier; the mice loved bran muffins more than he did and scurried quickly to take the crumbs and sit in the sunlight.

Meanwhile, Chet's steady hand moved the controls that placed the large shipping container down flat in front of the seated row of world leaders and representatives from the major countries around the globe—the slight movements and dexterity of his wrists and forearms moved the container, and the ropes slid appropriately to aid the container's journey. It sailed impressively, and gathered attentions of allied soldiers from around the world, who had nothing better to do than to watch the dance. And they wondered what on Earth was in the metal shipping crate, for what was large enough to contain a train car could hold anything. The group waited with quiet anticipation for the promised cure.

An old veteran, a Russian soldier working with the British said, "This had better be worthy of coming out to your boat, Captain Thirst." The British Royal representative of the Crown consoled his comrade, "I'm sure the captain will impress us much.

Captain Chet Thirst leaned away from the control board that operated the large crane on his ship. The steamer was large and flat in spots to allow helicopters to gather there. It was another one of the inventor's ideas, as to avoid attention.

The container stayed untouched until Captain Thirst circled it, unclipping the walls of the container from its sturdy metal floor. One steel bar lifted and slid free of being bolted to the floor, and after removing several similar pieces of steel with his crowbar, he returned to the control board.

efore the crate rose to the sky for its elaborate unveiling, which would take place before a court of world leaders, and solders, and some reporters too—Before the crate would meet its patient audience, Oriel scaled to the top of the thick-blue galvanized steel, marble plated containing facility that resembled a modest shipping crate except for an emblem printed across the container reading, "SKY VISION." Oriel stood on top, still in his wet suit and flippers.

Chet lifted the lever that brought the container up. He adjusted the tension of the wire from the crane that supported the crate by turning a knob on the control board. The wench brought the wire in and wound it upon metal spools, like it was a thick copper thread.

The storage container lifted to the sky, and Oriel lifted with it momentarily. He rose just over ten feet high before climbing down its side, where he dangled and dropped to the deck. He made it to the strange contraption that was revealed before the spectators left their chairs to form a circle around it.

"You're one for appearances," remarked Captain Thirst, "You coulda landed your balloon here, you know."

"By now you should know I'm much too cautious for that, Chet. Besides," said Oriel, "I like landing on the rocks."

"So long as you know," said Chet, "there's room aboard for you."

"I say, 'You can never be too cautious.' Which is exactly why we're here," said Oriel as he approached the spectators. He noticed they were dressed in their finest attires. He said, "The real credit goes not to us but to a man that none of you will ever know."

"Why's that?" asked the Spanish prince. "Don't you trust us?"

"Not a chance, Prince Ascubar," said Chet.

$$ \text{―}(.^{*})\text{―} $$

The Staten Island Life Center staff starts making their preparations as Henry Edwards and Oriel wait in the hallway to see Adeline.

"Where's Emily?" asks Henry Edwards, even though they are used to long waits for Emily, the youngest of the children, so much so that Henry Edwards has started questioning the relevance and truth behind the stories his grandfather tells him, but they are much more entertaining than the magazines in the waiting room. Still, Henry Edwards wishes to himself that they were true.

"Why did you have everyone out there on the water if the inventor was in a farmhouse?" asks Henry Edwards.

"Great question, kid," says Oriel. "I can tell you're listening. We were prepared to deal with the transport of this rare stone, but none of the crew or its guests could have anticipated the follies of strange misfortune that would befell us. When we took the container apart we were prepared to transport it to the man responsible for its discovery; I was the one who physically lifted it from outer space with the technology made by Monsieur Hollindais, who invented the space craft and decided where I would pilot it. When I landed in the Atlantic Ocean with the crystal intact, everyone around the world knew about it, which we had anticipated already."

"The plan, according to Hollindais," says Oriel to Henry, "was to get permission from the world leaders when they saw the solution we had to restart the tides.

"Hollindais was intelligent but strange in his behaviors," Oriel tells Henry Edwards, who has been watching out the window for his sister. "Like my young grandson, the inventor was constantly distracted by the world around him, and for a good reason at times because sometimes his curiosity would pay off in a way that I can only illustrate by example.

"On one day in particular he was drawn to the natural world like a curious field mouse in a lab coat, but unlike his scientific hero Darwin, Hollindais kept his lab coat on his body and never intended to get his hands dirty in his quest. Darwin was known to be obsessive in his research though, and scholars have made claims[1] that the prolific scientist had a form of agoraphobia that shaped the way he dealt with the natural world that he loved to explore.

"Hollandais was in the field searching for the creatures that made their nests on the building where he made most of his discoveries; the strange looking owls that nested above the warehouse doors had intrigued him. He wanted to understand what owls were doing in that part of the world, and how his barn owls compared to the wild owls he found became a topic of his disillusion. Hollandais stayed in the field while we were on the steamer, but not long, since soon enough he was able to locate them. He heard the owls hooting and calling in the treetops above, even so much so that he thought the owls were onto him discovering things about them, and he thought they knew he hoped to eradicate the owls at the farmhouse. He lowered himself to the ground on his haunches to adequately take in their sounds. And he stayed there, listening until he could listen no more."

The inventor made his way through the forest that day. Despite how strange it could have appeared, he was alone to crawl around and look for small creatures on the ground and in the lower tree limbs. He wasn't searching for a strange cure or anything of the sort. He wasn't dehydrated during a nature hike, either. He was conducting his research by trying to imagine and go about life as he figured an owl must, but he was unable to hunt at night and swoop around the grass for prey, of course. He thought for a moment what that would be like though . . . .

Hollindais put his head against the trunk of a tree. He felt the ridges of bark, grooves running from root to treetop, and he noticed the ants there carrying tiny white eggs. He marveled that the ants were providing food for some great cause in the same way that the mice were providing the nourishment for the owls that wouldn't quiet down.

Hollindais understood the system he saw and did not doubt

---

[1] Kaulb, C. *Andy Warhol Was a Hoarder: Inside the Minds of History's Great Personalities.* (2016) Washington, DC: National Geographic.

it, yet he felt the owls above the door of his workspace were different entirely.

With a special lens he would equip on his binoculars at night, he was once able to see how the barn owls he observed were skilled at navigating by the stars and catching prey at night. Hollindais watched the barn owls at night, and he was even able to communicate with them through bird calls that he developed. One bird call resembled the hooting sound the owls made, and the owls would return with hooting of their own.

Hollindais once recorded the wild barn owls making sounds. He played with their sounds using effects on machines he built in his office. In one instance, he used a screwdriver to place tension on the recording tape of the machine that took up most of his desk and required the strength of both Oriel and Chet to transport from the field to workspace and back. He used the flathead of the screwdriver to effect the sound and slow it down, down, way down . . . to which he added a low *murmuring* sound that masked the owl hoot. He tested these techniques and recorded observations in a notebook he kept in his lab coat.

His observations were:

> *Great Grey Owl*
> *Scientific name: Strix nebulosa*
> *- Wild owl respond to strange sounds superimposed on the*
> *familiar sounds.*

> *- More curious to me, I find, is how the owls are drawn to*
> *the sound machines.*
> *...One owl even started approaching the speaker and*
> *calling to it as if it were a member of its own*
> *familiar brood.*

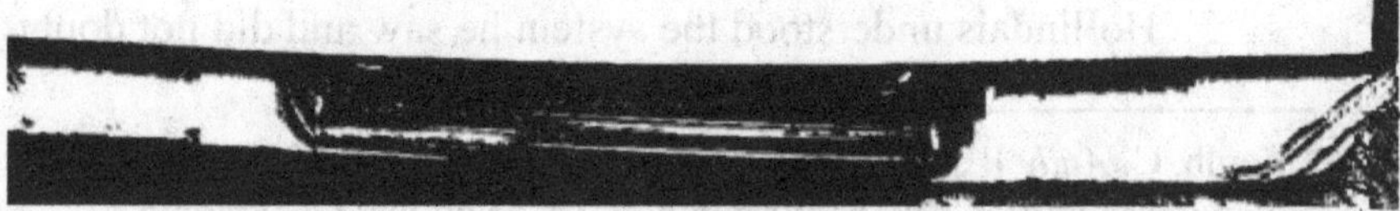

CAPTAIN CHET THIRST became a strange man in Oriel's eyes the moment he quit dating Oriel's sister and refused to divorce her, and yet, Chet still worked with Oriel, and they never had a chance to ever talk about Emily again. Oriel thought of Chet as no longer part of his family; he stopped seeing him that way. To be truthful, he never thought of him as a brother, even when he was devout in his relations with Oriel's sister. But he had been Oriel's friend for a long time, since the first grade when he helped Oriel out of a jam. And for that reason, Oriel was ready to talk to the crew if need be—or whichever dignitary even— if anyone thought the captain was too strange to follow his orders. He was ready to talk sense into them, which worked since Oriel already had their trust.

"Chet first helped me out of a jam," says Oriel, "when we were in first grade. I got caught making eyes at a girl who always got away with wearing dresses with flowers embroidered near the bottoms of' them, even though our private school had a strict uniform policy."

"In my school," says Henry Edwards, "they wouldn't let my friend Ralph graduate because he had too many uniform violations."

"Yep," says Oriel. "But what I was getting to, was the teachers . . . . Some teachers seem to live to uphold rules. The teachers at our school never punished this girl that I liked . . . but for me, all I needed to do was look at a teacher in a way they didn't like to get a slap on the wrist or afterschool detention. One time I remember playing hooky during the science fair, when I didn't feel like presenting in front of my class. They thought I went missing; the whole neighborhood was out calling my name. If I stayed missing any longer, we, Chet, the boys, and myself, would have gotten into serious trouble for having that fort built in the old radio station but we got away with our operations for some time thereafter."

Henry laughs and says, "You need a radio station . . ."

The radio station was how they first met Doctor Vanderfeld, a man whom they would only get to know quite briefly, but he would forever change the course of events with his wild inventions and discoveries—some for the betterment of human kind, and others for the detriment of a few individuals, particularly the inventor and the doctor's assistants . . .

At first—
          It was all pirate ship playfulness . . .
          . . . when they would put puppet shows on the air.
That escalated—
          To candy store sponsors . . .
          . . . that paid with sugar-pops.
In some time . . .

          As the boys become less playful and grew rather accustomed to getting on the air at the old station, they figured out how to use the equipment that was left behind.
          And as the boys matured out of their giggles and jokes, their material matured with them. They became known in minor circles of academia even, and eventually their town's city council voted to allocate the worn-out radio station for public use. This meant keeping it available for the boys to use. They rather enjoyed themselves for several months.
          They would call around to all the local lawyers and doctors to ruffle their wigs, but sometimes they would ask those bright questions that only a child's mind can come up with. Usually though, they called up retired professionals, plenty who were old and some who were senile, so plenty of the time they stayed on the air to talk with Oriel and his childhood friends.
          "We never got too rude with them," Oriel reminisces, "and we didn't really want to be malicious or cruel to anyone either. We just wanted them to take time to talk to us boys and some of them actually did take the time . . . ."
          There was Marvin Finley, the lawyer who put away one of

the most notorious bank robbers to ever step foot in their town; and they called the robber's attorney, but he failed to remember the case. They called a dentist who invented a new type of filling that all the kids were upset about, and berating him on the air certainly got some response from the class of children listening to the show.

They had to put their radio days to the side (and shut down the station for good) after one of the boys, Oriel's friend from around his neighborhood named Roger, proposed they call Doctor Vanderfeld. Unfortunately the doctor didn't appreciate the boys airing his professional guidance. However, to say that the doctor was too stuck-up to take time to talk to children wouldn't be accurate. In fact, he did take time to talk when they called his home that night, but he thought they were calling with the understanding that he was more than one of North Shore's most respected doctors—the physical therapist and sports medicine practitioner responsible for inventing a cure to get the town's football team off the benches and onto the field when a virus hit the water supply— didn't think they were calling him because he was a hero. He thought they knew his connection to their little private school class.

"We wanted to talk to him because we looked up to him," says Oriel to Henry, "like a legendary hero who hid from the newspapers that all sought to interview him. Not only were we excited about the opportunity, we had most of the boys in our school listening to our radio show that afternoon."

A nurse comes by to let Oriel and Henry Edwards know it'll be a little longer until the visiting room is open.

"Did the doctor tell you anything about waking people up from comas?" asks Henry Edwards.

"No," says Oriel, "I wish he had . . . . But he told us some other interesting information . . . . You understand?"

"I think so. And you just asked him whatever you wanted," says Henry Edwards with a passing twinge of disbelief.

"It was Roger who suggested we make the call, but during the interview it was Neil who suggested that we ask him if he was related to the girl in our class who had the same last name. We didn't do our research before the interview, and it never dawned on any of us just how close we already were to the town legend. During the interview Chet asked Doctor Vanderfeld if he was of any relation to Melissa . . . ."

"She was the girl with the flowers on her dresses," says Henry Edwards.

"Yes," says Oriel, "that was her. Indeed."

Suddenly it makes sense to Oriel why the teachers wouldn't tell her to go home and put on a different dress to match the rest of the girls in the school. Indeed, during the radio interview, the doctor said that Melissa was his only daughter, and Vanderfeld added, "I thought that's why you boys thought you could call me up like this."

What bothered the doctor wasn't that the boys were curious. Moreover, like plenty of his peers, Doctor Vanderfeld was pleased to speak to the children. He was happy to be educating young minds; however, if he had known the show was being broadcasted, he would have taken better care to only allude to his projects, especially a certain project involving a certain crystal.

The young boys had an audience of their own listening in, of course. Their class was excited to hear what they would do on their radio show each week, but another set of ears listened to the broadcast that day. The inventor listened to hear the show, which is why he would later intercept at that baseball game, before Chet could talk himself into an early grave by giving information to the press that could have placed him in imminent danger.

The inventor wouldn't be able to quietly sit on the information he found out. Because he, too, was searching for the same crystal that could fix the problems that the planet was experiencing with its tides, and Monsieur Hollindais decidedly became the one to find the crystal based off of the radio blabber of Doctor Vanderfeld.

The enthusiastic doctor was certainly upset to hear that his secrets were released over the air waves. He took it poorly to say the least . . .

Doctor Vanderfeld answered the call with a hint of agitation. He said, "Who is this nipping at my heels on the telephone?"

"We're in your town," said one of the boys. "Dr. Vanderfeld, we like what you did for our town when we needed help—Tell us what you plan to do next?"

"Strange," said Vanderfeld, "I don't remember setting up a meeting with the press. Who am I talking to?"

"This is . . . Oriel," said the timid young boy.

"Oh," responded Vanderfeld. He noticed the strange name from his daughter's class. "Well, let's see. I have a project that is a little off the books. If you don't mind sitting up tonight, kid, I'll tell you all about it . . . ."

Oriel smiled and Chet grinned. The rest of the boys jumped up and down in excitement.

On the other side of town, in his messy workshop where mice built their homes, the master of invention, Monsieur Hollindais, eagerly turned his radio up one notch higher. He was one of the fifteen listeners and the only adult apart from a farmer who wasn't in his right mind from being out in the heat all day. Those fifteen listeners were the first to hear Doctor Vanderfeld's plans to find a new alternative medicine that was buried deep within the planet's crust.

Hollindais listened to take notes on the doctor's exact predications of what the strange cure looked like and where to harvest the crystal, yet he didn't believe drilling for it would be the best course of action. He didn't agree with the sports-medicine doctor when he said, "The magnetically charged particles distributed deep within the Earth's crust were put there for the residents of Earth to redistribute as deemed necessary." Yet to the contrary, the inventor believed that doing such a deed, removing the particles from the Earth, would not only be difficult to accomplish but also have catastrophic results.

When Doctor Vanderfeld found out his plan was on the radio, he reacted harshly and abruptly removed his daughter from the school system. The family withdrew from society altogether. Nobody was sure what became of the sports-medicine doctor who was celebrated all throughout North Shore, and his daughter wasn't heard from again either . . . .

. . . . Until one day when the Earth's tides stopped their movements, when the moon stopped its rotation, and all life was feared to come to an end . . . .

Luckily, some off the world leaders brought this information to a particular inventor who had been working on a procedure to reverse the sudden stop of life giving forces. Monsieur Hollindais mounted a space mission to bring that intergalactic substance the doctor had spoke of back to Earth. Hollindais used the doctor's description to find the substance without so much digging. The goal was to restart the tides and rotation of the moon with extreme magnetism produced by the strange crystals.

The inventor couldn't do it on his own. By the time he was ready with plans for the ship and financial support, the boys were grown, so he asked for the help of the two young men that exposed the rare crystal on their childish radio show. It's for this reason that Hollindais cleverly timed his appearance at the baseball game with the reporter from Louisville.

"When the news eventually reached Dr. Vanderfeld," says Oriel to Henry Edwards, "that he was a part of our hooky radio broadcast, he was incredibly agitated and decided to buy the old radio station of ours to push it over with hired machines and workers in order to make room for a memorial park in his family's honor." The doctor fenced off the park and wouldn't allow anyone inside. "We felt responsible for the doctor spending a sizable fortune on the memorial, as it seemed to be a spiteful thing directed at us boys. Nobody heard much more about Doctor Vanderfeld until that tragic night that seemed to surprise us all."

"The girl with the flowered dress," says Henry Edwards. "What ever happened to her?"

"After we talked to her father on the radio," says Oriel, "it was late in the afternoon the following day that I worked up the courage to finally talk to Melissa for the first time outside of class. She was sitting in the cafeteria with a few more minutes left before the lunch bell. When I sat down next to her she offered me half of her peanut butter sandwich. What a plain, dry offering, I thought. But it was Melissa Vanderfeld offering the sandwich to me, so I gladly accepted it. We didn't talk much that day, partly because of how nervous we were, and partly because of how dry our mouths had become. But I knew she liked me."

Oriel gave that poor girl quite a shock when he asked to be her boyfriend through the means of writing a gushy letter composed of words clipped from a magazine and reassembled to read, "Will you be by girlfriend, Melissa?" It was too real for her to take; she didn't want to think about boyfriends and kissing.

She kept the candied hearts he gave her, but she declined his homemade card. He walked across the room that day to sit down alone with his torn heart in his hands. He placed it on his lap and quietly sat.

When his friends saw how badly he felt, two of them went to talk to Melissa on Oriel's behalf. Chet and Neil went over. Chet told her about the interview with her father and asked her a question about his line of work— one that a first grader could field an answer to.

Neil kept the conversation going while Chet snuck around to the other side of her desk. Chet took the candied hearts away from her. He said, "You don't deserve these," and he told Oriel, "Give these to someone who knows what's good for her."

"We never talked after that day—Melissa and I," Oriel says to Henry Edwards. "But that was how Chet Thirst first showed his true nature to me, and I'll never forget that. Part of me will always wish it would have worked out between him and my sister, Emily, but she wanted nothing to do with him after she . . . she transformed . . . . Their love on the downfall was fresh—it happened only a few months before the incident on the ship—a few months before that fateful day . . . ."

The blue crystal had been exposed to lunar charges that activated when compressed—the way that diamonds form from coal, but it turned blue when it held purely rotational properties that pressed the oceans astray to come back on their own when the crystal wasn't present, like a high pressure depressing forcefully. It erupted continuously, and like a healthy heart beating, it created ideal living conditions for all those close to the discharge.

Oriel's hammer went on to strike it, and bright blue sparks fluttered from the impact of steel on Elixiumbrium.

A natural misty steam coming from the shore masked what was happening aboard the steam boat. Unbeknownst to Oriel and his comrades aboard the steamer, the masked figure studied their situation. The masked figure could barely tell when Oriel was scaling the ship from how far away they were, but that individual would recognize the enormous container being hoisted away. It remained in the air, only swaying slightly and only perceptible to the masked observer.

Though the scope in their gloved hand wasn't able to get an image focused on the contents, the masked marauder noted the spectators being aroused and moving to get closer, which verified to the sly observer that the contents of the shipping container were just as they had expected.

"Mr. Oriel, please begin your demonstrations," motioned Chet.

He took a moment to prepare himself. It seemed necessary to get their attention from what had been unveiled and onto the goal at hand, which was to do something great and valuable for the planet that was suffering greatly ever since the tides slowed in the slightest degree. The tidal decrease wasn't noticeable to those outside of the scientific community. Government officials worked tirelessly with media correspondents to create misinformation and distract the public with other events.

"The moon landing, for instance," says Oriel to Henry, "was a stunt with the sole purpose of distracting the general public for their own protection. It was one of the covers we used, until we found a solution to the strange global predicament that gathered leaders from around the world that day . . . . In reality, going to the moon is as easy as jumping off a high building. It just takes courage and you'll—"

"Wait," interrupts Henry Edwards, "I don't believe you. You're saying the moon landing is fake. Then you tell me I should jump off a building?"

"Good," says Oriel. "That was just a test to see if you were listening . . . . Now, where was I?"

On a weekend afternoon, the Staten Island Life Center typically becomes busy. A few of the other visitors complained when they overheard Oriel's story, so the staff kindly asked the grandfather and grandson to wait outside until the rest of their party arrived, so they sat on a bench by the curb.

"You were saying," says Henry Edwards, "about the Elixiumbrium."

"Oh," says Oriel, "you're right. That cobalt blue crystal formation, no bigger than a car tire, was only a fraction of our discovery. The world leaders needed our guidance, mainly the inventor's guidance, and we needed their help keeping it safe along the way . . ."

In the soft glaze that covered the formation, one could see through it, and if one were to look hard enough, one could see a reflection of oneself. Oriel saw his reflection and the reflection of those behind him that gathered in its presence and were too astonished to speak to each other.

"What we have here, ladies and gentlemen," said Oriel at the top of his lungs, "is top-tier governments of the world uniting to keep themselves alive. Those who do not join us today will not know how far humanity has risen to keep itself alive. Because together we can control the rotation of a satellite larger than anything we thought was possible. Earth's natural satellite, the Moon, has a mass of about 73.5 quintillion metric tonnes. And one day soon we will have the ability to rotate the Moon. Or according to our plan—stop the rotation of the Moon."

There was applause to which Oriel said, "And one day we may have the ability to affect the rotation of the Sun—"

After his speech wrapped up a man in a white suit took Oriel's spot, and Oriel assumed he had a good reason to speak, so he went over to stand with Chet and listen.

The man in white said, "Ye finest water on Earth: it is our thought today, that all the water in our land has been developed for only our taste. If it were any other water . . . our taste would need be different. Thee Gods who bless'd these lands with their sweat and tears from heaven . . ."

"Great," said Chet. "They completely miss the point and made it religious."
The speaker continued, ". . . did not perspire in vain, Nay! These waters were given to us so that, we may worship in a way that pays homage to them, so that we may conquer land and do great things, so that we may be brothers and sisters to one-another—"

"Well," said Oriel, "we can always look at things differently— look at the bigger picture, Chet."
"What's the point of all that?" asked Chet.
"So that we may begin to wash away the evil that plagues man's heart," said the speaker to a receptive audience.
"Do great things," said Oriel. "Bless the lands—And they fund our billion dollar space adventure to get the crystal."

The responses of the world leaders came pouring out, like laundry from a clothes dryer, tumbling, bumbling, trying to stay fresh:
"Why, that's marvelous . . . ."
"Perfect," said the Russian.
"Extraordinary stuff," piped in another spectator.
"What exactly is it?" someone asked.

Meanwhile, on the rocky island where the balloon and basket rested, the masked figure made a signal to comrades of their own. It was time to begin the other phase of their operation.

"When you suddenly have the means to accomplish something that seems insurmountable on your own," Oriel says to his grandson, "the people who think they are in charge will sometimes have questions they ask to seem important. But remember this, if they're important enough, you will find a way to explain just about anything to stay in their good graces.
"We didn't need to assemble the world leaders. We could have carried on without them. In fact, it was my instinct to not

bring them in because politics can be as difficult to navigate as the environmental problems we were trying to reverse."

"The politicians that were on board the steamer were interested in our mission from the beginning. Either me or Chet only had to whisper in an assistant's ear about the problem and our extreme solution before speaking directly to each leader. It was the inventor's idea to pull the politicians along, for he wanted the security level he hoped they would bring with them. But nobody was prepared for what would happen when we opened that shipping container."

However much Hollindais argued to bring the politicians along, he refused to be involved in the correspondence or the presentation. The inventor was only there for the discoveries, the acquisitions, and the applications; he was a genius in that way, Oriel thought. He left Chet and Oriel to fend for the secret meetings being set up and presented with discretion. He felt that Oriel had a corporate influence already, a notion he presented when he interrupted their meeting with Danzel. In the inventor's words, "You have the media on a string already." He must have felt that Chet had enough connections too, with his extensive military and civil service positions. Yet, in actuality the inventor provided little contribution to the actually securing of the rare crystal.

"There was a major break in the water . . . right before our eyes," says Oriel, as Emily gets out of the car and begins rushing over to join her brother and grandfather. "The ocean ripped apart with the force of a windstorm coming from below. Luckily, our ship didn't take on much water, due to its commanding size. Yet, we were stunned to find the precious cargo we had unveiled was then lifted from us by way of a strange being I had never seen before. It was miraculous, since it moved quick and seemed to have no end but its source being the ocean."

Emily sits on Oriel's lap, and she says, "Why are you sitting out here?"

Henry Edwards urges her to keep quiet, and let Oriel finish.

"It came from the oceans," says Oriel. "A long tentacle reached above the ship's deck and splashed water upon myself and the rest of our crew, and a few of the political officials also became covered in the slimy, brown muck that fell on everything in the creature's way; it seemed to be the way the creature chose to defend itself, by secreting a substance from its suction-cup appendages."

"Ew," says Emily.

"Then, it wrapped itself around the strange blue crystal, and it took it back with it . . . into the ocean . . . ."

Meanwhile, at Staten Island's police precinct, Jerry is giving a speech, telling the precinct, including Sergeant Bruno Peters, "The place is always filled with cops and the most gorgeous people who want free drinks." About that Peters cannot stay quiet, so he speaks out: "You disgrace the badge," Peters says, and the affable Jerry doesn't get offended. "Would you like free appetizers too?" Jerry asks. Jerry wins over the crowd, people smile and laugh, something Peters cannot believe, so he leaves the precinct.

Bruno passes his sister, Joslin, outside near the municipal court building. She's going there to file for a warrant with a judge on behalf of Cary Oriel's office. Bruno tries to talk to her about his dilemma, acting like he's tipping her off about something else. He's dressed ridiculous, in a long coat and brown hat. Bruno says, "There's something wrong about this Loose Goose situation. Have your boyfriend look into it."

"He's my fiancé," says Joslin. "There's nothing wrong with the bar you're talking about. I go there all the time."

Bruno follows Joslin down the block. "Where are you going now?" she asks. "I'm coming with you to run your department for you," says Bruno. "You think you can shut that place down?" asks Joslin. "They own some people all the way to the top of the chain. All over. Look anywhere you want and you'll find out the Goose is there. Quack, quack. Take a nap and you'll see you're sleeping on his feather pillow. He's making airplanes. His company is piloting to other planets. The Earth is fucking over. And the Goose is the one to get off the planet. But he's still here. Do you know why? Because he cares about humanity!"

"If I found out you're dancing there," says Bruno as they step off the elevator on the fourth floor, "I swear, we're not making mom proud. You're not. I can't keep going on protecting your ass."

Joslin sits at her desk in the middle of the health department, with a dozen other people bustling around. She mixes a martini. She sips it down. When her drink is down to the olive, she says, "Not dancing. I wasn't. I promise." She wasn't and felt she didn't owe an explanation, so she left it at that.

When Joslin wasn't at work, or as she calls it, "spending time with Cary," she usually picks up free drinks just for sitting with the badges that stay around the Loose Goose. A group Bruno Peters thought were lowlifes. "Those people with their badges hanging out of their pockets. You think they're your friends. Huh? People with their mouths open. Disgracing the badge they wear," says Bruno. "They shouldn't wear it if they can't stand up from the bar without it sticking to the counter. I bet their bars have magnets under them. That's why they stay put there. Just watch them, baby sis. Watch them drool next time."

She goes out to that place at night and notices their expressions when she arrives. She loves their sinful glares and wants more. Cary can't stand to see it: all the thigh grabbing and ecstasy. Cary tries to confide in Bruno, in the lot outside the Loose Goose:

"You don't want to go in there and see her with those people," says Cary.

"I don't think she's going anywhere now that you're engaged," says Bruno.

"I can't stand to see her like this. Can you do something about it?" asks Cary. "Will you talk to her about coming here?"

"I ain't her keeper," Bruno says to Cary before going in to see who is sitting at the bar. Bruno doesn't stay there long. He looks disgraced and leaves before Cary can enter. Inspector Cary Oriel crumbles to himself in a booth, over the case he's working on. He drinks away his fears of heartbreak.

Chapter One

Closing In On A Family Legacy

AFTER the visit with Adeline, the children are interested in hearing more of what Oriel has to say, so he sits them down at his work bench with his photo album and a pot of coffee. He says, "Your Aunt Emily—that's who you were named after—She became a sea monster . . . . My sister . . . . Every year I visit her at the coast near Chet. Though they never reconciled their arrangement, it seemed appropriate to—"

From the next room over, Cary comes in to interrupt Oriel by saying: "Dad, I support you telling the kids about your brother-in-law. But Aunt Emily wasn't turned into a sea monster. She was involved with a bad man who kidnapped her—"

"Close," says Oriel, "but you're missing some details." He turns on a lamp and finds a particular page in his photo album. In a moment he finds the right picture of Emily, where she's standing

30

in a lab coat as long as her dress. "After high school she started working with an experiment and . . . a man that turned her into a squid of sorts."

Cary takes the photograph in hand to examine it closely while Oriel says, "It was her choice to be a part of the experiment. Get the details right, son. Emily volunteered, and . . . . Well, the Brood in our barn is a different story. He didn't have a choice in the matter . . . ."

After considerable efforts, Oriel has been able to gain support on the project, interpreting the data himself. He doesn't have trouble convincing people when the day approaches for a press conference at the Montréal Climate Control Summit. A day before the summit, the public is informed of the entire situation:

"Kimberly Wellington, from Channel 7 here, could you tell us more about the reports of the moon shifting or is it a rotation?"

"Thank you," says Oriel to a horde of reporters. "My peers scoffed at me for years. My own son wouldn't believe me. He still doesn't believe most things I say." People laugh and there is an uproar that unsettles his nerves.

Another individual is visiting Montréal for the convention, but he makes another stop on the way to talk to the Force in Montréal. The strange individual wasn't entirely welcomed there, but he paid to have their attention.

"Who does this guy think he is coming in to present about his restaurant?" asks Chief Inspector Howie Windhurst. "I got a promotion. I should be giving a speech."

"Well, let's see what he has to say," Captain Larry Stegner says to the newly appointed Chief Inspector of the Provincial Police Force of Québec. The presentation in the Montréal Police Department turns out to be a strange stunt for the owner of a restaurant chain. The billionaire entrepreneur made a presentation for everyone to see: "I'm so grateful to be here to attend the climate summit in Montréal. While I'm here, and while we're here on the final days of Earth. Before the tides quit moving altogether,

I figured I would show my support to your community with a donation of my own to your cause," said the entrepreneur.

"Don't you think they can fix it?" asks Windhurst. "Our brightest minds put to the test. You think you'd be one of them."

"Thank you for your time, gentlemen," says the entrepreneur.

"Everybody get back out there on the double," says Windhurst. "I need you to put a beacon out to find the dignitary that went missing."

"You read Bryant's report," says Stegner.

"I did," said Windhurst. "I'm sending McKindley and another out to check the scene. And you're on deck next."

Cynthia Valentico does not plan to attend the climate summit, nor was she present for the entrepreneur's presentation for the Force. She shows up afterwards and takes the discussion of confidential details to lunch to discuss with Private Detective Theodore Bryant.

Theodore takes a break from helping a few members of the Force in their attempts to recover a visiting dignitary, who was staying in the city to hear Oriel speak at the summit. Sometimes he tells himself that he needs to see Cynthia to understand where to go next with a case. He meets with Cynthia at a park bench nearby.

"This strange looking man I've seen on the news before—I missed most of what he was saying, but I saw his private podium, and I heard him shouting, 'Everyone here knows to go to the Loose Goose for a drink on me!' Can you believe his arrogance?"

"What's his angle?" asks Theo.

"I know. Right? What's he hiding?" ponders Valentico.

The man-bird hybrid made a special donation to the Force, so they allowed him to drop by for a presentation of his own, something he claimed to be doing all around the planet. "It's a way of giving back to those who serve in our final hours on Earth," he said to Sergeant McKindley, who was at the front desk when the Goose came into the precinct.

Ever since the Goose launched his stores around the globe, a chain of bars with quite large parking lots and secret underground chambers, he or his associate Jerry would make special appearances. They were, of course, following up on generous donations to police stations. Their speeches were rehearsed and sounded the same each time. Nobody knew what to make of their presentations, much like nobody knows what to make of the tides slowing down. But with the offer the entrepreneur has been extending to police departments around the world, plenty of tired, angry detectives have been celebrating the end by parking themselves at the bars to get free drinks.

It wasn't a problem until it got to the States. The Goose's assistant, Jerry, spoke to the Never York Police Department. He welcomed the entire department to stop by their establishments.

It seemed like all around the globe they had paid the right people and were making honest civil servants turn into crummy drunks. A free drink is a fine thing to have when you're tired of being shot at or sworn at by thugs and street vultures, and there's no way around that fact.

When Valentico told Theo about the presentation she missed, Theodore immediately thought the Goose was hiding something. "But the clever presentations went nearly unnoticed by everyone at the department," insists Cynthia.

While they are together they check in on where the Oriel Family is staying to make sure that the high profile family are safe in their rooms, but there is a police detail there.

"Just the old man and his grandson," says Windhurst. "Everyone else had better things to do."

"We've got it covered here," says Stegner. When Windhurst steps away, Stegner gets close to Cynthia and Theo. He says, "You too keep an eye out for Inspector Cary Oriel. He's coming to town later. Everything goes smoothly, the old man thinks he can restart the tides."

"Do you think he's right?" asks Theo.

"Does he seem in his right mind?" asks Cynthia.

"Well," says Stegner. "He has some stories. He has his memories. And I'll be at the presentation to see, so we'll see."

"I hope so," says Theo before he walks his wife to catch her train and return to her private office in the city.

Theo will return to search for the dignitary, but he'll think over everything Cynthia told him about the strange presentation at the department and how the Oriel Family is in town for a good reason. "Everything fits together somehow," he says aloud to himself. The entrepreneur nearly had everyone fooled.

It's a good thing that Inspector Cary Oriel was investigating the leads he received about tainted meat. He comes into Québec without gathering any attention from Theodore or anyone on the Force. Cary Oriel is late to the convention because he decided to pursue a lead he received from reporters.

The unsung heroes at the papers would have kept tipping other inspectors around the world to get to the Goose eventually. But Cary was the most obvious candidate for the information, because of his family status. After all Cary's father is the man coming to the public with the solution the world needs. The Goose left the Montréal Police Department after his presentation and went to the climate summit to witness Oriel himself.

At the Montréal Climate Control Summit, Oriel stands in front of the crowd, looking down at his notes on the podium:

Show slide, Take questions, Plan precisely.

He clears his throat and says, "My apologies as public speaking sometimes gets the best of me ... But hey, I'll pretend you want to hear this—"

"We do, sir," says a young reporter in blue shirt and yellow tie. He is standing in the back of the stadium in Montréal.

Oriel smiles politely and says, "We've arranged to have balloons take our miraculous magnetic substance . . . ." He demonstrates the crystal's capabilities in a small aquarium by dropping some specs of the substance into the water. He chips away at the crystal with a miniature rock pick. As the crystal falls into the water, the water stirs. "As you know, this is uncommon, of course. And the strange Elixiumbrium will ride along in my favorite vessel, a personal hot air balloon, until we reach a facility to extract the molecular constructs presented here in order to make something synthetic . . . ." He swallows and shows the next slide on the projector to be a cartoonist rendering of the world with dotted lines that show routes around the planet. "These routes present a projection to reorient the tidal forces placed upon the Earth . . . ."

He is stumbling through his speech, but it's typical for someone not accustomed to public speaking, and Oriel hasn't been speaking publicly for decades.

Henry Edwards lets his father in through the backstage door, but as they near the side of the stage they find that Oriel has been shot in the chest. He falls to the ground . . . . Cary runs out onto the stage alongside the security guard who says into his radio, "We have a Code Black-Nora-Nora-Nora. Active shooter. I repeat. We have a Code Black-Nora-Nora-Nora." A hooded figure from the crowd moves with great leaps and several bonds to the bottom of the balloon situated on the stage.

The hooded individual walks like a tiger on the hunt, and shoves the security guard away and onto his back like such a tiger would treat a turtle that stands in his way. Without spilling any of the strange blue substance attached to the pale at the bottom of the balloon the hooded figure takes off, knocking over everyone standing in their way. They run all the way to the parking lot, where they disappear into an unmarked van with tinted windows that moves fast to get away from the spectacle.

If you drive along the overpasses around Oriel Estates, the first thing you'll notice are the industrial sweeps of chimney tops billowing. While smoke smoothly rises from cylinder columns and electric-supplying power plants are as high and pointed as steeples of fine European churches, shipping trucks seem to float off into the sky. You'll reach the estate before crossing the Hudson River, before the Major Deegan Expressway that runs into the Bronx. Oriel Estates is surrounded by working class shipping professionals and endless fields of homogenized wheat grass mingling with garbage, mimosa, and other wilderness plants—not yet ready to be tampered back by cold weather and growing despite the awful low tides. The wheat takes over as much as it can in its final growth spurt, and it'll die because no one knows how to use wild wheat in Never York today. Yet, somehow Oriel Estates and Staten Island remain romantically intertwined with the unforgivable wholesome reverence of an island community located on the shore across from the major city.

Back at the warehouse, Oriel opens up a video feed of the event, and he says, "There's two bright ideas for you—"

"Are you sure you're okay?" asks Cary. "You're not even in shock that someone tried to kill you?" Cary examines what the bullet did to a seemingly impenetrable body armor that Oriel had discarded on the work bench.

"Not at all," says Oriel. "It would pay you to listen to my stories, son."

"I guess I just thought those were all *just* stories," says Cary.

"Yes," says Oriel, "well, they were stories. They were my stories. Do you think we just happen to have two dozen owls at our barn for no good reason, too?"

"I hear you, dad, and people believe you, obviously," says Cary. "They believe you enough to try to kill you and steal that stuff—"

"Then why don't you believe me?" asks Oriel as he reviews the tape. On the video feed, the hooded person was getting to the bucket, which prompts Oriel to say, "That stuff isn't real anyway . . . . My balloon—My first balloon is the only place I keep that precious crystal—Which reminds me," he sighs and says, "I still need to get it processed."

"Well," says Cary, "the authorities say it's best to let them, whoever that person is, believe that you have already died. So I'll have to step in to handle the foundation—"

"No way, young man," says Oriel. "I'd sooner let your boy take over and he's still a boy."

"I'll be discrete," says Cary. "And I'll be thorough. We'll handle the list of our benefactors together. Don't worry about it, Dad."

"I can do it myself," says Oriel.

Cary squints his eyes and says, "I don't know. These people tried to kill you."

"If you didn't believe me then," says Oriel, "then why would you trust me now? I know what I'm doing."

"Alright," says Cary. "I'll be there anyway—We'll set up a private convention for it."

Emily begins to ask a question, "So it sounds like that mad scientist—" Oriel interrupts with, "Who? Dr. Vanderfeld?" To which Emily says, "He liked turning everyone into sea monsters, huh?"

"Why, yes," says Oriel, "I suppose it *is* a nasty habit these days . . . ."

"What do you mean?" inquires Emily, but she is met with no answer from the old man, so Emily says, "But the man made of owls—" To which Oriel interrupts to say, "Please use his chosen name."

"The Brood," declares Emily. "And the scientist, uh— Dr. Vanderfeld . . . ."

"Good," says Oriel.

"He made the Brood and two sea monsters—"

"Correct," interrupts Oriel. "If you mean your Aunt Emily and the other squid we had chased at sea—"

"Are those the only ones he made into . . . ." Emily begins to ask about the creations of Dr. Vanderfeld, but she is growing frustrated enough that Oriel can tell.

"They are the only creatures I know of," Oriel says to clear the air. "Although you're going to think it's strange . . . . Oh . . . . Never mind . . . ."

"What is it?" asks Emily.

"I suspect," says Oriel, "Vanderfeld once failed to turn a man into a goose."

"That's rotten," says Emily. "A goose? But you say he failed?"

"Well," says Oriel, "he must have did something terrible to the guy . . . . He was a second generation Italian immigrant by the name Eugenio . . . . He goes by Gino . . . . He was the man who got away with all of Vanderfeld's fortunes when the doctor was . . . . rendered obsolete."

"A goose has all the doctor's money," says Emily with a great deal of timber and uncertainty in her voice.

"Not *a* goose, but *the* Goose," says Oriel.

When the great doctor perished by a stroke of his own ego, the fortunes used to fund his experiments went to a man who once assisted the doctor, but along with the money he won through lawsuits on Vanderfeld's estates, he also won patents to the doctor's work and Vanderfeld's research into the Elixiumbrium Crystals came with it. This was incredibly valuable, of course, because the Goose wanted to leave behind planet Earth altogether.

While they wait for the coffee to come to a boil, Oriel regales Henry Edwards with his story: "We left the deck in a hurry . . . . Even the commander of the Royal British Navy, a man who had lived aboard a fleet at sea for forty years of his life, was startled. We presently sought refuge from what monsters lurked in the vast oceans that we feared were all around us and found the steamer's parlor room to be an adequate space and natural place to reassemble our group."

The once luxurious parlor was still draped in red-velvet curtains and matching decor; the benches and tables were mounted to the floor to prepare for any type of weather, but they were covered with the type of mildew that accumulates on fabric at sea too long.

The room was empty when people shuffled in, apart from Prince Ascubar's daughter who was reading a book of poetry and the first mate who rushed in to check on her when the attack came. First Mate Brennan left to make sure everyone was accounted for from the deck, and Oriel counted heads to bring the total occupant count to twenty-four.

Prince Ascubar's daughter, Esmeralda, put her book down momentarily and asked, "What happened to the lot of you, by God?" Her bewilderment was sensible seeing as it was sunny outside before the creature appeared, and the steamer hadn't come to shore or capsized. Yet so much of their clothing dripped of a bile, so much so that they appeared to have swam a lap around the steamer before entering the parlor.

Prince Ascubar rushed to his daughter and told her what he was sure of: something took away the entire reason he brought her on the ship and they had to get away from the chaos.

The first mate returned to recklessly throw open the parlor closet door, and he piled towels on the arms of the servant, who followed close to the first mate. First Mate Brennan said to the ship's servant, "Help them dry off with these, will you, Minolo?"

The ship's servant patted towels on their shoulders, one by one, down the line of the drenched and slime covered officials. He handed towels to Chet and Oriel.

Chet cursed loudly about the entire event and the crystal being missing.

The young daughter of the Prince of Spain was old enough to withstand the foul language and only paused reading her poetry long enough to hear it was in English, a language that made her heart uneasy because she felt it was filled with business jargon. She had seen and heard enough, so she went further into the steamer, into the Captain's Quarters that were located just down below, through a door near the parlor closet. Esmeralda started to worry about her own safety, but she trusted her father as a leader who would stop the ocean currents by plucking the Moon from beyond the sky's grasp if it meant ensuring his daughter was safe on the ocean waters. She wrapped herself up in poetry and wouldn't listen to reality. She read to herself often, but it was then that she started reading aloud.

Ascubar saw his daughter's reaction and knew he needed to state his intention presently. He said, "Gentlemen, this time has become far too senseless for me to have my beloved daughter nearby. I will like to get her to a safe place before I consider joining you for an investigation."

Chet said that he knew what it was, but from his tone nobody could tell if he was serious. He said, "I've seen these things before. When I was on a bender one night, I thought they were calling to me from the deep waters. I thought I heard them talking. I didn't know if it was a mermaid or siren of the ocean coming to steal me away to their underwater love-palace . . . . It turned out these things were mating on the shores . . . . You can imagine my surprise when I took off my bathrobe and hopped in the water hoping to find a beautiful half-woman and instead, I felt its slimy scales on my shoulder."

The Royal British Crown Representative and his four foot-soldiers stayed on the ship and went with the crew to search for the monster, and they were joined by the US Secretary of Defense and his assistant. The Chinese ambassador agreed to stay and steer the ship since Chet's first mate brought out a harpoon and was the only crew member officially under Chet's command that was worthy of manning the steamer. The Chinese ambassador in actuality knew little up to that point about sea fairing but saw the look in the eyes of First Mate Brennan when he took the harpoon from storage. The young first mate's intensity must have inspired something within the Chinese ambassador to think he was adept enough to keep the boat from running ashore while the rest of them left on the hunt. He agreed to remain on the ship, alone, with the servant of the steamer, who knew where most supplies were stored.

Prince Ascubar was concerned about his daughter's safety above everything else. He brought her along to be witness to the great discovery that was to shape the Earth's history, but she hadn't hardly looked up from her book except for when the monster came from the sea.

"Oh, Captain Chet," said First Mate Brennan. "Please, I must oblige you reconsider allowing my departure with you and the crew."

"Reconsider, how?" asked Chet, and Oriel wanted to know, too.

Chet pulled his first mate aside, and Oriel could faintly hear what Chet said from the parlor room. He said, sternly, "Boy, don't question me in front of her. The ship. She won't tolerate that."

To which First Mate Brennan said, "To catch whatever anomaly that crept onto this deck is my priority, sir."

The captain must have saw and liked how First Mate Brennan of a town just a few dozen miles inland of North Shore had bravely challenged his employer, but he must have known his first mate would back down privately because Chet said, "You know we're after a rare thing that could fix everything on this rock. That's what the entire group of scientists around the world declared."

"I know, sir," replied Brennan, "but the girl will need me if this creature goes another route we don't know. We don't know—"

"That's her father's job then," snapped the Captain, and Brennan said nothing but looked glum, so Chet said, "I'll volunteer you to them for protection and see how the group reacts."

Captain Chet poked his head out into the parlor, and he was followed by First Mate Brennan. Chet said, "My ship's first mate would like to accompany any fleeing parties that require his assistance." The group of dignitaries all looked rather confused after he spoke and looked blankly back at Chet, who said, "Any takers? Prince Ascu—"

There was a sudden jolt on the steamer when it took a wave that towered its mighty deck. The water drained away, but Oriel began to worry about their situation when he caught a glimpse of the ship's tracking system to see the large mass that was recognized to be the sea monster had moved at a greater speed than they had expected. The giant squid was suddenly covering more nautical grounds than anyone anticipated, even surpassing those expectations of men who were of the ocean. Oriel checked with Chet when he saw the spectacle on screen, and Chet agreed that they should be on their way.

Chet had one last concern before leaving the steamer. He dutifully took the ship's servant aside and spoke to him quite charmingly. Chet said to the bright and eager Minolo: "I'm not here to do her medicine, so she gets three drops in each eye that must be spaced out at least 15 minutes—if I'm not back by nightfall."

Minolo took the clipboard and files about the dog's medicine and simply said, "Yes."

Chet looked to Minolo and to the other two staying on the ship, the Chinese ambassador and another volunteer, a Russian— To them he said, "Don't run the ship aground." Of course they did run the ship aground not long after the search party left the steamer, but they didn't have trouble getting it unstuck, for what the Chinese ambassador didn't know about boating, the Russian strategist who stayed with him made up for with his knowledge of sledding. Chun Lee and Vlad Kebob brought a few dozen dogs, that had been kenneled on the steamer, to their finest moments of heroism when the dogs pulled that steamer from a sand barge. It would have made a great story for the Louisville reporter named Danzel.

Chet saw the caliber of care that he was leaving in charge of the steamer when the brilliant Russian strategist who spoke hardly any language common with anyone else on the steamer was the first one to take the ship's wheel when the captain backed up and the first mate was searching for the torpedo.

Partially still recovering from the attempt on his life, Oriel tries to crank open the glass roof to let in some sunlight from above, but it won't budge. "It started to rain that day," says Oriel, "and wouldn't let up. Some of the crew put on rain gear to be prepared. There was the first mate hopping across the deck while putting his boots on, and I didn't hesitate to put on a rubber jacket myself. Chet didn't seem to mind the wet feeling, and at times he would take off his cap to let the rain pour along has scalp.

"Those several foreign dignitaries that weren't going on board the smaller ship to chase the blue crystal or helping man the steamer— dignitaries and their servants or assistants that weren't of use in our plan were huddled together and ordered to evacuate with Prince Ascubar's helicopter."

A few of the dignitaries had concerns about the weather conditions and leaving their own helicopters and other belongings as they fled. To which Oriel assured them that they were safe, and he even patronized them some when he said, "Your patience in this desperate time is appreciated."

Chet voiced his concern for losing sight of the monster, shown on the monitor as a large mass underwater. He thought they would lose track if they didn't move quickly, and Oriel agreed.

Prince Ascubar bowed as he was boarding his helicopter after everyone else going to shore was already filed away, and he made a promise, to return when his daughter was in a safer place:

"You men chase a creature that you do not understand," said Ascubar. "I am thrilled to watch you confront it." He shouted over the whirling blades of his helicopter before climbing around the cockpit entrance and piloting it away from the ship's deck, toward a dark, endless horizon, never to return to them again.

Chapter Two

It's Worth the Beauty Rest

OLD Oriel speaks loudly and with colorful tones near the sleeping Adeline, who does not stir. Oriel pauses only to glance at the woman and sees exactly why his son was hopeful and hopes, too, that the woman will wake one day.

Henry Edwards has a lot on his mind to get him through seeing his mother lie there. He wonders how Oriel made it out of the situation with the crystal being stolen from them . . . . "Did you get the crystal back?" he asks his grandfather.

Oriel smiles and nods. He is quiet and respectful when around his son's wife because of the sadness he knows his son has experienced through losing his wife. He supports Cary in his pursuit to find a new mother for Henry Edwards and Emily. More so, Emily is fascinated by the idea of having a female role model.

Henry Edwards sits and watches the machines that cause his mother to experience a breath of air in her lungs, and he wonders if the story is true. If so, had they fixed the Earth's problems with a strange crystal?

Henry Edwards had given up on his mother ever waking from her state as much as his father, but Emily is a different story . . .

The young girl never knew her mother at all, so she's the reason that Cary went to visit his wife for the past five years. Now that Emily is old enough to ask to see her mother on her own, Cary waits to let her make the choice. The still body of Adeline does nothing more to and for the world than does a bed-cover or comforter, thinks Cary, but he loves his children enough not to interfere.

"When are we going to see Mommy again?" Emily asks her father with all the joy a five-year old child can have for a parent that can't even play with her. She always wants to stay with her mother past visiting hours at the Life Center, past the point that Cary is able to hold back and fake smiling for his daughter . . . .

Some say it is a dream. Others say that it's cruel to leave her plugged into machines like that. Emily just wants her to wake up. She says, "Mommy, you don't have to dream anymore. You can take my dreams . . . ."

After her visit, Cary tells Emily, "Your mother is in a good place, sweetheart." He, too, wishes his wife was back in her old way of being, but her body and that blood clot ruined her chances of recovering after child birth— a gruesome reality that Cary wishes he could hide from Emily. For the past five years he has been a single parent, doing all the work to raise his two children, apart from occasional help from his father. And he misses his wife dearly . . .

Throughout the five years Emily has been alive, Cary has kept his promise to bring their little girl back to see her mother every week, ever since she was born to the world—when Cary spoke these words into his suddenly silent partner's ear: "You'll see her in your dreams, and I'll make sure she sees you too."

Something more than obligation keeps Cary bringing his daughter back, even back when Emily didn't understand where children came from. "Yes, it was more than obligation then, and now as well," thinks Cary as the child clings to her mother . . . .

45

The tiny heart that came from a place inside her beat, and for a moment Adeline was certainly full of life. She blooms like a flower when her daughter comes near, perceptibly so. Some people believe that a comatose patient experiences brain deafness when they are in a coma for a prolonged period of time. Whatever the case may be, Adeline hears those words and she keeps alive longer; she keeps alive to feel her daughter reach for her with love.

Traditionally, nearly every week since she has known who her mother was, which didn't take long at all, she has been asking to see her again. Several times each week for years, she would ask her father about when they would go visit her mother again, and she always received the same type of answer. When it wasn't time for a weekly visit Cary had to stay focused on work to keep himself from missing her too much.

The children help him keep from feeling gloomy about not having his wife around day in and day out. For instance, each and every day when Cary leaves work to pick his daughter up from daycare he finds his daughter has a glow on her face from the evening sun that reminds him of his dear wife and the gifts she left behind for him. Emily asks questions about her mother . . .

Some of those questions Cary can answer— "What was mommy's favorite color?" she once asked. "Turquoise."

"Who was Mommy's hero growing up?" — "Amelia Earhart." — "Who?" Emily asked. "The first woman to fly solo across the Atlantic."

"How did Mommy fall asleep?" inquired Emily one day. "She had an accident dear. But I know she would say that it's worth the beauty rest . . . ."

And there were times, as with most children who are developing at a young age, where Emily would ask a question and Cary would be stumped without an answer— "Where did Mommy go to Kindergarten?" — "I don't know. In Connecticut, I suppose." — "What did Mommy's mommy & daddy do?" — "She didn't tell me since she was adopted, dear." — "When will Mommy wake up to see me, Daddy?" — "I don't know, sweet one, but I'm sure she's dreaming about how your face brightens Daddy's world."

As much as he longed for her to return from her comatose state—
more than he wanted anything else in the world—In fact, want
isn't fair enough to say, for Cary yearned for the love of Adeline
with necessity greater than his lungs craved oxygen— his heart
squeezed with hope that she would wake out of it, yet it was no
use. For the doctor Cary brought in was one of the top specialists
in the world, and he told Cary that the chances of seeing his wife's
brain active again were low at best: "One in 3.5 million," said the
doctor.

Eventually it was too much for Cary to bare, seeing his
daughter grow up without a mother, so his mind wandered to
explore the possibility of bringing another woman into his
daughter's life.

One day Cary met Joslin Peters, when she was referred to
him by good authority, to work with him in his building. The
health department sometimes works with referrals from other
institutions. And it just so happened that the Never York Police
Department recommended Joslin Peters when a spot opened at
Cary's office.

When they felt a romance developing, they pursued it like
adults and Cary ended up getting to know Joslin well enough to
consider bringing her closer to his family unit; he saw that she was
pretty and that she seemed to care about him enough to want to
meet his children. Now, the day approaches when they will share
their first apartment together as an experiment . . . .

For five years his wife remained speechless and listless,
and it was finally over. He has decided to introduce Joslin to Emily
and Henry Edwards, too (although he hasn't been as concerned
about the boy since he's older). To prepare her, he said, to Joslin,
"My daughter is the rarest gem on Earth to me, so please
understand, my dear Joslin, I wish for her to see you only when
you are ready . . . ."

And Joslin said, "I'll step in to take the place of your dear
wife when it is right, love." And Cary said to that: "No one will
ever take her place, not in my heart either, not even in love." He
would tell Joslin about his love for his daughter too, but it was

never enough to bring Joslin into Emily's life, until now that they have made plans to move into an apartment together to try that out.

Still in his early morning routine, the butcher is not yet aware of the fetid odor behind his lips. The acidic quality of his cup of orange juice mixed with the burnt heels that finished the loaf of bread left from last night is a fusion that results in a whimsical moment for the butcher when he imagines a tale of acrimony aboard the tiny speck of breadcrumb within his cup. The butcher imagines what life would be like on the dusty world below, beneath his nose. His golden glasses twitch as if he nearly sneezes, but it is just a reflex to thoughts about dust that makes his ears move.

He thinks about the creatures that must live there. Imagines his monstrosity to the dust people. He dreams about taking their lives, to himself, so that he will live longer. And, oh! He does take their lives as he swallows the speck. At least he gargles and chokes a little in the end.

The butcher watches the customers arrive, every starting sit and first coffee. He watches them read and grumbles to himself low enough to not disturb their breakfasts. He puts together sandwiches and meals fast in the mornings, so fast the orders leave like they are being sold out of the back of a truck.

The man working the register is an ex-convict on parole for good behavior; the butcher hired the man because he was willing to work long hours for low wages and had experience handling money. He talks about jail sometimes and sometimes he talks about sleeping with women, but the butcher has trouble figuring out which he refers to when he breaks away from the long line of customers to talk to him while he is trying to put together a few choice cuts.

The cashier says to the butcher, "I told a pixie to lie for me. She only knew me, but she wouldn't lie for me. She set her own rules to be forgotten. . . ."

The butcher doesn't grasp the man's story, but he is an affable fellow who never complains, so he nods at the cashier to signal his understanding and comprehension, and the butcher says,

"The best rules are left aside to be never thought of again."

A beautiful woman holding an easel adjusts her blouse before setting up her studio on the bridge in front of the deli, and the butcher watches her adjust her hat to sit on the side of her bleached hair. Her finger nails match the pallet she works with, but the brightest colors in her color wheel never touch a brush because the light on her canvas is so bright all by itself . . . .

"The bees need more sugar sweets than flowers to liquefy their thirsty hive. They brought the honey. Do you see?" asks the cashier.

The butcher named Gino nods and smiles. He says, to the cashier, "Yes. They brought it from the place where it's made."

Minutes later, the cashier comes inside from his smoke break. He hands a flower to Gino. Gino puts it under the cash register when the beautiful painter walks in through the door. She has the same flower painted on her canvas. He sees this and removes the identical flower from beneath the register. He smells the flower in front of the woman. He keeps inhaling it and her but with his nose in the flower, and he groans. The woman is disgusted and leaves the establishment.

"More sweets for the bees?" asks the cashier. Gino nods and goes back to cutting the meat apart.

With his clipboard in hand, Cary walks into the Staten Island Delicatessen near the edge of the island. He looks prepared for an inspection of the place.

He approaches the counter and the cashier goes in the back room, leaving Gino to stand by himself. The place is empty apart from an old man watching the fuzzy television set. Cary asks for a sandwich: "I'll take whatever you'd like to make."

Gino doesn't know how to deal with Cary's request for any sandwich he'd like to make; too much could go wrong in the preparation, he thinks. Still, he tries. He makes Cary a sandwich with a lot of olives and feta cheese. He presses the sandwich like a panini, even though it's on a sub-roll. It burns around the edges. The bread crumbles like a sawdust, and the whole operation falls apart in the middle when the sandwich-maker wraps it in foil.

Cary doesn't have any preoccupations about what is on this sandwich since he ate just a half-hour ago and is picking this up for lunch for later. His appetite is already together after the shellfish he ate earlier that worried him some. Although people rarely get one over on Inspector Cary Oriel, his taste buds sometimes take over completely, guiding what he eats. And that pound of lobster tail from earlier sends a stream of panic racing around inside the inspector's gut. His spine jolts as he stands in the sandwich line he appears to be there to condemn.

The sandwich-maker rings up the order and asks him to pay, but Cary is distracted by an overwhelming smell of trash. He says, "Do you expect me to pay for that?" after the sandwich-maker tells him the price a second time.

The sandwich-maker says, "Don't be a prick here. I have to charge you sometimes to stay afloat."

Cary says, "I don't want to shut you down that way, Gino. But I have a rule. I never pay for something that doesn't look good enough to eat." The inspector writes something privately on his clipboard before continuing to say, "I never count on paying here. I can leave you holding that thing you call food along with a stack of paperwork involving code violations, occupancy variances . . . . The list goes on."

Gino puts the sandwich in a bag and slides it over to Cary. He says, "You're good. Just don't be a prick." The last time something like this happened Cary brought in a cart full of fresh bread; he baked it in a certified kitchen in the city, a space he rents just outside of town.

Cary stands there and takes a bite of the sandwich. He starts to say something: "So, Gino—"

But Gino interrupts to ask, "Hey, Friday told me you had to shut down the new kid who got with the gyros?"

"I did," says Cary. "News travels fast," he thinks aloud. "I saw the meat they were serving ... A writer at *Staten Island Review*—by the name of Danzel—he talked to a food critic and she tipped me off about it. Danzel does mostly sports writing these days, but he talked to this woman Elaine Pickard he knows that tipped me that the place . . . was foul."

The place Gino brought up was once a gyro place with about as much self respect as a stray alley-cat scratching at a can of tuna. Elaine Pickard wrote an article condemning the place and held back releasing until she felt justice was served. She told Inspector Cary's informant that the fish tasted like chicken, but it turned out the chicken tasted far, far worse.

"The young man was catching rats I take it, huh," Gino says while scratching his lumpy chin, near the mole that grows out of the side distractingly so.

"You'll have to excuse Friday for getting the information wrong," says Cary. "He's only telling you what I told him when he asked me the other day. The real story is printed in *The Review*. Pickard finally put up the story after the place got shut down two days ago."

Gino approaches a copy of the newspaper and thumbs through its information with his plastic gloves covered in shredded lettuce. He reads it over quickly when he gets to the part that mentions Inspector Cary Oriel shutting down the gyro shop.

"Something missing here," says Gino. "You don't say what the meat was really made from . . . ."

"Papers wouldn't print it," says Cary as he wraps up his sandwich for later. "Besides it would ruin all of our appetites."

"You're telling me, after all the money you made," says Inspector Cary, "you'd rather continue on as a butcher than leave the planet. That's noble."

"Well," says Gino, "what can I say? I love humanity that way."

"Why do they call you the Goose?" asks Cary.

"I made the Loose Goose bars, and I had the show where I cooked up some fine meals for everyone," says Gino.

"I guess you have the notoriety. And you've been helping keep the community together, right?" asks Cary.

Gino shrugs his shoulders, but they stay raised. "I'm here to be part of the end of it all. That's why I'm here. If they keep on calling me Goose, I'd rather swim out of the pond." Gino pulls something white and fluffy from the collar of his shirt and disposes of it in the fires of the grill.

Cary leaves the deli. Gino holds up his phonebook to see it in the light, and he dials his phone. Into the receiver Gino says, "Hi, Jerry. I think we've got a problem. We're going to have to keep a closer eye on our operations."

Dᴇᴛᴇᴄᴛɪᴠᴇ BRUNO PETERS deals with a call at the station. A voice says, "We need some of our restrictions taken back again." Bruno isn't sure what the person on the other end means, so he asks, "What restrictions?"

"You know damn well what restrictions," says the voice. Bruno replies, "I can't do anything if they keep shutting down your restaurants. At least your bars are safe if they stop serving food."

"That's not good enough. The boss wants to go out with a bang," says the voice. "You got cops drinking in those dirty mob-town saloons and that's not good enough? You've got to try feeding people to our city? You think I'm going to let that fly?" asks Bruno.

"Do something about Cary," says the voice on the telephone. "I can't," Bruno responds. "You know that's my sister's fiancé . . . ." He hesitates before saying, "He's persistent. But he's family . . . ."

Working late into the evening the night before last, Cary found a way to skip protocol. He worked with a judge to issue an order from the court calling for an emergency shutdown of Jimeny's Gyros. For, after conducting proper analysis, Cary found serious issues to cause panic. Normally, the management would be given time to amend issues, but the situation warranted immediately revoking all licensing from the establishment.

Tests were administered on samples of Jimeny's *Entre #4*, which the menu calls their "feature entrée": a delectable looking Chicken Kiev, not to be confused with chicken ala king. Chicken

Kiev, which is popular in Eastern Europe, is a cuisine that sources[2] attribute to being the concoction of a Frenchman who lived near the town of St. Petersburg in Russia, and so the dish was influenced by Russian cuisine. Also called suprême de volaille à la Kiev, Jimeny's mother would bake the chicken after rolling it in bread crumbs, but Jimeny was forced to fry his poultry to the point that it became unrecognizable . . . . It no longer looked like the tender breast that his mother had prepared for the family meal. It no longer looked like chicken at all . . . .

After receiving a tip about the food being contaminated he visited the place for lunch and left with the entire meal intact for proper analysis in his lab. Inspector Cary Oriel collected a sample of *Entre #4* without Jimeny's Gyro having any knowledge of a testing. He looked at the samples under a microscope and compared the tissue of the meat from the Chicken Kiev served at Jimeny's with tissue of a Chicken Kiev he prepared with help from a brilliant cookbook. His Chicken Kiev looked unlike the Chicken Kiev served in the restaurant. In fact, the Kiev from Jimeny's didn't look like chicken. The inspector feared it was human flesh, so he brought in a forensics analyst from the Staten Island Health and Public Safety Department who confirmed his fears to be true.

It was Zane Grey[3] that informed his readers of the term land pig once being used as a term for the plate containing human flesh, and it was certainly hard for Cary or the forensics inspector to go to lunch after the analysis was over. Cary agreed to handle the case and the forensics analyst took the rest of the day off.

Cary immediately informed his connection within law enforcement that their presence was required to shut down Jimeny's Gyros. With the test results confirmed, the police informed, and proper paperwork in hand, Inspector Cary Oriel picked up his keys to drive to the place himself to make sure not another meal would be served. It wasn't his normal protocol, but this was an extreme case after all. In the car, he meditated over his

---

[2] Stewart-Gordon, F. & Hazelton, N. (1984) *The Russian Tea Room.* Never York, NY. Perigee Trade.
[3] Grey, Z. (1953) *Tales of the Angler's Eldorado, New Zealand.* Lanham, MD: The Derrydale Press.

report, the envelope still awaiting its seal, and he thought about the letter he needed to send to the higher-ups in Congress.

Cary knew that Jimeny's Gyros was one of the establishments owned by a larger chain of establishments. Jimeny's Gyros, which was run by Jimeny would be shut down, but investigations will need to be done into the entire umbrella above the gyro shop. "The media will have their way with it," Cary thought, "but a formal letter to the district representative will ensure that the other establishments . . . are not serving up anymore of the repulsive dish."

He looked at the folder to find out what the parent establishment was that would need to be investigated. The company was called Goose Incorporated. Some quick research would tell him that Goose Inc. runs a saloon in every country around the world and nearly every state in the Union, seventeen locations in Never York City alone, including the sandwich shop Cary visited where the strange character named Gino scratched a mole on his chin and never grinned at the inspector once.

When the news leaked to Cary about the questionable entrée, the critic held back her article to give justice time to be served— He put everything on hold to make sure that justice was seated at the head of the table, and thus, it would be served first.

He put all other cases aside. When he found out his source was correct, he put all matters in his life aside: his family would have to figure things out, he thought. He told his father to pick up Emily, and the rest would handle itself, he thought. He found out the truth about Jimeny's Gyros, so he had to take hold of their operation and restrict their sales immediately.

He arrived at the scene to find his law enforcement contact, Detective Bruno Peters, sitting in his unmarked squad car. The detective said, "Nobody inside" when he recognized the health inspector with his frock coat and lanyard. Cary nodded and went to take a look for himself, but there was nobody left at the restaurant to disagree with the shut-down . . . . The whole place was left open.

"Looks like Jimeny and company took the fairy out of the borough," said Bruno. "Well, hand your report over. I'll take it from here, inspector."

"I take it you'll continue the investigations," Cary said. "I'll follow up with Judge Hiendler who signed the emergency shut-down this afternoon."

He firmly held onto the packet of paperwork as he said to Bruno Peters: "I want to hear back about this. I'll testify as an expert witness, no matter what it takes to make sure they're not serving that ... in our city."

Bruno nodded, and when Cary left, he made a phone call. Bruno said, "I'm here now." A moment went by with silence on the other side of the line. "There's not much I can do if the inspector is sniffing around."

Bruno Peters was in his office later that night, deciding what to do about Cary when a voice came on his telephone to give him fewer choices.

"I know who you are, you work for . . . ." Bruno trailed off into the receiver.

The voice replied, "The deal is . . . . Our boss . . . . You know the boss. He takes in people as a service to the community. It's like a mentor program, and you're the lucky non-applicant to get a spot on our campaign. It's not like you applied or entered some whacky lottery though. Nope. Our application process is simple . . . . The boss takes in people that can help . . . . And you just so happen to be a person in a position that can help. Are you listening, detective?"

By then, the computer system indicated to Bruno a location for the call. He looked worried. He said, "Anything Goose, right?"

"That's the place."

"You must be Jerry," said Bruno.

"Yeah. So what I tell you is—"

"Hey. I know you," said Bruno. "I know what this is. I know every guy from my department that sets foot in that place doesn't leave without his share of high-ball liquor, both of his hands filled with women, and whatever you do to pay off the lady cops . . . . I don't care, either. That's *baby bunny* stuff. I never thought I'd have to show *my* face," says Bruno. He wrote notes on a pad before he popped a strange red pill followed by a cup of brown liquid.

"Luckily for us," said Jerry, "Goose Incorporated sold Jimeny's Gyros before your inspection took place. I'll need you to agree to that, detective . . . . This is where you say, 'Of course you're clean!' I'm not feeling respected here, detective . . . ."

"I'm not here to show you respect," said Bruno.

Jerry laughed on the other end of the line, and he said, "The Goose himself notices that you're acquainted with a certain health inspector . . . . Is he your sister's boyfriend?" asked Jerry. "Stop me before I do everything for you . . . ."

"Cary," said Bruno, "he's my sister's fiancé." At that moment he knew it was no longer up to him or his department to determine what happened with the case that showed up when Inspector Cary Oriel called. He thought about his sister, Joslin, and he decided to do whatever it would take to keep Joslin safe.

Chapter Three

The Air Belongs To The Birds

THE lift is smooth. Henry Edwards knows how to operate the balloon better than his father, and according to his grandfather, the skill skipped a generation. Henry Edwards spent practically every summer on a balloon with his grandfather from age three on up. The eldest Oriel talks to Henry Edwards, teaching him everything there is to know about how the contraption works. The young mind of Henry Edwards absorbs the information, but he never wonders, never strays further than what is presented to him. He thinks, however, that this knowledge will come in handy if he ever finds himself on his own balloon adventure.

The contraption goes up in the air, and for the first time this year Henry Edwards rides the sky. "The balloon keeps going up like that until we get to the sky's limit, Grandpa?" the young boy inquires.

"No," Oriel replies, "the sky is a place where the stars do live. We're staying below them.

"We must. Do you understand, kid?"

"I think so," he says, "but the air is ours?"

"No," his grandfather replies and laughs. He says, "The air belongs to the birds."

"So then, why are we here in it?" asks Henry Edwards.

"You're onto something, Hen," says Oriel. "The birds own the sky. They let us use it. Birds are the only things capable of flight that is natural. Therefore, the sky is naturally their domain. You see?" He points at a seagull flying near their vessel. "I've got to have a plane to make it over the Atlantic, but they don't have to worry."

"You could make it over on a balloon," says Henry Edwards.

"I could," agrees Oriel, "but I wouldn't risk it, kid. Balloons can get into trouble making it over the ocean. Why, one bad sea storm and it would be time to put on your scuba gear."

"So that's why we brought the scuba gear? In case we crash in the ocean," Henry Edwards says fearfully. His sense of urgency grows as he peers over the basket rail at the rough terrain below, and the boy says, "We're not near the ocean yet . . . . We can't crash now!"

"No, no," says Oriel. "Henry, this marks my 400th trip, mostly alone. In the past year I made 400 trips in control of this thing." He holds onto the vertical rope leading to the burner system above their heads. Noticing the reading on the pyrometer, he adjusts the flame adequately. "I think I know how to steer away from the ocean," says Oriel.

"Then why do we have the scuba gear?" asks the boy.

"I'm going to throw you overboard. That's why," says Oriel, and he makes a stern expression. The grimace is out of character enough to make Henry Edwards smile, and he leans on the top rail of the wicker basket, feeling suddenly secure.

"Gee, young man, you'll never learn," says Oriel. "The only way to travel in a balloon over 20,000 times in your life is to bring a parachute every time."

"Yes, grandpa," says Henry Edwards. "But do we intend to use them?"

"I call it field testing of equipment. And it is a must," answers Oriel.

"Then, you have to factor in the parachute risks, or else you have a flawed statistic," says Henry Edwards.

Oriel takes the comment personally; he feels stumped. He scratches his head, and he shifts his weight around. He is becoming angry, and the young Henry Edwards is growing uneasy, so the old man turns on his humility: "I not think good on empty stomach," says Oriel as he opens a bottle of root beer. He takes the top off the bottle using the side of a toolbox located on the floor of the basket, next to the folding table. He drinks, the drink foams, and he belches.

"I'll pack my own chute, I guess," says Henry Edwards.

They set the balloon at a constant speed. It is moving quickly, but when he cuts back the burner, the balloon falls rapidly to the ground.

"Why is it falling fast, Henry Edwards? Do you know the answer?" questions Oriel.

Henry Edwards shakes his head.

Oriel lights the fuel to keep the balloon from dropping. "The point is to coast or . . . anchor," Oriel lectures. "Not many people know about this old trick."

Oriel drops a large weight, and as the weight falls the balloon lifts, keeping the rising motion accelerating quickly until Oriel cuts off the fuel by turning the valve closed. The weight is on the ground below.

There is plenty of slack between the weight and the balloon, which is done to avoid having a collapsed basket if the fuel is left on as the weight falls, because the balloon would raise more and not allow the weight to rest on the ground without ripping the basket from the ropes that connect it to the balloon shaped envelope above. This would be a tragically unfortunate scenario for the boy and his grandfather.

The anchor is dragging the fields, scratching the dirt and ripping apart the ground like the claws of a giant beast from above, bearing down into the world with ferocious tendency. Oriel tells Henry Edwards to control the balloon and pull the vessel higher to take up the slack. This happens in a matter of seconds. They watch the rope become taught from the closest knot to the anchor and back up to the basket where they stand.

"It's better to have extra slack on the rope to pull up and tie off, or raise up to draw out the slack," instructs Oriel.

"What if it comes short?" Henry Edwards inquires.

"I wouldn't want to be in the basket," grunts Oriel. "That's for damn sure."

They get back to the warehouse and load the balloon and basket into the display for the small, quaint museum. When they've finished loading, Oriel says to Henry Edwards, "All you know are the basics, my boy-o. You don't know my secret to being the oldest, most seasoned, and most handsome, I should say." Oriel wraps his tan scarf around his neck, and he pulls his flying goggles down over his eyes. They make a '*plop*'!

Through the hazy, yellow lenses, he can still comprehend his grandson cracking apart, like a hardboiled egg, with laughter. He smirks and remains stoic, and he says, "What do you think, boy-o?"

"I think your pot of coffee is ready, dad," Cary chimes in from the other room.

Oriel motions for his son to be quiet by waving his arms and saying, "You're letting everyone in on my secret. Then what will I do when this young man starts building his own balloon enterprise? Huh . . . ?"

"Dad, he's already signed a non-disclosure," says Cary. He winks at his son and says, "We had you sign one when you got your birth certificate."

"I did?" asks the earnest Henry Edwards.

"Sure you did," says Cary. "I thought you might not be mine at the time. I thought you were a spy. The son of my enemy!" He sits and watches them putting the finishing touches on the display. "Now I see it in you, you're my son, alright." Cary goes in to turn off the hissing coffee maker.

"He's better off flying than you, Cary," Oriel says with a snap. The coffee pot hisses as Cary pours two cups, and he returns with a mug for his father.

"We need to get those hinges back in working conditioning," Oriel says. He takes a swig of the steamy liquid that burns his tongue and sits the heavy mug on the workbench before making use of the caffeine.

Before he leans a ladder onto the wall to get to the hinges, he wraps a towel around its feet to keep from scuffing the wall, since the visitor center looks pristine. Its walls look clean and freshly painted in a yellow that glows when the sun creeps over the space, and it shines in through the teal glass-hatch. He takes a sip of the dark liquid before moving the extension ladder over to the wall where the ceiling is high, and into place on the highest rung. It snaps.

Cary walks over to hold the ladder for his father to climb it; he's holding a yellow can of spray. "I'll need the oil, son," says Oriel, and Cary shakes the can in front of his father. Oriel climbs while saying: "That's air freshener. Take another look before you leap, Cary." He's right; Cary looks at the can to notice its ornate design, and he sprays a mist of floral-concentration before searching for the oil can. He finds the can in a cabinet in the corner.

When the metal canister with its long spout is firmly in place inside a five-gallon bucket that is fastened to a rope and pulley, Cary pulls one end of the bristly rope to lift the bucket up to his father. Oriel waits near the top of the ladder, five rungs down, where the pulley is affixed. Cary says: "Dad, stop filling Henry and Emily's heads with nonsense about sea monsters and… whatever it is you tell them that isn't true. If you want them to go with you when you go to visit Chet . . . ."

With the bucket now empty, Oriel lets it drop to the ground: *'Buh-dhump!'* It lands loudly next to Cary who looks up in shock. Oriel says, "Would you pass me the flathead?" Cary moves with some haste, for he is agitated and wants to move on from this. He snatches up a screwdriver with multiple bits and pulls on the rope to raise the bucket once more. "I still haven't got this thing open yet, and it's almost opening day," says Oriel as he awaits the tool delivery.

"Dad, I need to focus on an important case at work," says Cary. "I want to be able to leave them with you without worrying."

"Don't worry then."

"The daycare will have Emily, but Henry is too old for plastic houses and tea parties."

"Relax," says Oriel as he pries open the hatch with leverage from the screwdriver. "I'll try to keep my stories to myself."

"Thank you. That's all I ask."

Henry Edwards stops looking at what he's been reading to comment: "I like coffee like Grandpa."

"Wow! I was in my teens before you told me your secret drink is just coffee," says Cary.

"It's not just coffee, Cary. Besides, I won't be around forever. And so I've got to pass some things on to the people that care," says Oriel. He looks over his shoulder and down at Henry Edwards; he sees the boy putting down his novel to look at Oriel's dusty photo album and smiles. "Try the switch now, son."

Cary flips a switch on the wall and the hatch opens mechanically. The gears on the wall expose the entire process that the electricity creates; the gears move, small and large ones, they rotate, and with the attached metal brackets between them and the spindle near the top of the ladder that twirls, the lovely teal glass hatch opens.

The basket is a good bit heavier with the magnetic crystals weighing it down. "Sandbags aren't necessary," instructs Oriel while he packs the crystals in plastic resealable baggies. "Fill those sandbags with supplies if you'd like . . . . We'll tie 'em tight with a bowline, so we'll have more room on board."

Upon the counter are all sorts of tools, ropes, gear, and equipment like binoculars and compasses. Emily decides to fill one sandbag with packets of *Borscht "Just Add Water" Soup* and a few small loaves of bread. Henry Edwards helps oversee her operation by sealing each resealable bag before she fills the empty sandbags, and Oriel takes care of the rest. They fill another satchel with cutlery and plates. There's a small table that sits folded down, attached by a hinge on the balloon's basket. When it's propped up on its leg it makes a pleasant place to have a meal on the ground, or in the air even.

"Well, we'll have all day tomorrow with our feet firmly planted. Do you suppose?" asks Oriel.

"I suppose we'll have to lift our legs sometimes," says Henry Edwards. "When we walk!" adds Emily. "Oh, yes! I'm afraid you're right," agrees Oriel.

"Well," says Oriel, "then, I suppose tomorrow night when we go to sleep we ought to lay down with our feet on the floor because the next morning they'll go wayyyy up high . . . ."

"Grandpa!" exclaims Emily. "We can't fall asleep that way. We'll wake up with cramps like pins and beetles!"

"Don't you mean pins and needles?" asks Cary. "Sorry to interrupt, I didn't want to miss out on where you guys are going on the big trip. Are you sure it's safe?" asks Cary. The blue crystal has a glare that catches his eye long enough for him to stop and stare.

Oriel considers it a moment before he says, "If we've come this far without any problems, then those people I thought were out to get me—"

"The ones who shot you," interrupts Cary.

"They must have wandered off like scared dogs by now," says Oriel.

"Yes, well, I don't know about this," says Cary with a small, quaint smile.

"So—our job was to make a high-energy deflecting shield capable of withstanding impact upon landing on the moon's surface," says Oriel. "Global warming is a shame, but—"

"Here you go with talking about back in your day," insists Cary.

"Well the tides stopped moving up and down," says Oriel. "And people missed the way waves normally would break. The water would become still if the moon kept spinning the way it had started spinning. Apollo missions were the way we built and tested for what we needed to keep the moon from taking its own rotation and becoming as evolved, in time, as other rotating satellites. In a sense, we kept the moon dark on one side, killing its potential to bare life . . . in order to give Earth its tides."

News reports are usually panging loudly over the speakers that are mounted around the big open areas that encompass the warehouse, where the balloons and all sorts of ballooning equipment is stored. It's where Oriel does most of his work. He claims that the sound is for disrupting anyone trying to listen in on what is happening in the space. This is Oriel's tactical surveillance counter measure, meant to nullify attacks, and it has worked like a charm for decades.

Oriel tells Henry Edwards a strange stories about the past. He says, "We were looking for owls with the ability to monitor our goings-ons. They were trained to do that. Someone is always watching what we do."

Cary interjects, for he cannot tolerate the stories any longer. He pops his head in through the opening in the doorway. He says, "This is what I was talking about earlier, Dad. Don't fill his head with that garbage. Henry, no one is listening to us— The government has more to do than—"

"We worked with the government," Oriel interrupts. He polishes his little coffee pot after wiping away the loose grounds with a clean rag. "We worked with leaders from around the world. The British. French, Russian Czars, Egyptian Royalty... They were the buzzards. They circled us like the giant birds and they picked our work apart. But we saw them coming. Those separatists were the real troublemakers."

ORIEL is always playing an AM channel that comes in clearly on the radio. It's a news station from the city nearby. Cary doesn't mind the radio because he's familiar with the host speaking. The light-hearted, sensible fellow named Joe Ortev sometimes has investigative pieces that peel back the veil of ordinary life to expose corruption in plain sight. Henry Edwards enjoys listening to the station instead of studying, and he finds it amusing when the host forces each guest to admit that he is the fastest talking host in all the lands.

The afternoon report with Joe Ortev comes on around the time Oriel has returned to his office. He typically stays there listening with his grandson. They often page through science magazines while listening to Fast Talkin' Joe Ortev give the latest scoop from a politician who is hard at work to end illegal smuggling of arms across international borders, or some other breaking news story. That's how Henry got his first glimpse of what the world was like outside of the Forgotten Borough.

One day a politician was wrapping up his spiel, and he said, "If you want further information, take a look at our reports on the internet." To which Joe Ortev replied, "What if our listening audience doesn't have the internet?" Henry Edwards heard this and his ears perked up since he was in the splendid minority to not have the internet streaming constantly. The politician said, "Well, I suppose the listening audience should turn on your show to hear the fastest talking reporter on the planet read the report to them over the air waves. What do you say Joe?" To which Joe replied, "Thank you, but I make no promises until I read the report for myself first."

After the radio show is over, they pack up for the convention Cary set up to explain to folks what happened after Oriel was shot and a thief made off with what appeared to be the Elixiumbrium. Not long after setting up their table, guests rush in through the doors. Reporters are there and camera crews, but Oriel backs away behind the curtains when he spots two particular individuals coming around the corner. "Great," says Oriel to Henry Edwards. "I can't go back out there. This test market is too risky for me, Henry Edwards. Get your father."

Cary had just arrived moments ago, since he had to put in extra time preparing depositions for the gyro case. The boy returns to the convention with his father where they find a table with literature about Sky Vision, but Oriel is nowhere to be seen.

A crowd of confused attendees rush up to Cary Oriel because he stands with the boy, or as one reporter puts it: "That kid—I remember you. Are you related to the old man who was just here a moment ago?"

"We want answers," another reporter demands.

Cary isn't sure what to tell people, so he assures everyone that everything with the crystals is happening on schedule. Most of the reporters are content with this information, but there is one guy who looks concerned. He says, "What if he's shutting down?" Cary has to assure everyone that the governments around the world have mandated the procedure so they can't shut down.

Two strange individuals, one stocky and one with red, slicked-back hair, come over to Henry Edwards while he is covering for his grandfather. He's seated behind the table, in front of the map they had printed to show all the places around the planet that Oriel intends on taking the crystal.

"If you take a look at the black dots," the boy's father says, while showing a map of identical proportions to a few spectators. "Here, and here. That is our latest warehouse and our founding location," he says with all the sales charisma he can muster.

"We'll have to visit for ourselves. Do you still see Oriel building contraptions in the backyard?" inquires an enthusiastic spectator with a purple baseball cap.

"No. My father was never the builder," says Cary. "That was his old business partner, and we don't speak much of him these days."

Done with waiting to talk to the man in charge, the two strange individuals make their way around the spectators. The woman with red, slick hair stands in front of Henry Edwards to see the large map up close, while the stocky fellow takes a smaller map and unfolds it.

"I bet you're very proud of your family legacy," the slick-haired woman says to the boy.

"Well, of course I am," says Henry Edwards. "Not many kids my age get to see the world from up high like I do."

"I'm not talking about vacations in Fiji or family trips driving across the country, kid," says the slick-haired woman.

"Easy," her stocky acquaintance says, and she calms down some.

"You think I don't understand," says Henry Edwards, "but while you are tying your shoes on the sidewalk, or taking a nap in your living room, I'm up there learning to fly."

The stocky man picks up a brochure, and he reads aloud, "Founder of the lowest cost hot air balloon fuel alternative." He closes the brochure delicately and says, "You think we don't know what's in it?" He slams the brochure down on the black cotton table cloth.

Cary stops in the middle of a sentence to get in front of the man. He places his thumb and forefinger on the chest of the stocky character. He put his arms up to separate them entirely from the table, and he says, "Good to see you today. Sorry, my son isn't a salesman. Maybe I could help escort you to a fine eggroll or slushy. How about some steamed cabbage or ice on your jaw?" He grabs their jackets and pulls them from the table.

"No. We were just leaving!" exclaims the woman. "Your kid doesn't know how he's going to have to go through it all." They stumble out together. But she turns to say one last thing to Henry Edwards: "You'll never know what hit you. One day, you're going to have to find out . . . for yourself."

The two strange individuals disappear. They're sucked into the crowds of people who want answers.

Henry Edwards wants to ask his father who they were, but he waits until they're finished their day at the convention. They're packing up the table before making the trip back to the Oriel Estate when Oriel comes up to them in the parking lot after they leave the building. Henry Edwards and Cary are the only two people there. He says, "Did they come up to you inside?"

"Who? Did who come up to us, Dad?" asks Cary.

"Those sons of bitches—I can't go on with this hanging over me," Oriel says. "What I've been telling you, every word of it is true, son."

"Were they the two from your story?" asks Henry Edwards, but Oriel is already walking off into the woods. Oriel says, "I'll meet you both later," and he's gone.

Cary shakes his head and says, "Don't believe a damn word he says . . . ."

They get in the car and make tracks in the sand on their way out. They fail to notice the woman with the slick hair is there on the sandy driveway. She picks up a handful of sand from the tracks they made on their way out. She looks over to see her stocky brother flipping through a series of blueprints. He walks off in the same direction that Oriel journeyed moments ago. The woman with the slick hair follows after her brother.

"We're going to have to call the trip off. I'm sorry, Henry. I'll break the news to Emily," says Oriel.

"I'll tell her when I see her," says Cary. "We're going to spend our first night in the new house."

Oriel doesn't let his spirits weep for long. He starts singing loudly to himself. Henry Edwards and his father can hear the old man sing:

"When at One,
one wonders what it's like to be a dove.
When at Two,
we wonder what in the world to do
About our lives
at Three and Four.
And at Five,
the world is alive.
Six o'clock,
a balloon between sun and moon.
At Seven,
we wander from clouds to dock by Eight.
At Nine,
be there to bed to rise and shine again."

Before Cary leaves, his son does a brave thing by confronting his father and asking who he thinks the strange people were and what they meant by what they told him about his family legacy. His father didn't know what to say . . . .

"Not everything is true that your grandfather says, you know," says Cary.

"Well, some things are," says Henry Edwards.

"Yes," says Cary, "but most of it is lies . . . ."

"So you're just going to leave us and go see that new lady," says Henry Edwards.

"It's not that simple," says Cary. "I'm picking up Emily. And I'm taking her to see your mother before she sees the new . . . apartment."

"Why?" asks Henry Edwards. "What's the point of seeing *her* if she's dead already."

"Henry!" exclaims Cary. "Your mother is still alive."

"Saying that," says Henry Edwards, "is like how grand-dad says things about being in outer space, near Saturn's rings and catching a nebula in a jar but losing it before getting back to Earth."

"Your grandfather is a screwball," Cary says dismissively. "But this is different, son. Your mother is still alive. Do you remember how she had to leave you? Well, she's still out there. I can feel it in my bones. I can feel it . . . in my heart . . . ."

"Oh Dad," says Henry Edwards. "She's probably looking at us from the stars. I think about her that way."

"Me too, son," the father says, while looking through the opening in the warehouse door at the sky filled with clouds. The door slams shut when Cary leaves, and Henry Edwards is left alone.

The alarm at the warehouse goes off when someone triggers the motion detectors at the edge of the property. Oriel and Henry Edwards are asleep in the loft when they awake to the screeching of the sirens. It bellows throughout the island.

The boy meets his grandfather in the secret room hidden

off of the loft built between the bedrooms. They go down the stairs that lead out of the facility entirely. Oriel has some trouble getting the door open; it's seized shut from rust that took a hold of its hinges; both top and bottom hinges succumbed to rust during the floods that hit the city over the last few summers, creating significant amounts of runoff that crept through the hillside estates of their community and washed through any facility that was under sea-level.

"That rust is to prevent intruders. We don't want anyone coming in after us, pal," Oriel says as he presses his shoulder against the door for extra leverage. He has no trouble recognizing the relief on the child's face when the door closes behind them.

There are cobwebs and spiders all over the place, but it isn't shabby for a place to take leave in a hurry. The inside of the safe room is carpeted in the lounge and sleeping area. Heating, cooling, lights, and all other electricity is supplied by a hydro-generator (situated on the bed of the Rahway River that separates Staten Island from Elizabeth and the rest of Never York that's to the west of the big city). And even though the river typically has low turbidity, the batteries pull enough off of the generator to remain well-charged.

Henry Edwards sits in the safe room on the edge of a bench that Oriel once snatched from a diner that closed, but when the boy notices all the webs he quickly gets back up to his feet. He helps his grandfather secure the door by pushing with him.

With the door firmly shut, they move quickly over to the surveillance station, where video monitors power up to display the feed of a few locations around the warehouse. There are cameras outside and inside of the estate, in the museum, in the shop, and in the warehouse. Their empty beds are on one screen, and another screen shows two masked individuals entering the side door of the warehouse, where loud radio broadcasts are still playing in an attempt to confuse and disorient the intruders.

Nevertheless, the assailants move swiftly toward their target.

Oriel is scrambling; he is unsure of what to do. He has planned for these times, and he even warned his family that he has secrets enough to make some very inconsiderate people come after him. This is why Henry Edwards already knew about the shelter underground. Cary would be there with them if he wasn't busy with introducing Emily to her new . . . home. As the old man watches the video monitors, his mind finishes coming up with a plan.

"Do you recognize either of them?" asks Oriel.

"No," says Henry Edwards. When he looks closer at the video screen of the individuals clawing at book cases and corners of the room to find the secret passage, he gets excited and says, "Those were the strange people that came up to us when you left today!"

At the Care Center to visit Adeline, Cary is alone with his daughter. She gets out of the car first, but Cary calls her back to the car. He says, "You forgot something, sweet one." Emily comes back across the drop-off circle and she goes into the back of the car to get a stuffed-toy giraffe. "Good girl," says Cary, and he kisses her forehead. "Tell Mommy about our plans to see the new house, and when you get done talking with her I have another surprise for you, my dearest."

Cary waits in the car. And Emily waits in the lobby while they prepare Adeline. Nurses have already administered enough medicine to assist Adeline in regulating her blood pressure, kidney functions, gastric functions, and immune functions. But Emily must wait while the nurses prepare her clean gown and move her to the Main Hall for family visits.

After the visit the girl returns to her father's car holding the giraffe under her arm. Cary says, "I thought you were leaving that with Mommy?" The child shakes her head and grips the giraffe tightly. Emily says, "Mommy wants me to have him with me."

"Okay, darling," says Cary. "Come in and have a seat." When she gets in, he says, "I've heard from the nurses that you're asking Mommy a lot about what it's like to grow up to be a lady, and I want you to have someone to talk to . . . ."

"Daddy, you don't have to worry. I'll keep asking my mother," says Emily.

"Well," says Cary, "I have a better idea of someone you should talk to instead, and I'm sure Mommy would understand."

"Who is it?" asks Emily.

"You don't know her yet, sweets," says Cary.

"Did she know my mother?" asks Emily.

"No," says Cary. "I don't suppose she did."

In a shrill sounding voice, the child says, "I'll keep asking Mommy and not bother you at all, Daddy."

"Well," says Cary, "I'd like it if you tried talking to my friend too."

"I'll be back then," says Emily. She gets out of the car and starts walking towards the Care Center when Cary asks her from through his open window, "Where are you going, sweets?" She turns to him and says, "I'll ask Mommy if it's okay to talk to your friend instead."

He waits a few moments for the little girl to return with her answer: "She says, 'No.' That's what she said." Emily shrugs her shoulders, and Cary thinks he better not pressure her further about meeting Joslin Peters tonight.

They stay the night in a hotel nearby. Cary makes pancakes for Emily in the morning, using the toaster. He goes to work when Emily goes to daycare.

Chapter Four

Nothing More Than A Dot Of Light

HENRY Edwards does not go willingly away from this place. He wants to stay with his grandfather to fight off any intruders, but Oriel wants his safety above all else. The next few moments Oriel acts out of desperation. For, the room they inhabit at the present is not going to keep them safe forever, but there are ways out of there that the intruders do not know. So Oriel comes to a resolution in his own mind to not take the tunnels in a last ditch effort to flee with his secrets and his grandson, and he decides instead that it would be easier for the young boy to slip away by himself through the vents, but he thinks Henry Edwards will not want to go alone.

He flips a switch at the work station in the safe room that controls a mechanism in the workshop to aid in their speedy get-away.

"We'll take to the vents and get out of here together," Oriel says.

"Not without you, Grandpa," Henry Edwards says.

"Of course, my boy," says Oriel. He makes his way to the large air duct near the door that was rusted shut. He notices on the monitor that the intruders have found the passage in his bedroom that leads to the hallway they took to get to the safe room. His hands move quickly to remove the large rectangular cover on the air vent using a tiny screwdriver from his coat pocket.

There isn't much room in the ducts for Oriel to fit inside, but he knows it is a straight path to get up to the main level of the warehouse where they will have a better chance of getting away. He welcomes Henry Edwards to get in the duct first; he says, "You're going now before it's too late. These men won't stop. If you're here, they'll use you to break me. I want you safe, kid."

"I don't want to leave you behind. We can both get away," Henry Edwards states with enough calm sincerity to cause the empirical wisdom of Oriel to stall out momentarily. The old man nods. They promptly venture further onward!

Oriel picks up a coffee pot that has been warming since they entered the space. There is enough coffee already in the pot for him to take a shot of it before squeezing inside the air vent: 'Smash!' and 'Clang!' sound the walls and floor of the duct as Oriel squeezes in through the opening.

Henry Edwards is already inside of the duct, waiting on instructions from Oriel about which way to turn when he reaches the first bend in the duct system.

When they reach the end of the shaft running parallel to the stairwell they climbed down earlier, they must ascend the massive vertical air vent crossing, or ventilation stack. Luckily, Oriel had a ladder installed for the occasional quick escapes like this one. It's dusty at points, but since the natural vents are in use for maintaining air pressures within the estates, there aren't an extraordinary amount of spiders waiting to greet them with webs. Still, Henry Edwards gets caught in a web when they reach the final section, and upon making it to the top he lets out a long-suppressed cough. They both freeze their movements completely.

The cough he made wasn't very loud. The intruders are at the safe room door, and they are prying it open with a crowbar. If only Oriel could know, his joke about the rust holds true! That door is harder for the intruders to break through. It takes two grown people a fair amount of time, about twenty seconds, of leaning their body weight on the tool to give them enough leverage to pry open the door.

Henry Edwards covers his mouth after spitting out the spider web. He moves on when his grandfather catches up to him. They are nearly to the vent opening that leads to the main showroom connecting to their workshop. When all of a sudden they can hear two distinct noises at either end of the duct. The sound of the radio station with sirens behind the static AM Channel, and sounds of the intruders reaching the inside of the safe room are at either end of the vent.

It doesn't take the intruders long to figure out that the man they are after has been taking them for a trip around the property. The intruders enter the safe room, they don't bother looking at the video monitors and other strange gadgets scattered about. The woman with the red, slick hair notices the chair nearest the door looks like someone was sitting on it because of the marks Henry made in the dust and spider webs.

Her stocky sibling takes to the seams of the wallpaper in search of another passage in the room to some unimaginable hidden fortress or a way out of the property. He's busy scraping and scouring the room until his attractive counterpart notices something. She spins around from the chair to examine a small scratch made on the surface of the vent leading from the room. She wiggles the screws loose, and upon closer inspection, she stands up and she motions for her partner to follow her up the stairs.

Oriel says to Henry Edwards, "The police are on their way," as he fiddles with something from his coat pocket.

They reach the showroom where the first balloon that Oriel built is housed for display; the balloon envelope is nearly completely inflated after Oriel flipped the switch for the burner to start warming up the air in the envelope. The red vinyl envelope is making contact with the teal glass near where Oriel had his ladder mounted to oil its hinges. The balloon houses a discovery that will shape the world, change their family, and it's responsible for placing both boy and grandfather in the predicament that they are troubled with presently. That balloon flew around the world many times. As old as the balloon is when compared with modern contraptions flown today, the balloon in the showroom— with its bright, thick, nylon envelope and its wicker basket made from bamboo Oriel cut down himself— is all ready to go on an adventure.

The adventure that was planned is one for this ballooning family to take together. They planned to fly from their town to the ocean to visit Chet. It looks like that trip will have to wait.

By the time Henry Edwards nears the opening and peers from the vent cover leading to the showroom, his distraction with what is beyond the vent has caused the boy to overlook what Oriel has been doing. His grandfather has clipped a simple, locking screwgate carabiner to his shoes, at the laces. And he slips a lanyard around the boy's wrists that he pulls tightly.

"What are you doing?" asks the boy. And with a thick rope he pulls from a hanging sign on the showroom's ceiling, a sign that reads, 'Ballooning History at SKY VISION,' Oriel makes with harnessing and roping Henry Edwards securely. The rope is strong enough to lower Henry Edwards into the balloon basket before he even completely comprehends what is happening to him.

To Henry Edwards, it feels as if he were a prize in a claw machine, and a claw has picked him to be in the basket. As soon as he knows what is happening, he receives a push from Oriel. He drops from the air ducts and he's lowered to the inside of the basket of the balloon. The boy lets out a holler, and he says, "What are you doing with me?"

Oriel says, "I'm making sure you get out of here." The sirens are approaching, but they are still far off, and the intruders are closing in on Oriel and his grandson. They are coming back out of the secret upstairs passage when Oriel pulls the lever on the wall that opens up the hatch on the ceiling. The glass turns from teal to sea-foam green as the windows open gently on their well-oiled chrome hinges. With the hot balloon already ready to fly off, it doesn't take long for Oriel to make it lift away! The very secret that the intruders are after aids in the quick lift of the balloon itself.

It starts to lift, and Oriel has to hurry to throw a pair of scissors into the basket with Henry. The balloon and basket make it through the hatch with the boy along for the ride when Oriel takes the lever and moves it to shut the impressive glass-hatch that sometimes brings spectators to the showroom for nighttime star gazing.

With the AM radio station still playing loudly, Oriel is certain the intruders haven't heard a sound of the balloon's departure or the hinges opening and closing the teal glass-hatch.

"You're working late, old man," says Bile, the man from the convention.

The tall, attractive, red-head named Sybil reaches the security camera and ejects the tape to take with them.

He's high above the property he knows well when Henry Edwards is able to free himself. He cuts his wrists free first, and then he's able to untie one of the shoes he wears, enough to slip it off. He works on unlocking the carabiner when he stands up to look over the railing at the scene down below his balloon.

He stays quiet and sets course for the spot where they had planned to visit on their trip, and he wonders what happened to his grandfather. The lights of police cars coming toward the workshop have been growing brighter, but the other car that the intruders rode in is gone from the property.

As he watches the sun come up to light a place for his balloon to travel, Henry Edwards wonders if anyone has seen his flight from the showroom. He knows he is able to guide the balloon, but he fears he will lose his bearings.

The boy brings out his compass and a map of the area. He locates Sky Vision and Oriel Estates on the map by finding the corner of town that he is most familiar with. He knows how to use the roads, local roads and interstate highways, to guide the course he sets. But he has never planned like this, so he hopes he will cover sufficient ground to justify landing the balloon to rest later on, before night.

They slip away, farther away from him until they are nothing much, nothing more than a dot of light that he can hardly see, and eventually, he forgets the dot was there; then, it isn't.

Chapter Five

The Goose's Nursery Rhymes

"**W**HERE am I?" Oriel shouts to an audience he doesn't comprehend.

"You're . . ." says a voice that trails off completely behind the humming fluorescent lights. "You're having a bad dream . . ." says the voice in a round echo quality.

Bile removes the mask covering Oriel's eyes, and the old man looks around, but he can't move much due to the restrictive shackles holding his wrists against the walls.

"What have you done?" asks Oriel.

"We were in your neighborhood and thought we could have a chat— I hope you don't mind the urgency of our little meeting," says the Goose from behind a white curtain dividing the room. His silhouette is still. "We've been looking for you for sometime—Jerry, take over, will you?"

Jerry approaches from the back of the room when the Goose moves out from behind the curtain. The big butcher with the mole on his chin, known by everyone as 'the Goose', sits upon a stool near the window where he basks in the sunlight. Jerry has a cigarette in hand, but he doesn't smoke it. No! He says, "The Goose is interested in having a partnership." He holds the lit cigarette close to Oriel. He asks, "Smoke?" Oriel denies the offering.

"We want to reach a peaceful negotiation," says Jerry, "and I find that smoking helps calm my nerves . . . . You look a little stressed out yourself." Jerry pulls smoke into his lungs and lets it out as he says, "Our idea is to control the means to distribute your product . . . ." Jerry rolls his eyes and says, "How does that sound?"

Oriel blows the smoke away from his face with short bursts of air. He says, "I've seen better negotiation skills when a pilot yells 'May Day!' and he's the only one with a parachute. I must say . . . ."

"Some people say smoking gives them yellow teeth. What do you think?" asks Jerry with his fangs showing in a wide, toothy smile. "What do you think is coming next?" asks Jerry as he holds the embers of the fag close to Oriel's outstretched neck.

Jerry is interrupted by a shrill quack let out from the man basking in the sun who turns the noise into words, to say: "Jerry, I have a better idea. Let's treat our guest to a nursery rhyme, shall we?"

Jerry backs off and says, "Whatever you say, Gino—I mean, Goose."

"Good—Once upon a time," says the Goose with a big-lipped smile and a spin from his high-backed stool, "because that's my favorite way to begin— See, the best things follow any sentiment that can only happen once. I find the words that follow the phrase 'Once upon a time' are always worth all the build-up . . . ." The Goose spins away from his stool to take down the top corner-edge of the white curtain. He reveals the slick-haired Sybil standing next to a small bed on a raised platform.

Sybil slides the bed closer to Oriel. Its wheels slide smoothly on the buffed concrete floor.

Oriel looks at the bed and gasps, for his dear granddaughter, Emily, is there asleep in the chamber.

"Don't worry, old man . . . . This is a happy nursery rhyme," says the frowning Gino, who continues to say: "For their once lived a girl with no mother,
Mother slept all day and . . .
. . . little girl thought she didn't love her.
So what did she do to get . . .
. . . her motherly affection?
How about we administer round-the-clock . . .
. . . opium injections..."

Oriel hangs his knobby head low, but the Goose is not satisfied with that, so he takes clear plastic gloves from his pocket. He holds the gloves in his hands to create a barrier between his hands and Oriel's cheeks. With that comfortable detachment, he's able to force Oriel's head to turn. He forces Oriel to watch. He says, "Don't miss the best part," as Sybil gives the girl a shot to keep her sleeping.

The excitement causes the Goose to quack a little, but that turns into words, to say:
"Is it destiny or is it irony?
That Mother and Daughter . . .
. . . join in a dreamy symphony?"

Oriel is unable to comprehend what has happened in front of his eyes. He says, "If you take all the crystals, there won't be enough of . . . to fix the problem with the tides."
The Goose smiles for the first time that day. It's a big-lipped smile. He says, "I don't care for the tides. Once I have your secret formula, Earth can stop moving altogether for all I care . . . ."
The Goose extends his neck to its most outstretched position, and from the back of his shirt collar protrudes a line of soft, white plumage, enough feathers to keep him warm on a cold winter day. He lowers his head and says, "Take them away." Jerry moves in and pulls all the feathers he can reach, while the Goose is sitting still on the tall stool.

After plucking is finished, Jerry applies a cold pack of ice to minimize the swelling that is inevitable. Oriel has seen enough, but he has nowhere else to look. A breeze blows each dancing feather along the floor, and most of them end up under Emily's bed.

Chapter Six

Strange Calls & A Secret Lover

AMONG the fuel tanks is a large crate that normally contains gear, but Henry Edwards remembers packing something else in the crate. He removes the photo album Oriel put together, and he thinks to himself, wondering what Oriel would tell him if he were there with him.

He opens the album to where his grandfather left off in the story . . .

"Will I always miss out on all the excitement, Pa-pa?" asked Prince Ascubar's daughter.

"You have your share of excitement already," Prince Ascubar said, "and I will rest tonight, no matter where I happen to be tonight, because I will get you somewhere that I know will be safe."

"I don't believe what everyone said about what came aboard the boat," Esmeralda said.

"It didn't just come aboard the boat. It ripped something precious from our clutches and took it into the ocean," Ascubar said.

"Something precious?" the young royal girl inquired.

"It's an orb that was discovered that could return Earth back to the blessed kingdom we know, and we're going to need it back," he told his daughter.

"Is that why the tall man and the ship's captain are so eager to get it back?" the girl asked.

"They are both clever enough to outwit an octopus or whatever is responsible for the loss," he said.

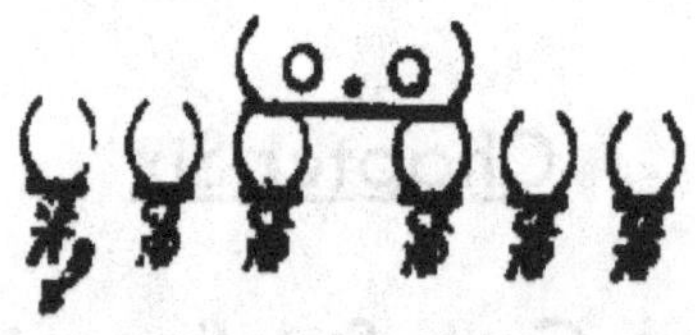

"Hey! Come up here and say that!" Inspector Cary Oriel yells with torment down into the trolley track behind his business place to a lunatic poking around in the bushes down below.

The fellow below once lived on the trolley track that runs along the island until his small shack was raided for narcotics one evening during the summer, when a few boys were playing too close to the tracks and stream. Since then he has been worse off. He's been talking to himself all afternoon.

Cary finally says something for the benefit of all the intelligent, hearing folks in the neighborhood that don't tolerate such a noxious predator living in the area, either. The lunatic has been saying things like: "I'll find you. I'll find out where you sleep. And I'll stand there by your window watching you, and when you come out of your house, I'll be there, waiting for you like I know you. I won't ask you nothing, but I am going to take something from you—not your fancy car or diamond rings, either. Nope. I'll leave you those because they don't do me any good. If I'm watching you like that, it's because I'm taking a part of you . . . . I take a part of your being and who you are every time I'm at your door."

Needless to say, people living and working in the neighborhood did not like to interact with the lunatic, and his heart hardened to prove how it feels to be shunned when treated with contrition by the parents who would cover the gazes of their children from seeing him.

"Hell yeah! What are you going to do?" the pained fellow shouts upward, and spittle runs from his mouth to cover his beard, like runny egg.

"It sounds like you're talking to yourself, since you don't have anyone with you," says Cary.

"I'm talking to you," says the lunatic.

"I tell you what," says Cary, "you come up here and say to my face the things you keep saying to us, and I'll break your fingers."

"I'm on my way," says the lunatic.

He finishes writing a report, condemning a case of strange lingonberry jam that has expired. After setting the report aside for Joslin to file when she returns tomorrow, Inspector Cary Oriel picks up the receiver of his tan office line and dials. "Hello, thank you for taking the call."

"9-1-1. What's your emergency?" the operator's voice seems to spring off the earpiece and into Cary's ear.

He pulls the phone away some and says, "I just told the man hurling garbage at my window, if he comes up and deals with me like a man, I told him I'll break his fingers."

"Sir, please calm down," the woman's voice says. She tries to remain neutral and says, "What's your location?"

"He's on his way up here already."

"Sir, please tell me your location so I can send a car."

"Public Health Works Building. Fourth floor. And send an ambulance while you're talking cars," Cary says.

"Sir, what are you going to do?" the woman asks.

"It's been a rough morning for me. But I'm a man of my word," replies Cary. He places the receiver on his desk. The operator hears the sounds of a door opening, followed by several loud noises, including the sounds of crunching bones.

On the old welcome mat in the hallway in front of 422 Manchester Avenue, Unit B, the door is ajar, due to the stack of two medium-sized boxes placed in the threshold. The top brown cardboard box is accurately labeled and contains kitchen items, but the bottom box has a label that has been scrawled out with black marker.

The bottom box contains stereo equipment. The top box gets pushed aside to get to the bottom box, which he unpacks while waiting for Joslin to show up with the keys and copies of keys. He untangles the wires that lead from speakers to the console, one set of wires with prongs twisted at each end for the right speaker and the other set for the left speaker. Upon stretching the power cord out along the full length of the room, he finds it to be adequate cordage to supply electricity from the outlet to the console, even if he keeps the console near the dining room; he thinks about running an extension to the cord.

He reckons the antenna wire will be useless, crumples the cord up, tosses it into the box from whence it came, and mumbles to himself about the lack of quality radio programming in the Forgotten Borough. The radio stations in Never York have been going downhill altogether, mainly because traffic reporting is useless in the city since there is constant traffic at all hours in most neighborhoods. But there is a certain news station that broadcasts groundbreaking stories . . . .

He leapt to the box to untangle the wires. He hopes to catch part of an investigative report before Joslin arrives.

He turns the console on to Fast Talkin' Joe Ortev.

✢

Meanwhile, Inspector Cary Oriel crowds the door of a phone booth outside of his place of work; he left before the ambulance arrived to cart away what's left of the lunatic. On the way down he had to wait for the fur coat wearing older lady to exit the booth before entering. He lights a cigarette, picks up the receiver, and dials.

"Hi," says Cary, "Please put me through to the fastest talking news anchor in all the land— Hi, Joe? Are we live?"

"Joe will be with you shortly," says the operator.

"You're live with Fast Talking Joe Ortev," says another voice.

"I already told you once, Joe. You're the fastest talking anchor in all the land— just ask the other guys. Never mind they're taking forever to respond—"

"Alright, caller. What can I do for you?" asks Joe Ortev.

"I have a favor to ask you," says Cary.

Joe lets out a howl and laughs before he says, "Gee, Cary, is that you, ol' buddy?"

"It is, and happy birthday to you."

"Thank you, but I have to ask for the receipt," Joe retorts. "We'll be right back, folks." The station cuts to commercials before Joe says, "What can I do for you, Cary?"

"I need you to try reading the report," says Cary. "The calls always come in. This time . . . I'm going to record it to show you."

"No. I don't . . . ." says Joe; he sounds far away. "Listen," he says, "we're coming back from commercial soon. I can't keep reading that piece you sent me over the air. It bugs my producer and creeps out listeners, or else I would."

"Read it one more time, Joe," says Cary. "Will you please? I'll give you first dibs on any story that comes of it." Cary pleads with the news anchor.

"Yeah, but I have plenty of stories already," says Ortev.

"How many times have I listened to your tips?" asks Cary. "I've shut down city blocks when you've worked up a story to fit the order."

"You're welcome," says Ortev.

"I make your stories worth something, and it keeps you employed," says Cary. "I'm not dumb. You need me the same."

The speedy delivery of that wiry Spanish man comes to a slow fizzle; Joe can't come up with anything to say as a rebuttal.

"I'll record when the call comes in and let you hear," says Cary.

"Okay, but I won't be able to listen to the recording . . . . That's not for me, Cary. I can't get into it," Joe says.

"That's up to you, Joe," Cary says. "I'll send the shorter

version to read on the air—"

"Yeah," interrupts Ortev. "Keep it short."

"And I'll see if she calls," says Cary.

"If who calls?" Joe asks. He motions to his producer, who is stalling on the air; she's good at vamping into a microphone, so he isn't worried yet.

"Take a look at your email," says Cary. "I sent it before I left the office. Won't take long—not for you anyway."

"You can say that again, but I'd probably beat you to the finish," Joe says before Cary hangs up the other end.

Meanwhile, Joslin enters the apartment at 422 Manchester Avenue to find her secret lover fiddling with a broken antenna wire. The static fills the space and spills into the hallway.

Joslin says, "Are you expecting guests?" as she pushes the leftover box of kitchen supplies in through the doorway to give room for her to enter.

Her lover lifts the box and places it on the kitchen counter to unpack. She places her grocery bag next to the box and removes a half-dozen bagels in a plastic sleeve.

He takes a box-cutter to the tape on the moving box. When finished, he conceals the blade inside its metal sleeve. With a few quick motions more there's a toaster on the counter and its plugged in.

"You look surprised that I knew there would be a toaster in that box," he says.

"I'm surprised that you're bold enough to unpack my fiancé's belongings . . . without asking me when he would be home. And you're shirtless. That's why I'm surprised," Joslin says while blushing. It is hard for her to remain pale when a man as alluring as he stands buttering her bagel.

"That guy don't stand a chance," says her lover.

She joins him by removing her shirt and breaking a bagel apart. She presses her broken piece against his buttery piece, and then, she presses the lever down on the toaster. The toaster starts humming as it warms up.

"You know you usually put the bread *in* the toaster before you butter it, right?" he asks her.

The toaster clicks and shoots its metal coils back up again. "I know, but I love feeling things warm up," she says, and she presses the lever down once more.

He takes her hand away from the toaster. There's room for him to play, so he holds the lever down without letting it back up. He watches the heating coils turn cherry red.

"Aren't you . . . special," Joslin says and plants a kiss on his cheek.

She walks away to leave him there examining the bag of groceries.

"You bought whole wheat? I thought you hated whole wheat, Joslin?" he asks her.

"Well," Joslin says, "it goes great with the jam I brought home from work. I don't care for it, but I thought you might like to try it."

"This?" asks her lover as he holds up a jar of purple berries. "It smells rather tart."

"Yes," she says, "I suppose it does."

The first time Cary walks into the apartment on Manchester, the place they mean to share until their marriage, the first place they share as a couple—the place meant to test if Joslin is the right woman to be there for Cary's children—the apartment is empty.

"What do you think of the stereo being set up over there? I know . . . it's far from the living room," Joslin says as they walk through the door.

Cary pauses and looks at the console of the stereo for a bit. "I think the sound will travel to fill the space." He notices the antenna is missing. "I thought I packed an antenna here somewhere."

Joslin comes to his side and says, "We need a new one. I threw away that one you packed." Of course, she remembers what happened to it when her lover bent the wires back and forth until the prongs broke off, and he had no idea how to strip the cordage to produce more wires from the line. *He* tossed it in the garbage.

She kisses him, and Cary asks her, "Do smell lingonberry?"

Joslin doesn't hide her surprise. She replies, "You can smell well today, Cary. Can't you?"

"I love the smell of lingonberry, Joslin," he says. "But I didn't know you knew where to find them around here."

"Yes," Joslin says. "Yes, I do. Oh, at the market on 25th. *Friday's!*" she says.

"Yes," Cary agrees, "Friday's is great. You know everything, Joslin. You're quite cultured."

"Thank you," Joslin says while taking some glasses from newspaper wrappings.

Cary watches her in the clean reflection of the stereo console. He turns the dial that moves along the red slider to show what station is selected to play. As his idle hands move the knob, he says with a great deal of conviction—enough to raise a dead horse— "What on Earth—the CD player is busted—I probably should have packed some bubbles over top of the door. I think it slammed when they closed the gate on the moving truck." He stops futzing with the knob and goes to the actual CD player door. Taking out a shiny reflective object and holding it low, below the door, he sees what part of the door is apart and pops it back in place. His eyes move to the door's reflection, and he sees her standing in the kitchen; she is picking her teeth with a napkin.

When they meet it's to the sound of smooth jazz guitar. "The disc works, I see. Sounds like Mozart had to wait," Joslin says.

"I have it, but I save the classics for when I want to unwind," Cary says.

"But the day is still fresh," Joslin says.

"I know. Listen," Cary says, "you're fresher. If you only knew. You're a darling." He breaks away from her.

"You know what to say. Where are you going?" Joslin asks.

"To make a phone call," he says before exiting the apartment for the first, and final time.

"Listen," says Cary, "don't do it because you feel like you owe me. You don't know what's about to happen."

"Cary?"

"I'm here. I'm good now, but I might not be in a few hours."

"You're alright," says Ortev. "Listen to me. I got to go, kid, but you'll be fine. I'm making the call on saying your announcement for you—for your family. You'll find them."

"It's not that . . . ."

"Then what Cary?"

Cary crumples up his necktie and removes it. He says, "Check your email, Joe."

"I can't. I'm not there in the office."

"I can't explain everything. But I've got to get out of town now. Everything is falling apart."

Joe clicks his tongue and says, "You got to straighten up a bit. Get your act together. You just moved in with Joslin, right? She's making you sleep on the sofa already, huh?"

"She's nothing," he says and pauses. "I shoulda known when I found out what her brother was like. They're a family of louses. But I thought she was alright . . . to take the place of my wife."

"Right."

"Well, I was wrong, alright? Lay off. I have to get going, Joe. Read the email and tell the story. That's your job."

Joe hangs up and hops back on the air. "You're out of time, Bonny… That was Bon-bon A-loo-loo with her consuming autobiography. Now it's time for some actual reporting . . . .

"Get up and get out! When you're through talking, you're through in this studio . . . so leave," Ortev says and looks around the room; everyone is waiting to hear where this goes: "I'm kidding but seriously—Let's give a warm thank-you to Boo-Boo for sharing her life story—I wasn't really paying attention to be perfectly honest with everyone— I had an emergency . . . . My ears . . . started bleeding . . . when she . . . opened her mouth . . . ."

The last guest is not the slightest bit amused. In fact, she turns bright red. "No. I won't sign diddly-squat," she says as she slams a ball-point pen down on a clipboard. It goes '*Thwack!*' so hard even the listeners can hear the slap of the pen. The decibel is high enough that Joe turns to her to show her that he is going to keep going even if his rant didn't go well, and he doesn't cut the feed because he knows this drama is good for ratings.

The guest tries to leave out after asking the producer: "Why did you even ask me on the show? Just to ridicule me? I've had a hard life, but nobody— nobody needs this treatment."

The producer—she's used to it—She tries to calm the guest down, or at least she tries her best to slow the guest down from leaving, while Joe makes the microphones more sensitive. He opens up the email Cary sent his way. He reads the email to himself while the guest keeps expressing her unsatisfactory experience: "I've never been treated with such hostility . . . in all my years."

Joe reads to himself: "I'm going to have to hang low, Joe." Meanwhile, the guest continues ranting: "Real professionals know how to treat their guests . . . ."

Cary's email continues to say, "They've been watching me closely and I feel like they're closing in," . . . .

"I'm a lady!" says the guest, and viewers start turning their knobs to the highest volume to hear the guest shouting. The producer writes her comments down in an attempt to show the guest that she is being heard. "Put this down: 'Learn to treat women with respect.' We're interesting too, jerk!" The guest stares at Joe, but he is fixated, lost in the email that carries on loudly in his head:

"All I know is I can't trust the woman I thought I could . . . Joslin. And my wife . . . she's the only woman I ever trusted but she can't hear me when our children are in danger. I feel like I'm in danger being here too. I hope you know it has to be something bad to cause me to leave. Yours, Cary."

Joe sees that the guest is gone and the air is dead, so he switches gears, like a professional to say, "Folks, I want to read a special announcement today. I promised a friend that I would keep putting the story out there. You know it already if you listen to my show, but if you have any information on the whereabouts of the Oriel family that went missing: Grandfather and two children.

You'll do a great service to the world by bringing that information forward to authorities and the media. I am in touch with Mr. Cary Oriel, and I don't believe what I'm starting to hear . . . in the news." He turns the computer screen off and closes his eyes for a moment before saying, "Our lines are open. Thank you everyone.

"Let's get on to our next guest . . . . I suppose you've gotten your car washed this past year, but have you gotten it spit-shined? The newest carwash on Main and 14th is open to clear the pollen from your eyes and your mirrors . . . with fluids the Earth provides . . . ." He turns the microphone over, and he looks at the email once more before deleting it.

━━━O,O,O━━━

The voice sounds like this: "P-sh-pppp-shhhh-pppp-hhhh— I've been dreaming—ppppp——sheeeeeee— I've been awake. I've been saving my dreams to be with you . . . ."

On the fourth floor of the Staten Island Health and Public Safety Department, outside of the commercial capital of the eastern seaboard, Inspector Cary Oriel sits at his desk. The state-commissioned health inspector is known most exclusively by judges, lawyers, and several unlucky business & property owners throughout his district. But needless to say, Cary Oriel does not know how to respond to the strange phone call. There isn't much activity left on the line apart from a strange whirring sound, but in the background he hears a murmur.

He flips a switch on his desk. The switch next to the phone controls a tape recorder mounted under the phone in the top drawer. The capstan and pinch rollers spin lively as the electromagnetic strips of the cassette tape are held in place. The tape is fed long the reels inside the tape recorder. The tiny electromagnets inside the device begin recording the sounds on the phone line as the murmur becomes silent.

93

CARY gasps and says into the receiver, "This isn't funny, whoever you are. If you have information on my family's whereabouts, come forward . . . ."

All at once the line goes dead and the overhead lights turn off. Cary feels around for the curtain rod and gives it a twist to let some of the crimson evening sunlight fill the space. He opens the top drawer of his desk before nudging the tape recorder. He opens and closes the tape deck before reaching the phonebook.

He takes the phonebook down the street to use the booth on the corner of his block. Cary dials, and the voice of the man that picks up the other end says, "I'm about to go live, Inspector. Can this wait?" It's the voice of the quick-witted radio show host again.

"Do you want me to go run with the story again?" asks Ortev.

"No, Joey," says Cary. "It worked. She called. Don't run the story anymore. Run it tomorrow, maybe. I don't know. But I'll pay double if you meet me for coffee."

"Great. You'll pay double, and I'm not even tipping you off about anything today. I'll have what you're having," says Ortev. He pauses before asking, "Do you want me to tell people to keep their eyes open?"

"You could do that. Do it a few times since you're the fastest talking guy around."

"Meet at the usual spot then," says Ortev before the line disconnects.

After Cary's call ends he stomps out a lit cigarette before going back into the building. On the way up the stairs, like a marble statue, stands the pretty, thin woman he was planning to marry. His fiancé shares a resemblance with a certain actress who starred in action movies where her clothing seemed to get torn to shreds in the cuts between scenes. But unlike her Hollywood doppelganger, Joslin dresses conservatively, for she is at work and must keep most of her cleavage covered by a paisley, cotton scarf.

They kiss, and when she leaves, he watches her scarf get caught in the door on her way out. But she was in too much of a hurry to notice, and the scarf stays behind hanging and flowing with the breeze. He picks it up, and when he gets back upstairs to their office, he places it on the upright support of her desk chair. And that's where it will remain until she returns for it another day.

"Now it might sound a little bizarre," Max Orefield says, speaking to the young intern on her first day at the station, "I know it does, but trust me." He continues, "I can't get around how strange it feels listening this closely to the sounds of people talking, but if you're careful at doing your job, hmmm . . . ? Then you will be able to exactly pick out the sound of the tape running, sounds of machines buzzing, and anything extra that we might want to filter out of our broadcasts. Do you think you can handle that?"

"Yes," she says while placing the large noise-canceling headphones over her straight blonde hair.

"Well, alright," Max says and starts moving back to his work station. "If you know what you're doing, then I'll spare you the details of how to do it. If you get your job done, then I don't even need to hear from you, unless there's a fire."

She clicks around on her screen and adjusts some of the audio levels. Then, she inserts a disk that she brought with her. The disk in the computer buzzes away and spins wildly. "I'll be back in a few," she says casually to Max.

"What are you doing?" Max asks as he rises from his work station. "We're about to go live."

"I know. It's already working, so you can relax."

"What's working?"

"My program I installed," says the intern. The grinding disk in the computer gathers a considerable amount of attention from others in the studio.

The intern leaves. Max picks up her headphones, and he listens for a moment before turning to another audio engineer who is listening in on his own separate listening devices. He asks the engineer if it sounds alright, and the other engineer nods in agreement. Max makes a comment about the young woman being a trailblazer before listening to the content of what is being broadcasted:

"—you know this guy through the work he's been doing whenever myself or my colleagues give him a tip. Not every public official is a scoundrel. Any information on the inspector's family is helpful—"

Back at his own work station, Max flips on his microphone and speaks into it: "Your sign-off sounded good, Joey, but could you repeat it?"

Ortev's voice is muffled on the other side of the sound-stage window, but Max can hear him clearly. "Great, Joey. And one more time," Max instructs.

"If you have any information pertaining to the location of the Oriel children, call our station right away," Joe says, and he gives out the phone number with great speed and accuracy.

In a short while, several blocks over, Joe Ortev is out of the radio station and loosened up. No longer is his tie at his neck, but it sways at the loosened Pratt Knot below an unbuttoned and exposed neckline. The lump on the front of his neck twitches and a rich, crisp sound fills the coffee shop.

He says, "Cary! What are we having, espresso?"

When Cary spots Ortev coming in through the double doors he has a spark of inspiration to lean towards the waitress and raise his forearms summoning the young woman with a couple waves. Cary says to the waitress, "Two espressos. Better make them double."

"Right away," says the waitress.

Cary goes on about business and how his job isn't as much about reporting as it is about serving his community. Cary says, "The city needs health services from me, not my opinion on matters. That's your job, Joe." He can tell that sort of patronizing behavior has little impact on Ortev, and he knows it already, but he can't resist reminding his old friend of his important role as one of his informants.

For once the fast talker doesn't say much, so Cary works to fill the silence by telling about the story he has been dreaming up for Ortev to work on. Ortev is already set to report on it before Cary was brought on as a consultant. And Cary's signature alongside the signature of a supreme court judge means one of the largest rings of underground gambling will be shut down. It started with Cary's official report on poor ventilation in a couple of row homes that were being renovated, and now it is reaching into the seedy jurisdiction of organized crime, drugs, and prostitution.

"Anything to get Cary's mind off his missing children," thinks Ortev to himself, so he gives Cary his undivided attention.

"You were right about the dive bar on Victory…" says Cary. "It's infested. My niece told me she saw maggots in the ice cubes in the freezer when she worked there for a week."

"That's nothing after the tip on the gyro shop you got from Danzel," says Ortev. They discuss the analysis that brought Jimeny's Gyros to a sudden halt. Joe is sincerely interested in how it happened. He says, "I heard Jimeny was found belly up after running from that mob."

"He's dead?" asks Cary. And on that note Cary grows quiet. There's only so much he can talk over cases without feeling like he's getting off track from figuring out his own personal matters. Cary gets to it when he says, "I thank you for the bulletin you put out on the radio for me and my family."

"Sure," says Ortev, and it seems obvious, so he asks: "Is there something more I can do for you?"

Cary explains the strange phone call that came in after the radio announcement aired and how plagues of electrical surges followed the call.

Ortev asks if he captured any sounds, to which Cary mentions the tape recorder in his desk. It was switched to record the call, but he doesn't have the tape on him at the coffee shop, so Ortev says, "Come by the studio when you can. I won't be there tonight, but I'll clue Max in to know you're coming by. Talk to him. Tell him everything you told me. Let him listen to the tape." And Ortev goes on talking as quickly as sounds can form and noise can spread.

He never claims to have seen anything out of the ordinary. Even Ortev agrees that his office seems to be a perfectly safe, sane place to work. But the strange calls have come in every time the announcement has aired. Talking to Ortev in the coffee shop with occasional cold glances from his journalist informant to long periods of self reflection with his coffee mug, alone on his side of the booth, he is marred by pressure and stress that accompany terror and anxiety. Being there with Ortev is comfort to Cary. He realizes that his ally will soon part ways, so he asks a question that he can't possibly keep from asking:

"Joe," Cary says, "How did you carry on when your son went missing?"

Ortev sips the tiny espresso cup with its caramel foam still holding together. He starts speaking at his usual innately clear but quick rapidity, "My mind draws blank when I realize just how much I have overcome and how many pieces of the puzzle are still missing today." His pace slows and his voice actually wavers once: "Let's be clear. You're not claiming the sounds you heard were some supernatural or universal *being* of some sort."

"I know someone or something was there, Joe," Cary answers.

"Well, Cary, if you want someone to give it a listen, I suggest a guy I know personally and professionally. He's from Trinidad, but his vernacular doesn't extend to Creole. He speaks English better than you or me, in fact." Ortev changes his expression; it pains him to continue but he drives forward anyway. Ortev says, with a grimace upon his face and brow crunched together, "The thing is he doesn't have a lot of clients, you see."

"Is he good at what he does?" asks Cary.

"My word! He is indeed good at what he does, Cary. I wouldn't have suggested him otherwise. I'd say he's at the top of his *field*, Inspector."

"How can a guy with not a lot of clients be at the top of his field then? Do go on, please, Joe."

"Well," says Ortev, "hummff. I should say he only has one client."

"One client at the top of his field?"

"Yes," Ortev says convincingly. He adds, "It should stay that way as long as the client keeps paying him. My ally from Trinidad makes enough money with one client to cause him to not care about getting paid by anybody else. It's part of the agreement he has with the client."

"I don't understand," Cary admits.

"I wouldn't expect you to, not yet anyhow," Ortev says, and he finishes the espresso in one gulp. He says, "Some serious nut-job is paranoid that someone is after his billions, so he gave half of his fortune to Max—the Trinidadian— He is distributing the money in micro-increments, you see. Max gets paid as long as he keeps the guy from feeling paranoid that someone is after him."

"Sounds easy."

"It isn't."

"Did your ally try using a safe to keep the money from thieves?" Cary asks without much thought.

"I mean it when I say the guy is strange, Cary. He thinks the phones are all bugged... Technically, he's right to have suspicion, I suppose. I know plenty of cases where the government used wiretapping, and those cases are publicly available. I can show you some," says Ortev. He makes a quick reach under the table to retrieve his leather briefcase.

Cary stops him and says, "No. I trust you, Joey."

"Okay. I'm just warning you in case you witness some strange behaviors," says Ortev.

"You're warning me?"

"Why yes, Cary! I'm a busy guy," Ortev says before rising to leave. Then, he says, "I've a few more visits and calls to make before I get to see my wife. I've got to run, Cary."

"Thanks, Joe. I won't be a bother for you. I can promise you that."

"Why is that?"

"Because I have to pack and leave town. That's why," Cary says. "It's nothing too serious, unless you count the pieces of my broken heart."

"I haven't got a remedy for that. I'm sorry," Ortev says.

"I'll see your guy before I leave town," Cary says.

"He is likely at the station now," Ortev says.

"Good. Then I shall go tonight," Cary says.

"Good. Good luck, Cary. It will help," Ortev dares to claim. "If it's not her voice, if you can prove it, then you can put that behind you."

"Of course," says Cary. "And if it is her voice? What

then?"

"If my ally proves it is her voice, then things are going to get very strange for you, my friend."

"Indeed," says Cary.

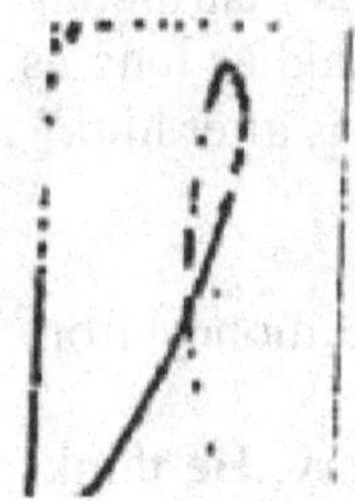

ndeed, it was an unusual philanthropist that encouraged Max Orefield to practice certain arts. Witchcraft allows for him to wear a crown upon his head for measuring frequencies that human ears cannot perceive.

As Fast Talkin' Joe pointed out, Max is funded by a private investor, but what Ortev failed to mention was that even Max has serious doubts as to the validity of his practice. Yet, his one and only client always seems pleased. The job started as a simple counter-surveillance task, since Max has a past with the Regiment, an integral part of Trinidad's Ministry of National Security. The Regiment was headquartered in the city of Chaguarama (pronounced "shag-ha-rah-muss"), which is to the west of Trinidad's capital city of Port-of-Spain. That's near a known fishing village, known by locals as "the place of silk cotton trees," but Max Orefield knew the village as his home.

As the client grew more paranoid Max was forced to incorporate some popular occult practices into his routine, such as listening to white noise for hours at a time.

While looking for ways to secure his client-relations, Max even went as far as to develop a line of promotional products to keep his client appreciative of the service that Max provides. He knows that as long as he keeps the client anxious and fretting he will be well-off financially. Over the years, he's sent everything from stress balls to t-shirts to help remind the client that Max is at his disposal whenever he feels uneasy. Promoting his business is just as important in his strange line of work as it is in any other. Max's crowning achievement to lure his client to the phone often is a simple keychain with a tiny built-in tape recorder installed that gives the client an easy way to record strange sounds for his employee to review as soon as he can get to the device. The client, located in the Bronx, calls Max with a lead on a strange sound, and he says to Max on the phone, "Maxie, get over here," or some more paranoid sentiment before hanging up and cursing the very device that connects their voices across the five boroughs.

Max doesn't need to convince Cary Oriel of anything, however. Cary is in a cab on his way to the studio to try to catch Max before he leaves for the day. Cary doesn't believe in the other-worldly ideas that are often thought of and brought up when discussing the deceased, but he knows that his children are out there somewhere. He thinks, if taking a few tapes to some modern-day soothsayer of sorts will get him closer to finding his children, then it's worth trying. He admits to himself for the first time, in the cab, that he will try anything to get to them.

There is no limit to the amount of his own finite resources he's willing to spend; Cary brings with him an ample supply of money to persuade the audio engineer to listen to his case, even though Ortev prepared him differently. Cary understands no other way to get someone to listen quickly when matters are pressing. "Perhaps," he thinks— "Perhaps, the strange guy Ortev referred will be willing to cooperate if he sees a few stacks of cash." Cary brings a paper bag full of cash that sits next to him in the cab; it's everything he has to his name.

Max is in the sound studio when Cary arrives. The audio engineer is capturing sounds of a banjo player recording a debut album called *Another Night on the Range* to be released when he tours the country. Max is able to do two things at once here: help an artist with his album, and use the tonal waves produced as a reference for measuring sound produced on the tapes he is screening for his paranoid client.

The recording goes as you might expect it to go. The sounds will be remastered later, but as it is recording, Max has the sound feeding into an advanced audio editing software that allows him to alter the key signature that is being produced by the banjo player and his twangy instrument. In the editing software, Max watches the timestamp, the number used to show the current place of the recording. When the live sounds of the banjo are coupled with the prerecorded white noise coming from the tapes given to

Max by his paranoid client, the mask of the instrument creates a sort of empty space for other voices to be heard.

It is rather unusual to occur, but one of the signs of a disturbance on the prerecorded tape—either the phone being tapped, or some other entity listening to the call—will be indicated if the timestamp displays inaccurate numbers in the software. When this puzzling anomaly occurs, it is a prompt for Max to investigate further, and Max always finds a good reason why the timestamp changes, so his reports to his paranoid client have concluded that tampering and foul play are unlikely. Max Orefield has never had reason to suspect something out of the ordinary has occurred.

"Alright. Give it another go, Jeffey Rey," Max says over the personal audio system that allows him to communicate with the musician on the other side of the glass.

Without missing his cue, the banjo player holds onto the microphone, he grips it tightly, and he gives a yodel that could shake boulders loose from tall mountains. Max knows hardly anything at all about yodeling, apart from what Jeffey Rey taught him in the studio and when they went hiking in the vast Central Park. But this tech-savvy Trinidadian knows how to record it; Max knows exactly how to match Jeffey Rey's pitch with that of his twangy four-string banjo.

Jeffey Rey's voice shakes the dividing glass: "Yodel-a-eee . . . a-a-e-a-e-hoo!"

Max leans in to adjust the levels on the studio sound board and listens closely to the tape playing white noise in his ear. It is a gentle static that could put a cranky child to sleep, and the tape continues to prove Max's doubts further each time he examines the software. "What an easy job," he thinks to himself. All he has to do is document his process enough at the end of the day, every day, and his paranoid client will part ways with half of his fortunes.

Jeffey Rey positions himself on the wooden stool as he plays. He notices some bright flash of light coming from the other side of the glass. For a moment Jeffey Rey considers that Max might be signaling the performer with some sort of flashlight to let him know that the recording session is coming to a close, for Max offered his time as a favor to the young artist, and he knows Max has abruptly stopped recording sessions for friends of his in the past. But he sees that the flash of light is surely coming from the door in the sound space that leads out to the hall, where a few other businesses, studios, and a few accountants work with the station.

The light glints sharply from the two-foot square, a wire lined peephole used to check if the spaces are occupied when they aren't already signed on the whiteboards located outside each studio. Jeffey Rey watches the reflection and sees a figure block the window to look inward.

Cary Oriel had to check a few other studios before he saw Max's name on the clipboard. He knocks lightly before entering discreetly to observe Max at work.

Max turns to see Cary, but he figures Cary is just another record executive coming by to check on Jeffey Rey's album, so he prepares something to tell him about the album's progress and release date. When he finishes recording the musician, and when the performer finishes playing, Max looks back to see Cary has assembled two stacks of cash on the folding table nearest the door through which he had entered.

"I've never seen an exec offer such a per diem," Max says.

Cary approaches the sound engineer with a cassette tape in his hands, and he moves forward to pass the tape over to Max. Cary says, "You don't know me, but you can help me by telling me about what's on this tape. I'll give you one stack of cash today and another when you find out something that will get me closer .. . to-to my-my-my children."

Max puts everything together in his head, for he knows that taking possession of the tape brings with it some responsibility. Max asks, "Did Joe send you?" He accepts the tape, dismisses the banjo player, and listens to the details of Cary's predicament.

Max asks Cary, "Do you believe your children are still alive?"

"Listen for yourself. Someone is out there," Cary says in a loud voice. The commotion causes Max to completely unplug the white noise he has been absorbing for his paranoid client.

"You'll have to excuse me, Mr.—"

"Oriel," Cary says.

"Yes, Mr. Oriel, I will not be able to accept your generous payments due to a conflict involving my contract with a client," says Max, giving out his typical speech that he gives when propositioned for a job he wishes to perform without accepting a fee. For, anything outside of pro bono suggests a breach of his contract. "This free job," thinks Max to himself, "will be no different in the scope of what the client is used to, no different than having Jeffey Rey record something for his album."

This thinking is, perhaps, Max's one mistake.

Before plugging the tape in to take a listen to it, Max closes the curtain to cover the glass in case someone comes in to practice in the space. He doesn't want anyone disturbing the delicate process. Max even looks out in the hallway to make sure that there isn't another audio engineer waiting to use the space before he gives the answering machine tape a listen.

Max's heart beats heavy in his chest as he plugs the cassette into the player. He feels a considerable amount of pressure since he is accustomed to listening to tapes that he hopes do not lead to further investigations; he is pleased to report to his client on a daily basis to assure the man he was likely suffering from a vivid imagination. But for once Max hopes that he will hear something.

He never believed in anything resembling ghosts, even growing up as a child when he was raised by a woman who was connected to the spiritual realm. Max's childhood caregiver was a woman that was barren all her life, but she practiced the craft of voodoo in hopes that she would unlock an ancient energy capable of lifting her body to the great divine and granting the gift of a child. The woman did not conceive a child, and that image of her bleating and lonely in the village known by locals as "the place of silk cotton trees"—near where Maxwell learned tactical surveillance and counter-surveillance procedures from the Ministry of National Security in Trinidad—seeing his caregiver in such a state left Max feeling pragmatic and unable to believe anything resembling spirituality. Max offers up an explanation to the unusual events that tend to revolve around him like laughing ghosts of children seated on a carousel; he explains away the sounds of organ grinders with science or remarkable coincidence.

"I've heard Joe read your messages on the air. Wish me luck, Mr. Oriel," Max says staring into the gaze of the blank-eyed father.

Cary sees Max plug his earphones into the tape player and press play. He doesn't feel it necessary to wish him luck. Inspector Cary Oriel knows the sound of his wife's voice when he hears it.

In Montréal, the husband and wife duo had been racking their brains to come up with a way to pay for their needs after Theo left the police force. "We need more exposure if we are going to grab our market enough to actually help the world," says Cynthia. She flips through a newspaper and says, "Nobody is advertising what we do in the paper these days."

"How on Earth do you—" Theo says before his coffee runs over from the dispenser. "How will we advertise all over the place if we can barely afford to have your office in this overpriced, self-righteous historic district—"

"Stop it!" exclaims Cynthia. She closes her paper, and walks to the window to look out at the doorman near the street feeding pigeons. She can hear him talking to the birds and talking to the person coming from the building. "I love this place," she says.

"I love it too," Theo says. "These are tough times for businesses in these parts. Perhaps you ought to learn French. There are a lot of French speaking people you're turning away . . . ." He drinks some of his coffee and notices the coffee mug is the same one he once used when he worked as a detective, and just like that—he realizes a way to get word out about their business venture. "My dear, you may . . . let go of your fear . . . ." he says before producing from his wallet a small key with a round head.

"When is the next time you have a consultation at the station?" asks Theo. "Tomorrow," says Cynthia. "Okay," says

Theo. "There's something I need you to look at when you're there."

They plan to show up at the police station at night when the cleaning crew is buffing the floors because the crew will have to leave the back door propped open for ventilation, Theo recalls.

After Cynthia checks the schedule, they know to arrive at the stroke of midnight when the crew will already be at work.

They get to the station and the door is open, so they go in and Theo uses the key with the round head to open the sliding, drop-down gate that secures the supply room where all the department's top-notch electronic gadgetry is kept in storage. Behind the beekeeper boxes that never actually collected enough honey to make a profit (another one of Stegner's lesser ideas that came back to sting Theo but this time quite literally), there they find enough surveillance equipment to meet their needs. They only take what they need and what they know they will use. They leave the weaker components and outdated systems for the cops to use before leaving the station to return to the world as better prepared concerned citizens that run a *consulting firm* out of their home office.

Once they're in their car, Theo immediately takes to the scanner like an old friend reunited after a tragedy. He says, "You poor thing. Let me see what you want to tell me." He plugs in the scanner and picks up chatter about the strange happenings among the Oriel family, concerning the disappearance of young children.

By the time they make it to Staten Island, they find Cary leaving his office for what might be the last time. They follow him to the studio where he meets Maxwell, and they plant a seed in the situation, hoping to get involved in a personal way.

Using one of the gadgets they brought with them, they are able to beam a signal into the recording station for anyone listening in to hear, and it just so happens that one avid listener, Maxwell Orefield, is meeting with Cary Oriel this afternoon . . . .

A voice on the radio says the following: "My husband was a sergeant on the Force, but he's not wearing that badge anymore.

As a private investigator, he helps me solve cases I come across, which is why we're able to help people all over, using web cams to figure out what's wrong and treat your disorder if you have one to treat—"

"I don't have a disorder," says Cary.

"No," says Maxwell, "but listen—"

"Send us your video/audio of your interview and we'll analyze it in twenty-four hours for no charge—" says the voice on the radio that winds down to a cool sound of a jazz saxophone.

"One of my goals with 'Therapy For You' is to bring our professional practice to anyone who needs anonymous assistance," says the prerecorded voice of Dr. Cynthia Valentico. "We do this through consultation. And we're not afraid to come to you if the situation demands our up close investment of time," adds detective Theo Bryant.

After the commercial airs in the studio in Staten Island, Cynthia says to Theo: "We need to make clear that we're not active detectives but consultants."

"We need more exposure if we really want to cover enough ground," says Maxwell.

"I'll cover as much ground to find them as possible. Until my shoes run thin and my feet turn into miserable stubs. I won't stop—" says Cary. He turns to notice the beautiful blonde woman walking down the hall outside the studio looks eerily familiar in the way she moves, familiar enough to remind him of his wife... But the blinding light from outside the studio hits his eyes, and he questions what is going on around him. All he can see . . . are spots.

Maxwell clicks around on the computer screen to raise a few different bars that change the audio levels, and he experiments with different filters, but he does not look happy with the results when he returns to Cary with: "There's something there, but even with my equipment, I can't hear . . . a damn thing."

Cary, with his hands on his hips, says, "What do you recommend?"

"Perhaps," says Maxwell, "you will profit through another medium."

"Do you mean that I should video tape the call . . . . or," Cary begins to ask, but he is at a loss for words.

"Not necessarily, but that wouldn't hurt . . . but that's not necessary. What I'm saying is that maybe I'm not your guy . . . . There's only so much to achieve through looking over audio files this way . . . . I mean, I've seen my fair share of *strange* doing this, and when I see something . . . that needs more attention," Maxwell talks while scrambling for something in his desk drawer. "If I find a red flag, I tell my client and he shoots the file over to someone to be a medium for any . . . . entities that might be hiding out." He hands a blue business card to Cary. The card has a twisted emblem and metal outlining.

He reads the words on the card aloud: "Take it to the river." He looks at Maxwell for an answer.

"That's the guy I work for. He'll understand why you're calling," says Maxwell I told him about your story, and he already heard Joe talkin' on the radio about it and asked me anyway. Anyway, he knows you're going to call . . . so get to it."

Maxwell turns back to his computer screen to play around with a file when Cary takes the card and picks up his coat to leave the studio.

Maxwell removes his headset and says, "Trust me when I say that some of the things I hear aren't so great. I'm hearing a lot of wrongdoings that I can't handle. Someone is going to try to get back at this guy someday . . . .

"When he hired me from college I thought I would be analyzing codes or encrypting data, but he has me listening to his tapes and signing off on forms to say I didn't hear suspicious surveillance or any unidentifiable entity, but I'll tell you what I do hear is extortion and corruption—"

Maxwell storms out, leaving Cary standing alone and uncomfortable.

Cary peaks through the curtain, and he watches a musician packing away his instrument to settle his nerves. But Maxwell comes back moments later to give Cary his tape back and says, "I don't hear anything there." He sits the tape on his desk next to the keyboard and walks back out.

The next day, in the afternoon, Maxwell Orefield enters the luxurious estate of his client.

"Well, it appears you're running later than usual," says the client.

"Sorry about that. I was having to deal with a musician that forgot his sheet music, what can I say," says Maxwell.

"Not at all, Maxwell. Take your time, as long as you're listening to something good on there," says the client. He tugs at Maxwell's headphones that are playing loud rap music.

"Right," says Maxwell, "I desperately want to have a look to see if there's something we can use for a backdrop—"

Maxwell takes a copy of a musician's CD from his messenger bag to show the client who nods in agreement. Maxwell says, "This guy is coming out with a new single and a video shot here would really set him up."

"Take as many photos as you need," says the client. He leaves the room.

When a call comes in from Cary, Maxwell sounds discouraged. He says, "I heard back from the people we sent the recording to. Yeah. Unfortunately they weren't much help. The reply I got is . . . . Hold on . . . ." Alone in the main hall of his client's enormous mansion, Maxwell flips through his notes at a pedestal made of marble and covered in a gold outline. "Ha . . . . Here it is. The message they left with us after I sent the recording from your machine . . . 'If you are sending a prank, please find a better way to spend your time . . . .' It's signed by a detective . . . Theo Bryant."

"Well," says Cary, "I was really counting on some good news…"

"The good news is my special client is open to discuss being a psychic medium for your wife to use, like an antenna. Apparently, my client is curious about what it is I'm doing and he was so intrigued by the particulars of your case. How does that sound? Cary?"

Cary had left his city, left Staten Island and Never York altogether. He's been working through the fear for his loved ones with hope that Maxwell could offer a suggestion as to where he should search for them . . . . The hope Cary has had throughout the train ride leaves him, and he is left with an empty feeling. He wonders how his father feels, if he feels responsible. He says, "That sounds great. Whatever you can think of to help . . . find out where . . . ."

"My client is here now. Would you like to talk to him?" asks Maxwell .

"Who's there?" asks the disoriented Cary.

"My client who I've been telling you about," says Maxwell. "The guy who needs all my surveillance measures. Tell me you remember my client who will spare no expense to make me feel important. Can you talk to him a minute, Cary? It's the least you can do."

"Huh?" asks Cary. His head is spinning. "Now?"

"He's interested in your case," says Maxwell. "What else can I tell you? Here he is. Please hold . . . ."

"Hi . . . . I'm so glad that Maxwell brought your story to my attention, Cary. What a strange circumstance. Hi, Cary, my name is Mr. Drake. Can you hear me on your end?" asks the client.

"Of course I can," says Cary, and he feels like he's going to be seeing the bottom of his stomach. He wants to feel some grain of . . . hope.

"Sorry about that," says the client, "but we record all our calls, so sometimes the line goes flat. Where was I? Oh yes, may I be a conduit for your dear sleeping wife?"

"Not that I don't believe in your conduit idea, but I feel like . . . . If my wife . . . . If Adeline is trying to speak to me . . . . I'm listening, so she doesn't need a conduit," says Inspector Cary Oriel, with a proud timber in his voice.

"Certainly, sir," says the wealthy client. "Good luck finding . . . your father."

"Hi, Cary," says Maxwell. "I am guessing that didn't go over well. I'll listen to what you guys talked about later, but for now, just know I did all that I could, and good luck," says Maxwell Orefield.

"Is he gone?" asks Cary.

"Yes," says Maxwell.

"Good. How did he know my father is missing too? My father is officially dead," Cary says, and he continues: "It was only reported that my children are missing . . . ."

"That's strange. I'm not sure, Cary. But if I find out," says Maxwell, "I'll let you know about it on point."

"Thanks, Maxwell. I feel like you're someone I can actually trust," says Cary.

"Certainly, sir," says Maxwell, and his voice vanishes when Cary hangs up the phone. Cary says to himself: "I'm listening, Adeline."

Maxwell stands in the middle of the marble floor in the main hall and looks up. He uses his digital camera to take a few photos. He plugs a battery in underneath a bench and says, "I hope you don't mind if I charge something here . . . ." He tugs at another cord leading from the wall, and curiosity has him follow it to its source. The cord goes along the polished floor and under a long red, floral carpet before leading to the crack under a door, behind the stairwell.

He has trouble getting the door open at first, but after a little jiggling of the knob he is inside a small broom closet. He says, "What have we got here . . . ?" He finds the cord leads to a projector, and on the projector is a plastic transparency with the layout to the Oriel Estates.

Chapter Seven

Adventures Away from the Tribe

A mouse squeaked, nibbled, and hid out of sight before Henry Edwards knew any better. He had hid himself away in a section of the wicker basket that was coming apart after taking back with him only a morsel of what the boy had been eating. Earlier today, it was a loaf of bread and borscht, but the borscht is a soup that doesn't taste good later, so the mouse took an extra bite while it was still plentiful and at its freshest temperature to please his palate. The mouse lapped an extra thimble's worth of borscht broth before biting into the bread that was stale; had the mouse known that the bread was stale, he wouldn't have bit at it at all because stale bread is hard on tiny mouse teeth.

The mouse thinks it would have been smart to stock up on more of the bread in the kitchen cabinets of the warehouse before going on a balloon trip, but he wasn't paying attention when the balloon took off.

It was easy for the mouse to hide its bite marks, since the

loaf was already broken apart. That fine hard shell, with its glazed, buttery surface, would have made apparent any scratching or denting if Emily hadn't broken it apart while helping pack the supplies. But chewing apart the inner bread meat, still doughy enough to swallow with a mouthful of broth from the borscht, made a splendid meal for that tiny stowaway.

Henry Edwards thought he was spending his first night alone on the balloon up in the sky . . . until he awakes from a dream . . . the stars talking. Unfortunately, there isn't anyone around to share in analyzing what dreams may mean. A voice had said to him in his dreams, "Those stars could be anything at all. They would live like you if they wanted to live that way, but they choose to stay high in the sky, where they know they are in good company."

One star grew more luminous than before; it came forward to say: "I'm the brightest."

And another star said, "No. You're faint. Why, you're fainter than Henry even."

"No. Henry isn't faint. He's only asleep," said the first star that came forward in Henry's dream world.

"You're dull, and your laugh is of an imbecile."

The laugh echoed throughout the heavens. And the second star said, "Listen to your laugh. How hideous." Even the stars have their problems, reflects Henry Edwards.

The first star replied, "I came up from a small bit of fire, but I'm red . . . . I'm a red dwarf. I stand at the center of the universe, I tell ya'. When I explode I'm taking the rest of you with me, you're darn tootin'."

"What's the point of being a star in the sky?" a voice asked Henry Edwards.

Henry Edwards answered in his dream. He remembers saying, "The stars guide us. The navigators, ancient ones, used them to find their way. The Biblical Stories used them too, because the Gods were quiet about where they should go, but the stars were bright . . . . At least they were bright when they were the only real lights in the sky."

That light in the sky laughed like an imbecile and wondered why we're not looking up at the sky more often. We're stuck looking at the lights coming off the screens surrounding our living quarters, artificial light coming from TV boxes, when the only thing we have to do is look up to the stars to have all our wishes come true.

"My son, great hunters move to where the game does go. We do not overhunt to extinction the animals, but we conserve so the resources—so the spirits of the animal kingdom might have a way to find a path for expression," says the wise old leader, King Grass, to his son.

The herds have been maintained that way. Meat was smoked when the animals had been hunted to preserve meals for future seasons. Abundance has been the rule of the land and it had been that way since King Grass was the age of his son, Tall Grass.

"It is the way of our people," King Grass says as a steamship passes near their shore.

They hear a tour-guide on the steamship say: "This is as close as our tour goes." A child on board asks the guide, "Why? Are you afraid of the savages?" The tour-guide responds after turning away from his lapel microphone to have private, discrete conversation. The guide says, "No. Unfortunately for us, but fortunate for South Shore, we don't trespass on the land for we allow their people to remain uninhibited." The child licks a lollipop and smiles. He waves to the natives of South Shore.

"And it is the way of our people to care greatly about the outsiders," King Grass says to his son in their native tongue, which sounds like, "Clik-clik a-woo-ah woo-ah." He continues in English, "The man who visited to research the animals here . . . we allowed him . . . into South Shore. He told of the caribou population having problems existing in outside communities, and since then we have worked with the caribou here and look at them thrive . . . . You must go, my son. Tell our ways. Help the animals and spirits coexist with those of humanity."

"I will father, and I will return with a gift for our people. I promise I will return with added abundance," Tall Grass says before going to his family and friends to tell of his imminent journey to North Shore.

Off on the land goes the solemn son of a native chief. He is a boy, only a few years older than Henry Edwards, yet he celebrates his first teenage year by leaving his luxurious family home to prove to everyone, what he needn't prove at all, that he is already a man. He vows to bring back proof, something of substance for his tribe.

"You'll know when I return, Miss," he calls to his sister with admiration, "when I return with trumpets sounding my arrival."

"They'll play loudest for your youthful departure," his sister says. "We shall rejoice in premature loss of an inaccurate marksman. We'll have a celebration with the finest jeweled maidens, and I will marry a prince before you return, young brother." He thinks how this will be true if he cannot find ways to return in adequate time. "Surely," he thinks, "my sister will marry in a year or so to her suitors, and good for her!"

"You're not yet ready for a shave, Tall Grass," she teases him, for she knows he will cut his long brown hair, so evenly woven. She knows his resilience after leaving the sanctity of South Shore is to be tested.

The water surrounding South Shore fades into the deep purple and blue sky. The next shore is not well known by his people. They only know that its inhabitants are strange beings that make strange creations. He sits on the bank of the River Majorilis and cuts apart his hair. Beads, wrapped in shiny brown threads of hair, fall to the ground; some of those amber and turquoise colored marbles roll away. The one he takes and places in his satchel resembles a hollowed-out cat's eye marble. "For later," he says, "I must present myself once again to my people."

He shoves off into the River Majorilis that feeds into the Sinking Oceans. On his small boat he prepares a feast with his horse, Windsor. The wise old horse belongs to his father, but Tall Grass would go to feed him every day as he grew from a child. He knew his father would not protest the horse's accompaniment. Windsor goes willingly and with his father's support. They sit on the dugout canoe and eat.

When they reach North Shore, the balloon carrying Henry Edwards sails high above the young warrior and his horse. "Our village has never seen anything like that. What a marvel, I bet it flies high enough for man to visit the Gods above," Tall Grass says aloud to Windsor.

He takes aim with his bow and arrow. First he draws the quiver back to his ear. Then, he lets it fire. He misses entirely. The arrow flies over a tree branch, ricocheting and shooting upward off of the trunk of a mighty oak tree. It goes up in the opposite direction before leaving the silhouette of Tall Grass below the canopy. The bark above his head splinters and drops onto him. He steps one foot forward with a bend at the waist, and he pulls back the arrow along the tense bow-string leveraging the weight of his back leg.

He feels proud, not that he is accomplishing any of the reasons he left home in the slightest degree, but he thinks to himself, "I'm living with honor defending my neighbors against the brutal fantasies of what creature hovers like a red monster." The arrow releases and lands close by, its point impaling the winding root of a sycamore tree. A third arrow covers the sky in its trail. It fades off in the distance, going over the balloon altogether.

Suddenly, the balloon is high, too high for Tall Grass to see. Henry Edwards is unaware of the threat below the canopy, and Tall Grass can only make out the red contrast above the trees until even that quickly disappears. He has a hard time following the balloon, climbing down to the bottom of the ravine and across the muddy river bank to proceed.

There, on the muddy river, lives a man who used to hunt with packs of dogs until the dogs trapped his neighbor in a tree by the dog trainer's mistake. Elvis, a strong hunter in the area, is out with his dog when Tall Grass goes on his merry chase for another shot, or even a glimpse of that fascinating monstrosity above the treetops.

By the early dawn Henry Edwards experiences his first sunset on the balloon, and he thinks it seems like a peaceful place to make his landing. The sky is a rich red. This is the signal to use when ballooning, he remembers Oriel teaching him. He makes his landing in a clearing with plenty of cover. The basket touches down in a pasture of overgrown millet, near the forest edge.

A sweet sound comes from the trees. The forest creatures sound loudly and let their calls reverberate, surrounding Henry Edwards in what can only be described as a lullaby. He feels tired, even with the way the birds are making noise. The birds are talking loudly in chirps, caws, and calls. They speak to each other; their voices grow intensely as the daylight lessens and soften as the signal of the sun's red glow changes to a final farewell of the darkest possible purple imaginable. Gentle bands of indigo form following the sun's departure, lingering in a hue that will soon fade on the horizon.

Spring is not yet a status, so the birds quiet down when the night settles in for several hours as the planet rotates. Life becomes nocturnal. Since human beings have to defeat darkness, so does Elvis: he has the advantage of electricity, which assists the loading, unloading, and polishing of his rifle.

Human beings may have found ways to defeat certain laws of nature, but there are laws of their own that will not sit idly by. For instance, it is nearly hunting season in North Shore. "Close enough," Elvis thinks, "to test my guns out." He likes to get a couple targets set up on the ridge and make holes in them. Late at night, he's sighting in his scopes and getting a feel for the action on his rifles, for tomorrow is opening day of hunting season when all the hunters in North Shore will start claiming game.

Elvis has friends who stop by to shoot when they hear him testing out his rifle. One friend comments, "Look how clean that action is . . . like he spent all summer . . . getting it ready." The group always tries to impress girls with their trophy kills afterwards. Of course, the ones that shoot the biggest game on opening day land a smack on the lips from the girl of their choice.

"Hey stud, you're going to get in my way with that sight looking primed," says a friend to Elvis.

"Not a chance, scrub" says Elvis.

"Oh, right," says the friend. "I forgot you're stuck on Lucy the lawyer."

"Well," says Elvis, and he's about to blush, but he doesn't hold back—he says, "She's a law student."

"Alright," says the friend. "My mistake. Look at you defending your gal. Pretty soon Lucy the lawyer will be defending you!"

"It's late, El," says another friend. "We're going to roll." And the group of camo-clad compatriots part ways.

For several hours the planet spins, and it is dark in North Shore. The robin get up from their nests to see that spring is not nearly ready.

In the morning, Elvis puts on his boots and clothes. He wears leather gloves that are still covered in a polish because he was taught to care for his firearm as if it were a sacred tool. His father took him shooting when he was nearly a grown man, but his father was always away at war. Elvis misses him and wonders if he is safe. What would he do if he found out otherwise? "The war isn't over," he thinks to himself. "People still die over there or become missing." What usually worries him throughout the year doesn't get to him the same, for he senses nature calling.

The hunter named Elvis could sit down and cry. He probably should do something about the sadness in his heart, for his father hasn't returned to base near where he was stationed, he read in a report. A report stated his father ". . . was not with convoy . . . whereabouts unknown . . . ."

The hunter gets his mind away from those thoughts in the only way he can: by cleaning his rifle. And he thinks about the girl who he wishes to kiss on opening day if he can win her affection. There's a girl Elvis has loved ever since they first spoke, but she didn't know he cared about her until recently.

Elvis creeps along in the shadows, keeping low along the path from his house in the town to the public forests used for hunting and trapping. He notices the grounds are beginning to lose their own lush covering; tiny chutes from seeds of pine trees that have been stored in the ground by last spring's careful squirrels, or dispersed carelessly by the birds, have rooted themselves. A few chutes will turn into saplings in the following years, then a few saplings will grow enough to become healthy adult pines that produce their own offspring, and the cycle continues. Elvis feels connected to this natural process, so much so that he's glad he waited until opening day to fire his rifle at game. He checks to make sure the rifle's safety mechanism is engaged before climbing into his tree stand.

High up in the tree, on his stand made of two-by-fours and rusted nails, there, the hurter named Elvis sits alone. The only company he keeps is the picture of a woman in the locket around his neck. Each time he needs to feel purpose, he feels for the locket. He feels for the picture of Lucinda-Lee. The locket is secure. Its clasp is closed and kept in place by sliding the tiny, protruding metal ball which penetrates the hairpin-shaped outlet of the clasp. It seems to be securely frozen shut, and he likes it that way. He feels a certain security in knowing the precious photo of his blue-eyed lady won't slip away. He also feels secure knowing that someone else on the sideline of his life won't make the discovery that he is after Lucinda-Lee Price. He keeps her colored yearbook photograph hidden, out of fear of competition from the hordes of other males; he considers his peers that could have spotted Lucinda-Lee when she moved to town. She arrived two years prior to care for her aunt when she fell ill with a case of the mumps.

Elvis likes that Lucinda-Lee cares for her family to such a great length that she picked up her entire life. She uprooted herself before finishing out high school in her hometown because she felt that she was needed in North Shore. That type of selflessness takes its toll on Lucinda-Lee, however; it is evidenced by her stern brow-ridge that guards her deep, blue eyes.

His secret locket-love is busy all around town. When Elvis walked to the post office one afternoon, she was there on her way to the library, she told him. They smiled and exchanged pleasant greetings. She was there in the library looking at a book when he walked by. That Friday afternoon, Elvis was on his way to the trading post in town to get rid of a few fur hats. (More libraries should take note of the way a woman can draw men to their shelves.) So he started going to the library every Friday afternoon in hopes of running into Lucinda-Lee again. And after investing only one month's worth of Friday afternoons, he tasted the fruit of his labor.

He read every book he could find on hunting, so he moved on to read a book of fiction. It was a collection of short stories about swashbuckling pirates and pioneers on the ocean. He was carrying the book and reading a chapter called "Heroism on High Tide" when he turned a corner by the rare book archive at the same moment that Lucinda-Lee just so happened to be coming in the opposite direction. It was far from fate or destiny, however. For, he had planned out every possible thing to say before that moment. He planned out how he felt it should go in his mind, so much so that when they actually bumped into each other he lost his chance to say anything more than asking to be excused.

"Pardon me," Elvis said to Lucinda-Lee.

"Here," she said. "Let me help you back to your feet." She took his hand in hers and countered his weight. She noticed how his eyes took her in, and she became a tad nervous when she noticed how he took focus on her newly developed laugh lines. But when he first noticed the imperfection of her facial features that day, he became even more attracted to her. He assumed she was constantly trying to please people with her smiles. Smiles, like laughter, are contagious; he wants to smile more while she's around. While she's around his troubles and worries seem to float away on the breeze that sweeps through North Shore.

Suddenly, to Elvis it seems like Lucinda-Lee is gone out of his life, like she was when she left out of the library that Friday before he climbed into the stand on that sturdy tree. He tests his rifle and is shocked when through its scope appears the horse belonging to the young warrior. Though, he still feels like he did when he stood there smiling that day at the library as Lucinda-Lee went out the front door. And some part of that warm feeling comes over Elvis whenever he thinks of her.

With a quick click of the clasp, Elvis closes the locket and seals away the woman of his dreams. He tucks the locket away under a layer of camouflage fatigues, a uniform left in his father's closet. And just like that his love for Lucinda-Lee Price is hidden away, like his face hides under layers of green and black charcoal. He carefully removes the bright yellow florescent vest, a remnant of his last job with North Shore's road service crews, and he folds the vest up to stay hidden from the horse and its rider. His peers are out there, too, hiding in tree stands of their own; mostly every person in North Shore who is old enough for a hunting license and owns a rifle is out there testing it.

Elvis shifts his weight and holds onto a branch that grows forth from the tree that supports his stand when he hears the sounds of great puffs of air. Rapid breathing comes from a large animal that seems to be under a considerable amount of stress. It gives Elvis plenty to sight with his rifle. The short, exasperated pants come from the nostrils of a horse trying to keep calm after being tied to a sapling. He is farther down the trail, where the wooded area truly takes over the terrain, and the brush makes it difficult to see ahead of the next bend in the path.

Even with a densely vegetated landscape thickening at all sides, Elvis sees the horse before the creature notices him or stirs on his behalf. He sees Windsor with his own eyes, but he uses the scope of his rifle to get a look at the leather saddle. He notices the careful engraving along the throat and girdle of the saddle are the work of a craftsman; he sees the way the horse recognizes the rope and bridal tethering him to the sapling without pulling the rope taught. The horse awaits the return of the blustering Tall Grass, but Elvis does not know that. He watches the horse strictly out of curiosity.

The young man, who knows enough about hunting on his own, knows this horse belongs to a great hunter of some sort, for the horse is no ordinary horse with an ordinary appearance. The star, stripe, and snip on Windsor's muzzle, forehead, and face give him plenty of personality. Windsor's mane is adorned with jewels, and the saddle is so equipped to accommodate a hunter with bow. The arrows are there too, apart from three that Tall Grass used to attempt to take down what he imagined to be a great flying monster in the sky.

Around the same time in the morning, Henry Edwards wakes from his deep sleep. He failed to notice the arrows bouncing off nearby trees and the commotion on behalf of his arrival in the bright red balloon. Perhaps the agitation could have been blamed on the color red and the response the color elicits in humans and other animals. He landed it just fine, however. The landing was without notice to the possible perils that could befall him.

The balloon landed in a grassy pasture, where it was covered from all sides by thick, burnt blades, burned by a sun that hadn't let up since one of the driest springs the little provincial land felt in decades. It has been so dry with the chaotic nature of the unsteady, unpredictable ebb and flow of the tides that people talk a great deal. People of the areas talk of the end of times, and others talk of rebuilding anything nature might wipe away in its motions.

Tall Grass is from a group of people that don't waste time or energy fretting about the changes of the season. They don't talk about them, rather they deal with them as they begin to take shape. It is as if the society he is used to living in is one living their lives with a paddle to steer a boat; they steer with whichever current meets the bow and however the wind meets their sails.

Though it's not the growing season, and Tall Grass feels he could be useful to his new community by planting some crops there for next year. Tall Grass realizes this when the great flying monster disappears over the canopy before his eyes, and eventually, he gives up searching. But if he cannot find a way to help the people in this land by destroying that great red monster from the sky, he feels the need to plant and contribute to this strange place he inhabits. For, it is the way of his people to respect the seasons when they change by contributing to the Earth's bounty. He must do this by putting in seeds of whatever is at hand to grow. After all, it is the law of nature: to reap, one must sow.

Without wasting any more time looking for the monster in the sky, Tall Grass starts walking back. He must follow his footsteps in reverse to find his way back to Windsor. He's already convinced himself to end the chase, and he begins to doubt what he saw all together. "It was a sight that must surely have been caused by dehydration," he says aloud to himself. By the time he ends the chase, he feels that it is absolutely necessary to pay tribute to his people with an act of planting and resolves the way to honor his new home will be setting up future harvests. If his seeds will take to growing in this untested, foreign soil, he will rejoice. Returning to his horse seems like the only logical solution to a young man who holds the Earth's cycles on a pedestal, as would Demeter, the Greek Goddess of Harvest. Tall Grass has the impulse to return to Windsor when he realizes he left his rucksack containing seeds tied to the stallion's halter rope.

On his way to Windsor, Tall Grass imagines how his father and sister will be proud knowing that Tall Grass has remembered to honor their people. While out on his mission to search the lands for what is most valuable to the ways of all life, he has become captivated by the notion of spreading seeds. He imagines a big swooping heron flying with its mouth full of trout that the bird drops further upstream, if only nature could care so much.

When Tall Grass reaches Windsor he is not entirely alone. No, in fact, he is being watched by a careful eye from up high in a tree stand. Elvis doesn't look through his rifle scope, but instead, he uses binoculars that he has become accustomed to using for bird-watching during the parts of the year when his rifle was not welcomed in the canopy around North Shore. Elvis is able to focus in quickly to see what the suspicious character on horseback is doing in his town.

Tall Grass tugs apart the end of the rope keeping the rucksack tied to the halter rope. When the knot breaks loose the rucksack falls to the forest floor, and the halter rope gains slack enough to calm Windsor down considerably. Elvis watches Tall Grass offer Windsor seeds from his pack, and the hunter wonders what else the intruding young savage will produce if he keeps watching him.

All is peaceful in the forest. Elvis thinks he might have an upper hand on his intruder—when Tommy Rottingham comes across on the portable radio. After a loud static-click, Tommy's voice says,

"There once was a hunter named Elvis . . .

. . . whose tree was shaking so bad . . . .

. . . that . . . I could see it . . . from . . . across town . . . ."

After a moment of no reply from Elvis, Tommy shouts, "Coming at you, boy!"

Elvis pays the transmission little attention, apart from winding the radio's knob to turn it off. Suffocated by the lively sounds of nature, the torments of his rival did not sound loud enough to disturb the boy at his horse.

Tall Grass sorts his seeds; he carries two types: one for planting, and one for consuming. He spills the seeds meant for planting onto the small satchel from where they were stored. They came from his bag that's made of the same type of hide as his rucksack, and the satchel is attached to the rucksack in case the satchel drops free. The satchel holds to the rucksack by way of a strong, handspun cord that's weaved through the mouth of the satchel to act as a drawstring for the bag.

He finds brown seeds with small white dots on them and a split down the middle of the shell. Tall Grass feels the soil to tell if it's moist enough to plant the seeds, and it is satisfactory. He blows on them once to get rid of the dust and dirt, and with his hands cupping this time, he blows on the seeds once more in an attempt to give the seeds a piece of his soul. He plants them there in the moist dirt.

Tall Grass spends all of his attention focusing on the little gifts bestowed to him by nature. He places the seeds with great care in a perfect spot where the soil seethes healthily for growth and the sun is plentiful. He knows that spot has the best chance for the seeds to start growing; "They would have rotted in my rucksack and aren't nutritious enough to eat on their own," he thinks to himself. It is the plants that grow from seeds such as he held, those that have been great enough in bounty to provide a staple for his people back home.

"I'm going to shake you out, boy!" yells Tommy Rottingham over the West Hills. He comes with a sledgehammer, a wailing iron fist. He wails on the tree trunk below Elvis, and the tree stand wobbles.

"I saw the way you look at her, but she's mine," says Tommy with a voice that rings out loud enough for Henry Edwards to hear the group nearby. "She don't know yet, but I'm going to get her family to give her away to me,"

"Then you better know," says Elvis, "you rotten devil, her family are good people. They like me, and neither she nor they believe she is anything but free to decide who to be with or not be with. You see this locket? She gave this to me."

"Oh yeah? Why you out here looking for a big ol' kill to prove it to her then?" questions the menace.

"I'm not tryin' to prove anything. Now, would you please stop hitting that tree?" asks Elvis.

Tommy stops hitting the tree long enough for Elvis to peak into his binoculars to see that the young savage and his beast have vanished. He can't search for them now because he has to hold on and brace himself as Tommy Rottingham keeps at whacking the tree enough to loosen the nails holding the stand to it. The whole stand starts to give way beneath his feet.

"I told you before, Tommy Rottingham," says Elvis, "you and your whole clan of Rottinghams can rot and decompose for all I care. Don't hunt on my land, either. If you want to stay alive and on the topside of the soil, you'll go back home."

Elvis puts the safety on his rifle as the tree shakes so much that a few leaves fall from the branches. Elvis thinks Tommy Rottingham might try to bring that ancient tree down to the ground with his hefty tool, wailing at the tree over and over at the same angle, mangling its bark.

The hunter in the tree holds on for safety. To protect his own life, Elvis resorts to clinging onto one of the other sturdy thin trees that holds together his hidden tree fort.

"I'm surprised you found me here," taunts Elvis while his legs do dangle. He supports himself only by using sheer upper-body strength in his arms, chest, and back. The tiny veins in his wrists and forearms begin to bulge, and his grip begins to loosen, so he lets go of the rifle that was making it harder for him to hold onto the tree. The rifle makes a clatter when it falls to the ground.

Tommy hears the rifle fall, and when he sees where it went he takes out some of his rage on the long-barreled firearm with his steel mallet. The rifle is mangled beyond recognition. The hunter is too late to save his instrument, for Tommy's aim put the mallet precisely on the barrel of the gun, and its brutal penetration of that once mechanical fortress tore apart the gun and brought its sighted scope to never be seen again.

"You brute!" Elvis exclaims. And try as he might, Elvis cannot hold on. The stand falls on top of Tommy Rottingham. He is stunned. Elvis is lucky enough to land in the bush below. He has catapulted off the trunk in a way, and in another instance, he's lucky to land next to a sharp granite boulder and not hit it.

Tommy Rottingham shakes off his condition. After being hit by something falling from above, he decides to leave the trees alone. He puts the mallet over his shoulder, at rest, and he reaches for Elvis' other prized possession, the locket with Lucinda-Lee's photograph inside.

Tommy has no trouble getting to the locket, either, since Elvis is still feeling stunned from hitting the ground and seeing his family heirloom destroyed. The events take an emotional toll on Elvis. Tommy brings the hunter back to reality and away from his gun that is in pieces—so much so that the Hunter is in a shock like he has a cold drip of water rolling down his spine. He is taken off guard, so Tommy has no real resistance when grabbing the locket from his neck.

Tommy snaps the thin locket's chain, and that pulling motion brings Elvis forward onto the leaves and twigs that broke his fall earlier.

"I bet I know what's in here," Tommy Rottingham says before opening the locket. "Yep. It's the pretty girl you watch. I told you. She's mine."

Elvis gets to his feet, and he holds the broken barrel from his rifle over his shoulder, opposite of Tommy Rottingham. Elvis questions Tommy by saying, "That girl . . . ? What do you think you know of her? Enough for her to be yours?"

"I do. I reckon," Tommy spits out.

Elvis is far from convinced. He shrugs and says, "Well, even if you think . . . you might . . . know her."

"I said, I reckoned I do," Tommy says.

"Or reckon," Elvis says. "If you reckon you know her,

how come you don't know she isn't anybody's anything?"

The hills and forest are quiet enough to hear wildlife moving in the bushes. If Elvis and Tommy listen carefully, it's possible to hear Henry Edwards unpacking his balloon and readying the basket. But instead their silence is shattered when a screeching bird-call is made by Tall Grass, and he says, "Don't move."

Both the hunter and his antagonist stay still where they stand. Tall Grass comes in closer to them to reveal that he has his bow drawn and ready to fire. "You with the hammer," he calls to Tommy Rottingham. "Give this man back what you took from him."

After a moment of deliberation, Tommy reluctantly gives up the locket. He tosses it over his shoulder, back towards the path that leads into town.

Tommy says, "If you want it, go get it. I'm off . . . to get the real thing." He decides that he would rather get his own picture of Lucinda-Lee. Tommy's mind begins to make rapid leaps in logic and imagination, and it leaps in the worst possible directions for a human mind to go.

Tommy slumps the mallet over his shoulder and leaves in the opposite direction from whence he came, away from Henry Edwards, and away from the shores; the menacing young man marches into town to look for that pretty woman he aims to steal away from Elvis.

Tall Grass lowers his bow when Tommy Rottingham has cleared away from the area. He thinks to himself, "This hunter I saved should be relieved." But to the contrary, the hunter still looks perplexed.

With Tommy Rottingham strutting into town to try to win the girl he so admires, Elvis feels at a loss. He says to Tall Grass, "Don't you have your own problems to figure out?"

"I do," says Tall Grass, "but you looked . . . like you needed my help." And the young foreign traveler takes to his saddled horse. Windsor's strong, straight legs move with action that show his superior breed, and his ribcage has a moderate spring to its boney fortress that supports Tall Grass and his belongings.

Tall Grass needn't pull sharply upon Windsor's reigns, like the horses he rode when he was too young to know how to get a horse to walk. All Tall Grass needs to do is ask, "Let's go, Winnie," and the horse canters when he pulls the heels of his moccasins gently towards the horse's ribs. He shifts his weight forward and in the leading direction. Windsor canters like a strong, muscular, controlled machine.

As Windsor and Tall Grass pass by the tree in front of Elvis, the hunter parries. Elvis takes to what is left of his tree stand in an act of territorial combativeness. He gets higher than the young boy and his horse. Elvis says, "You'll have to watch where you step that thing. You put hoof marks all along the trail leading from where you left, I bet."

The hunter doesn't know how careful Tall Grass was to make his trail disappear most of the time. It is something Tall Grass does to keep from being followed by friend or foe. For he had considered how a member of his tribe could have been with him, following him to ensure his survival and mission success; and he fears that people or creatures he encounters may not always be the merciful kind but the hungry kind. So Tall Grass thinks deeply about the comment Elvis made and thinks it was particularly inaccurate, but Tall Grass still proceeds with a certain degree of caution. He speaks with great conscious considerations to Elvis and his needs. He speaks in the common language of the land they both know. For, his people have some knowledge of society outside of their villages, enough to prepare with a common language to communicate with each other.

Tall Grass says, "I have a home, too, so I help spread for the new growth." Tall Grass shows the satchel of seeds to Elvis, but he can tell the hunter does not approve.

Elvis says, "I saw what you were doing. Don't think for a moment I didn't see you putting that junk in my dirt." The hunter climbs from his tree stand in a few thoughtfully planned leaps and bounds; he stretches his own limbs to reach the ground where Tall Grass buried the seeds. Elvis kicks a large rock, a boulder big enough to cover the seeds, and he places it down when the boulder is finished rolling. He places it on the spot above the seeds. It covers the seeds, so no nourishing light will have a clear passage to penetrate the soils and push the seeds to the surface. That boulder is large enough that it will not budge by natural or accidental force; it would require a deliberate maneuver to clear the way for the sun. Alas, these seeds will never grow; the Goddess will not shine on this harvest in North Shore.

To that act, the young rider clicks his tongue, and Windsor walks.

But Elvis isn't through; his pride is still hurting from what his hateful neighbor had done to him and plans to do with the woman he cares for. The hunter could go into town to find Lucinda-Lee before Tommy Rottingham, but he misplaces his anger and directs it towards Tall Grass. Instead of writing a love song for Lucinda-Lee, or impressing her with something else so pure and worthy of her admiration, the hunter chooses to prove a point that day about national pride. It seems noble in his mind (it really seems like a good cause to Elvis).

Elvis leaves in a hurry. He says, "I'll show you what I mean. I bet I find your trail, after all. I bet your people need some talking to about your coming here to spread your seeds."

When Elvis runs off toward the river that brought Tall Grass in, the boy fears the worst, and he immediately tugs at Windsor's reigns, for he wants to stop the hunter in his pursuit. But the horse is stuck in mud. "Yah!" roars Tall Grass, but alas, the poor horse isn't able to climb out of the mud.

It's nearly nightfall and Tall Grass still can't remove the horse from the trampled muddy grounds. He begs and pleads with the animal to move. He sees the pain in the straining animal's eyes, so he gets off his back to take a look and relieve Windsor of his own bodyweight. The horse's hind feet and right forefoot are completely submerged in the mud that otherwise provides a clear path along the hunting grounds. Windsor pulls his left forefoot from the mud and pulls against the hard ground adjacent to the muddy trail, but it's no use. To top it off, the horse has been growing tired in the struggle.

Tall Grass does everything he can think to do, including pushing the horse from behind without getting kicked in the process, which isn't too much of a worry since the kicking legs of the sturdy horse are cemented below it. He tries to pull the horse's bridal and reigns. In a hasty effort to gain some leverage, Tall Grass anchors himself on what he thinks is a vine coming from the tree above to give him some leverage. And he pulls on the reigns with all his might while leveraging his bodyweight on the supposed vine.

At last, Tall Grass notices an important detail of his situation that becomes presently clear to him upon inspection: the vine is not natural but constructed by man or machine. He pulls the rope once more and it comes loose from the other end.

Tall Grass promises Windsor that his departure will be brief, and he leaves to inspect where the rope has its origin. He discovers the recent target of his arrows: a big red canopy that has descended downward, covering the bamboo basket below it. He is so fixated on the balloon that he isn't even aware of its pilot, Henry Edwards, standing next to him on top of the hill.

"I . . . . I am in the presence of greatness," Tall Grass stammers. He looks both horrified and grateful. "Please have mercy on me, dear holy spirits of the sky."

"I don't know if the spirits heard you but I did," says Henry Edwards.

Tall Grass looks up from the balloon below at the young balloon pilot that is close to his own age, and he feels silly for what he has said. But Tall Grass does not let his shame spoil this meeting. He brushes himself off from being on the dirt and crunched leaves, after throwing himself to the mercy of something he did not understand. He asks what questions he finds within himself to gain the understanding he wishes to have.

"Is that your horse . . . ?" he feels silly asking Henry Edwards the truth about the deflated balloon envelope and basket.

"Basically," says Henry Edwards, "except my horse doesn't have a name."

"I'm sorry," says Tall Grass, "but I aimed to kill your winged horse." He points to the arrows stowed away in a quiver on Windsor's back. He mimes shooting his bow in the air.

Henry Edwards understands what he means, and he sympathizes with Tall Grass, since the strange young man seems harmless and honest. He takes notice of the situation Tall Grass has acquired, however. After collecting his rope in a coil around his shoulder, he says, "Let's get *your* horse loose. I've used this rope to anchor my balloon, and it held up tons of weight itself." He looks at the end of the coil of rope and wonders about it, since it looks frayed.

The mouse responsible for the frayed rope-end peeps his tiny whiskers out of the crevasse that concealed him in the balloon's basket, and he begins to fret that Henry Edwards will catch on to him being stowed away in the bamboo. The mouse feels guilty after chewing through the rope that was once tied properly to the basket.

Henry Edwards thinks to himself and can't come up with a good reason for why the rope wasn't hooked properly in place on the basket and concludes that his grandfather must have untied it. Then, he pulls it between his hands to test its tensile-strength and concludes that it seems strong enough to adequately hold a horse.

As it turns out, the mouse hadn't been greedy enough to ruin the rope, only hungry enough to satisfy his appetite, and rope isn't all that filling for little mice. So he wishes luck to Henry Edwards with a few tiny squeaks and squalls, too small for Henry Edwards to hear, of course. Then, the mouse takes off to discover what North Shore is like . . . on his own, and his adventure continues elsewhere.

Henry Edwards pauses to measure the distance from Windsor to the nearest limb extending from a sturdy tree. In the meantime, Tall Grass makes a harness for Windsor out of one end of the rope.

Henry Edwards cuts a large tree trunk with an axe he finds near the tree stand. Henry Edwards nearly fells the heavy tree he found before he stops cutting.

"Quick! The mud is starting to dry," says Tall Grass, worrying that his horse will forever be stuck in the ground where he stands.

They hurry to fell the tree, carefully letting it drop with no slack in the rope, as to not jerk the horse when it falls. That tree is large enough to provide enough weight, which transfers to lift. The weight of the tree, along with the force of gravity, pulls the horse out of the mud.

Windsor seems grateful, something Henry Edwards can tell instantly. He watches as Tall Grass goes not to his horse . . . but to the fallen tree instead.

"Count its rings," says Henry Edwards.

"The planet needs a spark in order to return to fertility," says Tall Grass. "The plants grow until they reach their maximum height, and then, they wait to die. My people say that it is man and woman who are responsible for the planet and for the change of energy on the Earth. The people can tell when it is time for the planet to return to ashes from where it once started. After all, Earth's literal meaning is 'dirt.' When I was assigned the task of slashing—of killing the largest tree in my village—of bringing it to meet the horizon forever—I left with little salty tears that ran from my face, and I pricked from my finger with the edge of my sharp axe blade to spill my life with the life that the planet asked for. The tree remained living for days. Weeks. Years. It's wood and rings were green and would not burn until it let go of its own life."

When Windsor is finally free, Henry Edwards must bid a fond farewell to the young boy who is still looking perplexed by his flying machine. Tall Grass is truly enlightened by the experience. He wants to bring this gift of flight to his people, but he doesn't know how to put it in words that they would understand, so he washes his hands in the river to clear his mind and body of the obligations this experience holds for him. He embraces the idea of finding new inventions and ways of living that have been all around him.

Meanwhile, Henry Edwards returns to his balloon. When he starts the burner the red nylon envelope starts to fill but a seam lets out and the balloon won't hold air. Upon inspecting each section to figure out why it won't hold, he half expects to find an arrow. Instead he finds the top of one section to be torn. A large tear runs all the way down the balloon, one that needs to be repaired before attempting to fly again. So he looks in the toolbox in the passenger-basket and finds a patch kit that he has used before to mend much smaller holes. But the kit is small, and unfortunately, the glue is all dried up.

It is then that Henry Edwards sees it: the locket that

Tommy Rottingham tossed over his shoulder in spite is hanging in mid-air from a tree branch. It is this culprit that tore his balloon. The sharp metal clasp holds the locket shut and seals away the picture of a beautiful woman desired by more than one man.

Tall Grass intends to stop Elvis before he returns to South Shore, the village that Tall Grass knows as his home. He thinks how the hunter will anger his father and worry his sister, but everywhere Tall Grass looks along the shore he cannot find a single track that Elvis had left behind. He finds the slip for a boat on the river that leads out towards the Sinking Oceans. That river brought Tall Grass from South Shore. But the boat itself is nowhere to be seen. He imagines it must belong to Elvis.

It is near the empty slip by the water's edge that Henry Edwards sees a bird land upon a branch so sturdy it does not shake, even though the swallow itself far outweighs the branch. The swallow keeps his body close enough to the trunk to avoid breaking its perch. Henry Edwards tells the bird, "How lucky you are to have a perch on the ground, and I am lucky enough to perch in your skies."

Soon enough he catches up with Tall Grass and agrees to help him find the hunter in exchange for assistance repairing his once mystical, now fallible, flying machine. Tall Grass remarks, "From the heavens, a charmed creature doesn't need help . . . regaining flight. Not so charmed but humble, I suppose."

The horse travels in good spirits even though it was injured. Windsor pulled on his left leg too hard when he was getting out of the mud before Henry Edwards lent a helping hand. The horse and its rider look forward to relieving the animal, even briefly. He's a warrior's horse, so he's not entirely unaccustomed to pain, but this is not a battle. Their ability to rest in South Shore will come as a relief to Windsor. Henry Edwards is glad it wasn't his fault. "If it's all the same, I'd rather not get on this horse's bad side," Henry Edwards thinks to himself. He worries about his grandfather and hopes his father is safe, and Emily too.

They agree to take a boat when the next sun comes out.

Meanwhile, Cary Oriel is being questioned by police who find it strange that his children and father went missing and he is left to run Sky Vision all by himself. The police couldn't be any more wrong. In fact, in the morning when Henry Edwards is getting ready to go with Tall Grass on a boat, Cary is waiting for his lawyer to arrive. He isn't happy about the situation: his sleepless night in the police station is spent worrying about his family's safety, not knowing what happened to them, wondering if his father was right about some of the strange secrets he talked about openly—

Cary begins to ponder, "Was my father telling the truth when he talked to Henry Edwards about his voyages and all those secrets he knows?" He doesn't feel proud of his father's legacy since it just might be why his family is in peril after all. He certainly doesn't know what to believe—He didn't even make it into the house when they disappeared. Emily wasn't at daycare, Henry Edwards disappeared, and . . . so did Oriel.

He wonders if talking about the trip Oriel had planned and asking if the balloon is missing would help the investigation, but he doubts that there is a coincidence. "There is more to this puzzle," Cary thinks, so he doesn't talk to the cops. He doesn't have anything to add to their investigation anyway. The officers that responded to the alarm saw Cary pull up in the driveway.

Those flashing neon lights bounced off his car the same as they bounced off the teal glass-hatch when he pulled into the driveway. He tries remembering the glass-hatch on the roof. "Was it ajar?" he asks himself. "What if it was open and they could all be on a trip somewhere safe," he tells himself. "But what if the balloon is still there," he thinks. "What if Oriel flipped the switch as a sign for me to know something was happening . . . ? Or as a sign to look at the sky . . . ?"

It's as if . . . some force compels Cary . . . to look into thin air . . . .

The police who told him about the disturbance at the scene asked him questions on the spot, and they eventually took him into the station. They had probable cause due to the evidence that seemed to pile up: the shop was a mess, and Cary would inherit the Sky Vision fortune. But the police have trouble finding a motive behind the disappearances, and they know someone tried to kill Oriel over his inventions once already.

The detectives on the case don't introduce themselves or care much about Cary's rights. They slam him in the car and put him in a cell while they wonder where the family went, or where their bodies are hidden . . . if Cary went mad. But luckily for Cary, Bruno has arrived. Joslin's brother helps Cary get out of the station and back home.

Chapter Eight

Tracking Psychos & Mending Hearts

IN North Shore, the desirable young woman named Lucinda-Lee is used to getting attention from men. Most of the men who know her think she's unfair, however; she seems to put her career above romance, so much so that even looking at a man in a physical manner is unlikely. On the contrary, all men can help to do is catch a glimpse of her radiance, her sun-kissed skin. Other women question how she stays looking so very blessed by sun alone, using neither lotion nor surgery. Her appearance comes as a surprise since she spends much of her life tucked away in buildings: libraries, the clerk's office, and places where she can assist with the legislative process that aids social services, like those assisting her aunt. She has been working with low-income folks in North Shore while helping her sick Aunt Mitzy find the help she needs, enough to make her own personal recovery.

Mitzy was once in an auto accident that left her with weak knees, a problem Lucinda-Lee has not encountered thus far. Boys wish to be men when they see Lucinda-Lee; they put away their toys and pick up books, guns, or anything they can use to impress the Lito beauty. It is the boys who have weak knees when Lucy comes around.

When Tommy Rottingham took off from the forest he was set on finding Lucinda-Lee to prove that he's right for her in spite of his neighbor, Elvis, whom he hated with all the growing envy of a less skilled rival hunter. Even with a busted rifle, Rottingham couldn't outhunt Elvis, so he spent the night picking through new ways of impressing Lucinda-Lee.

Tommy Rottingham finds Lucinda-Lee, there among the stacks of books, between the 792 thru 856 stacks and the 857 thru 902 stacks; she's reading a law book to prepare for an exam when Tommy walks up to her and picks up a book in the same row as the one within her grasp. He makes it so the gap in the bookshelf becomes larger with one more book missing from it. Lucinda-Lee, as usual, is far too engrossed in her studies to realize that she could be missing an opportunity to shack up with the man in flannel who stands next to her— she's looking through her notes on cases she has been studying all semester and checking to find the appropriate example of a case to fill in her study guide. She's looking for cases where courts have ruled in favor of discrimination being used in the workplace when she is intersected by the ravenous hunter.

Tommy Rottingham, who has been building up an argument to interject, clears his throat of mucus built up from not dipping tobacco for a few minutes; that sound gets her attention, and he thinks it's a good opportunity when she turns. He says, "So sorry. You don't know about land use, do ya'?" He waits a moment for a response, and another moment goes by where she could respond, but she doesn't say anything, so he says, "My buddy is trying to buy himself some property and—"

Lucinda-Lee interrupts by saying, "I can't give unsolicited advice but—" She reaches into her small leather-strapped purse. She uses a slender hand, decorated with nail polish, to quickly hand him the card. She proudly says, "This is the guy I work for. He should be able to help your friend with his questions about the law." Just like that, she smiles, he smiles, and she's off leaving Tommy Rottingham with a lump in his throat. He's less than satisfied with how an encounter he hoped would be romantic turns out to have been trivial and rather mundane. Still, he sees what Elvis likes about her . . . after that first encounter, and he decides he must talk to her again soon.

Tommy thinks to himself, while blaming the girl: "Lucinda-Lee Price, with her dark-hair and rich Caribbean blood line, has got me thirsty and eager for more."

Unfortunately, Elvis doesn't realize how much trouble the apple of his eye is in, but who would find him at fault?— No, the hunter from North Shore is filled with pride and purpose. He's driven to step boldly into the land called South Shore to show those indigenous people what an outsider is capable of achieving, a notion he vexes wildly to himself on route to the land across the Majorilis. Some romantic fantasy takes over his being; it could be the waves or the gulls and the salt water that bring Elvis to a deeper understanding of his situation. For, he hopes for something more than proving the young trespasser named Tall Grass to be a foolish and unkempt errand boy. His voyage gives him time to gather the value he will bring conversing with people who don't care to understand modern technology; he fancies they will worship him like an early conquistador was worshiped. He thinks to himself, "They'll certainly treat me like Cortez."

In the morning, around the time Lucinda-Lee leaves the library, Elvis runs his boat onto South Shore. "There, this must be the place where the thorn in my side lived," he thinks. And he's right. Stuck on the ground before his feet is a clump of clipped hair. He recognizes the color. Elvis picks up a single bead from a clump of one of the locks of hair that used to belong to Tall Grass. He looks through the toothpick-sized hole in the wooden bead to see, where, on the other side of the miniature scope, exists the path that young Tall Grass took a day earlier.

After stewing for a few moments, Rottingham takes offense over not being seen as astute by the woman he wishes to charm; he knows Elvis got through her icy demeanor because once he saw them laughing together, and he feels he didn't deserve to be dealt with so hastily. He's getting angry over it. When he sees a few high school teens studying for exams, he thinks how happy they look and how content they are in their own world. He wants to wreck their lives and bring them to a dark sadness. When he gets to their study place, in the atrium before the door leading outside, he knocks their books from the table and even topples a chair over on his way out.

He shows his anger just like he showed it to the pigs at his father's farm. Oh, how he loved to watch them before snuffing out their lives. The pigs were full and pale from being kept in pens, where they were fattened up for the slaughter. His father wasn't mistaken either, for he knew something was wrong with his son— He even told him in front of company when he saw him caressing that knife and looking out the window above the kitchen sink. Tommy Rottingham was looking out at the pigs and creeping everyone out when his father confronted him, by saying the following fatherly advice: "STOP playing with monsters, boy!" It was the best he could muster up for his son.

His father was referring to the monsters in the seventeen year-old's head, of course, like the monsters that told Tommy he didn't need to pretend to wince at the spilling red that covered the slaughter-house floors. He saw what his son was becoming and how the disturbed young man enjoyed depleting the livestock. After he saw that Tommy was robbing the animals of what keeps them alive, his father took him aside to tell him the following: "That's the devil, boy. You have the devil in you." Try as Mr. Rottingham might, he was not able to reach his son, so he forbade Tommy from touching steel in his presence.

But when Tommy picked up a gun to go hunting on his own, his father didn't have it left in him to stop the terrible tormentor. Tommy had grown strong from all the boxes he lifted, working at the shipping yard for a furniture warehouse. When his father witnessed the wing-tips of his shoulders broaden, and how they had gotten round like cannon balls—how his son could lift a quarter-ton box over his head, the humble farmer conveniently lost interest in teaching his son. For his own safety, he lost interest in protecting the world from Tommy Rottingham.

After scaring the students out of the atrium, Tommy Rottingham stays indoors because he thinks he might be able to ogle some more of the most sought after woman in North Shore.

He thinks of how polite he must seem to stand looking through the library window with a barrier of glass in between him and his plotting. He isn't careful either. Tommy leaves traces of himself all over the place. His fingers leave greasy smudges and his breath fogs up the window, while he thinks of a way to get his competition completely out of the picture. Images that come to his twisted mind are those of taking a knife to Elvis while he's on his knees with ropes around his wrists. He fantasizes about this until the security guard from the library approaches him and properly asks him to leave.

"You're scaring people around here," says the guard. "We've gotten reports saying you threw a chair. Are you hearing me, guy? Hello! . . . ?"

Tommy Rottingham beats his chest with a right hand fist coming at his meaty breast, with the force of what his hammer swung at the tree that held Elvis up high. He swipes his foot on the ground as well, like a cat scratches to mark its territory. The guard secures Tommy's wrists, but Tommy takes the guard down with a shoulder to his ribcage. The pinch Tommy issues to the guard on his neck is enough to give him a neurological disorder that could come with weeks of headaches.

All passersby cease their movements, and everyone in the vicinity looks toward the action. Tommy Rottingham hightails it by getting in the driver's side of his work truck. The box truck he drives is an ancient machine with bright-yellow, sun-dulled paint that's chipped all over. He shoves his smelly work uniforms over to clear the passenger-side bucket seat off completely and sets off a racket of beer cans rolling out from the floor of the work truck.

"Better get things tidy if I'm thinking about bringing in company," torts Rottingham.

The blue Elixiumbrium Crystals shimmer in the first light of the morning and wake Henry Edwards from his dreams of stars and families reuniting. The magnetism of the crystals cause vibrations to be sent out. Emanating from each center is an emission of a certain magnetic charge. The charge is imperceptible to human senses, but it is monitored by a mechanism placed around each crystal. The mechanisms around the crystals are equipped with magnetic compasses, voltmeters, and magnetic pole identifiers, which relay the information gathered there to a transmitter that sends the data to the system in Grandpa Oriel's workshop. The only person with access to that system at this time, of course, should be Oriel.

But alas . . . . When Detective Bruno Peters helps Cary get out of being questioned for the disappearances . . . the sly badge takes over the system for monitoring the rare crystals as well . . . .

Henry Edwards approaches the shimmering blue crystals while Tall Grass sits up from where he fell asleep next to their fire, and Tall Grass says, "This carriage is cursed. What do you suppose?"

"No," says Henry Edwards. "I don't believe in curses." But he removes the monitoring system that tracks the balloon. He plans to toss it into the waters when they get to the ocean. He leaves the Elixiumbrium in place, however.

"Thanks for agreeing to take a look around," says Cary.

"No problem," says Bruno. "You've got your hands full . . . I guess. You're almost family, so we got to start looking after each other . . . ."

"Yeah," says Cary. "I'm not . . . so sure."

"What's that?" asks Bruno. He's found the software monitoring the tracking system, but the tracking system stops transmitting a signal when it is removed. The screen reads, "SYSTEM MALFUNCTION." Bruno shakes his head and says, "This is no good. No good at all." He pushes the desk chair in and asks, "And you don't have any idea where that balloon might be headed?"

"It was nice to get to skip out of the jail cell," Cary thinks to himself, "but I'm not sure what he's up to." Cary resists the urge to tell Bruno about the family trip they had planned and how his son knows how to fly a balloon. He simply says, "That old balloon probably wouldn't make it off this property."

HENRY EDWARDS doesn't realize the twists of fate at play, which isn't surprising because twists of fate usually don't reveal themselves to those being twisted while they're in such moments of deliberation.

Actually, according to a poll taken by a reputable publication[4] 52% of people surveyed admittedly believe in fate. Either fate or coincidence is surely at play when Henry Edwards boards the canoe with Tall Grass and his muddy horse, for they are bound for a land where the chief's son is familiar with all aspects of life, and where he stands the chance to meet a hunter who is also in unfamiliar territory.

On the canoe, Henry Edwards considers talking to the authorities as soon as he is able to repair his baboon, but then he remembers all the people after his family's guarded secret. He doesn't know if he can trust the authorities.

"I told him to sit. He came here on a metal boat—"

"It's carbon fiber," says Elvis.

"Junk!" shouts King Grass. "He cut his foot and he looked to us for help, but he said we are bad people for putting out you, Tall Grass, into the world."

Elvis rolls around in pain. He's under a shady palm tree on a peninsula of South Shore, on a cliff that faces his home.

"Did you help him with his wound?" asks Tall Grass.

"My son," says King Grass with a smile on his face, "I knew you did not return to harm this man. I told him to sit on his rump—to take pressure off the foot."

A shaman nearby is humming and waving. He says, "A-puna-mayte," which translated means, the body grows from the ground.

Not long after their arrival, Henry Edwards leaves with Tall Grass and a barrel of sap from palm trees. The people of South Shore use this sticky substance as a sweetener in cooking

---

[4] Harper, J. (2015 July 15) Majority of Americans believe in fate poll. *Washington Times*. Retrieved from https://www.washingtontimes.com/news/2015/jul/13/poll-61-percent- republicans-believe-fate-horosocop

but also for patching the roofs of their homes, which are ornately constructed from ocean boulders, wood from palms, and a substance similar to this sap but more like concrete. With a low rainfall and low humidity the sap lasts as a temporary solution for shelter.

Elvis declines an offer Tall Grass makes to give the injured party passage on their return voyage. Elvis says, "That'll be too rough on me today, for the tide is high now and the wind keeps changing direction . . . enough to make use of a sail difficult." Tall Grass leaves him some water and a knife in case the foot turns green, he thinks. Tall Grass says, "Cut a coconut if you need food." They leave on a much smaller dugout canoe, one with no room for a horse.

When they are nearing North Shore on the return voyage, Henry Edwards thanks Tall Grass before going off on his own to repair the balloon. Tall Grass says, "Now we are even." He does not get off the boat but watches as Henry Edwards takes the barrel of sap onto the grassy shore and into a thickly covered swampland.

Henry Edwards remembers Oriel telling him how to fix a tear in the balloon: "It's called patching up a sheet," said Oriel to Henry, in a field somewhere close to home once. They were out flying when the balloon they were riding hit a snag because they were running too close to a tree branch. Oriel claimed the maneuver was done on purpose, of course, to teach his grandson how to mend the material. He taught him to sew: "No different than that. Thread a needle and darn a sock, but only we're using a different needle and thread is all."

With that over-simplified notion in mind, Henry takes to sewing. But it was a tiny hole they sewed that day that wasn't much bigger than a frock-coat button. Now, Henry has a much larger tear to sew, and he must mend it with the sap in place of glue.

Chapter Nine

How and Why Inspector Oriel Left Town

THAT jar stayed sitting in the Staten Island Health and Public Safety Department for a full weekend to weekend span.

It was absolutely baking in the sun that came through the blinds on the fourth floor during the day, but the air conditioner helped keep the rather delicate lingonberries from crystallizing during one of the hottest autumn weeks in the history of Never York's Forgotten Borough.

It resembled the way summer does heat the pavement, giving it a glow enough to reflect the fluids evaporating from it, and some would notice gasoline evaporating when mixed with water; this happened all around the building.

The oils seemed to radiate evenly in the mid-day sun, except when a heavy dose of acid rain came through the isolated borough to wash it away.

That jar stayed on the desk in Cary's office for a week.

Meanwhile, at the Manchester St. apartment, enough time had went by with no signs of Cary. Joslin sleeps pretty on a thick mattress made of what her med-student lover can afford. Her new suitor that came into her life amidst her engagement to Cary is an affable sort of fellow. He's gentle and kind, but he lied about being a dentist. He is still studying for his degree, and she feels ashamed to be with a student since she is a woman in her late-twenties. She feels accomplished in her career as an office manager enough to pay her way in life, and she hasn't had trouble keeping money coming in. The feeling of independence rings true as Joslin starts viewing her new suitor as a temporary engagement after realizing his little lie about his job title.

Miss Joslin Peters goes to the fourth floor office, where she was recently situated to work with Inspector Cary Oriel until he stopped coming in and failed to report to his supervisors. She goes in the fourth floor office area to pick up office supplies and look for the shawl she dropped when she realizes she left a few other belongings as well.

Seeing the crate of jam next to the dried up plant in Cary's office that has been raided reminds her of the words of her lover. On and on, for weeks, her med-school lover had asked her about the berry jam like it was the antidote for a poison that had taken control over his central nervous system. He quivered with hunger in the mornings when he was confronted with plain muffins, but he was still in good health then. Still, he went on thinking things like, "That jam would go great with a slice of fresh-baked marble rye bread." Another day he even threatened to go buy it himself, saying with hostility, "I'll get the damn jam myself if I have to."

She finally agrees to fetch it from the office where it is being kept cool in the air conditioning. Knowing that she's fulfilling his request causes her med-school lover such a relief that his belly even distends some from the sense of upcoming satisfaction to have proper satiation. Joslin takes an unopened jar of lingonberry jam from a shipment Cary had confiscated. The hole she makes is easy to cover-up since the cling-wrap winds tighter, wrapping the berries in another suffocating layer of insulation.

Joslin takes her belongings from the office with a crate that fits in the backseat of her white convertible. The crate is full of *Woman's Daily Life Magazine* subscriptions from inside the drawer of her desk, and a coffee mug with the following vague expression, printed in Comic Sans: "Not every Monday is dreary as long as you stay the hell out of my way." And there was the shawl that Cary placed on her chair when she left from their final encounter. The box fits well in the backseat of her luxury car, with plenty of fine literature to support and surround the glass jar of jam as it rides with Joslin to a nearby strip mall. The sexy adulteress makes a stop there to get her a manicure and a pedicure of white outlining the tips of her fingernails and toenails.

Joslin's French manicure dries perfectly and looks stunning by the time she picks up that polished, silver butter knife. It's still warm from leaving the dish washer. Her suitor can't wait another minute; he can't control himself. He tries to remember what it tasted like but can't pinpoint . . . the correct parts . . . of his pallet. He longs for the taste of that rare jam . . . so much so that it surrounds the deep, dormant parts of his subconscious mind, so much so that it has affected his sleep even. But to some incalculable degree each night, the memory of the lustful, red, juicy texture on his tongue's sweet sensing taste buds have caused the craving to manifest greatly, far greater than the average addiction.

He loves Joslin because of it, and they love each other despite her feelings toward him being a student and telling lies about himself being a dentist already. They make passionate love that night for the first time since Cary put everything together about Joslin and her suitor.

Plenty of romantics say, love conquers all. Romantic medicine people and travelers will admit, love heals wounds and crosses the sands of time when with the right person. Couples counselors romanticize over love bringing together two people for more bliss than one person can experience on their own; it can bring nations together, says . . . the romantic optimist. But even love is not ahead of the curve when it comes to detecting pathogens on their way through a healthy human body, says the thorough mortician.

FRIDAY's Corner Store has a visit from Ms. Joslin Peters after her lover finished the contents of the poorly preserved jar of jam, and Friday is the seller of an unopened container that is dated with a satisfactory sell-by date.

Friday guesses she is in a rush to get somewhere when Joslin leaves her credit card behind on the counter by the register and rushes out of the store. So he does what any sensible shop owner in a struggling economy would do when trusted with someone else's financial information: he takes her card to the nearby gas station to fill his tank, in an act of supporting local business. Then, he disposes of the evidence before she returns looking for it. Ol' Friday knows what Joslin did to Cary and thinks that he'll help him get back something, or at least that's what he told himself in his head.

Luckily for the dishonest shopkeeper, Joslin believes she might have dropped the card elsewhere when Friday denies seeing it all. He quickly covers his tracks: "My card reader is down, so you must be mistaken." Meanwhile, the newly purchased jar of jam waits in her convertible while she argues with Friday and shows him her receipt. The ordeal doesn't take long, and afterwards she goes back to the apartment to wait for the jam-loving man she shares her home with.

She stocks the pantry while she waits for her lover's arrival, and she even has time to set the table for dinner before the call comes in that her med-school lover is no longer living. Not long before she gets the call . . . a few glasses of white wine are spent thinking about the past few days and about how it ended with Cary . . .

It didn't occur to Joslin how much pressure Cary was under because she never met his family. She almost met them, and she saw plenty of pictures of his children, but she never actually saw their faces.

"It feels like Emily, my little girl, guiding me," Cary thought to himself on that final day in his office before he left town in a hurry. "I can see her there, baby, like she's alive. I think, whatever it was, I don't say ghosts," he spoke, imagining talking it through with his sleeping wife, Adeline. He didn't believe in ghosts. His disbelief is calculably correct seeing as according to another poll[5] only 42% of people believe in ghosts.

"But Emily's spirit was up and visible in the shimmers of light all around me," carried on the inspector inside his own head, "like she was keeping the evil away."

Cary spoke to himself aloud: "My baby girl might be gone. She might not have made it past five. Our babies . . . . And do you know why? Because their dad was out looking for some greasy gyro-chef low-life."

In his own head, he started replaying everything Adeline once told him: "You blame yourself too much, Cary." Her voice was calm and smooth. It rolled over his mind like a soothing breeze tussles blades of grass. "You didn't do anything wrong," said Adeline's voice in his head, "I'm sorry if you still hurt, but it— Talking to you— It sends me in this downward spiral." The breeze got stronger, and his mind raised with how tormented Adeline was when she said, "I love you, but the pain is so bad that we can hardly carry on like this."

"Adeline, wait!" he remembered calling to her back when she was awake enough for them to have a fight. "We have each other—"

"I'm sorry, Cary," she said. "Goodbye." And she left him alone in their house filled with sparkling new appliances and clean carpets. She left, not knowing what would happen to the man she loved.

The feelings she had, she kept them in the same place— The love for him was contained in the same part of her heart as the

---

[5] Broxson, B. Why so many people believe in ghosts. *Real Simple*. Retrieved from https://www.realsimple.com/health/mind-mood/why-people-believe-in-ghosts

love for the child they cared for until Adeline went to sleep for a long time.

Cary woke from his dream on the couch in his office. "It's okay Emily, baby. Don't cry. Emily, baby . . . ." he whispered. He was awake, tears rolling down his cheeks.

He got up and went to the copy machine. The machine was jammed. He took his original out and went to visit the copy shop down the street. After he finished making his copy, he visited a corner store to investigate something that had been troubling him.

Under a streetlamp, Cary Oriel left behind the breezy city street to face his fears in Friday's Corner Store. The door slammed back on him, but he managed to sneak by, though it was close to trapping his coattail. The sound of the short square leather bits of laces, those burnt-looking ends of leather that friction caused to agletate—His untied moccasins alerted the cashier to his presence, and he watched Cary walk down aisle three.

Cary looked to see if his hunch was right. He saw a peculiar thing in his fiancé's desk drawer. He was sure she didn't buy it herself. She showed him how much she disliked the jam herself; when he ate some of it, she even made an elaborate effort to avoid kissing him with his sticky, sweet face.

He knew how hard it was to get that jam. Lingonberries are a select variety.

When he didn't see it in the appropriate place on the shelf, he checked his facts: he approached the store owner and said, "Hey Friday, I'm looking for my favorite jam."

"Yeah?" asked Friday.

"Yeah," replied Cary. "It's made from a strange berry. It's a rare import, comes in on a boat, I think . . . from Europe. Do you know anything?"

Friday spoke casually: "First time I came to America, my father, he told me it takes all the world to bring me here, that the reason we left our country . . . was because the world we knew, our town and the people we lived with in my home wanted us to be born again in another place. Our people saw us leaving, and I saw them rejoice, so . . . it made sense to me. It wasn't overwhelming and unbecoming, either; they weren't happy to get rid of us, and they certainly felt no sense of desertment to either party, no . . . .

"They felt responsible for birthing a people who would represent their country. My father's name you could not pronounce, but we spoke French too, and I learn English, but my father made a point to show our new country what our people stand for . . . with his goodwill and service. He too felt responsible. I don't . . . . I watch more than he. I view like a bird, and I don't get involved in what you think about all day. Getting ahead in life by bringing others down— That's you, boy. You should be . . . ashamed at getting ahead, Cary. You here to put me out of business, too?"

A silence fell over the store. And Friday replied, "The jam you seek is normally in aisle three."

"That's where I was just now," said Cary.

"Well, I guess you're out of luck unless you drive to my other store in Poughkeepsie," said the smiling shop owner.

"I'm not doing that," said Cary. "How long ago did you sell it?"

"Hmm," thought Friday. "I guess around same time yesterday."

"You're certain?" asked Cary

"Mister, this pretty girl came in . . . looking good," said Friday. "I thought I was 'bout to pass out. She was perfect."

Cary could tell he was talking about Joslin. He asked, "She bought it, huh?"

"No," said Friday. "She met with some guy near the front of my store. And that guy bought it."

Cary remembered telling her how much she would love lingonberries. Now, he suspected she had tried it already, and she's spreading it on more than a piece of bread.

"Was—were they together?" asked the daring inspector.

"She kissed him, I suppose," said Friday. "I saw he had the most, the biggest forehead I ever saw." Friday gestured.

Cary caught Friday up to speed on who Joslin was to him, and Friday shook his head in disgust and shame. If she's spreading jam for the man with the big forehead, Cary was determined to find out the truth.

Back in his office again, Cary tried to imagine what it would be like without Joslin. He pictured her in bed wearing a red lace lingerie. Her hair was dark enough to put out the sun; it made her fair skin appear even paler than it would otherwise.

His chair leaned back so far that it bumped into his desk, and from atop a jar of jam— one she brought to him with such arrogance— a sticky butter knife fell flat on the mahogany desk. '*Claaang!*' it rang out loudly.

Such reverberations of metal upon wood did something to jog his memory, for Cary thought about her that way she was when she first came into his office looking for work. But she never wore red . . . at work. She reserved that color for nighttime affairs. She said that red makes the biggest splash in men's eyes. Until that moment for some very odd reason, Cary had successfully imagined every man's eyes plashless when Joslin was around. But suddenly the truth was eating at him.

Eventually, Joslin took off her brown shawl before creeping over to the copy machine. She couldn't help but notice Cary staring out the window longer than it normally took to look out at the majestic world of pavement and high rises.

Cary couldn't deal with not having sex. And up to that point he was willing to put everything on the line to bring meaning back to life through that powerful physical release. But it suddenly felt wrong, and he felt like it was foolish to move on from his old life. He wanted to reclaim everything he had with Adeline. "That woman is waking," Cary thought to himself. He wanted to visit again, one last time before he left town. But he knew there wouldn't be time for that.

The smell of perfume entered his office. It was a sweet smell of familiar intoxication that blew around inside his nostrils and radiated a part of his soul in a way that Joslin's lofty department store fragrances had never suckled to his senses; it shined bright to his soul in a familiar way that only one other person had accomplished.

"Joslin . . . . ." said the entranced inspector. "I don't see myself needing to further ask for your services."

"You're going to call and set your own appointments then?" asked the peckish woman. "Fine by me."

He started turning in his chair when she said, "You're acting cruel—"

Promptly, he took from his lap a stack of photos. He placed them on top of the empty plate on his desk with so much force that bread crumbs shot off in all directions. And he said, "What is cruel is caring about you and then you go sleep with the filthy mug next door."

She was in shock. With unapologetic desperation she said, "We . . . . We were just messing around, Cary." She looked down at the photos of her with the other man, when something inside caused her to shudder: the thought that it wasn't even a passionate affair she was having.

He wanted to throw her through a window; he was furious because she, Joslin, burned him with her passion and promiscuity. He no longer trusted her, and moreover, he had started to develop this temper towards her and her lover. "What diseases have they brought to my loins?" he wondered aloud in his own head.

She took the engagement ring he gave her off her finger. She extended it to him. "Here you are," said Joslin."One last kiss before I pack my things then?"

"I can't resist you," Cary told Joslin. He swept his arms around her waist. She leaned back, and he folded her hand closed with the ring inside. "Keep it," he said, "as something to remember us by."

He never had a problem getting started with her when they were intimate, but that was because he was telling himself all along that the mother of his children was dead already. That the woman on the bed with the tubes running in through her wrists and throat was already gone, and what was left wasn't the person he loved before. But when he heard Adeline's voice, or what he thought was her voice, he assured himself it was her calling to him from her sleep in the skies . . . . He couldn't look at Joslin the same way he once could. It felt wrong all of a sudden.

The sweet, beautiful tantalization that crept around his office and his lungs, lived within the shadows of all consciousness. Something else . . . entirely.

He was no match for it. He was neither rage, nor lust, nor . . . anything really.

He was a slave to the smell of desire. Adeline called him one last time. The phone rang. But he didn't answer it.

Joslin was on his desk one last time, but all he smelled was Adeline.

"One more time," he said, and she nodded.

He pulled her legs closer to him; they stayed there. He pleasured her with one gentle touch of his finger, deeply and firmly. She will never forget it. He left the office before she could catch her own breath.

He will see her once again, years in the future. Her hair will be frizzy from too many chemical treatments. And though she was once agile, her years will progress unkindly. He'll temporarily lose sleep thinking about how awful life would be for him if they had stayed together.

He gathered up a few belongings and got on with what felt right.

She canceled his cards and called in her brother and whatever bulls he could bring with him before Cary could get out of town. After all, being close with the police is how she got that desk job in the first place.

As Cary made his way home he predicted some trouble or a shakedown from the cops. He decidedly took the alleyway all the way back. When he got to his home in the city he took the corner building's fire escape to the roof, and then, he got to his building from the roof access. But he made a mistake by taking the elevator, which took him down to the lobby.

He might have never made it to his home at all, but the security guard at the front desk of his building gave him a tip. "I've been hearing your name tonight, boss," said the guard, holding his hand-radio high. "You better get going. I have to call it in and I got to make it look good on the tapes, like I'm trying to stop you."

The big guy behind the desk was there waiting for him when he left Joslin at the office. He was already coming at Cary. He ducked when the guard took his first swing. The guard was fast, and his punch landed painfully on the wall. After giving him a quick elbow to the back, Cary had the guard on the floor in a choke hold.

"Damn. I bet it was Joslin," said Cary. He held the guard's face on the shag carpet. "I just confronted my fiancé about her infidelity. What are they after me for? Murder? Extortion?"

"They said you're wanted for tax evasion," said the guard before going limp on the carpet.

"Well, thank you," said Cary. He dropped the guard completely to the carpet. "Give me a five minute head start before you call the bulls."

"Boss, it's just tax evasion. I'd give you twenty— even if it was true," he said, sinking further into the shag.

He took a bag and went to the train yard. When it gets tough . . . you can't stop and get off. If the case keeps moving, it means it's getting good. So he kept moving, but it wasn't enough.

When Inspector Cary left town he didn't give his opposition much to work with: he left his car where it sat in the parking garage. He made it to the main train station in Never York by taking the mid-day ferry at St. George Terminal to get off the island. He would have boarded a passenger train at Grand Central Station by using a fake ID and passport that he had. He was ready to travel as Frank Greenburoughs, a real estate and financial planning coach, but his undercover plan drifted to the wayside when he saw that the trains happened to be completely full. Yet, when he looked around the station there didn't appear to be many people.

Cary asked around and found out that somebody came to the station and purchased all the seats. He wondered who would have the billfold large enough to buy up a dozen train cars.

There wasn't much time to think about the options. There were only two ways to go from the box office where they sold tickets down to the trains themselves. Cary couldn't sneak past the conductor who was standing, waiting to tear the tickets. He saw the conductor and considered him too bulky to sneak past since he was taking up enough space with the swaying of his arms for two people of his size to stand there. That's why Cary decided to take the other way out: there was another stairway that looked like it would spin around a few times before it let off below, on the ground level. He saw the lights downstairs were flickering and imagined it smelling of soot from all the boxcars that were transporting coal, and he was right.

Inspector Cary Oriel only had to wait for the right moment to leave for the stairs. He waited for the bulky conductor to turn to look at the empty cars he would have to haul, and when he did turn Cary snuck down those stairs. He even got on a car without anybody noticing he was there, or so he thought.

But they were there already, on the empty car waiting for him. Eight male officers and two female officers—operating outside of the law— They wanted to beat the poor man until they thought he was close enough to death that he would do anything they wanted him to do.

Detective Bruno Peters made the call when they cornered Cary in the train that day: "We'll bust you up before you go away, Cary. That'll give you something to think about on your trip— which, by the way, hey Cary, where you goin'? You . . . look a mess. I guess we all do."

By the end of it all Cary Oriel's blood would be on them, on their fists and on their shoes. "Don't bother cleaning up none," Bruno told the rest of the dirty cops. "Joslin needs to see I did right for her after he cut her loose like that."

Looking back, Cary thinks about how they looked smug, like they own the place. "How come they thought they owned that train car, too?" He thinks hard but can't figure anything out.

"You know you're wanted—" said Bruno

"I didn't touch my family," interrupted Cary.

"Yeah," said Bruno, "that may be so, but do you know anyone by the name of Maxwell Orefield?" Cary looked at Bruno with a blank stare.

"You know Max?" Jerry asked the inspector. "See, I know

Max is loyal, but I've gotten tired of his taste in music. Too many loud drums . . . ."

"What are you talking about?" asked Cary.

"What if I write a report for Officer Peters to turn in . . . 'Trinidadian found stabbed in the chest—"

"What?" interrupted Cary.

"You seem surprised. Course you shouldn't be. Your fingerprints are all over the scene," said Jerry. "Aren't they . . . detective . . . ?"

"Might be right," said Bruno.

"And you're the last one to call his cell phone," Jerry added.

"I saw Max this yesterday morning, but— You know me, Bruno. I didn't do that," said Cary.

"I thought I knew you," said Bruno.

Jerry said, "Officer Peters is in critical condition over what happened—with his baby sister and you."

Bruno raised his jaw and his jowls pulled downward before he blew his cheeks out with the following phrases: "Orefield is lucky. What happened with my sister makes you a dead man."

"She-she let me down first," said Cary. "You have to believe me. She's been seeing some guy, I just found that out—"

"Not true," said Bruno. "You broke her heart, Cary—"

"Fine," said Cary. "Let's face the music. There's only one woman for me— That was my mistake all along."

These were trying times for Inspector Cary Oriel, as he laid his unconscious head in the blood from a wound contracted out of pummeling fists moving past his raised arm-block. His elbow threw off their stances, since they hadn't any real training apart from what training the dirty cops received at the academy, but that was years ago for all of them, and they don't usually need to use their fists because people tend to give in to them when they take charge of situations with their crumb-covered badges and sticky hair-triggers. They hadn't used what little training they had, not regularly, only when beating on brats from out of town, or when ganging up on any person who stood in their way; they couldn't be stopped.

Even at that rate, Cary put in his fair share of punches before they took full control of the skirmish by overcoming him as a group. In one instance, they took up each of Cary's limbs, and the leader, Jerry, dropped his ego momentarily to let Bruno get out in front of the group to say a few fierce words.

"You made my sister call me up and complain to me about you leaving her based on something you can't control," said Bruno. "That's love, real love, Cary, and you'll get buried in it here today." He stopped speaking when Cary raised his head. Bruno saw the final fleeting mental faculty Cary had left, draining there on the freight car floor. Bruno asked, "Do you have anything to say before I cut you open?"

"Wait a second, Bruno," said the inspector. "Don't do anything you can't take back!" pleaded Cary when he witnessed the way the greasy detective held a three-inch blade like he was going to carve a turkey. Cary thought how he might have a chance if only he could convince Bruno to make the right choice to let him be.

Without cowering, Cary Oriel kept his eyes trained on the big man holding the blade as he raised it above Cary's head, but he didn't bring the blade near Cary. For, all the noise in the practically vacant platform area alerted the conductor of the powerful locomotive, and a burly man, with glasses and an official uniform cap to cover the top of his hairless head, became interested in what was going on inside the freight car. The conductor's voice rang out loudly, above the creaking and clattering sounds coming from the train car where Cary was being held. The conductor said, "Jerry, is that you and your boys causing troubles on my train again?"

They heard the conductor's voice hollering from close to the front of the train, near the engine. He was checking on the cars when he only made it as far down the line as the second car. The conductor picked up his pace when he realized that there could be more occupants in the trains than he counted coming through the station.

The group of dirty cops had to pause their wrongdoings. Their boss, the man who organized the gang of troublemakers, wasn't running the entire city by any means. The boss was a retired ring-leader from a mob that habitually smuggled goods, so the dirty cops were already privy to how it was done in the train yards. But they hadn't set up a system at Grand Central. So they were out of their jurisdiction that night. Back with the mob, the boss had a guy in another city ready to pick up contraband from train yards before the train reached that station, where authorities lurked. Everyone along the way who wasn't part of the mob was getting paid for turning a blind eye to their operations, or else they were threatened for not turning a blind eye and usually caved in sooner or later. That was what the mob boss once did, of course, but it wasn't happening when Bruno took the eight men and two women on the train that night.

The conductor thought he knew well what was going on already. He was ready for a bribe, but he wasn't ready . . . to clean up a bloodbath. "Let me set you straight," Bruno Peters said as he hopped from the train car, and the leader of the group of dirty cops went with him to talk to the conductor.

"Not you. I only speak to Jerry," said the conductor to Bruno, and he pulled the leader aside to say, "Jerry, get your boys off my train before somebody breaks something, okay?"

"We're leaving," says the incredibly affable Jerry. "Jim, have a night on us. A nice night on me." He patted the conductor on the shoulder and took out his wallet from the conductor's back pocket without him knowing. He slipped a roll bills taken from the conductor's wallet and exaggerated the movement of putting them in the conductor's shirt pocket. Jerry repositioned his gaze by gently spinning him around with the friendliest touch.

Even though the conductor refused the money, Jerry started walking while holding onto the conductor's shoulders as Bruno picked the poor man's other pockets to find the train departure and arrival schedule.

The entire gang leaped, one by one. All eight men and two women leapt from the train car where Cary was holding up his side of the fight. Cary had nearly turned the tables when he had one crooked cop in a chokehold. That ended, of course, when one of the women took point with a pistol to Cary's forehead.

"Let's go," said the woman who whacked Cary with her gun, and they were all off the train before the conductor could spin around to see where all the noise was coming from.

Considering they're in a train yard in a city of eight-and-a-half million people, the crooked crew of cops looked innocent when the conductor finally got away from Jerry's forced march forward. He didn't pay the group any attention: the conductor thought, "I bet they're another group of delinquents that mean trouble for me." He thought he'd better stay out of their business and let them take their orders from Jerry. The group of crooked cops didn't try to hide their façade, for they were still doing a few things to further incriminate themselves. However, their palm-ground fists and spit hitting marble floors was of minimal interest to Operator Jim.

The conductor locked Car #243, and he would have left Cary's car unlocked because it was nearly empty but he wasn't dumb. He knew those delinquents were up to something in the car, and he wasn't getting paid enough for that kind of trickery, so he locked it and kept it locked until the train left beyond the city limits.

Inspector Cary Oriel looked bruised and bloodied. He was relieved that the conductor didn't see him for his own sake, but once Cary saw the door closing he lost consciousness; he was still holding on up to that point, in case he needed to fight for his life. He laid with his eyes shut at least until the train got to the border into Canada.

Before the conductor reached the next car, Bruno was there waiting. He spun the conductor around by pulling on his shoulder. The conductor backed away to get ready for a wild punch; he weakly tossed his hands up to block his face and shield his glasses from impact.

"You dropped this," said Bruno.

"Oh," acknowledged the conductor. He retrieved the crinkled train schedule from Bruno's outstretched hand. "Thanks," he said. He attached the schedule to his clipboard and went on with his job to get away down the rails.

"We'll catch up with you later," said Bruno while outside Car #537. "Ohhh Cary!" he taunted and knocked on the train car's door. The sounds, which echoed inside Car #537, caused not a single stir from Cary.

On their way out of Grand Central, Jerry took Bruno aside and said, "Look, Bruno, I like you. Yours is one of the few real badges I like to have hanging around." He took Bruno's badge hanging around his neck and tucked it into the officer's shirt. "You were here before we arrived, right?"

"Right—" said Bruno

"And you fell in line like a God damn good domino," said Jerry. "Alright, you did. But I'm going to put you in a full body-cast if you don't wise up and get after that guy, alright?"

Not more than a week later, after Cary left town and things were quiet for Joslin, they don't stay quiet for long. When she gets the call and finds herself on her way to the morgue to identify the body of her lover, she's in her car with her white-tipped nails clenching the steering wheel tightly— so tightly that her grip drains some of the blood from the rest of her body. She looks pale. She is worrying about her med-school lover's death having something to do with all the terrible things her brother, Bruno, is involved in. But she doesn't know that Bruno is miles away in chase after Cary. Part of her mind is worrying that all the sinful behaviors have caught up to her too.

When she finally reaches the morgue she finds out that the mortician summoned the sheriff. When she sees the county car belonging to the sheriff she starts to fear the worst. She immediately thinks, "Bruno, if you're involved in this somehow . . . I'll never forgive you." When she is inside, the sheriff pulls her away to a back room to question her, but she holds strong.

"Have you been ingesting any insecticides, Ms. Peters?" questions the sheriff.

"Of course not," says Joslin with red, crying eyes.

He thinks to himself that Joslin's tears take considerable effort to make, and he thinks she seems off, so he threatens to take her to the station to hold her for questioning.

Before they make it to the car, when she's in cuffs and the

sheriff starts reading Joslin her rights, she cuts him off. She lets him know about her brother being a cop, in a ploy to gain some leverage from the sheriff.

The sheriff laughs and tells her that her brother's unit is already being investigated for the disappearance of Inspector Cary Oriel, among other crimes. "It didn't take long for me to put it together," says the sheriff. "Figured I would mention Oriel since it turned out you're going through men like you do."

She stays quiet while the sheriff finishes reading her rights.

"I didn't know that jam was poison," says Joslin. "Seriously . . . ? How could I have known that?"

"You're being charged for the murder of one . . . Mr. William Lately," says the sheriff. "May Mr. Lately rest in peace."

"You haven't any proof," says Joslin.

"We've got plenty," says the sheriff. "The jam is the same that you stole. You might remember it from earlier. After all, you were filing paperwork for the shipment that Cary had confiscated from Friday's Corner Store."

"I didn't know it would become poisonous," says Joslin.

"The report signed by Inspector Oriel came through your office," says the sheriff. "You were the one to type it up and send it over. You ought to pay more attention to what you type up, miss."

He hands Joslin the thirty-page report. He flips to the middle of the packet, where one line is highlighted in yellow, clearly stating, "if left in direct sunlight for longer than twenty-five minutes . . . the rare berries may deteriorate. May produce noxious odor . . . fatality assumed."

"I don't read the stuff that comes through," says Joslin. "That's not my job!"

"Tell that to your judge," says the sheriff. "Unless you have proof it wasn't you . . . who typed the reports."

"I don't know if you're familiar my brother," says Joslin. "He's connected." She talks in between sharp breaths that resemble panting.

"Why do you keep bringing up your brother?" asks the sheriff holding her in custody.

"Bruno Peters," says Joslin. "He's a dignified . . . badge, but he's getting in deep with . . . you-know-who . . . ."

"Who?" asks the sheriff.

"The—" She makes a loud, abrasive quack. This sends the sheriff into a deep state of contemplation about what life will be like for him . . . if he holds onto Joslin much longer.

He thinks how he will say something like, "I swear. I didn't know." In his deep imagining, the guy holding and questioning him will probably be the one who did most of the foul business that goes on, and he knows that's Jerry. Jerry might say: "Well, you're going away . . . when the Goose gets back from across the pond."

He thinks he might say, "Please! No. I swear I didn't know she was related to one of you." But Jerry won't be so easy to reason with. No, the sheriff thinks he'll say something like: "You didn't know? She's on our list, right? Did you run Joslin's name?" The sheriff thinks how he will tell Jerry he ran it for prints but she was clean, and Jerry might say something like, "Of course she was clean. Now I get to explain why this ugly duckling couldn't do his freaking job and stick to the list we provide to each and every badge under our belt."

He imagines the Goose walking in through what he recalls to be a bamboo-beaded curtain that will clatter as he *saunters* through it. He might even smile greatly with muscles that make his ears move a little in separate directions, with their long earlobes dangling on either side.

Jerry will likely treat him with utmost respect upon his entrance: "Mr. Goose, this guy isn't respecting the list." And the Goose will say something like, "What happened? What was the result of his incompetence?" He will want the full story, thinks the sheriff.

Jerry will likely tell him everything in as few words as possible: "Eh, just the sister of one of our crew was picked up. She called looking for Bruno . . . to bail her out."

The Goose will likely try to show how reasonable of a man he is by saying something like, "Well, if she's out, then there's no harm. Perhaps we will remind this officer one last way . . . . Think of a way."

Then, he will likely leave the room through the beads he came in through, while Jerry might tattoo the entire list of names on the sheriff's chest.

After considering this entire scenario, the sheriff runs Joslin's license, he sees her brother in the database, and he lets her out of his custody with haste. He takes off her cuffs, and she is free.

When Jerry finds out about Joslin being detained, he calls Bruno off his search for Cary. They meet at the Loose Goose Saloon.

After a rather warm greeting, Jerry launches into: "Your miserable tramp of a sister is behind bars, and she'll stay that way if you don't catch up to that guy soon." Jerry is good at bluffing.

When the Goose comes out of the backroom to join their table, Jerry places Bruno's conversation on hold. "If the old man . . . Oriel won't talk," says the Goose before trailing off. He stops talking to bask in the sunlight that is coming in through the slanted windows.

"We'll keep plucking his nose hairs until we hear something we want to hear," says one of the women from the private sector. She leaves to the backroom in a hurry, pulling surgical gloves up to her wrists.

"Wow," says the Goose.

"You're telling me. Do you see what I have to deal with?" asks Jerry. "Torturing old people shouldn't be so slow and agonizing. Bunch of numbskulls." He walks over to the bar and shouts, "Oh, Bruno. You still here?"

Bruno joins him. He says, "I'll get started looking for Cary-uh-Oriel."

Jerry holds onto his compatriot's shoulders, stops holding on to brush them off, and he brushes off the back of Bruno's coat too. Jerry says, "We've got to keep you looking good out there!"

"Just don't hurt my sister," says Bruno.

Jerry steps lively at Bruno and Bruno jumps a little. Jerry says, "YOU have the power to keep baby sis out of harm's way. Get to it."

Bruno talks to Joslin once to assure her he can follow through: "If I know the guy, he's got two kids he don't know where they are— he's going for them first!"

"What about his wife?" asks Joslin.

"He was with you," says Bruno. "Wife ain't opened her eyes since she popped out their last kid. She's probably hooked up to all kinds of tubes with nurses and shit. He's basically forgotten about Mrs. O."

the phone and controll
the top drawer. The
ant.

Cary gasped and sai
ever you are. If you hav
come foreward..."

All at once the line
turned off. Cary felt aro
crimson. evening sunlight
then he nudged the tape r
before reaching the phone

He took the book dow

Chapter Ten

Help from Strangers & Meeting Miss Vinter

INSPECTOR CARY ORIEL dusts his jacket off; what was once a nice overcoat is now covered in blood, and dust & dried leaves from sleeping on the floor on the train. He wants to wash the past from his sleeves and lapel, but it is holding on tightly to him, like a bad cold that won't leave but aches in every corner of the body. He thinks to himself, "The pigs at the station in Never York, they didn't rob me of anything but my pride." He is too afraid to use a credit card, for Bruno would try to track him, he thinks. But Cary isn't paranoid enough to stay away from checking up on the tape he dropped off to get analyzed by a certain audio engineer from Trinidad.

It's as if the tape senses the danger Cary is in when it falls from Maxwell's shelf. It lands on his keyboard when Maxwell is true to his appetite and goes out for lunch with the cute new intern.

When Maxwell finishes lunch, he makes a call to his banjo playing friend who is recording later in the afternoon, and he rushes to get the pictures of the Goose's home printed out for the musician to take a look at. He thinks about what he found, however. Maxwell can't help thinking that the Goose is a bad person to be involved with. He carries a folder with the pictures of the Goose's estate and inside that folder is the blueprint he found that reveals the layout of the Oriel Estate.

On the way into the recording studio Maxwell sneezes from being in the sun, and by the time he recovers to find his keys he notices the door is open and the banjo player is waiting for him already. When the room is unlocked the banjo player warms up with a ballad of his own creation that is too twangy for Maxwell, and when Maxwell hears the musician "Yip!" into the recording studio's microphone—he takes out the folder he brought with him.

From inside the folder Maxwell produces a printed copy of the plastic sheet he found. He sits the copy on his keyboard next to the tape that fell. In an incredible twist of fate, he picks up the tape to notice that it is not what he expects—it's not the one from his client but rather it's the tape Cary brought to him.

Maxwell thinks to call Cary since he planned to inform him about his strange finding at the Goose's mansion, but before he can move to the phone—"FLUB!" exclaims Maxwell, since Jeffey Rey is now on the other side of the studio glass. "What are you—" Maxwell starts to question Rey as the musician stabs him with the bow of his violin. The barbed, thick metal pierces his heart and Maxwell falls.

"Maxwell, I hope you liked the sound of that—" says the musician. "I think the Goose will be taking back this, of course," Jeffey Rey says as he takes the folder with the layout of Cary's family estate. He leaves.

Maxwell sees his phone vibrating on the edge of his desk; he blinks— In a miraculous leap of faith, Maxwell reaches his phone to answer Cary's call—In a quick attempt to relay information he says: "Cary, you got to listen—"

"I'm here," says Cary.

Maxwell grunts in pain and says, "I might not have much time, but what I found is my client is after you Cary—"

"What does that mean? Maxwell? Maxwell I have your tape," says Cary but the phone cuts out.

166

His phone doesn't stay out for long. It buzzes with a call from a restricted number, and Cary picks up the call.

"Shame about Maxwell," says the Goose.

"Yes," says Cary, "but how'd you know about him, Gino?"

"I know a lot of things," says the Goose.

"Like what?"

"I know you're innocent," says the Goose. "I thought Maxwell would be more useful to me, but he . . . didn't work out."

"What? How do you—" Cary starts. "How do you know about Maxwell?"

"He was working for me until he got wise," says the Goose. "You're lagging behind, Inspector. He was supposed to help me get to you."

"You don't know where I am," says Cary. "And you don't know where I'm going—"

"No," says the Goose, "but when you get there, I'll be ready."

"I'm not afraid of you or any of the people you throw my way," says Cary.

"If you turn yourself in," says the Goose, "I'll let the girl go . . . ."

"What about Henry Edwards?" says Cary. "What about my boy?"

"If he's not with you, I take it . . . he's with the crystals," says the Goose. "That's not . . . such a good place to be."

The line cuts out. Cary tosses his phone from the moving train to avoid being tracked by the Goose and his cronies.

There are plenty of police officers hanging around the Anything Goose Saloon; the bar itself is lined with cops getting free drinks. The banjo player, Jeffey Rey, is seated at the table with Jerry and the Goose.

"What a shame about Maxwell," says the Goose. "Who's going to fill their ears with all the tapes I keep recording?"

The Goose stops recording one tape and switches to another. "The more powerful I become the more I want to record every second. I don't know what you'll say about me . . . behind my back. And I don't exactly understand what the spirits are saying about me either."

"We found this on his machine," Jerry says before plugging a tape into a second player that he brought with him to the table.

The Goose listens to the tape with headphones on. "You came prepared," he says. "It seems like there's some interest in going out of the States."

"We don't have any Feds in here. Do we?" asks Rey when he gets a look around at all the lowlifes. "Too bad . . . ."

"Yes," says the Goose. "Very bad. Who do we have in Montréal?"

"No one yet," says Jerry.

"Yes," says the Goose. "No one . . . yet. Thank you for seeing this through. You will both be rewarded."

"What if I'm listening to the train fly wildly around a mountain bend from the cold belly of a still car?" asks an old rambler sitting near Cary on the train. "I know the conductor saw us but he doesn't care. He just shut the door . . . on our car . . . probably because he would feel bad to put us out like that in the middle of nowhere . . . when the weather is starting to freeze as much as it can tonight. We can toss around an old beanbag I brought to keep blood flowing and give us something to aim for besides sleeping one-eye-open."

A beanbag slams upon Cary's chest. Looking down through a cloud of steamy breath, he sees the dirty beanbag caught in his gloves, but he can't even feel his fingers. They're numb. He shakes and grips them before tossing the beanbag to the old rambler. And Cary says to him, "You'll let me use your phone when we get a signal?"

"Yeah, my friend," says the rambler. He echoes Cary's words: "Use my phone when we get a signal."

They are moving fast and already two-hundred miles from the last town, and Cary didn't check the map at the station before darting down between two rows of cars on tracks and climbing into the same car because he knew it was empty.

"You say you have a brother back east?" he asks the rambler with the scraggly beard of grey.

"Yeah," says the man with the beard. "I've run out of money. I suppose I'm heading west to where I find work. Probably farming . . . . I know grapes well."

"Introduce me sometime, my friend," says Cary, eyeing the longneck bottle protruding from the man's pile of belongings. He lets a smile hit his face for the first time since losing consciousness.

"I'll introduce you now," the old man says. He gets his pack open to bring out the vino, an unmarked glass bottle with cork inserted.

"I have a mess kit my son gave me from when we were camping when he was younger," says the scraggly bearded man to Cary. He combines the bottle of wine with mulling spices, consisting of whole cinnamon sticks, cloves, and dried orange peels. It heats over a small fire. The scraggly bearded man hands Cary a blue polyurethane cup. The man finishes pouring his serving into an aluminum pot.

The aroma of the wine relieves them both. They had been enduring the putrid pig guts, and whatever other foul smelling animal remains that are being kept frozen in the packaging on the other side of the wall in their car.

"You're tasting last year's harvest. Still sweet," says the old rambler.

"Oh, yes. Very fresh. I taste the sour," says Cary.

"I am humbled by your friendship, but I must nod off while we have quiet," the scraggly bearded man says, leaving Cary standing by the partition door. The man goes to roll around on his pile of belongings. He settles into the pile with a blanket wrapped around his body, like a squirrel escaping snowfall.

The scraggly bearded man stays nested there even after the door opens electronically. The train car door opens when the button is pressed by the conductor in the locomotive. Cary wakes his friend, politely making eye contact, and he is the first one out of the car. They do not exchange words.

The pack Cary supports on his backside feels heavy to his body that didn't get much rest at night. "It would be hard to run," he thinks. He thinks of how he might have to leave the pack in a ditch or bury it. Instead, as he prefers, he keeps everything he needs to survive on his person.

But he recalls when he was last on vacation in this part of the world, when a stranger introduced him to the idea of paying for a survival retreat. The stranger was trying to sell tickets to get his referral bonus in a marketing pyramid scheme, and Cary was gullible enough to attend the survival retreat.

The retreat had a name printed on pamphlets and t-shirts, called "Be Your Own Hero," and when Cary got enough people to go on the retreat his ticket was free. That was how he first learned the difference between mapping the stars and pointing at the sky. The stranger at the retreat looked at the stars one night, while leading the group through harsh wilderness conditions. They struggled that night, so the stranger mimed connecting the constellations. "That's Alpha-Centuri. That star there. It connects to . . . that one . . . there." He lead the group that way, but you would have known he was making everything up. Cary noticed when the star he referred to started to blink and move. It was a satellite in orbit, thought Cary.

He thought about how ever since then when he goes out on his own he need only bring a knife. The pack on his back is a luxury, a luxury that weighs on him.

Inspector Cary Oriel carries a blue karambit, a knife that folds into itself. Originally used for farming purposes, the karambit looks like the claw of a tiger. The knife is used in styles of fighting as well. The fighters make fists and fight like tigers; they can go on pretending, but we all know tigers never farm.

"The karambit is all I need if the pack wears too heavy," he assures himself. The straps of his pack hug his waist and fit under his arms, but he pulls in the straps to adjust the pack and synch everything even tighter. When the pack is formed to him as an extension of him, Cary feels full of energy. The warmth building inside his boots moves forward as springs of perpetual energy turn into a jog.

Cary looks over his shoulder. He can barely make out the

appearances of a few uniformed conductors approaching the train where a mere shadow of the drifter from the train finishes lacing his boots on the edge of the platform. The drifter presently takes off with great speed in the opposing direction that Cary walks.

With no eyes of people in the town of Ottawa, no friendly eyes casting on him at least, at least none that he knows, Cary talks to no one, even when a homeless man jumps in front of him. Construction workers laugh at his poor understanding of French, so he leaves a café and the homeless man outside gives him change for his American money. The street names all looks the same to Cary, who knows *rue* to be French for street, but he can't make sense of the map enough to find his way out of town to Montréal, to visit the investigators that Maxwell sent the tape to. For, he trusts Maxwell's instinct and doesn't know any other investigators outside of Never York City.

     Feeling properly disoriented and alone, Inspector Cary Oriel takes shelter for a few hours in the earlier part of the day, before noon, with a few families in Ottawa's brightly lit bus station. The families are there waiting for the next bus out of town. He blends in as a weary traveler, but he fears the pity that could come his way; he only wants to lay flat on the floor for a few hours. So Cary stays there on the floor until the bus arrives and the flickering of overhead fluorescent lights wake him up from his slumber.

     With his stomach already in knots, it doesn't help when Cary sees them looking at him in the glass; a set of eyes and Adeline's unforgettable rose-colored cheeks appear in the sliding doors of the bus station. He takes a walk to see the frozen river nearby, where townsfolk skate, and one pleasant fellow along the way assures him: "The river is popular enough with activities of all kinds that you might just see a celebration!"

     Yet, there is not a celebration of any kind when Cary marches toward the Rideau Canal that is frozen with thick ice. Walking down the snowplow'd Catherine Street, he passes by the Ottawa Police Station. There is some visibility there, and he can tell the paths leading into the frozen canal are open and passage is permissible. A tiny shack has a sign welcoming people to come try beaver pies, but Cary has no appetite or curiosity for such strange foods, and he thinks how every town must have their own unique problems with health and human services.

"What would the provisions for using a beaver tail be?" Cary wonders to himself as his makes his way to the passage where the street and sidewalk connect to the canal.

Still, Cary is open to anything that can get his mind off the dreadful memories that take him over. He rests his pack on the canal's edge, and he walks out onto the ice a lighter man. The voices of children, enjoying a run, and playing, trumpet from somewhere nearby. The children pass in front of him, and he feels surprise. He's glad to be around such youthful vigor.

Cary finds a spot out on the river where there is no snow. The ground where the snow doesn't cover is incredibly thick ice that has been swept clean of debris and snow at some point, recently, to make room for wintery activities. A single pair of skates are tucked under a bench made of pine on the opposite side of the canal. Cary notices the laces on the ground.

The ice near the bench is decked in scars from skates passing over it. Cary's fear of ice skating leaves him entirely when he notices the skates are small enough to fit a child, but there's no child around to claim the skates. In fact, all the children he saw earlier have gone somewhere else. He assumes the skates must have belonged to one of the cheerful young kids that ran past him moments before he sat down. Only briefly does Cary entertain a delusional thought of there being something sinister afoot. The thought only comes to him when he imagines how it would look to someone noticing that he was traveling and could plot to attack him when he is alone, weak, or tired.

Luckily for Cary, he is brought into a safer reality when the sweet tone of a woman's voice warms up next to him.

"Have you tried to skate?" asks a Swedish woman in a neighborly tone.

"Yes," replies Cary.

"Recently?" asks the relentless Swede.

"I have not," says Cary, "not since high school."

"Oh," says the woman. "Were you embarrassed?" she asks and laughs. Her laugh sounds familiar to Cary. His ears perk up, and he feels safe talking to her.

"I fell in front of a girl I was trying to impress," says Cary.

"Oh no! Tragic," says the Swedish woman in a calming voice. Cary thinks how her voice sounds flirtatious. And it *is* rather melodic. She calls to him like sirens call sailors out at sea. She continues, "When boys do things . . . to impress girls. It is a pity you fell."

"I failed by falling," admits Cary. "I had a concussion and Tommy D'Angelo swooped in to ask her out to prom, and they're still together to this day. I vow not to fail again." He smiles sweetly at her, but she seems not to notice. And if she does notice the smile, she doesn't act like she cares.

"I bet they are both greasy and have five kids by now," says the woman.

She notices what he's holding. The skates are smaller than Cary would wear, it seems obvious, but they are large for a child. She brushes past him to pick up the skates. She looks in the shoe of the skate at the tongue, while sitting next to him on that lovely bench in front of the frozen Rideau Canal.

"My understanding isn't good," says the Swedish woman. "Can you—"

"It says 'Thomas' but someone crossed it out," says Cary.

"What then, does it say under the crossed part?" asks the woman.

"It says 'Johnny'," says Cary.

"Oh," says the Swedish woman in a strange tone, but she does not go on to explain her thinking on the matter.

"You're not from this country?" Cary asks, hoping to get her to talk more.

"How did you know?" asks the woman.

"I put things together for a living. I'm observant, I suppose," says Cary.

"Wow . . . . You look like . . . wild dog," says the Swedish woman, and she helps him look less mangy by pulling out some of the ice that is frozen where his hairline meets his forehead. She feels warm and radiant, and he doesn't know why but he wants to trust her. She has blue eyes, blonde hair, and tan skin protected by a fur-lined jacket. He notices how she always keeps her back to the wind to lower the wind chill.

"Pardon my appearance," says Cary. "I'm if the process of relocating." He starts with a lie to preserve anonymity.

She doesn't seem convinced. She says, "To where will you move?"

"I haven't decided yet," says Cary, and he shifts away from her to focus on where his belongings are located. Upon seeing the pack he left is safe on the other side of the canal, he shifts his weight on the bench, toward the woman.

"You are troubled," says the Swedish woman.

"I will be," says Cary, "until I find . . . until I find my children." He could not contain himself in front of her.

"You will find what you look for, I hope," says the woman. "What about your wife?" Cary feels a brightness radiating from the Swedish woman that he hasn't felt for a long time. "What does she think will happen?"

"I'm not sure how to put it," says Cary. "I feel her here sometimes. She guides me."

"I don't understand," says the puzzled woman.

"Well you see," Cary hesitates. "My wife has been in a coma."

A few moments later the Swedish woman is on her feet and takes the other skate that Cary holds from his grasp. "Come on," says the Swedish woman to Cary. "I will drive us. My car." She points to a blue sedan that is covered in salt and frost. It's parked across the canal.

"Where to?" asks Cary.

"Thomas," answers the woman.

"You mean Johnny," says Cary, and he holds up the skate by the tongue with its inscription showing.

"Oh right," says the Swedish woman. "It crossed out."

"Right," says Cary. "Thomas—do you know him?" He follows her across the ice, each carrying a skate.

"He is my neighbor," says the woman. "His father is police officer. You must meet, you must."

Soon enough they are walking to pick his pack from the snow, before getting in her car. In the car she thanks him for going with her to do a good deed, and she says, "More people ought to be good neighbors." He understands and shows it with a warm smile that comes from the center of his mouth and presses upward; his cheeks raise and become bright red the longer he holds the expression.

They drive through a slate grey snow. And snow covers the grass in a blanket of white. The side roads aren't plowed; still, under the Swedish woman's direction, the car drives speedily along until they make a stop for gas.

The inspector goes into the gas station to pay. He uses cash to buy the gas, and he asks, "Is it permissible to hang a poster here?" He shows the attendant the poster he wants to hang of his children and a description of their appearances when he last saw them. The attendant agrees to put the poster up himself.

After a moment, Cary walks back out to the car while the Swedish woman, who tells Cary her last name is Vinter, is finishing fueling the car. Miss Vinter notices the sign on the window being hung up as promised and begins to wonder about her new associate.

Chapter Eleven

Only So Much Luxury She Can Take

NEITHER Johnny nor Thomas are home when they arrive, but Johnny's father is there. Larry Stegner is flipping through television stations when Cary arrives with Miss Vinter. She rings the doorbell and the father answers.

Captain Larry Stegner is not dressed in uniform, but his loafers and starch ironed shirt tell of his disposition towards order. "You look lost," says Stegner to the inspector.

"Please, it is good to meet you," says Cary to the towering man who stands on a stoop, giving him the appearance of being even taller than he would appear on flat ground. "This is a lovely town," continues Cary, "but I feel like I do not belong. I am only passing through."

"Where ya' from?" asks Stegner with an outstretched arm for greeting Cary.

"That's not so important for me to relay to you at this time," says Cary.

"You're a wise-guy, huh," says Captain Larry Stegner while removing his hand from greeting Cary.

Miss Vinter worries about the level of discretion and presently holds up the ice skates. Stegner takes the skates and he says, "How strange . . . . Johnny will be relieved," and he stands there waiting for Cary to add something to the conversation before kicking the door back and saying, "Strange indeed. Well, you can come in but you're going to have to loosen up, alright?"

"Alright," says Cary. As he pauses by Stegner, he comments about the name being scratched out to which Stegner adds that he and his son share their vacation home in Ottawa with another family. "Johnny and Thomas are often claiming each other's belongings," he says.

Inside, the Captain offers drinks to his guests, but neither Miss Vinter nor Cary accept anything. They sit at the large wooden dining table with Captain Larry Stegner at one end and Cary at the other. The television talks in the background: "News by the hour . . . . A seemingly dismal day in the stock market, as Sky Visions . . . drops off the Never York Stock Exchange . . . after the recent arrest of the primary share holder . . . . And his family is still missing, including his two children . . . ."

"They say that guy is involved in the disappearance. It's hard to believe people are like that," says Stegner, and he sips from a mug of coffee with a fury of steam coming from the brim.

Cary takes from his pocket his fake passport. "I am from North Ottawa," says Cary. "I lived in Montréal, but I was living in Never York City until something brought me here." Cary holds onto a flyer similar to the one noticed by Miss Vinter at the gas station prior.

The police captain takes the flyer, and before Stegner can read, he says, "You? Hard place to be losing someone you love."

"How'd you know?" asks Cary, gripping his fake passport.

"I saw how you tensed up when the news told your story," says Stegner.

"I've seen some things and I can hardly sleep now," says Cary. "I am listening for a sign."

"What kind of sign?" asks the captain.

The power goes out for a moment; it blinks on and off so

quickly that the lights don't stay out long, but the television does not turn back on after the surge. Stegner puts the flyer back on the table and slides it to Cary. In a low tone Stegner says, "Well, I wish you luck in your search. Are you headed anywhere in particular, friend?"

"I am heading— west. I was on my way," Cary lies, and he tries to scramble for a story to give the captain. "Going to my brother's vineyards to work. I will head west again, I suppose," says Cary.

The police captain walks them to the door, but as he opens it Johnny runs inside. The boy pushes past everyone to turn on the television. Miss Vinter sees him and her eyes light up, something Cary notices as he watches the scene from a few steps back.

"'Johnny, we found your skates!" exclaims father to son.

Johnny ignores them and flips past the news station where the pictures of Henry Edwards and Emily are still on screen. Johnny changes stations to a cartoon channel.

Miss Vinter watches Johnny enjoying cartoons. Meanwhile Cary remains a few steps back, and Stegner tries to act like he doesn't notice what he's observed already. He's picking up on observations surrounding Cary's guilty association with the missing children.

Stegner thinks to himself, "The man could be quickly overcome, so I could try to get a rise out of him." So Stegner says, "I see it in your eyes. That's why I invited you in. You've seen something or been somewhere, buy yer not trying to get back."

In an instant Cary shakes his head, and he says, "No," but for some reason he lies because he's worrying about whether the Canadian police captain is trustworthy, so he only tells some truths and eventually says, "In Never York, my plight looking for my family got derailed due to some personal matters that tied me to some crooked cops, but you seem alright around here. That's my full disclosure."

"Your case, whatever it is— It's putting me in danger," says Stegner.

"Is that true?" asks Miss Vinter. "What do you tell me that is true?" She stands between the men and the child. She suddenly changes the way she looks at Cary, and her mind is clearly focused on something entirely different than anyone in the room is prepared to address. Her eyes are distant, and she holds onto her ring finger.

"I'm not sure," says Cary to the Swedish woman with her face pursed and ready to explode with emotions. "A group of crooked cops are part of a mob that nearly killed me, but I got away on a train when the conductor locked me away in a car for my own good. And that's how I ended up in your town, Captain."

"I don't know if I believe all that," says Stegner. And at that point he shines a flashlight in Cary's eyes to see if he's intoxicated or lying. He can tell . . . he's not been drinking at least.

"I'm operating outside of the law," says Cary.

"Johnny, go to your room," says Stegner, but the boy turns up the television.

The television blaring loudly and the father growing frustrated causes Cary to think the environment will be chaotic if he stays around, and he remembers how the police captain already expressed that his home is in danger.

"I want to talk to you both, but is there someplace—a diner—that we could go to?" asks Cary.

The police captain takes Cary and Miss Vinter in his car to visit a small diner outside of Ottawa that has chrome, polished fixtures. It's bright and busy that time of day with a lunch crowd from all around town. Captain Larry Stegner orders a pot of coffee for the table, and he says, "That's it." They aren't there for anything but to talk. They don't even touch the coffee until the waitress comes to check on them again.

"You've been kind to me, but I don't need you to stay. I trust you, and that's why I could talk to Captain Stegner in front of you. I wanted . . . you to know. But you don't know too much yet, Miss. You can still get out of here," says Cary to Miss Vinter.

Stegner nods. He picks up the pot of coffee and pours a cup but doesn't place the pot down yet.

Cary gets up from the booth to let her get out without a problem. But the Swedish woman says, "I might like to help."

"What's going on?" asks Stegner.

Cary snaps out of it for a moment. Suddenly he realizes that it's just Stegner at the booth with him. He says, "She is always visible to me. I see her nearby." He looks out the double-pane window, and beyond the dewy glass, beneath the glow of a neon light, it is snowing. Cary says, "I can see her glistening in a snow bank now. She has been trying to get my attention . . . ever since I left the city."

"He was clear minded for a moment," thinks Stegner, but now Cary sits down. And it appears to Cary that Miss Vinter is sitting beside him.

Oddly, Miss Vinter thinks Cary should clarify what he is trying to tell Stegner, so in her own way, she asks him to be more clear: "Is it the death of your children that caused the spirits to haunt you?"

"My children are alive," says Cary sternly.

Stegner finally places the coffee down when he thinks Cary seems to have snapped out of seeing Vinter, or is at least coping with it better. Cary says, "I believe they are alive. They're both beautiful, just like their mother. And I believe it is my wife on the other side . . . calling to me with help. Their mother went into a coma while giving birth. It was like she died to me that day. I am lucky that she surrounds me, I know she does somehow, but do not understand why."

To that Miss Vinter shakes her head and says, "It would be a cold woman to turn her back on her child, after a coma . . . even after death. A parent is . . . bound to their child in that way. That is . . . truthful . . . and most kind."

Getting up from the table is Captain Larry Stegner who has heard all he can tolerate for one afternoon. So Stegner thinks up a lie to avoid making a scene at the diner. Stegner says, "You will do best to sleep off your anxiety in the inn down the road. I'll drive you."

"Don't go to the inn!" exclaims Miss Vinter to Cary.

Cary spills his coffee some, and he says to Stegner, "I can't go *there*, not with you, I guess."

"Why not?" asks Stegner.

"She's telling me not to go," says Cary.

"Oh," says Stegner. But he drops the act of keeping up

with Cary's lunacy when he asks, "Who's telling you what now? I am normally on top of the situation, at least I usually know where the situation is going. Although I have experience dealing with other-worldly, supernatural entities, once . . . I am . . . typically able to easily explain things in the end. Like, saying it was hot water pipes that caused the wooden floorboards to creak at night, not a demon beneath the surface. My wife was superstitious. She probably still is, but I wouldn't know . . . now. Now, she is my superstitious *ex*."

"It could be the cold making me see things. The freeze slows my thinking," says Cary. "So it is certainly a possibility that I am seeing incorrectly, Captain."

Whenever the bell above the door leading outside rings, Cary alone notices Miss Vinter turns her head to look to the door, and one times she does the turn most eloquently, so eloquently that Cary more than glances in her direction. She notices the inspector's fixation on her, and she says to him: "I wonder if they will find the boy and find Emily."

From one look at Cary, Captain Stegner can tell he is not talking to him or anyone else in the diner, and so the police captain snaps into his normal call-to-action modality. He says, "You need to settle down, Cary. You're talking like there's someone there but there isn't!"

Of course every conversation in the diner apart from the one happening at their table has abruptly stopped to listen to the commotion Cary has started.

"It's happening again," Cary says, and the inspector sits solemnly. "Ever since . . . my wife. I lead you the wrong way with what I was saying earlier, Captain Stegner," Cary says, and the Captain knows he is confessing the truth when he sees his pupils change. He knows he will need to ask plenty of questions if Cary doesn't keep talking, but, luckily, Cary wants to talk it over with his new confidante: "Ever since my wife—that's my only omission of truth, apart from protecting my neck by showing you a fake passport earlier," says Cary. He removes his passport from his jacket pocket to place it on the table. "You can't be too careful with who you trust when you're dealing with the type of people—

the internal decay that is destroying the police force in my city . . .
. My omission was that my wife didn't die, sir, but I sure thought
of her that way . . . . I even got engaged once to move on, after my
wife—she fell into that coma." Cary looks down at his passport
and over to Miss Vinter with eyes fixed on her like before. He
smiles and says, "But first she gave birth to our daughter, my little
girl, our Emily . . . ."

The captain, along with anyone within earshot, is certainly
confounded. Stegner is utterly speechless, so Cary continues. He
says, "My wife appears to me in beams of sunlight . . . . She didn't
. . . die. But she's been here . . . all along. And now I see her as
someone—someone new and real to me. I'm afraid I might be
crazy."

There are several long moments of silence for the diner that has
already heard all the news it can handle. The people around find
the way of the world again, and the sound of the diner picks up its
distinct mid-day clatter of dishes being cleaned and serving
battered food up to tables of chatty eavesdroppers that go back to
being talkative once more.

"I don't think you are crazy, Cary. It's really me," says
Miss Vinter, and she reaches into her pocket to remove the
diamond pendant that Cary once gave to Adeline. She puts it on
the chain around her neck and reaches over to touch the top of
Cary's left hand.

The inspector passes out in the booth at the diner from the
excitement brought on by Miss Vinter and her touch. He has
wanted her to touch him . . . since they met on the frozen canal, but
he didn't realize why it mattered . . . until that very moment in the
booth.

The waitress comes by to see if everything is alright to
which Captain Stegner says, "No, Dottie, ma'am. I am not a
professional in regard to tell you if this man is alright, but I know
someone who would be able to tell me all I ever need to know
about his mental . . . well . . . facility. I need to use your phone to
call up an old friend. Do you mind showing me where that phone
is?"

"Of course," says the waitress, and she leads him behind

the counter, where people are lined up to eat breakfast foods and coffee drinks are flowing.

"Uh-huh," says Stegner into the phone. "It's Larry. We'll need you both…"

Soon enough Stegner has a waiter help him take Cary out to the squad car. When they get there, he is able to talk in private on his radio.

When Cary comes to, he finds himself sitting on the back seat of the police car. Miss Vinter is on the outside of the car. Cary watches her spin in the snowflakes that are illuminated, on their descent, by the light pointing down from the diner's rear truss of the roof. She's under the fluorescent tubes that light up in neon reds and blues.

"He's tranquil," says the captain into his radio. "I don't know what he's seen because I ain't him."

"Well, I'm incredibly busy, Captain," says Cynthia Valentico. "I was nearly dragged to visit America. I've never been to Florida. Have you?"

Stegner sighs and his breath is visible. He says, "That sounds lovely. But when will you return?"

"Soon enough, I hope," says Cynthia. "We're nearly done making our observations of a new patient . . . . And she'll have to try some radical treatments for her . . . disorder. I'm at a loss here, really."

"Oh," says Stegner. "I do hope it—the, uh, situation betters itself. When you come back . . . ?"

Dr. Cynthia Valentico speaks into the receiver from her magnificent office space in Miami. She flips through a file box and says, "I won't kid you, Larry. This client is shelling out . . . a fortune, but there's only so much luxury a girl can take." She is frustrated in her search through her file box. She plops the box down on the floor for later. "In addition to my usual retainer and the usual fees, pick up the rent for my office and pay my husband something for his paper if you want me to have anything to do with skipping my protocol."

"I've already bought five subscriptions for me and a few guys at the department," says Stegner. He resists for a few moments before he says, "I'll see if our new cadets have read them."

"I knew I could count on you," says Cynthia.

"Yeah," says Stegner. "Mark me down for two . . . boxes of cookies."

"One month and a dozen copies should suffice for skipping protocol. Until I feel safe, you'll have him cuffed," demands Cynthia.

"I suppose so," agrees Stegner.

"Okay," says Cynthia. "Otherwise, go buy a web cam like I tell . . . all the other new intakes."

For Dr. Cynthia Valentico, things have been this way, keeping new clients far from harming her, for a long time before Stegner pulled her in to help . . . with Inspector Cary's curious case . . . . A case of worldly importance.

!(_.__)?

"I'm working with the local home-owners association to qualify your duplex for a new roof due to government grants made available. May I see that you qualify?"

"Alright," says Alice.

"You do qualify," says the phone representative. "I'm looking at your roof on satellite now. Let me see if we can get someone over to you sometime this weekend. Will you be home Saturday at two in the afternoon?"

"Sure," says Alice.

"'We'll have someone over to measure those dimensions in person," says the telemarketer.

Alice is in a skimpy dress with fuzzy tassels and trim when the middle-aged technician shows up with his tape-measure, wedding ring, and surprised expression. She makes one advance at him after a long day of board meetings and conference calls; she wants to get away from the life she leads, even the luxury of it all.

Cynthia sees Miss Alice Petchulia in person from the top of an apartment building near the park where Alice decides to go. She watches through binoculars. Alice isn't wearing pearls or a large sun-hat or diamond earrings either. The multimillionaire is dressed rather modestly. Yet, the way she sits on the bench on the hill is suggestive enough to reel in male joggers near her pathway, as if they have no other route to take.

Alice has an antidote only her eyes can deliver to any man or woman she passes over in her sudden glances. "They glare back at her constantly," Dr. Valentico says to Theo. "She can't help but look to someone else for help eventually."

Theo checks his watch for the time. He says, "It's been six minutes, Doc. We're more than halfway through."

She watches her patient and sees the girl is on the move; Alice takes a stroll around the flowers near the bench where she had been sitting. Valentico says, "There. She has her prey." Alice pulls a jogger in with one sticky, lingering glance that lasts until the jogger is the only accessory on her collar.

The two warm bodies in the park move closer to each other before she holds him firmly by the shoulders and plants a wet kiss on his lips.

"Well," says Theo, "you told her to sit and this happened."

"Well," says Cynthia, "perhaps she wants to show me she isn't a bitch you can train . . . ."

"You stand to lose everything you own, Miss Alice Petchulia," says Dr. Valentico. "Do you care about your fortunes in the bank?"

"He can take that to his wife to buy a king-sized bed to fuck each other exhausted and sleep, exhausted and sleep, like they were twenty years younger. I'm giving him a life," says Alice. "He can have the money. My accountant assures me any losses will be recovered next quarter . . . with my luxury stock price rising."

"Okay," says Dr. Valentico. "Let's say they only take half your money. I doubt, well, at least your lawyer doubts, they'll likely not get more than a million and a half at most—"

"So?" asks Alice. "I'm left with only one island and how many yachts?"

"Sure," says Valentico. "You'll survive. But your dignity. Your family name. That'll burn holes in your plans."

The phone line is quiet, but Valentico places hers on speaker when Theo comes in the room. He points out, "The board members on your hotel chain won't tolerate the risk you've taken, Alice. Your stocks might rise, but . . . they'll cut you off from all business deals. You'll turn into a silent partner . . . in no time at all."

"Okay," says Alice. "Heal me then doctor. I'm all yours."

"Good," says Valentico. "We'll start when you can sit unnoticed somewhere. You have to work on drawing less attention to yourself. Run and be a quiet girl, alright?"

The line is quiet until Alice politely says, "Alright."

"Alright," says Valentico, "I'll be able to meet with you in person *only* after you prove you're capable of such a feat—" The call cuts out—

"All ready to go on another picnic but where are the pickles?" wonders Alice to herself aloud. She fluffs the satin fabric around her basket in order to prepare it perfectly for an outing that was decided in her mind to be an exploitation of euphoric tranquility. She seals the basket by closing the two hinged top pieces. Hand-woven whicker pieces fit together snuggly when she pushes them. The two top doors conceal the lace lining, a pink, embroidered scarf that once returned upon her lap when she made the long plane voyage back to America after visiting France last year. The memory of that trip is sensuous enough to make up for not having pickles, alright.

She feels content leaving her house neat and orderly, shoes line the door, and ceiling fan spinning, spinning to create a comfortable breeze. She knows that any guest to arrive at her home at 1325 Freedom Way will feel at ease without any tiresome considerations whatsoever, in spite of the noisy hustle and bustle of the marketplace connecting to the alley behind her home. And without further preparation, she enters the verandah that leads out, and, thus, she enters into the world.

She knows of the world as a bold, fun place with strange turns along the way. The prospect of whom she will run into and how they will spend the afternoon together excites her, so much so that along with the help of the cold air, certain proportions of her body present themselves to be perky.

She is Alice Petchulia, and Alice isn't just an average twenty-seven year-old living in Miami, where the ocean tides have stilled enough to create a tropical oasis on the same level of tranquility as described by great philosophers of Atlantis. In addition to living in paradise, Alice has recently inherited the preeminent luxury apartment complex in the city. It stands gallantly, on high, above the rest, sought after due to its multiple tennis courts, and private beaches with volleyball nets (not much clothing to mention). It also boasts a lovely full-service massage parlor. Consequently, growing up with such a lifestyle has left Alice without appreciation for such pleasures. She needs to get out, so she does what any carefree woman does with beauty and a tan.

Alice goes on her picnic. She dreams, during that sunny afternoon, about the times she has been abroad and makes several glances to strangers passing by. It feels strange being out of her complex, not hearing the crowds going about their shopping in her stores, and she is relieved to not be called upon for her opinion in all matters related to running the apartments, facilities, and marketplace. Indeed, she is swept away by the calm and surrenders to it by letting her body completely sink into the blanket and grass.

"I'm not going to get anywhere with anyone but myself today," she thinks to herself.

Nevertheless, Alice feels content enough to agree with herself to return another day, and during day dreams in the park, she lets her legs fall apart at the knees. As she does this a man jogging past can't help but notice her smooth thighs spilling over the edge of her blanket onto the sharp blades of grass.

What Alice Petchulia doesn't know is that for the second time she is being watched from up high. This type of surveillance is made possible due to the high price Alice is willing to pay to bring the doctor and detective out to help her avoid slandering her family name. This time Dr. Valentico has nothing to say about her behavior. Alice has turned down the advances of the handsome jogger, and she returns to her solo picnic. "She's ready," Theo says. "She must be ready, I take it. I'll set up an appointment for her to speak with you in person, Doc." Cynthia nods and says, "Perfectly fine."

The next morning Alice Petchulia eats breakfast and is surprised to find just how quickly the waiter takes away her empty plate, like a steel discus moving along a guided pulley system that has its destination bound for another man's hands.

"Anything else?" asks the waiter with a smirk upon his face when he returns to her table. She feels his flirtatious smile is an invitation for more, but she resists taking the bait. She asks him for a drink, something with rum in it. In return, he asks, "How about a coffee?" He puts vodka in the coffee, and she . . . nearly gags.

—(♠)—

So Alice says, "I don't trust a man who gives you alcohol that you don't ask for. I need *that*, at least. What if I was allergic to *cherries* . . . ? Well, you don't put cherries in coffee, but you know what I mean." She pauses to take a breath before turning to her therapist during her twelve o'clock appointment.

Dr. Cynthia Valentico, amidst a thriving local practice, yearned for more than the job she had at hand, but she is able to remind herself about the big picture plan they were working on, and this reassurance kept her there to help Alice. After careful observations, such as the one-sided video chat via the internet camera and the times they viewed her in the park, the young woman finally made it to the final part of Dr. Cynthia Valentico's intake procedure.

After intake, in just a few short appointments (if Alice can resist showing signs of sexual aggression) Dr. Cynthia Valentico will recommend to the board of her complex that she be readmitted as its president. Even though Dr. Cynthia Valentico shows a strong passion for helping others, she herself must cope with a severe trauma in to her professional pursuits.

Dr. Valentico must cope with severe trauma while assisting the same type of stressed out, upper class clientele completely and thoroughly. In prepared dialogue, she starts helping the buxom entrepreneur, Alice Petchulia, feel satisfied

188

with her role and gracious for her large lot in life.

She reassures Alice that patience is more likely to bring results that the young woman desires. Dating just any man will slow her down; furthermore, it could stunt her career if potential suitors date her primarily to suck up her inheritance. She helps Alice plan completely.

Dr. Valentico provides financial coaching and emotional support that even extends to handling extra large deposits in the bank; she even agrees to accompany Alice to the bank while she is in Miami if she needs company, but Alice insists, "I don't need a chauffeur." Even after the property managers take nine-percent, Alice still has plenty of money coming in. She says, "I need help not spending all of my money on clothing, jewelry, and exotic finer things in life." The kind doctor has a lovely way of slowing down her spending at a mere two-hundred-and-fifty dollars an hour (plus travel expenses).

After she observed her once, Dr. Valentico recommends Alice to go back out on another picnic-date to celebrate life. Now in a lovely, rented Miami office space, Valentico watches Alice sit in the chair and move her legs from side-to-side. Alice noticeably straightens her legs to untuck her dress and get more comfortable any time the doctor asks about her plans for her *next* picnic; the young woman relishes in getting comfortable. Dr. Cynthia Valentico notes when Alice says that she doesn't have any plans she grows restless and needs to untuck herself to get more comfortable.

A sudden source of relief causes her pale skin to turn colors to a rosier pink. Her heart races, and a tiny smile creeps across her face as Alice thinks of the men who might jog by next time she spreads her blanket in the park. "They will want to dominate my mental forces," Alice thinks loudly to herself. She stirs but contains the thoughts. The doctor notices her stirring incessantly while lost in such strong feelings.

Dr. Valentico hesitates a moment before she says, "You're blushing, Miss Petchulia. Are you thinking about a gent?"

"No," says Alice. "Well, no boy in particular."

With the young woman seemingly so exposed, Dr. Cynthia Valentico thinks over two options: "Tell her to settle herself, or give her extra space," Cynthia thinks to herself.

She realizes how hard it must be to suffer from Alice Petchulia's disorder, and upon this remembrance she gives her patient some extra space by rotating her desk chair towards the file box. She decides to give the files some extra attention while she has the rented office space. File boxes love when they get some attention; one can practically hear folders, dividers and the rest of them huddling together and jumping out from the drawer to be organized. A messy file box can signal character traits as much as an overly organized file box, come to think of it. Dr. Cynthia Valentico thinks of a few speculatively characterized file boxes while gently pulling apart the elastic band of her traveling accordion box: "Oh, how Andy Warhol's file box was probably packed since he was a hoarder, and well, the OCD that Howard Hughes might have suffered from would have likely helped him to keep his file box organized, and I bet the narcissist Frank Lloyd Wright likely had a wooden-file box filled with letters about his own achievements," Cynthia thought to herself. Her file box's lid lifts open on its free hinges, something that the doctor simply enjoys to witness.

Accordingly, Alice Petchulia takes a few chances and makes a few changes within and around herself when the doctor's attention seems to divert, since she feels the additional space to do so. She takes a few chances. For starters, she takes a new top from a shopping bag she brought with her and makes the swap with the perfectly fine top she wears. She pulls the tags from the top before taking . . . her second chance.

The second, more risky chance comes from the feeling of exhilaration she experiences from feeling vulnerable and from the return of the idea of going on another picnic without any clue of who she would run into along the way. Alice Petchulia thinks . . . about it . . . the possibility of embracing someone new.

She thinks to herself, "If Dr. Cynthia Valentico is a good doctor, then she won't mind if I experiment in feeling the pleasureful sensations that rightly accompany such an exhilarating feeling." So Alice feels along the seam of her long black dress. She searches for the zipper. And when her narrow fingers reach it, they open it some, along the side facing away from Dr. Valentico, of course. Alice is daring and unafraid. "Feeling pleasure in front of another woman . . . . Any good doctor should understand," she thinks to herself. Alice Petchulia slides her comely hand across the soft skin around her naval, and she shifts her weight, stretching the dress some to allow for the full expression of movement.

Alice thinks of the gentleman she was seeing when she traveled after graduating. "He must have pegged me a minor . . . but I would have done anything to feel his love." She remembers kissing him to say goodbye . . . before getting on the plane to America.

"What are you feeling about your current state of affairs?" asks Cynthia, flipping through manila folders with her long, blue fingernails. The delicate files stack end to end, like dominos waiting to fall.

"What am *I* feeling?" echoes Alice, who is fixated on the tiny hairs that she feels with her fingertips. She can't help but think about the tiny, springy hairs in need of wax even after bikini season.

"What are you feeling about the picnic?" asks the doctor, finally coming to the folder she searched for.

"I suppose it's good to experiment. I'm always doing new things," says Alice while openly fiddling around with the hairs in her wax-zone. Luckily, the paper shuffling in front of the doctor is loud enough to distract her from any sound of soft vocalization Alice makes.

"Absolutely," says Dr. Valentico. "Experimentation is how a bird learns about flight." She cracks open a folder that seems to be glued shut and closes the file drawer she had been leaning on with a '*Slam!*' hard enough to be heard in the hallway outside her office.

After she realizes the doctor is coming back to her, Alice stays quite still, as to not seem too aggressive in her pursuit of feeling her own self, but her fingers feel the moisture that falls from her body.

Dr. Valentico rolls her desk chair nearer to Alice and notices how the young woman grows uncomfortable. She becomes very still, indeed. It's around this time when Alice realizes . . . how very infectious love can be. "Even though I've never thought about a woman in a physical way before," she thinks to herself before admitting her attraction to Dr. Valentico. "Her physique, her toned hourglass frame and the way she always keeps her hair in a little bun that constantly becomes unraveled," Alice Petchulia vexes to herself. She feels for the trigger of calmness and finds that sensation.

Indeed, Alice feels a calm come over her all-embracing body, complete with euphoria. As the doctor gets up from her chair to retreat to the door, Alice wonders if Dr. Cynthia Valentico will do something drastic, for she really fears being made out to be a fool. It's an unstoppable fear, almost as unstoppable as the thrill of touching, rubbing, and gliding over her body the way her Parisian-lover once did.

Upon noticing her patient's actual state of affairs, at last, Dr. Cynthia Valentico turns the lights dim, and she pulls the door closed. She whispers, from the outside of the rented office, in the crack of the door, "If you're feeling anxious about your new experiment, perhaps it went too far already."

The doctor shuts the door and the thick wood makes a '*Slam!*' against the metal frame. With a look of disgust all over her face, she carries a folder marked, "Erotomania," which means to become mad . . . from love. Cynthia must decide whether or not to bill her patient for getting her rented office space cleaned— "The chair she sits on will need to be steamed for certain," Cynthia thinks—but given the interests of Petchulia, it is worth it to help the client.

Alice doesn't let a door slamming bother her. She could buy the building and pay a therapist to watch her masturbate if she wants to, she thinks. So Alice enters her own body with two fingers, deeply but not forcefully. She feels like she has earned it after waiting for so long. She tries hard to picture her lover when they met on that first day in the market, but all she can see in her mind is her American ex-boyfriend's stupid looks and how he looked disappointed whenever they made love. Sadly, she can't keep going with this day's experiment.

She leaves the therapy session early to allow for enough time to get her curly hair trimmed. Her hair stylist is delighted with her situation and her flowing and glowing energy, he is.

Meanwhile, Theodore Bryant has caught up to Stegner and Cary outside of Montréal, near a popular ski resort called Mont Habitant. He found them after passing Stegner's cruiser on the road, where the radio signal was poor, and they got out to transverse the longest trail of the resort, called La Cabane Ski Trail.

Theo gathered they went on foot to the resort to call for a tow-truck. Theo follows their trail and agrees to keep them company while they get assistance. For, he knows as much about auto-mechanics as Stegner, and both men combined know little about helping Cary sort out his thoughts.

They're walking along the ski trail and take what Theo believes to be a shortcut, until Stegner loses faith in Theodore's sense of direction. "You'll take the lead again. Don't give up, Bryant. It'll be a warmer day I give you clearance to take the lead," says Stegner.

"I knew it was only a matter of time before you tried to annex my ideas for your . . . superior ones," says Theo arrogantly.

Captain Larry Stegner shares something he has been holding back: "Imagine my surprise when I read the reports the US officials kept hidden. When I was starting off as a detective they put me on a case that took me on a search around the continent, from Canada to the US, to discover one of the most notorious criminals and find his lair. My unit was approached at the Québec City Police Department in the fall of 1980. We were geographically estranged from the capital, Washington D.C., where the first victim was discovered. The police detective in Washington was removed from the case when one rookie detective made a mistake that compromised evidence that could have brought the perpetrator to justice swiftly and smoothly . . . before that individual was able to cause more harm.

"They didn't have any leads, and the detective who lost the evidence was placed on probation, then a minor investigation started, but his disappearance is what prompted the FBI to call departments around the world to examine the case. Our fresh perspective came with a price to our city of Québec and our department . . . that the US Federal Government would never be able to repay.

"Not to mention, I left Québec City shortly after the incident to fill an opening at Montréal Police Department . . . . I left one thing to take up another, and so did you, Theo . . . . I brought you here today because you're a good sleuth," says Stegner.

"My partner was about my age when I started at the academy, and when I was a rookie, McCoole—Alfred McCoole, he lead the international investigation from our precinct," says Stegner. "I thought I was a lead weight the entire time. I didn't know much outside of writing tickets for moving violations and sitting in patrol cars, so I was ready . . . to listen to McCoole's instincts.

"We investigated the city, starting with the National Monuments in Washington, specifically looking at camera footage to see the last victim of who the papers dubbed 'the East Coast Body-Snatcher' and the latest disappearance was a bus driver, a gentle old man at the end of his days with spectacles as thick as a glass-bottom beer bottle. We watched the victim board his coach on the camera footage we found at the monuments. After everyone had their bag stowed underneath the bus, from a camera near Jefferson's head, the old driver was last seen taking the bus out to Virginia.

"The bus made it to its yard, but the driver never signed it in," says Stegner. He recalls what it was like visiting the yard and speaking with the management there: "He's the type who wouldn't leave until the bus was inspected for damage, cleaned up inside & out, and soaps restocked. He was thorough about everything," claimed the pudgy manager.

"Back then," Stegner tells his captive audience, "not many places had . . . tapes." The bus yard manager only had luck to wish Stegner and McCoole on their investigation; the manager didn't have surveillance over his operation.

Without the footage, McCoole looked for another reference to prove the driver was indeed the victim and not another scenario. The manager insisted, "We've only been running two trips each week. Mr. Markot was my oldest driver. He's been here since my dad was alive running this place. I'm sorry to hear about him, and I'm sorry I can't be of further assistance in the matter. Good luck. Are your accents from the Midwest?" asked the manager to try to lighten the mood.

"No. Up north. You mind if we take a look over Markot's log book? Which routes were his?" inquired Stegner.

"Our drivers go all over the place," said the affable manager. "We've taken busses up to Never York, over to the Great Lakes. You name it— So whereabouts up north are you?"

"That's confidential, sir," snapped McCoole, and he made his way to the file cabinet. Larry Stegner stepped in and said, "We're going to need to see his past years worth of routes and next month or so." The manager looked at McCoole who stopped rummaging and said, "Yep. That should do it. We're here to see if we can help your boys in blue. Sorry if that's all can tell you."

McCoole stepped outside for a cigarette, leaving Stegner with the manager, who said, "He talks too fast. Have him checked out when you get back wherever you came from." Stegner said, "I'll take that into consideration." The manager said, "Yeah, okay," and he went to find the books in another room altogether.

The manager came back with a few log books and a desktop map of the Continental United States. He moved his fingers across the Midwestern states. The bus yard manager said, "He came from taking a group through St. Louis and passing Lake Michigan on the return. That's in there."

"He slid the log book to me as McCoole got comfortable in a chair in front of the manager's desk," says Stegner to the other two gentlemen as they bided their time on a hill of the trail, still awaiting Dr. Valentico's arrival.

On the pass of a mountain, Cary is listening and finds Stegner's true-crime tale interesting enough to pass the time. Though Theo has a different outlook on Stegner's story. He keeps his composure, but he doesn't care for Stegner's style of storytelling. From the time Theo spent with the captain working on the Force before he left, he heard the best stories Stegner had to tell, so he thinks he could do better for entertainment by watching what's happening down below the mountain pass.

Cary adds, "Oh, weren't you the responsible type to take case evidence without showing your badge."

"Well," says Stegner, "you see, McCoole didn't know anything about geography. He didn't care where the hell he was either. As long as the objectives were met, we could have been floating on sea horses through the tip of the Bermuda Triangle."

"So it was up to me," says Stegner, "to have . . . an active role in the pursuit. Just by keeping track of where we were. McCoole handled people . . . when he could and he kept his fire arms."

To say that he kept or readied firearms is an understatement because Alfred McCoole had one single bed in a two-bed motel room filled with all the equipment needed to care for a firearm; cleaning rods, brushes, guns, and ammo sprawled out on one bed with the curtains drawn, and "Do Not Disturb" sign hung on the outside of the door, while one of the two men was left to sleep on a cot every night. He had the motel towels rolled out to cover the sheet, and he would sit in a chair with a rag and bottle each night to ensure the chambers of each weapon were perfectly lubricated. He didn't seem to mind that the room smelled of gun powder, and he certainly didn't get bothered when he had to towel off with that same greasy motel towel, either.

So they drove Markot's last Tuesday route. They entered St. Louis the next day, but nobody remembered seeing the bus. When they found a Square-K Truck Stop near the Southside of Chicago, they met an attendant who recalled seeing a coach bound for D.C. pull through the truck stop. The pretty attendant said, "Old Markot looked his usual self."

It wasn't until they made it up to the last leg of the route, up through Virginia's Skyline Drive, near Shenandoah National Park, that they found something suspicious about the route.

"We pulled into a diner there," says Stegner, "and the mood of the place . . . shifted entirely. I pulled my pistol when the bartender ran out the back door, but I wish . . . I'd been quicker . . . ."

"Markot was excited," recalled the pretty lady who worked at the truck stop coming back from St. Louis. "His son-in-law had bought property over there, he inherited it from someone in Virginia, and they had some tourist attraction they were working on together."

"He and the son-in-law," restated McCoole to the attendant. "He said he was going into business?"

"Yes, he did say that. Are you boys coming from up north?" asked the attendant.

"You sound like, let me guess," said Stegner, "Wisconsin. Am I right?" The attendant looked puzzled and she blushed. She wrapped her hands around her narrow waistline and leaned in slightly to say, "Don't you know everything. And where are you from yourself?" McCoole silenced this flirtatious banter and they parted ways, the lovely attendant from Wisconsin and Captain Stegner.

Stegner adjusts himself on the cool mountain pass, his tie loosens and sleeves become rolled. He says, "We stopped at the Welcome Center for McCoole to pick up a few pamphlets. He picked up on our next stop when we made it back through Virginia's Welcome Center, which produced enough literature to fill several glove compartments. Luckily, my little, beat-up car only had one compartment for my partner to use and abuse . . . . He ruined my glove box, fellas."

The men laugh a little. Even Theo lets go of a chuckle.

Stegner holds out his hands to demonstrate: "It was only this big and he packed it full of sandwiches, ammunition, deodorant. It smelled like the locker room you don't want to stick around in. His rolled up, dirty socks. It was the worst! Anyway, we didn't add to it when McCoole saw a postcard for Shenandoah's newest addition, a park called 'Dig Up for Gold,' and we dug . . . alright."

They didn't have to get out of the car before McCoole's senses picked up on something out of the ordinary—"Keep driving," he said, and the rookie Stegner diverted the car from turning into the parking lot for the tourist trap they had intended to visit. Even though they didn't signal to enter, someone from the 'Dig Up for Gold' company came out of their little booth. A man with long sideburns waved to get them to come into the lot but they kept moving.

They drove out close to Ruckersville on State Highway 33 before going south along Highway 29 to Charlottesville and back around that way to get to their motel. McCoole put time into greasing up their guns enough before nightfall. As they waited to stalk their target, McCoole decided to clarify for Stegner the following: "Something was off about that place. That shed was put up in a hurry." Stegner could recall a new addition on the property and plenty of tarps laid out around the place. "We're going to find out why," said McCoole.

"He lead us out . . . at night . . . . McCoole did . . . to find the tarps were hiding mine shafts and an entrance to a gold vein the size of the Great Pyramids," says Stegner. His voice echoes off the walls of the side of the mountain.

After he ran out from behind the counter, they chased the bartender on foot until McCoole ran out of breath. He couldn't keep up, so he got back to the car in a hurry and let Stegner follow up on flat feet.

Stegner chased the bartender out of the park into Harrisonburg, and up State Highway 340 before McCoole was close by with the car. When he pulled up, Stegner got into the car. McCoole said to him, "I got lost, started driving up to New Market," but the rolling and rumbling spillage of pills in the back seat caused Stegner to get suspicious of his partner. He reached back to discover an empty bottle of heart medication.

"My heart . . . when we started running. We'll get him rookie, don't worry," said McCoole.

Stegner put a few pills from the backseat in his partner's shirt pocket, and he ran off to catch up to the suspect while the old detective took his time. The bartender was cornered, he took off his shirt to proudly display tattoos of occult mysticism and some of a nearby gang that was well-known for brutal beheadings of public officials. Stegner called for him to stay put, "Freeze, dirtball, unless you want to get someone to sew that ink back together," but the shirtless bartender leapt down a hole in the ground and out of sight. Stegner pursued, but it . . . didn't end well. The perpetrator was brought to justice, but McCoole was fatally injured in the process.

In the cave where he was shot, Stegner listened to his partner's words, as all the blood he had left his body. McCoole said, "It's alright, kid. You'll see . . . . You'll see what I mean one day if you get lucky enough to see a kid that is trying to capture something pure— to care about something enough to risk your life without knowing who you're protecting... Some things are a dead end. I don't know how to explain." The dying detective told his rookie partner, "Go write about it . . . . It's a massacre, what it is. All those innocent people but now it's over—" And Stegner held the man's hand as he jerked in sudden agony. "Tell me I'm lucky to be the last victim this time around. That's . . . all I want to hear."

"You're not," said Stegner. "Markot was the last victim." In an attempt to keep McCoole alive he said, "You're strong. You're going to make it."

"Nope. Look at me kid," said McCoole, trying to smile one last time, but his bottom tip wouldn't turn upward. "I've been through this before, on my end before. You don't keep getting this without it getting you one time around. And it's . . . my time. Today, the Snatcher from the East . . . is dead."

Stegner wraps up his story to Cary and Theo: "The papers ran with that story. My badge was worth more, so I started running the Force, you know." He says to Theo, "That's where I was when I dealt with the next international massacre, but you should talk to this half of one hell of a husband and wife force if you want to know about that case."

Theo turns to Cary and says, "The case he's talking about got covered up and distorted once it turned out the suspects . . . weren't human, of course."

"They weren't . . . ?" asks the stunned inspector.

"They weren't human, and they were none of my business," says Stegner as he climbs to be the first one out of the mountain pass where the trees were giving them shelter from the moon light.

"Once you step out of the city's main controls and into the towns… anything can happen," says Theo before leaving Cary in the darkness under the pine trees.' And in the darkness . . . Cary loses control of his senses . . . for enough time to draw Theo and Stegner back to check on him.

The bartender was identified as Vincent Malloy, a member of the Malloy Gang from across the Atlantic Ocean. He was upset when his brothers were shipped back home after a failed racket they were running on elderly people. They were caught tricking old-folks to give up their retirement funds. They used to dress up as used car salesmen since that racket only costs the price of a few cheap suits and a classic car that they kept polished and never parted with until they were caught. Vincent Malloy drove the car into a river to keep from joining his family because he didn't want to go back to farming in his old country. He took to the lam and started upping his antics to the deadly, less merciful degree, as depicted by Stegner.

After he was brought to justice, Malloy accumulated over $80,000 of stolen goods from the people he tracked, abducted, and took to the old mines. He discovered the mines while hiding in the woods, and he took out the owners, even assuming the identity of Markot's son-in-law . . . in the process.

Markot and his son-in-law were on to something when they set up their business venture. The place, with its unusual rock formations, looked like a fairyland made of glittering, ancient Earth, but Malloy ruined the sanctity of the place.

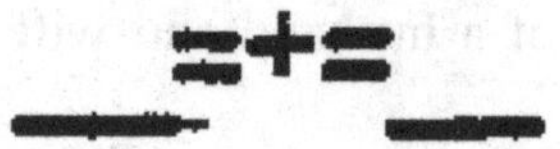

"Mr. Oriel, can you hear me?" asks Dr. Cynthia Valentico. "His eyes were open. I'll give him another moment."

"I'm here. Who is that speaking?" asks Cary.

"Mr. Oriel, you've been experiencing . . . . a type of

psychosis," says Valentico.

"Psychosis . . . ? Who are you?" he asks, and he looks about the space, but the room is dark.

"There's a lamp in front of you on the coffee table. Take a moment to familiarize yourself with your surroundings please." Cary follows the instructions he was given. Cynthia says, "I've been briefed on your situation already, and I'm here to help you straighten things out before your troubles worsen."

He notices the space: light coming from under the large, wooden doors at the end of the room, a few things on the table, books on shelves lining the windowless room.

"There's a glass of water and a pill to stop your headache. A proper night of sleep would do the trick, too, if only we were so lucky to have that sort of time to rest," says Valentico. "I hear you feel you're being followed. Tell me about your situation. Will you?"

"Where are we going?" asks the disoriented Cary.

"You're already where you need to be until we figure out your situation. I promise you're safe where you are. Captain Stegner and Theodore brought you here . . . to my office. Do you understand the things I'm telling you? Nod if you do."

"I understand. But where are you?" asks Cary.

"Unfortunately, you are in my world, so we must abide by my sort of gravitas. Are we clear?"

"Your . . . ?" Cary says and takes the pill with a big gulp of water.

"These are my rules. You'll have to tell your story . . . to the lens. Due to the pressing matter at hand, Mr. Stegner has offered to sit with you . . . if the camera makes you shy. But that's the only way I can begin to help you, Cary," she says.

He notices the camera at last, and he says, "That's okay. I just find it strange is all."

"Yes," says Valentico, "well, until we get to know one another, let's assume the worst about each other."

"Assume the worst? I'm just looking for my children. They disappeared . . . and my father too."

"Well, you might be right, but according to the papers.

You're a wanted man, Cary," says Valentico. "You're wanted for questioning back home, your home. Did you realize that you're a suspect in the disappearance of the very same people you are searching for?"

"No," says Cary, "but it doesn't surprise me to find out. See, I mixed with some bad people when I started seeing this woman— I haven't told many people . . . about her."

"A woman? Says here . . . that you're married."

"I am, but I was lonely with my wife . . . being the way she is. I told people on a daily basis that she was dead so I could move on . . . . But . . . now . . . ." Cary trails off and takes another big gulp of water.

Cynthia says, "Slow down, Cary. You said . . . that you were seeing another woman."

"And my family didn't know her yet, but I thought I loved her, until it turned out she wasn't the person I wanted her to be," says Cary.

"Sometimes we make people out to be more than they are. That's very true. Continue, Cary," says Valentico.

"Well," Cary says, "she was cruel to me. I guess no woman . . . could ever replace my wife. I wouldn't have looked at Joslin that way if my wife . . . were her old self. I swear . . . . But now . . . I can't even see another woman if I tried."

Cynthia says, "Are you referring to what Mr. Stegner told me— You're seeing your wife. Is that right, Cary?"

"Not this instant, but she was there!" he exclaims, and he grips his arms around a throw pillow.

"I bet it seemed real to you," says Valentico through the small speaker. "But Mr. Oriel, that was your brain's way of dealing with the facts as they came in . . . . You're overloaded with the threat of losing everyone you love."

Cary is sobbing.

"We'll see what we can do—" she says before cutting off her microphone. She says to the others: "He's not faking it . . . . I believe he does see her. At least it's real . . . to him."

"Hm . . . ." says Theo, and they look at each other in proximal silence with the sad sounds from Cary coming from down the hall.

DR. CYNTHIA VALENTICO finishes making her notes before she says, "My first impression is," and she notices Theo shifting his weight back and forth, so she says, "You look eager, Theo. Do you want to tell me what you're seeing on this one?" She closes her notebook.

"Well, uh," says Theo, "I was interested in hearing what you think, but this is your show now, so okay . . . . The fact that Inspector Cary—"

"Oriel—"

"The fact that Oriel claims to be chased by some group of crooked cops, that may be a connection," says Theo.

"They're an organized mob. How's that have to do with anything?" asks Captain Stegner. "I could care less about what he thinks to be truthful." Stegner snubs Theo with: "Now you got us here. Your job is done. You can go back to writing your sloppy paper . . . for my team to look over."

"You son of a . . . ." says Theo and he stands with enough force the chair he was on is now at the wall. "You go on using people, and some of us are trying to get to the bottom of something, Larry!"

"Gentlemen," Cynthia says, and she stands between them in the middle of the room. The corners of her mouth depress and that firm gesture speaks loudly on its own, but still, she says, "There's one thing missing . . . ."

"Yes. We don't know what they're after. And Cary—"

"Cary knows?"

"Nope. Unfortunately he likely does not know who is after him," says Stegner, "and that's what is causing him—"

"It's causing him to see his dead wife?! You think he's under that much pressure?" asks Theo.

"Well, yes," says Cynthia.

"Anyway," says Stegner as he rolls his sleeves back upwards, "his wife isn't dead. I checked, and she's in a coma, apparently. His story checks out."

"But," says Theo, and he looks away from Cynthia when he says, "at her stage, there's no difference." He looks to Cynthia and says, "You heard him, right? It's been years. He's tried to move on."

"But something won't let him," says Cynthia, and she looks at the screen of Cary Oriel laying on the couch with the throw pillow covering his face. His body shifts.

When Cynthia looks closer at the video feed she jumps a little. Her shoulders raise up and her breath shortens. Her wrists bend to an arch while her hands become truly exalted, and she says, "Look! Over here! Look! Quickly. Hurry!"

Theo and Stegner crowd by her shoulders to catch a glimpse, but they don't have the same reaction as Cynthia:

"Don't you see her there?" asks Cynthia. The men look to each other, and Theo shakes his head. They look from the screen to Cynthia for her explanation: "The woman. I see her sitting next to our dear Inspector Cary Oriel. How . . . curious."

Chapter Twelve

No Jurisdiction

IT turns out Tall Grass wasn't the only one to spot Henry Edwards in the sky. As Lucinda-Lee was returning from grocery shopping for her disabled aunt she nearly tripped over a bit of jagged chunk of asphalt and her grocery bag tore open.

Aunt Mitzy came to the door, and she said, "Babe, you having trouble?"

"It would seem that way," said Lucinda-Lee before she went to pick up a few items, "but I guess I'm lucky it isn't raining."

"That a-girl. Way to be positive," said Aunt Mitzy. She got her cane and helped.

As Lucinda-Lee was standing back up she looked to the sky, but she didn't say a word, so her aunt asked, "Are you having trouble again, dear?" When, she turned to see what her niece had been seeing, a bright-red haze behind the clouds moved its way across the sky, and with its movement went the strange shadows on the clouds.

"Oh dear," said Aunt Mitzy, and she went inside to call everyone she could think to call. A local news crew came by to make a short video, and it wasn't long before word traveled all around the shore.

🍷

"These reports about a strange flying aircraft might be worth looking into," says Cynthia.

"Oh, right," agrees Theo with a pungent bite of sarcasm. "Because light bouncing off of rainclouds and water combined with a balloon—"

"Yes," says Cary interrupting the couple's dispute, "We have all heard of that, but what does it have to do with my family?"

"You say that your father was getting ready for a trip," says Theo Bryant. "What if—Tell me, Cary, do you know how to fly one of those balloons?"

"I'm sure I could if I had to," replies Cary.

"Well, have you?" asks Cynthia.

"Not on my own," says Cary. "What's this a good time to make me feel low?"

"This might be at your expense," says Theo, "but do you know if your son or daughter knows how to fly the balloon?" Cynthia smiles over the progress.

"I think my daughter is too young for that, you know," says Cary, "but Henry—" He looks off in the distance.

"The child knows how to fly," says Cynthia. "Brilliant." She puts on her coat, and they look to her for an answer. "What are you waiting for? We have a lead on finding your children."

"What about Stegner?" asks Cary.

"He's napping," says Theo. "Let him catch up with us later."

"It's out of his jurisdiction anyway," says Cynthia.

The three of them leave Stegner asleep in an armchair in their home to go investigate a lead on a hot air balloon in the skies.

206

"
——
*

"Hi," says a voice on the intercom. The young woman who presses the button to speak isn't in the mood for guests and responds with the following: "Who's there? If you're another reporter, you can go to hell!"

"I'm not a reporter, miss," says the voice. "I'm looking for more information about the mysterious flying object." There is no answer back, so the voice says, "I think I can help figure this out, Lucinda Price."

"Lucinda-Lee Price isn't home I'm afraid, and Miss Mitzy isn't in good spirits today I'm afraid," says the young woman.

Approaching the door with the intercom system outside is Cynthia followed by Cary. Close behind, fumbling with gadgets in hand is Theo. Before they reach the doorstep, Cary stops in place and says, "Wait."

Cynthia goes back to hear from Cary who turns and makes his retreat known by her. Theo continues fumbling on the pathway in front of the building until Cynthia pulls him along. They stand behind a fence and look through slats of wood to see the building where Detective Bruno Peters stands. They watch Bruno buzz the intercom and get no response.

"That's the guy," says Cary. "He's after me— Him—"

"He didn't see you, right?" asks Cynthia.

"He's not getting in wherever he's trying to get," says Theo. "Oh, I heard something about clouds . . . ? And . . . ." Theo turns the knob on his device to listen at a different frequency. "There's a young girl's voice."

"Great. We need to get ahead of him then," says Cynthia.

"Now do you believe me?" asks Cary.

"Do you mean to tell me this guy just happens to be looking for your kids too? That doesn't exactly prove to me he's after you," says Theo.

207

"There's another way to find out," says Cynthia as Theo taps his device on a rock near the post at the bottom of their side of the fence.

Theo says, "Some girl on the intercom is messing up the transmission."

"What's she saying to him?" asks Cynthia.

"I don't know. I can only hear him or her, not both of them," says the urgent detective.

Cynthia takes aim of the amplifier, and she takes one of Theo's listening devices that fits in her ear, as Cary continues to look through the fence. Cary says, "The girl—There," and he points to a young woman on the fifth floor peaking through the vertical blinds from above.

"She's missing, too—" says Cynthia.

"Who?" asks Cary.

"Police suspect foul play," says Theo.

"Who? What police?" asks the puzzled Cary.

The audio amplifier raises to the young woman: "Maybe check around her school if you care so much? Why do you ca—" Cynthia lowers the device to Bruno's level: "Because I have the right to care. Now, tell me, can you ask the old lady about which way the thing in the sky was moving?" Cynthia raises the device to the room where the young woman was looking out moments ago, fifth floor and two windows over from the left, but the blinds aren't moving. All of a sudden Cynthia and Theo hear a loud thump on a wooden door on the fifth floor, and the young woman's voice: "Aunt Mitzy, it's your neighbor."

"What do you need, dear?" asks Aunt Mitzy. "I'm sorry to do this, but I need to get back across the hall to get ready for work, but I'm back here tonight. I hope—"

Cynthia lowers the listening amplifier and says, "I've got a plan." She takes off her glasses and lets her hair down before running past Cary toward the back of the building's alley.

She comes back to give Theo a kiss on the cheek.

Moments later, Cynthia appears on the inside of the building and opens the door leading to the front door step. "Thank you," she says, "you are really brave to look into this for us. I can't tell you how happy . . . Aunt Mitzy is. Even knowing . . . there's people looking for her niece."

"What's happening?" asks Cary.

"She can handle herself," says Theo. "All that matters is we have to keep you out of sight."

"No," says Cary. "He knows too much . . . about me."

"Do you have something to hide?" asks Theo. "If so, this is a really a good time to come clean."

"Well," Cary says, "let me just say he knows where my wife is . . . ." His mind races with guilt for having been with Joslin Peters while his wife was in a coma. "But she's here now," Cary says when he notices his wife next to him.

Theo has stopped paying attention to Cary; he has diverted all of his energy to the events unfolding before his eyes and plugged ears.

1

"He found out about this other disappearance. Maybe he's trying to do something good," says Cynthia. She is crouched down behind a row of bushes beside the apartment while Bruno is talking on his phone around the corner.

"I doubt it," says Cary.

"I'm partial to agree with Inspector Cary Oriel on this matter," says Theo. "I believe the man is following a hunch to look at a similar case of a disappearance in hopes that there is some connection—"

"Perhaps this is how we find out he isn't involved in the abduction?" says Cynthia, and she shares a moment locking eyes with her husband.

"Do you think you should follow him?" Theo asks, lost in Cynthia's gaze. Her eyes get big because she is thinking whether Cary is telling the truth from the beginning, but she nods and says, "I'll stick with him and have you as my backup."

"If you're certain," says Theo. They kiss, and Cynthia whispers to Theo, "Can we trust him?" He whispers back, "Yes."

Cynthia goes off to get in the car with Bruno, and they wait until they have a chance to get to their car undetected and follow them. The move takes some effort on Theo's part since Cary is fixated on watching Adeline through the vertical blinds in the fifth floor window.

They follow Bruno's car until he pulls off to get gas. When they pull in and get out, Cynthia catches up to the detective and locks arms with him briefly. Theo seems at ease with having her back. She backs up and takes out a radio from Theo's breast coat pocket, and she holds the button to say, "Larry, you there?" Captain Larry Stegner says, "Yep. I'm keeping your couch company. How's Cary holding up?" Cynthia notes how Inspector Cary Oriel looks like he's unraveling. He swallows and his hair still looks mangy. "He's holding up," she says.

The car Bruno drives is an unmarked cruiser with tags from Never York. Still, Bruno puts a light on his roof. When she gets back to him, Bruno says to Cynthia, "Thanks for joining me, Miss . . . ? You're so kind."

"Sure—It's nice to see someone actually taking initiative. The police around here keep scratching their heads," says Cynthia, and she feels a slight smirk take over her gestures and movements, so she tries to settle her nerves to avoid giving away her position. "I need calmness over me," she thinks to herself, and she counts in her head, "One-thousand & one—oh! That was a perfect resemblance to the voice coming from the intercom speaker—One-thousand & two—I can't believe I'm getting away with this—One-thousand & three—Keep positive and move on—"

"You put up a wall," says Bruno.

"I have to stop myself from thinking about it too much," Cynthia says with a great release of breath. "I think, what if it was me instead of Lucy?" She takes hold of his arm.

He keeps driving and says, "Hey, it's alright. It's Lucinda. Lucinda-Lee Price, right?"

"Right," she says, and she thinks to herself to pause and let him ask the questions.

"So are you from around here?" asks Bruno.

She lets go of his arm and says, "Not originally. I'm . . . Gabby."

"Well," Bruno says, "Gabby, I have some questions that

could get us closer to your friend."

"Alright," she says.

He doesn't say anything until they're through the intersection. When he stops the car on the side of the road, Theo and Cary pass by them. She bites her lip and feels the first twinge of anxiety coming back to her. "Right," Bruno says. "Okay. So you said the college. They've got to have a camera on."

"Yep," says Cynthia, "but it's like I told you, honey. The college won't even show us the tape, and her aunt—Mitzy," she says knowingly, with another twinge of pride. "She wants to have a look herself, you know?"

"I understand, and I want you to know that I'm extremely grateful for a woman such as yourself accompanying me on my investigation," says Bruno.

"What do you mean?" Cynthia says with a forced smile of bright pink lips.

"I mean," says Bruno, "you are obviously on your way somewhere looking like that. Now, we got to get to those tapes!"

"Oh my!" exclaims Cynthia. She puts her hand on his bicep as he reaches to shift the car into gear. She wonders how much she can get him to do without needing to sleep with him. "You can't just run into a building like that for me. You barely know me."

"I know you're good natured," says Bruno.

"They won't show us the tapes because they likely still have faith in the sheriff, but *pfft*," she says with distaste.

"Well, baby girl," says the gleeful, tight-lipped Bruno, "let me tell you what—that sheriff of ours is dipping into the Goose's pocket like the rest of the district." He shows a twinge of discomfort in his squint.

"Who's pocket?" asks Cynthia.

"No one you should need to know. Show me where to find the law school," says Bruno.

Cynthia nods, and says, "Let me check my GPS . . . for directions."

She looks at directions quickly. When her glance tells her the time is right, she types a message to Theo saying, "NS LAW SCHL - Security tape."

BRUNO pulls the car up to a large, white marble façade that reads, "Legal Studies Branch of North Shore University." He puts his arm on the back of the seat behind Cynthia, and she holds onto the seam that runs horizontally along her skirt for a moment. She settles her nerves in the time it takes Bruno to look around the lot next to them. They drive farther with his arm behind her, and she looks back in the mirror to see a set of headlights.

He finally puts the car into reverse to look for a spot near the administrative building. He uses his arm on the back of her seat to help him navigate, while smiling and singing along with the radio. He turns his head to look back and sings:

"You'd better move on, mister.
Move that barrel away from me.
Move on, mister. You—
You just wait and see-e-e-e."

"Bingo," says Bruno when they pull up to a row of vans belonging to the campus security, a few golf charts too. He parks the car, and they get out.

Moments later . . . they are denied assistance. While standing in the front office, the head of security comes out to greet them. He shows them the control room and says, "We've already shown the police—"

"Well, hold on a sec," says Bruno and looks to Cynthia for a moment. "Do you mind giving us a second to talk man to man?"

"Sure," she says and leaves out to the walkway in front of the building.

When the door is shut Bruno says, "Gee, I'll tell you . . . . There's a lot I'll do . . . to impress a woman. Do you think she's beautiful or what?"

"Oh, sure," says the head of security, and they look at a screen that shows the security feed of Cynthia out on the pathway.

"There's a lot I'd do to you to get to that tape," says Bruno, and he takes out a knife to show he's serious.

"I don't want trouble," says the security head, and he goes for a panic button, but Bruno is too quick. The man's hand is met with a blade instead. "Okay!" the man screams. There's blood everywhere from a deep cut. He plays the tape of the night Lucinda-Lee was taken by her attacker.

They watch a man with a hood covering his face walk up behind the young lady who is carrying a small stack of books under one arm, and they watch Lucinda-Lee fighting for her life. But the attacker was too strong, and he overcame her and cut off the supply of air she was receiving. He was wearing blue jeans and gloves, and there was a lanyard hanging from his pocket.

"Can you zoom in there?" asks Bruno. The guy behind the screen takes the camera recording closer to show a blurry, pixilated lanyard keychain necklace. The attacker turned when the victim lost consciousness. When he returned to face the camera he dragged the young lady a few feet before tossing her body onto his shoulders.

Cynthia sees Bruno outside in the parking lot; he is stalking about the area where Lucinda-Lee was last seen on the security tape. When she goes to greet him, she asks, "Well, did they let you see it?"

"Yeah," says Bruno. "And I see what we're looking for next—"

"Next?" asks Cynthia.

"Yep," says Bruno, and he kicks around some large rocks that were once part of the parking lot. "I'll know once I find it here," he says, and he is really going through some considerable efforts to lift the rocks in front of Cynthia. "The suspect had a lanyard keychain, and I believe it was removed in the struggle by the victim."

"Do you think she left us a clue?" asks Cynthia above an approaching police siren.

In their car, near the university, Theo turns up the police scanner: "All units responding to intruder at the law school." That prompts Theo to say to Cary, "Listen, sounds like there's been some action." Theo and Cary stay planted in the car, watching Bruno and Cynthia in the parking lot nearby.

"Yep," says Bruno. "We need to go, but not without that lanyard."

"Right," says Cynthia. She moves her foot and adjusts her weight on the flats she wears.

"Darling, not just to impress you, but I want to find this girl . . . to . . . you know, serve justice, and I think she's seen something more than a weather balloon out there," says Bruno. He digs in the dirt and becomes covered in that grass.

Cynthia marvels at how pathetic the man is as she reaches down slowly to pick up the lanyard below her flats.

The detective says, "You ever feel like giving up?"

She is ready to move from the area. But instead of using her stamina as a runner, she uses her training as a doctor to spot a serious call for help. Her maternal instincts kick in as well. All of her anxiety is gone. Standing there with someone she could care less about, she still can't ignore the cries she hears, so she stands there to listen to him a little longer for his sake.

"I mean, you play a pretty part—Come in out of nowhere and get involved—I want to know how quickly you would uproot from here to get involved more intimately," says Bruno. He turns to her on his hands and knees and says, "Because I'm looking for a partner—"

She thinks about leaving and calling for help. She knows how close Theo is, but she can't give up. She thinks to herself, "What if the pathetic man on his knees knows where to find this girl? What if he can help us find Cary's family?"

"Well," she says, "Look-ee what I found, partner." Her smile is a dazzling sight to accompany the lanyard in her hands.

She holds out the lanyard. It's for a place called "North Shore's Rumpus Room Décor," and it has a picture of a young shipping clerk.

Once inside the largest furniture store in all of the area, they try to blend in with the crowds appreciating the store's weekend specials. "BUYOUT ON ALL NEW PIECES - ONE WEEK ONLY," is printed on the banner above their heads, and other people in town must have received the message as well, for the store is packed with buyers moving furniture steadily out the door on flatbed, hand-pulled wagons. The wagons are low enough to the ground to sweep the floor, but those movers hold the furniture from dragging the ground.

Bruno leads the way, and Cynthia joins him in following the sounds of opera music coming from a radio in the back room of the furniture shop. The music is appropriate to the energy within Rumpus Room Décor, as Vivaldi's "The Four Seasons" comes through the speakers of the store and echoes loudly from its origin in the back rooms. The store isn't as busy at the music's source.

Once they go to the back, they are face to face with a large conveyer belt that leads upwards at an angle no greater than forty-five degrees. They hear someone coming from the loading dock and have no choice but to avoid getting caught by sneaking around back there, among the moving belts. One rolls forward steadily, and they get on the thick vinyl belt. They are pulled toward the ceiling, out of sight.

Meanwhile, in the parking lot on the front side of the building, Theo is getting impatient. He says to Cary, "Where are they? I can't see anything. I'm going to have a closer look." He turns to Cary and says, "Stay here, alright?"

The conveyer belt moves steadily across the packaging space and up above near the rafters. Way up high, on the belt, Bruno clings to one side of the steel girder that supports the sturdy mechanism, and Cynthia clings onto the other side. Bruno's nod towards the end of the conveyer belt, where a flap of plastic drags along the belt leading out into an area marked for incineration, is an expression of terror.

Cynthia could not be more at ease when she says, "Ready? One, two, three," and he lets go with her as they drop . . . downward . . . from twelve feet high.

In the interim, Theo is looking around the store when a salesman approaches him with: "Sir, you're in luck today. What can I—"

"Not today, pal," says Theo. "I'm searching for my wife."

They land on a stack of mattresses that breaks their fall entirely. They roll off the mattresses, one at a time. Cynthia rolls onto a carpet and keeps rolling to hide away, and Bruno takes a sheet of thick plastic used to cover furniture along with him to hide under. He says, "Good thinking."

"Coming our way, and he isn't wearing a nametag," says Cynthia. She sees a man moving around the corner, by looking in the mirror, mounted up high near the conveyer belt, and she tucks away.

Moments later they hear a *'Cl-ick!'* of the wheels being unlocked to roll smoothly, and the cart starts moving with Bruno and Cynthia hiding on it.

Outside, Cary is watching for Theo to come back when he sees the large man moving about. Out the back of the furniture store, Tommy Rottingham is loading up the truck. He pushes the cart from the loading dock onto the truck, he climbs down the small set of stairs, and he puts the key in the ignition to get it started. When the engine cranks Cary notices another detail. His wife is sitting on top of the truck, looking like she did . . . when they first moved in together and paused to watch fireworks . . . on the roof of their borrowed moving truck.

Theo unlocks the car door after making several attempts to get Cary's attention from outside the car. Cary says, "Theo—I saw her again—Adeline—My wife—" When he points to the back of the furniture store the truck is already gone.

Theo and Cary drive around looking for the truck, but they aren't able to find it. Theo asks, "Are you sure is was yellow?" Cary nods.

Things get less comfortable when Cynthia and Bruno are trapped in the back of the moving truck. The hills are steep around North Shore, and the driver seems to be hitting every bump in the road from North Shore to Canada. After unpackaging himself, Bruno asks, "How did you know to get in here like that?"

"I'm just following you around," says Cynthia.

"Like hell—" he says. Bruno is excited and more interested in Cynthia by the minute. He turns up his flirtatious manner and says, "Are you . . . into this girl who disappeared or something? You seem to have a natural instinct that is getting us places."

With her fake smile and batting eyes, Cynthia says, "No.

But I don't mind helping get her back to her family."

"Me either," says Bruno.

They aren't on top of each other until Tommy slams on the brakes and changes lanes—The furniture shifts, pinning Cynthia and Bruno against the cold metal wall of the truck. Cynthia is close enough to give Bruno a whiff of her perfume, and he can't decide which is more lovely: "The scent of her perfume . . . and the distinct . . . smell . . . of furniture polish." They resonate together within the confined space, he thinks, along with her shampoo and the smell of pine.

Her hair is loose from its usual bun, and some of it gets caught in Bruno's whiskers. Her lips puff apart and her face gets red as she fights back against the furniture that continues sliding their way. Only after she is successful in using her right flat like a doorstop, creating a wedge under the half-ton mass of boxed furniture, only then does Bruno lean in to help her stop it from sliding.

This part of the book is a lot like one of Captain Larry Stegner's true crime novels, a book called *The Seamstress and Her Headless Hens*. Except that book is 900 pages in its abridged form due to the meticulous index . . . listing the names of every individual on the case.

"I need you to say it—"

"No! . . . ."

"Say it, Lucinda-Lee, and maybe I'll let your hands free a few hours while we figure out what we're going to do when we run away together," says Tommy Rottingham.

"What we're going to do?" asks Lucinda-Lee. "You're going to let me go and get some help for yourself," she pleads. "Look—If you want money—"

"I don't need that. I *got* money for both of us," says Tommy. "I want you to understand just how grand life can be for you." In Stegner's novel, this is when the Seamstress would show her victims their filleted flesh, but lucky for Lucinda-Lee, Tommy wants to preserve her the way she is. "I can provide for you, baby," he says. He touches her hair that's wet from sweating so much in the hot kitchen. He closes the oven door. "Dinner should be ready soon, and I'll let you free for a while then. I promise."

He starts working with knives. He sharpens one that he plans to use to cut into a slab of red meat with the same delicate control that the Seamstress would use to thread her chicken-bone needles. Tommy pokes the meat with another knife that is longer, and the full tang of the steel knife is long enough to keep his hand from getting hot when he places the slab in the oven.

Lucinda-Lee has been working on the knots that hold her wrists together. One of the knots is coming loose, but she has to stop when Tommy turns to say the following: "I don't need your money. I need you to tell me the things you used to tell Elvis."

"Oh," says Lucinda-Lee. "Okay. That's fine. Tom, you're an excellent hunter—"

"Stop it," says Tommy. "Not like that. Besides if I was a good hunter, you'd of let me take you more willingly. I know that. I'm not stupid, Lucinda-Lee . . . . Just because I don't . . . go to libraries like you do. I mean, I want you to tell me the good stuff. If you want to be set free for dinner. Try to be detailed like you're reading a book to me out loud."

"Oh gosh," says Lucinda-Lee. "Tommy . . . . You know I love it when——"

"Try like you're reading. Sound natural," says Tommy.

"I'm not sure what that means," says Lucinda-Lee, and she thinks of Elvis. "Uh . . . . When my nights are restless and I can't find peace . . . there you are . . . ."

"That's better," says Tommy. He gets to seasoning the slab of meat he's fixing.

"When you touch me," says Lucinda-Lee as she works on the knots again. "When you touch me with your big, strong . . . muscles." She looks over her shoulder to see if Tommy is watching as she has nearly got the knot undone. He smiles at her in the reflection of his butcher knife. He says, "I would touch you, but I would want you to want it—Do-do you want me?"

"Oh . . . . Yes!" exclaims Lucinda-Lee when she pulls her wrists apart and spins the chair around to knock Tommy in the knees. He falls to the ground, but he doesn't stay down long. He's on top of her before the moment is over. He buries the point of the butcher knife—all the way to the tip—deep in the wooden floor, and Lucinda-Lee screams.

From out on the side porch, Bruno and Cynthia hear the scream. It startles them enough for Bruno to quit prying at the locked screen door; he kicks it in. It bounces off the frame. He finds the knob in front of the door to be locked. "What do you think that was? The scream . . . ." whispers Cynthia. "I don't know," Bruno replies, and he moves back a few steps to assess the situation.

After putting the ropes around her wrists and ankles tightly, Tommy goes to the kitchen window where he looks out into the darkness that exists beyond the shack. He polishes his butcher knife. "You bent the tip," says Tommy, and he turns to show Lucinda-Lee the butcher knife. She yelps through the gag in her mouth when she sees Bruno looking through the kitchen window behind Tommy.

"Don't move a muscle," shouts Bruno with his pistol raised from its holster. "Whatever you're doing with that girl— You better get out here and leave her alone. Do you hear me?"

Tommy Rottingham slowly brings the butcher knife to the counter, where he places it down. He slides his hands along the counter, grasps the rope of the blinds, and with the tiniest tug, the blinds are free to slam down, down, down in front of the kitchen window.

When she finally gets the screen door out of the way, Cynthia is able to turn the knob of the next door before stale air rushes through her nostrils. Bruno moves back around to the side porch where Valentico slowly creeps in, and he says to her, "This is exactly why I don't leave my city all that often." Bruno takes his badge from beneath his shirt and lets it dangle over his clothing. He approaches the kitchen and says, "Listen, son. I'm a police officer." He witnesses Tommy holding the knife with its straight edge pressing into Lucinda-Lee's jugular but not piercing her perfect neckline.

The tension is too high for Bruno, so he takes his weapon and places it on the floor, and he says, "I'm laying down mine, why don't you do the same." Valentico picks up the gun from where it slid, around the corner and out of Tommy's sightline. She nods at Bruno to keep going, so Bruno moves closer. He says, "I'm coming in, and I just want to talk."

The detective notices Lucinda-Lee has a gag in her mouth and her arms are tied together with a thin nylon packing rope. He reaches out slowly to place a hand on the giant man's trembling shoulder, and Bruno says, "We're going to sort this out, alright?" Tommy Rottingham lets go of the knife, his knees buckle, and he drops down to the floor. He's cowering in the corner saying things like . . . "She kept screaming," and, "All I wanted was her to talk to me," and, "I can't let nobody scream at me like that."

He finally looks up at Bruno, and he sees Cynthia Valentico untying Lucinda-Lee. "Go," says Cynthia to the young woman, who doesn't argue with her about leaving the place she had been imprisoned.

Cynthia breathes deeply and says, "I need you to sit next to him, so you can explain the whole thing to the authorities." She pulls the nylon packing rope from being wrapped around the chair and tosses it to Bruno. She yells, "Now! Get a move on it!"

As Bruno receives the message, shocks of disloyalty plague his being. The shock gives Tommy Rottingham enough time to raise an axe he had hidden behind a vertical support beam in the kitchen. Cynthia screams, for Bruno is too low to get a jump on stopping Tommy. He covers his face while curling away from being struck by the blade—

✦✦✦

"Enough of this!" exclaims Bruno. His arms are tied and so are his legs. He's losing blood but the rope acts as a tourniquet, for he was grazed by the axe.

"I knew it was too good for there to be much truth—But, hell, I didn't want much from you, honey," says Bruno. Trying to piece together what Cynthia is doing, he notices her cleaning the chair with a rag. "Of course, get your prints out of here. You keep

220

playing like a flower— You're going to get stung one day, honey!"

She stands, adjusts her hair back into a tight bun and starts for the door until Bruno says, "Come on. You're just going to leave me here to go help Cary, huh?" She stops walking when she knows he's onto her. "You saw what we did here. Listen, I'm one of the good guys. Just untie me and point me to Cary—You're not safe around him, you know."

Cynthia doesn't turn to Bruno. She says, "Cary's on a train heading south—That's all I know unfortunately—"

"I can tell a liar when I see one," says Bruno.

"So can I," says Valentico.

"You got to be kidding me— Hasn't he gotten tired of getting shipped from place to place?" asks the injured detective. "Cary Oriel—Ought to call him 'Cary Orient' like the Orient Express, get it?" Bruno tries to make one last jab at Cynthia, but the joke misses completely.

"You'll have to excuse me," says Cynthia. "I've told you all I know." She exits out the same door she came through moments ago.

Outside, Theo is parking the sedan and Lucinda-Lee is near the road, too. Dr. Cynthia Valentico shows up in her own time. She walks up the narrow pass in the dark. It's difficult, but she makes it without trouble. In fact, she surprises Theo and Cary. She's removed her jacket. She's wearing all black to hide away; and she looks extra slim with her long boots and her hair wrapped high and tight.

Cary unlocks the doors electronically to let Cynthia and Lucinda-Lee get inside the car. When the doors shut, Theo gives the sedan gas to get out of there fast, for sirens are loud in the distance; the police are on their way.

Before Theo can ask his wife what they have missed she beats him by presenting the following question to satisfy her

221

own curiosity: "How did you know where to find me?" asks Cynthia.

Theo can't hide his satisfaction when he looks in the rear-view mirror to say, "We had satellites search for blurs of yellow, looking for the moving truck, and we found it . . . thanks to Stegner, and Cary's dead wife, I suppose."

"She's alive," says Cary.

"Yes," says Theo. "My mistake. Cary's . . . wife's . . . apparition . . . ?"

Theo turns on the police scanner so he and Cary can have a better understanding of the scene they missed.

Lucinda-Lee still looks distraught; she leans over to Cynthia for what turns into a warm embrace. Cynthia says, "You're safe now."

They drive back to drop Lucinda-Lee off at her home with her aunt.

"
—
✳

The sirens are getting close. It doesn't look like a good situation to be in for Bruno. He squirms in the ropes to get closer to the axe that is covered in his blood. He gets his ankles around the axe's cutting edge; its bevel is sharp enough to start cutting the packing strip as Tommy Rottingham coughs and spits some blood against the wall.

"Damn," says Bruno. "She got you good, but it was either you or me, and this is your mess after all."

"I'm good looking, aren't I?" asks Tommy. He conserves what little energy he has left after taking a close-range shot to the chest— a bullet that should have killed him, but it slowed its fatal blow when the lead round got lodged in his sternum.

Bruno has his feet free enough to pull the axe by the knob on the end of its shaft and position the flat butt of the axe on the ground where he needs it to remain. He saws away at what binds his wrists to the vertical beam. He says, "Listen to them coming. Looks like luck might be on your side today."

"I just want to be good enough . . . for her," says the twisted young man.

"You are, son," says Bruno as he gets to his feet and ties the rope back around his injured arm.

"Then, why does she still choose Elvis over me?" asks Tommy.

"You're askin' the wrong guy," torts Bruno. "We both messed up by trustin' a woman to keep quiet. Yours got away because you're a monster. And the skirt I chased got cute. Real cute." Bruno leaves Rottingham tied up.

"Well!" exclaims Theo. "My dearest friend, look what we've brought upon ourselves with our meddlesome ways." Indeed, the shrewd couple brought themselves into such a tormented state of affairs. Oh! They certainly could have stayed with what they were doing, but the doctor and Theo have put all pressing matters to the side, including their young child who waits for their return.

As Theo parks the sedan in front of the apartment complex to let Lucinda-Lee loose, Stegner pulls his police cruiser behind another cruiser parked outside the shack. He parks and meets Lieutenant Ross McKindley by the side porch of the shack with the kicked in door. The tip came in and when they showed up it was just Tommy Rottingham there. He pulled up to the shack a few minutes after McKindley. Lt. McKindley explains how he saw Tommy Rottingham bleed out, but something didn't add up for Stegner.

After talking to Lucinda-Lee himself, Stegner finds that Tommy Rottingham was on the ground with Bruno and Cynthia standing about. The autopsy shows Cynthia's shot didn't kill him. Cynthia even backs up the story when Stegner asks her, giving Stegner reason to believe that Bruno killed that sick young man.

"Perhaps Detective Peters saw too much evil in Rottingham and decided to put him out of his misery," Stegner says to Cynthia over the radio.

McKindley writes up a report, and they start filing with the Director General of Québec City and District Attorney of North Shore to pursue Bruno.

"Please," says Oriel, "you have to understand . . . . I don't know how to create the Elixiumbrium myself. The man who invented it . . . he's . . . gone."

"I think he might be telling the truth," says Jerry.

"It's about time he does," says the Goose.

"Should I do away with them, him and the girl, I mean," says Jerry.

"Let them rot for all I care," says the Goose. They leave out of the chamber and into the hall. They pass Bile and Sybil. Sybil walks close behind to listen to what they say, while Bile stays put by the chamber door.

The Goose says, "If we can't get him to tell us how to make it, perhaps we can build a synthetic version . . . to attract the same type of gravitational wave."

"Brilliant," says Sybil. "We have to breach the surface for supplies. We can be back down here this evening to start . . . testing the process."

Bile waits until his sister and the other two turn a corner before he enters the chamber where Oriel is held. He doesn't even acknowledge the man chained to the wall, who shouts, "Stay away from her, you monster!"

"Silence," says Bile. He shocks the old man with a long cattle prod. His quivering hands reach for an IV bag, and he switches out the one that Emily has been feeding from.

"What . . . ? What are you doing here?" asks the feeble old man.

"I'm buying her some time," says Bile. He ensures the IV is dripping at a preferred rate before leaving the chamber and joining his sister.

Later that evening, out on the jagged cave floor, Jerry waits for the personal submersible elevator to return. His wet hair and sideburns cling to his face, still covered with some sand from his swim. Earlier, he had considerable trouble finding the entrance to the underwater cave on his own. The occupants of the "submerg-evator" seem to have had a safe trip. They came from the surface where they gathered the supplies needed to test the Elixiumbrium . . . on living tissue. They entered the Anything Goose Saloon to take the submerg-evator all the way down to the Goose's cavernous lair.

When the elevator dings and its doors begin to part ways, Jerry says, "Y'all are later than you said you would be."

"Old age has its quirks," says Bile.

"Not to mention," says Sybil, "being stuck on an elevator that took forever to dive. We would have been quicker putting our toes in the sand long enough for the currents to pull us to you." She kisses Jerry on the cheek at she passes by him.

"Hello," says Bile. "Don't expect anything . . . more."

Jerry lowers his hand from handshake height while he says, "I take it you know what this stuff is—"

"This stuff," interrupts Bile, "is our last evil deed before we . . . retire."

"Oh," says Jerry. "I thought you both were coming with us off this rock."

"My friend," says Bile, "I dream of nothing more than sandy beaches— even if the world ends while I'm on it—our contract is through— I'm retired after this."

"Well alright," says Jerry. "You can turn this place into an underwater nursing home for all I care." He looks at Sybil who waits with a nail file by the door out of the cave. "Although I wouldn't mind . . . getting to know you before I go." He opens the door and stands in the way so Sybil can't enter. He says, "Just a moment. I've got to check in with the Goose—I was on a swim before. I didn't have time to talk with our picky, picky, oh, so picky friend and financier."

"Wait," says Sybil to the man holding the heavy bomb-proof door with one arm. She wipes her hair along Jerry's muscular back and slicks it down to cover her left eye. "Now you can go."

"Oh-kay," says Jerry, "I'll be back for more of whatever that was, doll! I'll be back for more o' that . . . I can promise you." He leaves.

"What are you going to get his blood racing already for?"

asks Bile.

"I'm trying to keep climbing. Unlike you," says Sybil, "I don't quit . . . so easily."

"Suit yourself," says Bile as he fills the crevasse of the underground cave with smoke from his cigar.

The sibling team of Bile and Sybil Deville are soon busy at work filling out charts for each test tube of the synthetic formula they are making. Each test tube is ornately displayed in the round room with pristine white walls, and there is an elevated granite walking platform wide enough to get to each test tube that is labeled from 1 to 46. Bile says on his radio headset, "Let's begin. Send everyone in."

Bile turns away and fills out the rest of the chart while Sybil gleefully prepares her makeup in the reflection of metal behind the first sample of the formula. She applies a droplet of the blue, gooey substance . . . to the tip of a wooden tongue dispenser.

Jerry is accompanied by the ex-convict who was previously employed at the Staten Island Delicatessen. Together they bring a long line of prisoners into the round room where the formula is to be tested. The prisoners are chained to each other and blindfolded.

"Some of y'all gonna die," says Jerry. "That's unfortunate, because I'm the guy who has got to remove you from this here chain, which means our priorities must be off if we can afford to catch all of you but this is the system we have—"

"Let's get to testing," says the excitable Sybil with a ruby red smile that Jerry can't argue with.

"Building was pricey, mate," Bile softly says to Jerry.

"First contestant," says Jerry. "You are hereby removed of your duties going forward," he says to his helper from the deli shop.

"What?" asks the ex-convict just before Jerry clubs him. "We're cutting costs," says Jerry, and he opens up the guy's mouth.

"That's not how it works," says Sybil. She walks past Jerry and the unconscious guy he holds. He drops his body off the raised platform to be dealt with later if time permits.

"This place sure is cutting edge," Jerry says. He walks away from the line, and he cuts corners on his way, leaping into and out from the gutters along the pathway to find his place near the door.

Sybil says, "Good afternoon, and don't worry. You'll have the best care here under my watch." The prisoner actually looks relieved when Sybil unmasks him; he watches her lick her finger to tuck her red and grey hair back from being in her face. "These are being given at random though, so I can't promise you . . . won't get a strong dose." She holds the prisoner with one arm on his shoulder and puts the entire contents of the test tube in a syringe that she injects into the prisoner's pituitary gland. He resists the procedure, but afterward he stands there and looks fine.

He doesn't know what substance is coursing through his body and ripping apart his cells, of course. "The best way to test the magnetic circumference of our formula . . . human testing . . . ? What a sham," writes Bile in the log book.

<h1 style="text-align:center"><u>Chapter Thirteen</u></h1>

<h2 style="text-align:center">A Proposal, a Love-Letter, and a Curse</h2>

THEY spent some time talking to Lucinda-Lee to gather information on the strange sight she saw in the skies. When she got home, Aunt Mitzy was eating spaghetti at the dining room table with none-other-than Bruno himself. He winked at the young woman before he said, "Well, like I told you. There she is. If you folks need anything, don't hesitate to call."

Moments later Lucinda-Lee took her aunt aside to explain to her what confusion she is experiencing seeing the man who helped free her but was left by her captor.

Mitzy says, "He told me he was there and that you were being . . . cleaned up before being sent back to me."

Lucinda-Lee takes her aunt aside to say, "I'm not so sure which side he's on."

"What do you mean . . . ? He seems trustworthy," says her aunt, and she hugs the young woman tightly. "Well, I'm just glad

229

you're back safe, sweetie," says Mitzy. "I've told the man all he wanted to know. He just stayed around because I was fixing something to eat, and we all need to eat." When she returns to her house guest, Bruno is no longer present.

In the car, Bruno takes off his jacket and exposes his bloody arm, which he wraps with some duct tape he keeps in a tool bin behind the passenger seat. He doesn't have any trouble catching up to the sedan Theo drives. He cuts them off on the highway.

When they pull over with Bruno ahead, he turns his car sideways to say to them, "I've talked to the guys in charge. They have . . . Joslin. Not like you care . . . anymore."

Cary nods and stays quiet.

"We can fix this, I swear," says Bruno with desperation in his voice.

Theo backs the car up and off the road when he sees another car coming from behind. The car coming up beeps their horn loudly, but Bruno doesn't move his vehicle. "Listen," says Bruno, "the guys who want me to get you just want to get to that balloon—"

"They're after the crystal?" asks Cynthia. "Hush, babe," says Theo.

"That's right," says Bruno. "Good girl. It looks like you're brighter than you make yourself out to be . . . . The crystals—plural. We get those things and hand them over, the Goose promises to let your father and . . . Emily go."

"You son of a bitch," says Cary. "I'll kill you myself." Theo leaps across the seat to hold Cary inside, and Cynthia restrains his arms.

"Drive the car, Theodore," she says. "Got it, babe," says Theo and he returns to the wheel.

Bruno shouts, "The Goose doesn't care if you live or die, or if your daughter and dad live either! It turns out your father doesn't know how to make the formula because he stole it—so finding your son and what he's got on that balloon— That's all I care about . . . ."

Back in the Anything Goose Saloon, Jerry informs the Goose about the progress Bruno is making: "We have eyewitness accounts of the direction the crystals are heading, Goose."

"Great, but I'll need more than what's on that balloon anyway," says Gino.

"It's a general direction, sir," says Jerry.

"Good. Our operation in the lab is going swimmingly well. Do you suppose?" asks the Goose.

"Well, yes," says Jerry, "I suppose it is going well."

"Swimmingly?" asks the Goose.

"Why, yes," says Jerry. "I suppose it's going swimmingly well."

They share a hearty laugh, banging on the table between them, and their drinks falls from it eventually. When it gets too out of control, they quit laughing to catch their breaths and the usual banter in the saloon resumes.

"They're developing the synthetic formula to get us off this rock," says the Goose. "Hopefully before the world . . . ends. But if there's a chance to find the actual, organic crystals—that's a chance to make a fortune before we get off this planet."

The Goose goes with Jerry into a back room of the bar where they are joined by the sibling team from the lab. The Goose says, "We shall all march in that . . . general direction—and you and I, and what we have here will be the ones to walk away."

Sybil smiles, and she pulls her brother, Bruno, in to meet the Goose and Jerry near the center or the room. The four of them hold hands and look up through the needle point of the top of their rocket ship that is cleverly disguised as part of the bar. A blue cloudless sky reflects upon the glass nose of the ship.

"My proposition to you kind people," Bruno says as he makes eyes at Cynthia, "is to join forces before I bring in some terrible people to help me . . . take you down."

"Where did you find us—And how?" asks Theo.

"I'll be staying in the room next to y'all," says Bruno, "so try not to talk too loud."

On the car ride back to the motel, Cary is blaming himself for getting Theo and Valentico involved. "I just want my family back, and now we can't go back to our rooms with this guy on our tail like this. It's not safe for either of you," says Cary.

"No," says Theo. "Stop running. You're innocent—"

Beside Theo, in the middle of the seat, Adeline sits, and she turns to Cary and says, "Face your fear." She whistles loudly with her ringers in between her lips. This absolutely terrifies Cary. At the moment when the whistling is at its loudest, Cynthia interrupts to say, "Face your fear, Cary. Cary?"

There are a few minutes of silence while they drive down the highway. Finally, Cary breaks the silence when he says, "We need something . . . he can't resist." He starts writing on his legal pad.

Later on at the place where they're staying, Cynthia is dressed in black, sneaking around at night. She knocks loudly on the door of Room 173. When the man inside looks out, she kisses the paper she is holding before leaving it and backing away into the shadows.

Bruno reaches the door and finds a note that says,

Watch out. They're onto you. Take one last look at the train yard.
XO, Cynthia
—P.S. I promise you'll find . . . what you're looking for

"Oh! What a racket next door," calls the nosy neighbor who normally would have went to bed hours ago; still, they spy out of their blinds before returning to bed. What they don't see is that someone from a long way away has landed next door, on the roof of Perry Finster's home. The gutters are overgrown with weeds towering out of them, so much so that they will likely fall from their own weight before Perry Finster takes care of them. "It was only a matter of time," thinks Finster's neighbor, fearing the neighborhood children would do harm to the gutters soon enough.

Historically, children didn't have much respect for Perry Finster of 1001 Walliwick Avenue, where Pygmy People of North Shore live and thrive. But oh, how the children laugh as they nearly knock Perry Finster down when they often run past him! Why, one day, a bigger child was running ahead of the others, and he kicked a ball he was dribbling. It went up high enough for the child to juggle with his knees and feet. Well, the ball made an arch right near the archway of Perry's garden, so Perry made a comment about it, and soon enough the children have consistently been running through Perry's door-less garage and into his home with their mud-covered feet and no manners.

The neighbor is Sally Crawford and her husband is Jimmy Crawford, who is in charge of the village stables. They agreed to watch over Perry's home whenever he leaves for work trips, ever since they moved in last spring. They felt obligated because of the work Perry does for the village as the only spiritual object surveyor of the Pygmy Village of North Shore.

Perry Finster received his training, for the prestigious position, at the Pygmy Academy for Curse Relinquishment; he hadn't had any problem working his way through the ranks of plenty of humble candidates that still vied to uphold the sanctuary that separates North Shore from what exists even farther north. For Perry Finster, the process to get the position was simple because he understood the chain of events. All trash from the rest of North Shore goes to a waste deposit facility where gnomes go through it. Gnomes are not to be confused with pygmy people, mind you; making such a mistake is risky, and like the nursery rhyme declares, ". . . it might cost you the skin on the front of your meatier shin!"

The first gnome puts the garbage from North Shore on a processing belt, the next gnome sorts the trash, the next one has the difficult job of labeling each article with the owner's name, and the rest of it is a matter of spiritual belief. The gnomes don't mind helping find and sort the garbage; in fact, they rather like the putrid smell it gives their clothes and hair. The gnomes pass the labeled and sorted mess off to one pygmy, a rather small creature compared to a gnome.

Both races believe that people who die get reunited with their old junk in the *after-life*. So all the old possessions are preserved the way a curator would take precautions with a rare piece of art, for they believe . . . they're preserving and storing things for souls to use. Of course, sensible souls make purchase and use sensible things in *before-life*, like picture frames with memories, important notes, prom dresses or tuxedos, and stuffed animals that are cared for like livestock. Everything is preserved in a proper climate controlled vault that is waterproof and ventilated. Insensible souls, on the other hand, get things like keychains and old plastic baskets when they are alive, so that's what goes in their vaults.

Some of the objects are believed to carry curses. And, of course, there is one particular pygmy in charge of linking cursed objects to the events that cursed the object, and the Pygmy Village of North Shore chose Perry Finster as the one to uphold this role.

Perry isn't home for long before his mother pesters him about getting the hedges blessed; much like the weeds in the gutters, they have been overgrown for some time now. "Everybody in town knows you do so much to keep the balance around here," says Mother Finster. "Certainly, if ask you around, somebody will take care of the hedges, Perry. They're attracting so much dust they could really use the extra attention." The Pygmy People of North Shore believe dust is akin to negative energy.

"Yes, mother," says Perry with no intention of following through. He starts packing for his next assignment post haste.

"You're leaving already? But you've just arrived," says his mother.

"Yes, but my job is never finished."

When he gets upstairs he has a clear view of his rooftop garden where Henry Edwards and his balloon are still there. The attentive youth is not easily found out—Henry Edwards ducks behind a branch of a tree that is growing from the side of the house.

The lead on the balloon came as news from Lucinda-Lee and Aunt Mitzy. Although, the information was first told to friends and family and to a live television audience. After the horrible kidnapping was over, Lucinda recalled the scene only once more. She told Cynthia, Theo, and Cary in the sedan before they dropped her off to her aunt. Meanwhile, Aunt Mitzy told the same story as she remembered . . . to Bruno.

"I was at my home in North Shore when Lucy arrived," said Mitzy to Bruno over dinner.

"Try to remember," Cynthia instructed Lucinda-Lee in the sedan.
        "Well, it was raining that day, so my grocery bag cut out at the bottom," said Lucinda-Lee. "It fell apart when I got to the curb." She remembered her foot in red flats was nearly smashed by a can of tomatoes.

"I didn't see it at first," said Mitzy.
        "But then?" inquired Bruno.
        "I saw it . . . when my niece wouldn't stop staring up at the sky," remembered Mitzy.

"I can't remember the direction," said Lucinda-Lee. "It was over the trees, and that's where the train station is, so it must have been farther away . . . because it looked smaller than . . . a train car."
        "Farther north than North Shore?" asked Cary.
        "Yes," said Lucinda-Lee. "Before . . . the Tranquility Seas."
        Cary stirred when he said, "Past the land of refuse."
        "Yes," said Lucinda-Lee.
        "Even past the dumps and heaps of trash," replied Cynthia.
        "Nothing can live out there," said Inspector Cary Oriel. "The air is putrid, the soils are petrified, and the ocean is sure to be

contaminated with toxic waste."

They dropped Lucinda-Lee off to her aunt. Cary did what he could to quit fearing what might happen to any of his children on the balloon if they were to find themselves in such terrible conditions: "How do you suggest we make our way there?" asked Cary.

When they moved in six months back, the Crawfords agreed to watch over Perry Finster's home, but they recently decided it is too much responsibility to handle, since the rickety house looked like it would collapse at any moment.

Last week, Sally Crawford came to the door when she spied Perry Finster leaving his home. She pried open her door and said, "Mr. Finster, will you be home at all this week either?"

"I can't predict at all," says Finster. "I'm off to the city across the sea, so I will likely not return at all for a week at least." His furry brows twitched, and he said, "I shall send a message to your residence when I settle."

"Thank you, Mr. Finster," said Sally Crawford who stood out on her wooden deck. Her skin glowed that afternoon from being in the sun for once. "We approve of your lifestyle—you . . . bring pride to our land . . . . But I can't go on keeping your place safe. We've another on the way." At that moment her children just so happened to pass by on the deck and went inside.

"Well, can you believe that?" asked Finister righteously. "And you have room for a nursery in there? Do ye'?" He quickly examined Sally Crawford's home, which was much smaller yet sturdier than his own home.

"We do. We have den space to use," said Sally Crawford.

"Well," said Finster, and he made a final deliberation: "You know . . . you can use my den all you'd like."

"Mr. Finster!" exclaimed Sally Crawford with shock. She knew not whether to be appalled or appreciative of the offer.

"I have to go Sally," said Finster. "I'll send something your way when I settle."

"Safe travels to you, Mr. Finster."

Before going back indoors, Sally marveled at the splendor of the downhill slopes of wilderness on which her home sat. Near the joists that support her house's east facing wall, just before Mr. Finster's property starts with its hedges and shrubs, is a variety of flowers the like of a meadow; the spectrum of pedals and stems have surprisingly survived the crashing footsteps of neighborhood children.

For a whole week until he returned from his crusade, Mr. Finster worried to himself that Mrs. Crawford would talk with Mr. Crawford when he got home from the stables. Perry feared that, by the time he returned to the village from his crusade, Jimmy Crawford would be as easy to talk with as a gnome on vacation.

One week later, when Henry Edwards landed on the roof of Perry Finster's home he hadn't concerns of nosy neighbors, strange spiritual works of pygmies, or even the slightest concern over the safety of his belongings on the balloon or himself. He was thinking about his dear, sweet, listless mother. Like Perry Finster, the young boy wished there was a way to ensure that someone was watching after his mother when he was away.

Finster doesn't realize how fortunate he is to have his mother around in his life. Perry Finster thinks to himself, "If it wasn't bad enough being berated by mother about landscaping activities (activities that someone my age and position doesn't have energy for), I'm only home for an hour before a telegram comes in to get back to work!" Apparently, something on the surface is erupting; the message Perry Finster receives has a long list of names of individuals that are being investigated for crimes against all people of North Shore, but Finster thinks the perpetrator is likely of gnome origin, not pygmy, since there are so many . . . numbers in the message. "It seems urgent," Finster thinks, "since pygmy people of North Shore don't use numbers unless it is extremely urgent."

Perry Finster takes a stride around his home to gather what he'll need in his magical pursuits. He picks up his magnifying glass with a thick lens, twice the thickness that Perry's little fingers are round. He does this preparation while humming the song he heard playing from the windows of the Gathering Stone, the local pub; it is a song he heard on his long stroll home. He needed rest after the hours he put in *spooning* out summoned spirits and after all the strolling he did, of course. However tired he does feel already, he summons up enough courage, and he decides to forgo rest today. For, he remembers how wildly important this message does seem.

So he hums to calm himself. He hums and sings:
"Will it be-a daffodil?
What about-a pearl?
I coulda sworn it wasn't pretty,
but I gave it to-a girl!"
With his leather satchel buckled, he walks out of his home, slamming the door closed. He thinks how the wrought iron knocker needs a fresh coat of paint as it bangs loudly on the door. '*Ba-do-gong!*'
There's no time for his mother and no time for the Crawfords. He waves goodbye to both houses to cover any concerns that might be brewing over his swift departure without explanation.

When Perry gets to work, he has this conversation:
"You know how much I love blueberry," says Perry Finster to his assistant.
"No," replies the assistant.
"If you made me three-hundred and sixty-five blueberry pies for my birthday party, I would never need to make food again for the entire year," says Perry.
The assistant, a jovial, young pygmy woman, smiles and says, "You know blueberry pies don't last forever. Too bad you don't have a freezer."
Perry Finster is confused and says, "A *what*?"
The assistant looks up from the specimen they are working on, and she says, "A freezer. So you could freeze them pies for late-ah—"
The specimen is not cooperating with the summoning; it glows and vibrates. It hisses and spurts out a gooey brown foam. Perry says, "Just when I thought we had everything. Could we get

one hooked up?" The assistant coerces the specimen, and it settles down while Perry Finster uses a potion to heal it. The assistant says, "You don't have electricity though."

Perry finishes releasing the spirit they summoned, and the specimen is taken back to the gnomes for re-sorting and labeling. Finster says, "No. I don't have electricity, I suppose. But I have all the energy . . . known to the universe." He furrows his brow until the assistant says, "What do you mean? Where do you have all the energy . . . ?"

"At home in bed," says Perry Finster.

The shine on the blue Elixiumbrium causes Henry Edwards to stop looking at his map, as he attempts to chart his next day of flying. He drops the map to the ground. He stoops down to find a sandbag filled with all sorts of tools. He removes one bag from its tightly drawn rope, he selects a measuring rod, and he takes the measuring device to the back of one of the crystals that is affixed to the basket.

He pushes the narrow tool behind the crystal. He actually speaks to it; he says, "You're the reason my family is gone. I don't care if you do save the planet! You'll give me a home but take from me . . . all that I love." He leaves the rare crystals there on the rooftop.

At times, Pygmy People must enter society in ways in which they can remain hidden. This is not much of a challenge for the pygmies, for they are masters of disguise. For example, they masquerade as statues or inanimate objects; plenty of pygmies have went around as jack-o-lanterns during harvest seasons. Even if the pumpkin is tossed by a peer-pressured teen, the shell always seems to protect the pygmy inside.

Staying hidden when they want has never been a problem for a pygmy, but recent advances in technology have aided their quests to find the best camouflage. "What's wrong with my eyes, mamma? I thought I saw a man but it's nothing," called the oldest Crawford child, Mary Crawford, when she first saw one of the newer ways to hide. Her mother replied, "Yes. That was Mr. Finster—You have great vision, dear."

When Finster must go out of the village, he wears a cybernetic neoprene suit that allows for him to hide under any condition. In the rare chance that a person does see Finster, all the pygmy needs to do is sprinkle some of his magic dust he carries around, for dusting causes people to slip into a deep, dream-filled sleep. The entire encounter is unlike the usual dusting of furniture or bookshelves with rags and spray, but humans don't seem to remember it any differently.

The children from the Crawford clan that live next door to Perry Finster's house learned over time how to spot Mr. Finster well. They acquired the very same cybernetic suits to enter his home when he is away. Typically, the children would rearrange the house to drive Finster's mother crazy to the point of exhaustion. They would meddle, until she started cursing and saying, "This house needs to be cleaned free of spirits. It's those plants in the gutters! Curses!" But the Crawford children have been leaving the old woman alone since they noticed that Perry Finster was too busy to care.

The Crawford children take after their mother when it comes to the vastness of their attention to details. Not only do they know Henry Edwards and his balloon are parked on Finster's roof, but they notice the crystals he leaves behind when he goes.

When the Crawford children go to talk to the boy and ask what he is doing on Finster's roof, the balloon takes off into the sky again. The children agree to take the crystals to their parents, where Sally Crawford scolds them for being on Finster's roof. She says, "Now, you're going to have to explain to Mr. Finster. And we're going to have to watch his home and his mother. That's certain."

A hard-working pygmy like Perry Finster doesn't know how to control himself when he finds something as strange as the Elixiumbrium Crystals. Even with the camouflage suit on, he doesn't get halfway down his street before the neighborhood children spot him. They discover him like a pack of wolves on a hunt for food. They would typically tease him and trip him while using their own camouflage suits to hide on the street and around corners. But instead of trying to foul up his days, the children come to him for help:

"There was a problem on your roof," says Mary Crawford.

"Oh! I hope mother isn't getting exposed to the elements. I know she is a little moldy but you didn't have to worry me like that, child. It's not yet raining," says Perry Finster.

"No," says the child, "we found something on your roof."

"You were on my roof, were you," says Finster. "At it again, you were. And at it on my roof, I bet, and at an instant. Well, what did ye' find?"

"You have to see it yourself," says Mary Crawford.

Of course, Sally Crawford is there peeping out between the shutters from the window above her front deck. When Finster goes to his roof with the children, Sally Crawford even goes to watch from her bedroom window on the second story. She pokes her head out of the window when Finster is climbing up his stairs and out onto the roof from his own window. She finally says, "Those glowing things have been worrying us ever so badly."

Perry Finster takes into his hands the shattered pieces of the Elixiumbrium that were left by Henry Edwards. Sally asks, "What can you do about that, Mr. Finster?"

"The only thing to do, Miss Crawford," says Perry, "is to return this substance from whence it came." Without further consideration Perry Finster puts the Elixiumbrium into his satchel. He makes a quick dash in through the window, leaving the children on his roof. He gathers what he needs from his home before kissing his mother goodbye.

He skips to work because skipping is faster, for tiny legs at least.

And he sings:
"Oh my, oh my!
    Well, I wake and I die,
  But somewhere between
    I'll take a break
    And take to what you've seen!"
He makes one stop at a tavern on the way to his work . . . . to process the crystals.

At a train yard, north of Lucinda-Lee's home in North Shore,

Detective Bruno Peters reads over the note Dr. Cynthia Valentico left for him. He indulges himself; his fantasy makes him feel alright enough to do what he needs to do. "I'll turn Cary over and give it all up, and move in with this broad to try a new city," he thinks to himself. He thinks he's outgrown one of the largest cities in the world, as he passionately stares at the red smear of lipstick Cynthia left on the note and believes it will all be okay.

"You never could resist falling for a pretty woman, even your sister, I bet—" says Cary a few yards ahead. He comes from behind a loading platform that only a train-hopper could have discovered.

"You're referring to the girl I saved from being filleted alive," says Bruno.

"I bet you were shocked when she pulled the gun on you," says Cary. "They're good people, and we're working with law enforcement here to do the right thing. They believe I didn't do it. Now, Bruno, it's your turn. Come join us."

"If I wasn't already expecting this, I'd be offended," says Bruno. He rolls up his sleeves. "But I think I still have the upper hand."

Cary takes out the blue karambit. The blade sweeps open with gravity assisting, and Cary uses that same momentum to toss the karambit and catches it with his already jabbing right palm. He brings the knife along the jabbing motion. The blade pierces the air like the claw of a tiger rips through flesh when it strikes its prey.

Bruno touches his sidearm and says, "I was thinking I'd lay down the law with my hands on you again, man. But look what you're packing. What is that?" He takes his revolver off the strap on his chest.

"They used your sister," says Cary. "They used her . . . to get closer to me and my family and what we have, but I don't have the answers."

Bruno Peters stands in between Cary and an approaching train car. They're on the train tracks and the train coming their way is honking and slamming on its brakes.

Bruno shouts over the noise: "There's nothing left for you, Cary. We already have your father . . . . And I thought kicking the piss out of you once would be enough, but you know, it's a—there's a hierarchy—" But before he can finish his sentence Cary tackles him to the ground, and the two men tussle in the middle of the track.

Cary chokes Bruno with an arm pressing on his throat, but they have to move apart just before the train gets there. It comes in with its brakes pressing hard to get to a stop between them. As Cary catches his breath, Bruno shouts, "See this through to the end because if not, they might hurt her . . . ." Even though they only catch glimpses of each other on opposing sides of the track, Bruno can tell Cary isn't backing down; he's standing and waiting to attack Bruno.

On the other side of the train Cary shouts, "No! They used her once, and they'll use her again . . . . Show him. Where's the file?" Theo appears; he stands behind Bruno so he hasn't any room to move back, and he passes a file to Bruno.

"Oh you're here," says Bruno. "What a surprise."

"You'd better quit talking and listen up," says Theo. "My patience for you is dwindling."

Bruno does as he is instructed. He opens the file and removes the pictures of Sybil and Bile from inside."These two," says Cary. "They abducted my family. Brother and sister, they are. They came up to me when dad took—the . . . invention to the public. Little did I know they're working for the same man who turned you against me."

Bruno says nothing.

"So you're going to rub out my family's entire existence," says Cary. "Is that what you're trying to do?" The train is nearly stopped between them. Cary jumps on the car that slows down before him.

"I'm . . . not," says Bruno. "I'm going to end it here today." The train has a few more feet to go before its stop is complete. Bruno releases the file. Theodore grabs it on its way to the ground, and he can tell why Cynthia felt like sticking around Bruno to help him before, for he's a man . . . on the edge of existing. Bruno kneels on the crushed gravel, next to where Theo stooped to grab the file folder. Bruno places his head on the rail while saying, "Leave the rest up to fate, I guess—"

He hits his head on the wheel before Theo is able to rip him away from the train. There is blood on the tracks that causes Cary to slip as he finishes climbing between the two cars.

As they figure out what to do with Bruno, Cary's mind slips into thinking for a slit second about the old wine-o. He hopes he's somewhere sipping his homemade cabernet, but he feels the scraggly old ramble is perhaps feeling a bit lonely on his own.

"What on Earth happened to him?" asks Cynthia when she sees the man her husband is lifting through the living room is badly wounded.

Cary tries to explain, "He just bumped his head on a rail—"

"—ing. On a railing," Theo says and puts the broken man down. "Remember what Alan did when we brought him home from the hospital. He'll have a big ol' knot on top just like our boy did when he started out. And Alan seems like he's doing alright, right?"

"Dear, as much as I wish we were with our son at home," says Cynthia, "making this hotel room feel like a nursery is not going to make it any cozier. Your job was to stay with Cary for backup when Cary went to the train yard. He's the bait, and you're the brawn. But at no point in time were you supposed to let this man get run over by a rail car." She feels compelled to assemble a stack of linens and towels for their bleeding guest.

They leave Bruno tied up, on the couch, in front of a webcam. Dr. Valentico is at the monitor in the other room while Theo and Cary prepare to go off to search farther out than North Shore, near the sea . . . in the land of the pygmies.

But first Theo has time alone with Bruno: "We could flip you back around to the police if you don't cooperate," Theo says clicking a pair of clear plastic salad tongs around in his hand with the skill of a Japanese Hibachi Chef. He pinches Bruno on the cheek with the tongs and says, "Think about your options, alright?"

When Theo joins Cynthia in the next room over she tells him, "Please don't leave me with him again. I don't feel safe— Besides, they're looking for Bruno all over this place, since he's wanted . . . . Cops over in North Shore have probably already called in every station on both sides of the Canadian Border."

"He's scared," says Theo. "He tried . . . to end his life."

"Do you think you'll find the boy?" asks Cynthia.

"I don't know," says Theo.

"Do you think he has the crystals they're after?" asks the irritated doctor.

"I don't know that, either," says Theo.

"What about the rest of Cary's family?" asks Cynthia. Cary passes by the window that opens out to the parking lot. He waits near the sedan. "Do you think they're safe someplace?"

Theo takes a moment to look into his wife's eyes. He moves his hand along her hair, and she begins fixing it into a bun. He says, "Once again . . . . I don't know." He lets her hair go, and it floats down to her shoulders in springy formation. He kisses the top of her head.

"Well," says Cynthia. She looks in the monitor at Bruno. "Are those ropes tight?"

"Of that, I am certain," says Theo.

Bruno doesn't stir. He sleeps with ice on his bruised and bashed head. When he moves in his sleep some of the ice cubes crumble to the floor.

"You fly that thing well, son," Cary says to Henry Edwards who is waking from his slumber beneath a tent made of his balloon.

Cary hugs his son and tries to focus on the positive gain in finding his son. But the lack of his daughter's presence frightens him— He says, "Emily—she was with you?"

Henry Edwards shakes his head and says, "No. And grandpa isn't either."

They take the balloon up under the boy's supervision, but Cary does take over at one point. Theo watches the pygmy village from above, and he thinks about places where the young girl and her grandfather could be held. Theo says, "We're going inland. Let's take a trip out to sea. Shall we?"

Before they continue searching, Theo and Cary take Henry Edwards somewhere he'll be safe. "Your son will be safe here, as long as our boy is here. You'll have to trust me," says Theo.

"You think we'll find where the Goose has my family on the ocean?" asks Cary.

"I do," says Theo, "but I don't know where to start looking. But I bet we know someone who could give us . . . a good idea of where to start." And they return in the sedan to the inn to pressure Bruno for a lead on the Goose's hideout.

When Stegner finds out where they're staying, he has a few detectives join him on a stakeout of the inn. The police watch in order to get an idea of what Bruno is holding up with or if he has a hostage of his own before they are able to rush in. It is their protocol to proceed quickly and diligently to apprehend Detective Bruno Peters when they gain they information they need.

"Yo," says Bruno to Theo, "you got to keep that skank out of here. That flirting, conniving skank . . . . Ain't nothing good about her. Ain't nothing good about a woman like that. Like her."

"Careful what you say," says Theo. "She's the only thing keeping me from roughing you up beyond recognition now."

"I didn't know she'd lay down with someone beneath her station in life," says Bruno, but Theo tries not to react. He keeps busy to himself, figuring out a way to get information out of Bruno before Stegner arrives to take him away. Even with ropes around his limbs and a gash on his arm, Bruno persists, saying, "I said, I'm better than you, pal—"

Cynthia rushes in to say, "No. You're not." She could take no more of hearing the mad Never York City detective bash her Theodore. She says, "Your whore of a sister is the least of our concerns. I hope the Goose is sleeping with her too."

"Oh," says Bruno, "look who showed up to talk to me—"

"I told you I can handle it—" says Theo. "He'd say anything to get out of those ropes—he's going to tell us everything he knows—"

"Why should I?" asks Bruno.

"Because it'll keep us all safe to have whatever crystal got stolen returned to the scientists who have some clue how to use it," says Theo. "And there won't be a sister for you to keep safe, and there won't be a couch for you to lie on . . . as I make you scream until you give us the location of the Goose's hideout." Theo adjusts an iron fire poker in the fireplace. "If we don't get to the Elixiumbrium soon, hell, none of this will matter when we're all dead." The fire poker is warmed up enough and Theo takes it out. He says, "Are you ready to talk?"

Theo puts on the glove and takes the red hot poker. His work glove is burning and melting because of how extreme the temperature of the poker is. When it gets to Bruno's hairline, he can smell it burning at the ends. Bruno shouts, "Okay!" When Theo backs away Bruno says, "Hey, while us fellas talk, can she put on something a little skimpier and write me another love letter?"

"Shut up!" yells Cynthia, and she storms off through the door to go outside to get some fresh air.

Cary comes in when she leaves to say, "Actually, I wrote it. I just remembered all the times that Joslin . . . told me she loved me. All those times I thought she cared."

Bruno says, "She must have. Once upon, when you were first together. She loses interest easily . . . Men are like projects. To her . . . it's like the people flipping houses. She thinks she makes guys better and . . . lets them go."

The old innkeeper thinks he solved all his problems when he discovers a hidden melody of life, a way to acquire all the gold in the world. He thinks he knows exactly how to speak to every guest in way that will coerce them to spend the most money they could possibly afford. To help with his pursuit he mixed up the prices with affiliate travel agencies, and he posts a sign on the front desk that reads, "If you do not know, ask for our special rates." The game is set, and he waits for a sucker to arrive, like a spider watches the web.

He greets a guest that had trouble sleeping the night before: "Excuse me, your teeth look yellow. Do you need some free floss with your stay?"

"I'll have *you bought*!" yells the irritated guest. "I'll have you!"

"What?" asks the innkeeper.

"Is this a place you call work?" asks the guest. "Is this a place you own that I may purchase in order to ruin your life in this town, or is this place your employer that I may buy out to ruin you like a seagull drops from thin air above?"

"Excuse me," says the innkeeper. "I was only offering you floss at no extra charge as a way to say thank you for staying here."

"Oh, okay," says the guest. "Because if you were talking about my teeth, I would take you out," says the guest who happens to be a dentist on holiday. "I'll use my hands, and your eyes will watch as I make off with everything you have and hold dear. I'll watch you sleep in your own bed. And when the lids of your eyes open to see, it won't be me. I'll be gone . . . before the cops get to see why I'm in town. But I'll leave you with something . . . . Something pretty drilled into the teeth I let you hold onto." The dentist moves quickly toward the innkeeper to give the old chap a real jolt, and he says, "Stop looking so closely," before taking his bag and leaving the inn.

Cary passes the dentist on his way to the desk. He decides to get another room for himself. It was a long trip on the balloon with Henry Edwards; he found a safe place for the boy to hold up while Cary keeps searching for the others. And Theo talked the whole way back to the inn about taking up the queen bed. It was either get a new room or sleep in the same room with Bruno, so Cary makes his way to the front desk with his clipboard in his jacket, tucked under one arm. He leaves his other belongings outside on the bench near the door of the old inn that hasn't been updated since the decade before at best.

"I'm a health inspector in another country," Cary tells the old innkeeper. The innkeeper holds out his hand to shake Cary's like most proud business owners will do when greeting a professional in Cary's industry. After all, Cary could seriously hurt or help the innkeeper with the right review. But Cary says, "I'm not here to rate your establishment, actually." Cary hands the man his fake passport for Frank Greenburoughs and he doesn't suspect a thing.

"I'm conducting a seminar tour for my training classes," lies Cary. "I put up the seminars for entrepreneurs around the world, and I would like a room tonight, and perhaps, another room for everyone teaching at my seminar if I'm happy with the place."

He has a business spirit, the innkeeper does. He smiles and hands Cary a metallic-blue business card and gives instructions to call him anytime. He checks Cary in before giving a quick tour of the old inn.

Finally, Cary is alone in his room, but he is not please with the state of affairs he is witnessing. If he had been inspecting the inn or even traveling for pleasure, he would write reports to the right people to make sure the doors remain closed until repairs are made on the sink cabinetry growing mold, floorboards missing, and door with neither lock nor handle.

He hopes to get some peace and quiet in his room alone, enough to think about his daughter. He think about how the police captain with the ice skate leaving son and the Swedish woman brought him closer to the couple that helped him find his boy. He wonders . . . if they can find the rest of his family.

Inspector Cary Oriel takes time to think of some person to get in touch with about the crooked cops and the possibility of their involvement in the heinous crimes committed towards his family and whatever happened at that gyro restaurant he was once investigating. He remembers how the place was serving tainted meat to its customers. He knows a congressman to help with the case, one that represents his district. He thinks it is a good time to send word to their office in Washington, D.C. via the post office.

He feels that he can trust the strange couple, the ex-cop and the doctor. For some reason, he feels they are on the level, much like Stegner. He thinks about the spirits contacting him and his wife appearing, and it all seems to be less than coincidental. He breathes deeply and wishes for Adeline to be there with him. "Even if you are still asleep. I'll love you," he says.

Inspector Cary Oriel tries not to worry any longer about trusting the faceless politician whom he has never met; this congressman had helped with a few benchmark cases in the past, Cary recalls, but he doesn't know for certain if the politician will come to his side. Therefore, he has trouble giving too much information in his letter about who he is or where he's located.

He finds the address for Congressman Bob Schnyder when there comes a knock on the door. He walks over to see who is there, but nobody is present. After all the appearances of his wife, he feels uncertain whether or not he has even been hearing things correctly. He doesn't like the door not having a lock on it, so to feel safe he tries another strategy of protecting himself.

Cary spins around, looking for something to barricade the door. He spins and turns and finally comes upon a set of chairs that he thinks are perfect to place in front of the door, which he thinks leads out of the room and into the inn's parking lot. He brings the chairs over one-by-one, and he places them in front of the door next to what he assumes to be the closet. "Certainly, the closet needs repair also," thinks Cary. But he plans to see those conditions later. For now, he must find peace.

He piles sheets and blankets from the bed on top of the chairs, and he moves the mattress itself over in front of the chairs.

"That should do it," says Cary to himself.

When he takes off his hat and coat, he reaches into what he thinks is a closet for a coat hanger for his jacket to wear, but when he opens what he mistakes for the closet door, he finds instead that it isn't a closet but a door to the outside.

"Your bag," says the innkeeper, who is standing just outside Cary's room. Cary feels some need to explain his puzzled expression to the old man: "I thought you were in my closet for a moment. Give me time to remove the barricade from the door."

The innkeeper is certainly at a loss for explanation and acts grateful to gain some degree of understanding. He says, "May I look around the room actually? A guest stayed here last week and is looking for her earring."

Cary puts an arm across the doorway to guard its threshold, and after placing his belongings inside, he closes the door with the innkeeper still present.

"Very well," says the innkeeper in his native language that is a similar sound to the language spoken by people living in

Turkey, but it's a cross-dialect between that and something less recognizable.

The inspector moves the mattress into the corner where he hopes it will easily block off entering either of the outside doors. And having hung his hat and jacket on one of the chairs, like a proper gentleman, he sits. He unties his shoes and casually tosses them into the center of the room.

The innkeeper finds himself in his office alone, and he is sweating. He tears at his phone book and dials the number he was given. The old man says, "Hello," and he waits. "Yes," he says. And he waits. "The guy tried to use a fake passport, but I know it's your guy." He waits to hear instructions on the other end of the phone. "Sure," says the innkeeper, "I'll do anything for the right price."

When he finally has some spare time, Inspector Cary Oriel writes a letter to describe and make record of the issues he feels need attention.

It's a letter that Legislative Correspondent John Framingham will get the next morning in his office. He'll open Cary's letter soliciting John's concerns. But John won't be in the right frame of mind to work that day; he's been on the fence about whether or not to go through with signing the divorce papers he was served, so he will barely be able to concentrate on the inspector's letter, despite its clear and concise manner. He'll politely ask for some assistance in the matter by turning to his officemate.

An eager woman will come to his aide to read the letter. Felicity Malgrove has had some experience dealing with health inspectors already, seeing as she once managed public relations for one of the largest meat & seafood packing facilities in the District. Now, she works as a Legislative Correspondent for Congressman Bill Schneider, a politician who treads the line of corruption. She'll finish her task of penning a letter in reply to a public school teacher, who is asking for help finding money for new textbooks for an accelerated afterschool program for children interested in business entrepreneurship. Indeed, the letter Felicity Malgrove will write to the teacher will be promising.

After she writes her letter, a cup of coffee will help Felicity switch her mental delineation to the inspector's letter:

Dear Congressman Schneider,

This letter comes to you from a location I cannot disclose at this time, but I am working with the local police here to bring this course of recommended action to your attention. Prior to inspecting the premises of a particular gyro vendor, whose address I will disclose, I had received reports from customers and critics complaining about tainted meats in the chicken kiev.
Upon investigation, I uncovered a storm of aggressions that put me in my current state.

Please advise and send correspondence to my PO Box to be routed to me.

Yours truly,
Inspector O.

252

Chapter Fourteen

The Creation of the Brood, and Oriel's Ocean-Tale Resolved

EMILY ORIEL starts to wake. The drip from the bag of fluids Bile hooked to her is a saline drip that hydrated the girl without doping her up the way the Goose had ordered in the past. The old man, Oriel, chained to the wall in the chamber under the sea, notices the girl stirring. He speaks to her: "Emily, are you awake? Can you hear me, sweetheart?" She stirs but doesn't move. He goes on to say: "It's alright, dear. Just relax. We're going . . . to get out of here."

She stirs and makes a little, sad moan that frightens Oriel terribly. He calls to his granddaughter, "Em . . . ? Hey Em . . . ? Emily!" She only stirs a little.

Suddenly she speaks in a low voice: "Grandpa, is that you?"

"Yes, sweetheart," says Oriel.

253

"Can you... tell me a story?" asks Emily.

"Sure," says Oriel. His ribs hurt him, but he fights to stand and speak. "Anything for my little angel. What do you want to hear?"

"Just tell me a story," says Emily. "Tell one like you would tell me . . . and Henry."

"Well," says Oriel, "Okay. Let's see. We . . . were out on the boat . . . . Captain Chet and the First Mate Brennan, and we were with a bunch of other folks that didn't all belong at sea. We were after that dang monster that stole the crystal from off our ship. Do you remember?"

"Yes," says Emily, "how could I forget? It's a sea monster, right?"

"Yes," says Oriel. "Glad you remember."

"You said I was named after Aunt Emily," says the child, "and you said she turned into a sea monster."

"She was," says Oriel. "The same type of sea monster actually. We weren't chasing your aunt, but it was the same crazy scientist, Dr. Vanderfeld, who put together the diabolical machine that turned her and his assistant into sea monsters. We were after the sea monster that was still loyal to the doctor. Because that ugly thing stole something we needed to help keep the world safe."

"How did you get it back?" asks Emily.

"The crew members made a few crude jokes when the US Secretary of Defense, Jim Barker, made his way onto the steamer. Secretary Barker was overweight for his height, and I recall First Mate Brennan telling the ship's servant that the way physics works the ship would be able to hold a deck full of men the weight of Secretary Barker. 'I won't worry the slightest,' said the servant with a sneer in return.

"When we boarded the small vessel to chase after the beast, it was then that I saw the first mate make a bold call. He decided that the generosity of the US officials to keep with their quest was likely slowing down the group's capability to catch up with the monster."

"What was slowing you down, Grandpa?" asks Emily.

"When our ship's tracking system recorded a large mass moving out to sea, First Mate Brennan turned to Chet and me to say: 'We're carrying too much cargo.' We looked in the cabin and it was clear there were just far too many people on the boat. We put First Mate Brennan up to the task of telling our guests that one of them must take a life raft while I navigated and Chet took the course I provided."

"That's silly to go on a raft in the ocean," says Emily.

"Yes," agrees Oriel. "We had trouble keeping a straight face when we heard Brennan tell the US Secretary of Defense that the lifeboat should hold his weight, and if not, he said, 'You'll have to swim to shore.' "

Emily smiles in a tiny way and says, "Did he know how to swim?"

"Secretary Barker's one functioning eye twitched; his other eye was covered up by a patch he wore. In another crude moment after boarding the steamer earlier in the day, the juvenile first mate told me the patch was to keep Secretary Barker from getting distracted by too many hamburgers."

Finally, Emily smile turns into a joyous laughter, and Oriel continues, "Chet replied, 'Hunters sometimes cover one eye to keep the other locked on the prize.' But we found out the truth about Secretary Barker's vision when his loyal assistant interrupted our chatter to inform us that the patch is to cover up the surgery Secretary Barker went under when he had a detached retina."

Emily asks what a retina is, and Oriel tells her without much detail. Emily remarks, "How was he going to swim and stand around on the boats with just one eye?"

"Luckily Secretary Barker possessed a lower center of gravity, for that low center aided him when the storm picked up severely, and as Brennan confronted him."

Secretary Barker slid on the deck but caught himself on the rail. He protested leaving the ship in the storm. Outside of the covered awning the rain poured down. The inside cabin stayed dry apart from a few leaks. As the storm worsened it became crowded inside of the cabin, so the first mate went to ask everyone not responsible for the ship to stay back under the covered awning, where the lip on the ground of the deck made water flooding past their feet a non-issue. But the rain did come in under the awning some, in the form of a cold mist. Most people had rain gear with them, and to those who did not have their own, rain gear was provided in the form of cheap ponchos that had been stowed away on the ship.

"We started coming up to a much smaller mass than the one we were following. Something appeared on our monitoring systems," Oriel says to Emily. "And it turned out to be a small sailboat that had turned upside down. Upon further inspection, we saw it to be a catamaran, and we saw one survivor with the vessel that played tricks with my eyes," Oriel reminisces.

"It was a woman," Oriel says and he lights up with a warm glow. "That woman looked strikingly similar to a girl I once knew and dreamed of loving. There she was, Melissa Vanderfeld, and she was in need of rescue."

"Did you help the lady?" asks Emily.

"She was there in need of help. She was different though. The years she spent growing up on the coast must have changed her. At first, I didn't recognize her, and I probably wouldn't have known she was once the girl who tore up my valentine in grade school if it wasn't for the soggy flower dress that gave her away. I wouldn't be able to forget those patterns. Even then, I was kept alive in knowing that there was a girl in rose patterned dresses who smelled the same as flowers do in meadows during springtime.

"I was haunted by knowing she was out there, until there she was when we found her on that strange capsized vessel she was riding that wasn't much larger than a modest dinghy, even as small as the shipping container used to hold the crystal before it was ripped away."

"We saw her stranded," Oriel recalls as if in a trance. Emily is growing more attentive; she listens to his story: "She called to us with the waving of a flair in the air when we were miles from the shore. If we hadn't found her bobbing up and down in that water, she might have spent a day and a half there before another vessel saw her drifting.

"She was so relieved that she must not have realized who I

was and didn't see Chet yet. She asked us the moment she was aboard, 'Will you take me on shore with you?'

"I told her, 'Yes, but you'll have to wait a bit.'

"She said, 'What's the wait? We're not far from shore.' The vessel we rode sped up once again, leaving behind her catamaran, and she watched it sink to its grave to which she asked once more . . . what the wait was to get to shore."

Melissa Vanderfeld's arms made fits in the water, causing her muscles to become more decadent by the second. She held on, kicking and flipping most limbs in the air. When she was picked up, she was dry like an eel without a reason to towel off because the damp was so damn becoming to her senses, and everyone aboard knew from her lack of shame for her disheveled appearance and lack of introduction that she had an intensely wild, unchecked disposition that was full.

She was the type of woman who loved testing the energy of everyone around her before anyone could grasp her own. She had more will than most men to stay afloat in those waters without a lifejacket; her veins looked large enough that she looked like she could have choked any man on board, too. Had they rescued an Amazon woman? It had seemed so. But she hadn't ever choked anyone, not even beneath the sheets because she wasn't one to give men what they really wanted. But she remained polite somehow.

"When Secretary Barker realized we took on an extra passenger, he dismissed the undertaking, of course," says Oriel to Emily. "He threw his arms in the air and said, 'You can't be serious. You nearly push me to the fish, but we suddenly have room for this woman?' He was getting aggressive."

"Why?" interrupts Emily. "Didn't he want you to save the lady?"

Oriel presses against the chains. His fettered fingers grip at nothing. His wrists are weary from supporting him. He is lost in pain and seclusion, but he's hiding the surges from Emily. In his delusional state of remembrance, Oriel vexes aloud, "That man had no right. The Secretary had an assistant with him, Jon Federlane. He was in charge of ensuring mission objectives were met at each summit the commanding officer visited, and he was in charge of Secretary Barker's overall safety and quality of life. He made sure Barker had a dry place to stand under the awning of the ship, and he came into the parlor on the steamer only after he was sure the strange creature that stole the crystal was out of sight. But even the secretary's assistant—he did not stand up for Secretary Barker in that instance.

"Federlane would have rode the lifeboat with Barker to shore, or taken any other order given, but he didn't think Barker was right when it came to complaining about saving a poor, stranded woman, so he turned away when Barker objected."

The rain kept pouring down, waves kept crashing on the deck, but Chet kept the vessel going at good speeds to catch the large mass on the monitor that was still holding onto the crystal.

Secretary Barker thought his assistant was still next to him, so he confidently threw arrogant remarks around without thinking twice about how his words were affecting everyone on the boat.

The first mate was helping navigate, and Oriel could tell the ship was in good hands from where he was standing, so he stayed with them to sort out the ordeal. That's when he heard something foul and needed to get involved.

"Secretary Barker was upset that the woman we rescued wouldn't address him about her name or where she lived," says Oriel to Emily. "He started accusing her of being an improper woman."

On the boat, Barker said, "You're looking like you've seen better days, too. It looks like you've been passed by a few sailors today already." Secretary Barker tugged at Melissa Vanderfeld's ripped flower dress, and Oriel knew he had to step in, so he took one swing at his round stomach and a second. His left hook was enough to knock Barker down when he could hear no more of that behavior.

"Thank you," said Miss Vanderfeld, "but I have to ask again, what-what-what for-for what reason can we not go to the shore?"

"It's too difficult to explain," said Oriel to the woman in

the flower dress. Chet saw what happened and came over to talk to her about it. He was able to quiet her down, and he met Oriel back near the first mate, who was steering the vessel.

They still had the steamer in view when they stumbled upon Miss Vanderfeld, but it disappeared out of their sight when they started pursuing the creature at top speed.

"We were moving in the precise direction as indicated by our equipment," says Oriel to Emily, "and First Mate Brennan saw a tentacle rip through the waters ahead of us in a way that would be unusual for a creature that lives deep in the seas."

"Is that when you realized it was the assistant turned into the sea monster?" asks Emily. She sits up and moves closer to her grandfather.

"Precisely," says Oriel.

First Mate Brennan reported: "It moved with direct intention of a shark with a taste of blood enough to split the surface waters with its pointed fin."

The ship's deck was wet and crowded. On board was the captain, the first mate, and Oriel, and passengers numbering seven conscious and one unconscious—But nobody aboard had ever seen a sea monster before.

"Grandpa?" says Emily.

"Yes," says Oriel. His head is hanging low, causing the child to worry some.

She thinks of something that might cheer him up and says, "What are we going to do about the owls in the barn?"

"Oh," says Oriel, "you must mean my old friend. The Brood . . . ."

"The Brood?" she asks. "The flock of owls in our barn has a name?"

"Yes," says Oriel. "They weren't always a flock of owls.

Once upon a time, those owls . . . were a person."

Without luck in any instance was Mr. Hollindais when he attempted to keep owls away from his secret headquarters. This was where he did all the testing before launching his first ship to space, and it was the place where he observed all the space flights. The place was well hidden and looked abysmal from the outside.

It was an old stone farmhouse in need of repair. It sat awkwardly close to a non-interstate highway. The front door was mostly for show, as it was broken and never able to fully close. The sign that belonged to the realtor who sold the place was propped against the stairs to the front porch, and mold covered the sign and wood planks of the porch, to the degree where it was actually quite dangerous to walk upon the side entrance to the farmhouse. The house was positioned upon a cliff so that entering the front porch brought in some fantastic views of the rocky summits in the distance, and many times painters desired setting an easel on the planks, but they usually became shy about it once they realized the drop from the rickety floor boards was certainly painful.

During his last day at the shop, Hollindais found bad luck in the form of broken glasses. The inventor did not scorn the owls that were after the mice in the farmhouse, for he didn't know the true nature of the unnatural birds. Although, he had to take mice aside from time to time to warn them of being prey. No owls were permitted inside the shop, which made the interior of the farmhouse a safe haven for mice to live.

"It's a wide world," Monsieur Hollindais said to the family of owls above the shop's door jam. "Do you find what you need? I hope so." The natural birds stopped nesting on the shop when the mice traffic became low, but the strange owls . . . were persistent and stayed around. It is a wide world, indeed, and it is a world of potential consequences for any action. As he went inside his glasses slid down his nose and cracked on the ground at his feet.

When the mice moved into the shop it was to escape cold weather and because owls and other birds did not typically fly inside. They would build nests in the rafters—the unnatural owls would—it was certainly on the tiny mice-minds. But the inventor would never allow birds to nest inside. He built homes for them in the fields around the property; that was where the native birds went to live. But the unnatural owls stayed close to the farmhouse shop that was used for inventing the flying machines. They preferred the nests on the rafters along the top of the roof because of the prime vantage points. Because of this threat, the mice found the indoors to be a private place of sanctuary.

The inventor knowingly provided sanctuary for the mice. He knew they were there. He even knew they were chewing on ropes, which is why he would always have Oriel prepare for launch by first checking all coils and ropes. He would say the same phrase often: "Prepare for launch by checking ropes," and when they added the first electronics to the balloons, he added, "and wires" to his request. It was the first electronic gadget, after all, that provided a way to communicate with each other.

"My God, what a lovely orange glow in the distance," thought the inventor before he reached the sylvain edge. He didn't find any glasses in his search about the car, but the colors of the sky seemed to soothe his transgressions some. He prepared to leave the Wimble Brook State Forest on his way to read the weekly report from Wimbley University, where he planned to show support and to give a speech he had prepared. It was an honor to serve as an advisor to the science program. It was the closest the inventor ever got to being a teacher, and it was his anticipation to continue on a path to make tenure someday. But that was before his disappearance, and his life would change forever. It happened suddenly . . . .

The fire seemed odd to him, and he knew that foul feet find the way to wealth. Though he carried little of value to common thieves—not a jewel, watch, or piece of fine linen even— with his collection of discoveries, gifted mind, and celebrated notoriety, it's no wonder he was targeted. The fire that August was enough to distract Monsieur Hollindais to let his guard down in the area of the Wimble State Forrest where no other person happened to be that day.

When he got closer to the orange glow he noticed it to be more than a beautiful sunset, yet the ball of flames didn't worry him. He had seen the smoke up close before. But he had never been bamboozled. Still, with his high profile he carried a loaded pistol under his seat when he wasn't accompanied by his patient bodyguard, Tyre, who had the weekend off. He saw the turn to go south from the main highway, where the forest broke apart— The fire wouldn't find him there, he thought.

He took the car off the road near the highway exit, not going quick, but he bounced off the guard rail still. The smoke was like fog, making it hard for the inventor to see in the swamp filled land. However, he had no problem getting focused enough to make it back on track after that sudden jolt of adrenaline. When he reached the top, a new orange glow, with red and white flickering sirens, got louder the closer he came to the engine.

They seemed like fire engines whizzing by, they sounded that way with their cawing loud noises—screeching like sirens giving way for destruction, for when the fog cleared, it became obvious: no heat or flame caused the orange illumination. No, it was a trick. It was all a trick, and the inventor knew it at that moment. He shot his pistol out the window. The bright orange winged creatures were everywhere. Hooting and hollering, they circled the car in mobs. With the inventor's car being completely surrounded by the winged creatures, it resembled a ball of flames, certainly. With the window rolled up, the inventor felt trapped. He removed a piece of chewing gum from its wrapper, chewed quickly, plugged his ears with the rubbery chew and shot through the roof a few times with his pistol. The noise was still loud, but he wasn't stunned.

They scattered ever so slightly during the shots, but he only hit a few birds, and he was sure that more had joined the flight, more by the second. He knew the road was winding around bends, but what chance would there be to get out and get pecked in the eyes?

There had to be a way to stop them, he thought. There had to be a way to free his car long enough to break away into town; he wasn't far away at all. "Just over the hill is the town filled with people," he thought, "and surely the owls will be afraid of the bustle and hustle there."

He drove under some structure, which he could tell was an overpass by the way the light around the mob of wings was darkened immensely. His car crept along the pavement, bending the metal guard rail at times with its front bumper, front quarter-panel, and passenger door, but he could feel the ground where the pavement let off before the guardrail became uneven. He could tell he had drifted under another overpass because of the way the cloud of orange, red, and brown— the layers of wings, tails, and beaks —The sky became dark again.

They hooted and the inventor shouted back, "You're mad! Villains! To think I'll give you a mouse if you don't behave!"

The car kept going forward. It kept accelerating at an even pace until it started slamming against the guard rail, and it became violent then, that even the owls were frightened from their formation to scatter.

When the car was free of the birds, it spun wildly from the metal rail and got some considerable speed before plummeting off the hill. On the hillside below it landed sideways, the wheels in the rear kept spinning fast, forcing the car to spin on its side. It wound around again and again until smoke poured from its engine. The floor of the car hinged open and moved like a door, and the empty compartment was revealed to the owls.

The owls sat on tree branches in the forest, surrounding the smoking machine. They were watching it like one giant eye controlled by one thought. They were looking for the inventor.

When the car looked empty the owls spun their heads around looking for the driver. The inventor ducked back behind a pillar of the overpass before they could see him. He took his pistol and cocked it, but he was unaware of the shadowy figure behind the pillar, waiting for the chance to pounce on Monsieur Hollindais.

"What happened to the inventor?" questions Emily. She rubs her thighs with her palms to wake her legs some and says, "I can almost . . . move my ankles."

"Just sit tight, kid. Take it slow," says Oriel. "The inventor, he was trapped then, just like this. But he was trapped under that overpass. Trapped . . . by those maniac birds and well, unfortunately he was taken by a bad man. That man was just here."

"He was?" asks Emily.

"He was," says Oriel. "I saw him here. And he might have stopped being so bad now. That's exactly why you can feel your legs again, kid. I think the tides are shifting. I can feel them." Oriel cranes his neck and feels the wet caves ceiling dropping on him.

"He stopped being so bad?" asks Emily.

"I think so," says Oriel. "The man . . . who helped you wake up."

The shiny black Cadillac could have fit nicely in the funeral processions that drove across the Brooklyn Bridge any other day, but it crossed alone and at night with sleek reflections of headlights crawling up its narrow hood before reflecting in the driver's eyes. His eyes were behind thick frames with thick clear lenses. His brows were thick too, like furry caterpillars, and like hungry caterpillars, his brows grew animated with his thoughts about the job he was assigned. He was not ready for that day. He worked a job that had been thrown his way, like meat to a hungry dog, and he could not resist sinking his teeth into it.

"His name is Bile Deville," says Oriel to Emily, "and he took that job and the terrible things he's doing— I bet he's still taking those sorts of jobs to make his way back to a normal life for he and his sister."

Bile was sure not to harm the guest that occupied his backseat. He followed orders he was given, which indicated not to harm the inventor unless absolutely necessary. The windows were tinted beyond the legal limit to prevent any onlooker from approaching the vehicle and identifying a battered and subdued individual in the rear seat. On the passenger seat was a zippered leather purse containing $10,000 to be delivered to any cop that might approach the vehicle. The purse sat next to an electronic weapon on the passenger seat. Luckily for the driver, the car made it past two police officers sitting near the south end of the bridge, despite the muffled screams of the hooded guest on the backseat.

Remaining focused, Bile kept two hands gripping the steering wheel in the appropriate positions to brace himself for the potholes in the road. He was ready for anything, and he remained calm when the car did break down temporarily. When the tire went flat he prepared to calmly pump the breaks. He slowed the vehicle to a stop. The Cadillac went from 40 miles per hour to a complete stop in a matter of 10 seconds. The night air was crisp, felt by Bile when he opened the door. The cold air urged the backseat guest to grow louder when the guest felt the door open.

The screaming caused Bile to panic a little, and in a frenzy he ripped the backdoor open. Bile gripped the door's frame, and with his other hand, he took his electric cattle prod from its retracted position to its full lanyard length. The zap from the metal prongs was immediate torture, and a second of electrified pressure on the temples of the backseat guest was enough to cause the car to become completely quiet.

"What kind of a name is Bile?" asks Emily.

"His parents thought they were being clever and doing him a favor by naming him Bill instead of William, until the attending physician's cursive 'l' was mistakenly printed as a cursive 'e' by the nurse who must have been having a stressful day, so his parents let the name stay. Because, well . . . they thought Bile was a name worthy of a strong personality on its own.

"It wasn't until Bile's sister, Sybil, was born two years later," says Oriel, "that he began to grow into having a great deal of responsibility to be her protector when dangerous people came calling in Merdeville, but he felt it was his responsibility to guide he and his sister through working with the gangs and crime bosses. He put everything on the line to keep Sybil happy and alive."

In the heart of Merdeville, a hand-painted sign spelled out trouble: "City took our money, and We need water!" A man drove by yelling out his window in an aggravated, shrill voice: "Relax!" Under the sign, towards the street a little, where the bushes were mostly trampled, grew a single plant. It was the poisonous, dark green leaves that grew around the black foam seat on a child's bicycle that had been lying there long enough for the chain to rust, and its red painted body looked almost new. One decal peeled away already but another clearly read, "Rocket." Even with rust on the chain and a decomposed foam guard wrapped around the narrow handlebars, it still looked like it would have moved quickly on the cracked sidewalks.

Bile brought the inventor to his estate, away from Never York. They drove south to his estate in Merdeville, where people acted like they wanted to run each other over just to advance themselves; but they wouldn't actually run anyone over, they'd just ruin anyone's day that got in their way. In fact, most of the people who lived there— when someone actually did get run over, they'd mourn the loss of life— Even wildlife got people mourning in Merdeville . . . . Why, even Bile's neighbor the week before had some cathartic release when Bile pulled up to his home on the corner of Bland Avenue! He saw the neighbor examining road-kill. A squashed squirrel breathing rapidly its last rich taste of life; they mourned together in his driveway after moving the tiny, twitching body from the avenue.

When Bile pulled the Cadillac up to his estate with the unconscious prisoner on the backseat, the area appeared clear enough to bring the bound body of the inventor into his home. Up! And over! He carried the feeble man across his lawn on strong shoulders. And Bile remembered to lock his car door, too.

"The inventor was brought in to see Dr. Vanderfeld," says Oriel, "the doctor who would analyze the inventor's brain. With a machine called 'the Deep See-Diver' Dr. Vanderfeld looked at his deepest desires, thoughts and other things."

"What did he see?" asks the inquisitive young Emily.

"Things like what he feared most," says Oriel. "He gave

the inventor a choice in the matter. They were in the courtyard with Sybil & Bile in the adjacent room and nothing at his side, no tool nearby, his shoulders were strapped to the table and the probe was deep in his cerebrum, and he knew that even a minute movement would kill or paralyze him forever, so he held as still as he could . . . while Dr. Vanderfeld whispered something into his ear."

Dr. Vanderfeld said, "For taking what I have created . . . for destroying my dream . . . I am somehow still able to show you kindness today, for I give you a choice between giving your consciousness to me . . . or joining your fears. My dear Hollindais, I will turn you into a brood of owls . . . with the pull of a lever." He held onto the red-nosed lever labeled 'FEAR REACTOR.'

Vanderfeld said, "What do you choose, monsieur?"

The inventor stayed still, and he dropped his jaw enough to utter: "Well, if I have to make such a choice, then, c'est la vie. I choose nature—such is life to make me into an owl. I'll live with what I fear after all— Anything to . . . ." He lost consciousness.

"Not one owl . . . a group of them," said Dr. Vanderfeld, and he laughed victoriously.

"Group," muttered the inventor. "A group . . . ."

"Yes," said Dr. Vanderfeld, "it's alight. I'm sorry to tempt you but leaving you living in any form is a loss of life . . . for the world."

The inventor confessed: "It was wrong to steal it . . . . Your idea. I'm sorry. It was yours. And I'm sorry for what happened to you . . . and your family. Killing me . . . won't bring back what you have lost. But if we work together, beautiful things can happen for the world. You'll see. If we work together."

"I'm sorry," said Dr. Vanderfeld. "It would never work being partners. It's too . . . late. Your days of running off with other people's inventions are over."

Dr. Vanderfeld's thick, acid resistant gloves reached to pull the other lever on 'the Deep-See-Diver,' a blue lever marked 'REMOVE DATA' with a skull carved into the panel next to its label. He only stopped himself from transferring the half-pound of pressure required to pull the fatality inducing lever when he heard: "Hoo-ch-a-hoooo!" He turned to see the inventor flapping his lips to make the sound.

From the sky outside came the owls he had been observing out in nature, and they busted through the windows of the estate on Bland Avenue with ease and curiosity to see who called them. They came from all around. A brood of owls frightened Dr. Vanderfeld, and he leapt to flee the courtyard and join his associates. But in the process of crashing and dashing around the space, the red lever got hit, and Dr. Vanderfeld turned to watch the inventor become the Brood.

"The Brood," Oriel says to Emily as he leans along the wall, trying to conserve energy; his legs hurt him from standing and his shoulders ache from being held in place by the metal shackles.

"Yes?" says Emily. "Grandpa?"

The old man lifts his head to say, "The Brood is a moving force controlled by the crystal clear consciousness of what used to surmise the entity known as Monsieur Hollindais. The collection of owls came down in an onslaught of talons and beaks. No longer did the inventor fear owls, no! The Brood ripped apart Dr. Vanderfeld, leaving no trace of human flesh, only bones and hair. The owls that came to the inventor's side managed to crush Vanderfeld's skull . . . before his still-beating heart emptied of blood."

Bile and Sybil made it out of the estate and away from Bland Avenue for good and forever.

When they found the bones in the backyard, future residents on Bland Avenue mourned the loss of life, as usual, but nobody knew what had happened and there was only one person left who would ever ask— the only human being who would ever care to question the disappearance of Dr. Vanderfeld, the once idolized doctor of medicine —No, not his daughter Melissa. The only person who would ever question the doctor's disappearance was the last colleague Dr. Vanderfeld had— his assistant who agreed to test the machine on himself and was turned into a giant squid.

"Sorry about your boat," Oriel said to Miss Vanderfeld. He finally felt it was appropriate to speak openly with her. He couldn't hold back his words.

"It wasn't much of a sailboat," said Melissa. "I'm used to large yachts with mid-sails as great as a mast can support."

The large indicating blip on the ship's monitor stopped moving, and the first mate called that they were closing in on the Elixiumbrium. He readied his harpoon that was no larger than an elephant musket. It was mounted to the ship with a seat that the first mate occupied happily. He was eager to catch whatever monster was responsible for taking them off the course that they had set. After all, it was an interruption of what could have been a remarkable scientific presentation.

When First Mate Brennan was sure he would have the creature in his sight momentarily, poor weather and exhaustive maneuvering had brought on some engine failure that caused the boat to lose all forward movement.

Captain Chet patted the first mate on the shoulders and said something the rest of the ship could not hear, and the captain made way to a paddle rack on the stern of the ship. He returned with a paddle for each set of hands. To Miss Vanderfeld he said, "Welcome aboard, miss. It appears you can rely on the wind the same as we can rely on our engine."

"You can't be serious," Melissa said. "Are you considering rowing?"

"No," said Chet, "but you should." He went to the monitor to see if their pursuit was still progressing and he steered. Meanwhile, the rest of the ship, including Brennan, took to the water with slices from their paddles.

The first mate called for everyone to row and he did double-time with his motions, but Oriel noticed how he called out only every other one of his pushes and pulls with the oar he maneuvered.

"You rowed together," Emily says. "Was it easy? Did the lady join in?"

"No. Miss Vanderfeld did not join in for the rowing," says Oriel. "She held her oar on her lap, and I noticed her dress had lace ruffles on its bottom that looked pristine, even near the tears in the fabric above."

Chet set the course steady in the direction suggested by their equipment and tended to the engine. He added oil to the motor and gave it time to settle inside. He came to Oriel's side to whisper his concerns when the motor wouldn't start. The sounds of rowing and Brennan's commands covered the captain's whispers, as Chet told Oriel he was growing weary with anxiety. He warned Oriel of his suspicions surrounding the girl they picked up as well. Chet said that rescuing her that night was no coincidence.

The motor kicked on and the rowing stopped, but it was loud enough still that Oriel didn't need to cover up his voice by whispering. Oriel told Chet how he was sure that he remembered her from grade school, and Chet agreed. He said, "She bares an eerie resemblance, but I wouldn't had placed her if you didn't say something."

"Well, Chet," Oriel added, "there's more to consider here . . . if that really is the same woman."

"Wait a minute," Chet said. "Isn't she a Vanderfeld? I saw something in a report earlier. A cop had me bring a dog out into the city . . . to investigate the scene of a crime where a victim was strangled."

Training K-9 units was within Chet's skill set. He started a training facility when Mr. Hollindais warned him to keep away from exposing the cover-ups involving the senator having a cellar filled with dead bodies. The steamship had enough K-9 detectives to sniff out and hunt down all the criminals on the shores all day and night, non-stop. When Chet would need a break, one of the other crew members on the steamer would take over for him, usually Minolo. Chet would always look forward to that feeling he would get when climbing the rope on his steamer, knot by knot, vertically, until he would reach the panting, growling and sniffing that would usually take place on the deck. That is how the deck usually was, apart from when dignitaries came to the ship. When the ship had company the dogs would be safely and humanely kenneled below the deck.

Worth mentioning is the community's response to Chet's efforts. They went as far in their appreciation of the K-9 service that cleaned up North Shore as to give Captain Chet a special place to dock his steamer on an island off the shore.

"They liked that guy, huh?" asks Emily.

"They liked him a lot," says Oriel. "That special place is . . . where we were going to go to visit Chet. I go there every year to . . . pay my respects and visit him."

One pier is still marked with a slip for the unnamed steamer, and the slip has a sign that reads, "Reservation for U.S.S. Dog Catcher." It turned out to be a good story for Jackie Danzel to use in publications instead of the one that the inventor interrupted at the ball game. One of Danzel's tamer columns at the time featured an analysis of new businesses each month and Chet was able to help him fill one month with a delightful story about turning bad dogs into good ones.

The report written by Jackie Danzel is called "Teaching a Street-Dog How to Roll-Over."

Here's a piece of Danzel's report: "Chet said: 'What we have here is a mutt with no manners.' He took a feisty dog who wanted to spill his blood on the sidewalk—He took that dog into his arms," wrote Danzel, "like a wounded lamb, and it seemed to be released of some rabid-demonic possession."

The boat was forty nautical miles from the U.S.S. Dog Catcher when the engine resumed working, and Oriel knew Chet's chief concerns were finding the Elixiumbrium . . . because he had made no mention of getting back to his beloved K-9 units.

Up until this point, Oriel and Chet recognized that Melissa was innocent of any accusations surrounding the case. "She was innocent, but that's probably why she got out to sea," declared Chet to Oriel, privately. Melissa Vanderfeld was indeed trying to stay out of the public eye, and Oriel would learn enough about her to know that any accusations of her being involved in grievous matters, such as matters that involve the strangling Captain Chet had spoke of investigating with his K-9 patrols.

It was merely a matter of coincidence to be found out. Much like the young woman's return into Oriel's life altogether was a matter of coincidence. They just so happened to find Melissa while she was fleeing from her old life.

As the creature neared the open ocean First Mate Brennan swung around the ship's starboard side. Around the next island they went before putting it off, and they plunged their gaffs into the water that was shallow enough to touch bottom.

The monster roared when it was cornered, a noise that pierced the thin air. The unheard, somber melody was an attempt for the once human messenger to communicate, but it was in a tone that none on board could decipher, for their ears were dry, too dry to hear a message that travelled on watery vocal cords.

The violent cry was an attempt to save its own life. "Killing the creature wasn't our intention," Oriel says to his granddaughter, who is suddenly starting to look restless. "The loathsome Secretary of Defense had another plan, however. Barker pulled his assistant aside to say, 'Whatever happens with the crystal I want that thing taken back alive.' That fool!"

The creature wrapped its pink, pulsating tentacles around the Elixiumbrium, and its fleshy, round disks gripped tightly. It pulled the Elixiumbrium toward its center, but the Elixiumbrium was in its whole form, too large for the creature to consume. With nowhere to go, the creature's death-rattle slowed to a hum before they tossed a net upon it, and it was trapped near the beach.

"Upon close inspection, the eye of the creature squinted with a level of comprehension that it must yield to our threatening advances," says Oriel.

"Oh," exclaims Emily, "because the monster was a person like Aunt Emily," and she pulls her knees close to her chest to place her head upon them, getting quite comfortable now in the damp cave chamber.

Upon the monster's realization of being trapped, it released the crystal. Chet and Oriel both dove in the water for it. They began to attach enough rope and harnesses to the crystal to haul it from the water as Brennan kept steady his grip on the rope holding the net over the creature.

"You can let her go, on the count of three—" Chet said. Brennan nodded and held his place, while Chet and Oriel climbed from the water and onto the ship again. Together, they started hauling up the slack on the rope for the Elixiumbrium, and when it was taught Chet started the three-count, but he didn't get far before:

"Take your hands off that net," said Barker. His assistant didn't help him with his demands.

Chet said, "We're letting it go. We have more important matters at hand. Two!"

"I said, take your hands off," said Barker as he raised the harpoon gun high.

Chet saw the threat, but he said, "Three . . . ! Release the creature. That's an order—"

"Yes, Cap," said Brennan. He let the rope go so the net could loosen.

The creature was free long enough to watch Barker fire and miss with the torpedo. He did, however, hit an oil line, and a spark from that abrasion started a fire.

"What did you do when the fire started?" asks Emily with a slight jolt of her being.

"Something inside of me leapt forth," says Oriel. "In the confusion and chaos I did . . . what I couldn't do when I was a boy."

He took Melissa by the hand on the boat that day, and he was briefly taken back to their shared peanut butter sandwich. But in no time at all, the fire had erupted. Chet and Brennan went down with the ship that day.

The creature, though fatally injured from the blast, had enough energy reserved to rip Barker apart limb from limb.

Melissa, Oriel, and the rest of the passengers aboard swam to shore, and it was a group effort to bring the Elixiumbrium along with them.

D ANZEL's report to *The Worldly News* went like this: "Sea-sank captain told all before he and crew drown at sea. Corrupt police put behind bars . . . along with a certain senator who gave the orders."

"I was able to dip off the radar to figure out what to do with the Elixiumbrium," says Oriel to Emily. "And eventually, the Brood was able to figure out a way to communicate with me, mostly by speaking to his loyal bodyguard who kept faith in the strange man. He was able to tell me enough . . . to let me know the inventor was still there to help. And as for Melissa, we kept our relationship going, for even more peanut butter sandwiches when your father came into the picture."

Through the pain Oriel forces a smile, and Emily says, "Grandpa, where are we?" Oriel relinquishes his smile to say, "We're together, dear. That's what matters." She tries to stand up. He says, "Be careful on your feet, darling." The girl shakes her head, she falls back to bed, and she says, "My legs feel like jelly!"

"Well," says Oriel, "when you're able to move . . . . I have an itch on my nose that's been bothering me something terrible." The girl cracks a tiny smile. Oriel says, "I bet your father is on his way."

"Do you think he can find us?" asks Emily. "You're here," says Oriel, "so I know he's got to find us, Em."

Chapter Fifteen

A Crooked Cop Gets Away And Another Straightens Up

AFTER he finishes writing his letter to Washington, Inspector Cary Oriel finds his room in this inn cramped and unwelcoming. Despite the advice from Theo and Valentico, Cary decides to wander outside. His wife looks out at him as he leaves along the path from the rooms to the front desk. He ignores the glow she creates from inside the sanctuary of his unlocked room. He tries to ignore everything about her one last time when he tells himself that it's not really happening.

He notices a sign that caught his eye earlier, back when he didn't have time to pay attention. He decides to pull the chain on the bell of the cottage that is near the inn's front desk. The sign reads, "Paranormal Investigative Services." It is just what Cary wants to tell himself once and for all: that he has been seeing things that aren't really there and it's all in his head. He thinks to himself how he wouldn't mind someone else who knows about spirits giving his situation a look. "Perhaps this person is a professional," he thinks.

Bruno comes to, tied up and looking up at Theo, who is eating some sardines from a can. "You hungry?" asks the ex-cop.

Bruno turns to his side, away from the open balcony, and Theo slides a small basket over to him that Bruno tosses up into. "I guess not," says Theo. He tells Bruno, "You've lost a lot of blood, but that's all I can do for you now. I think you'll survive."

Bruno's badge is wet with his blood, and his expression tells Theo that he understands his circumstances.

"I have a family who needs me," says Cary to a man with a long, white Dali-mustache, whose points are parallel to the horizon so that when he talks his teeth look like car headlights coming through a tunnel at night. "I don't know where they got to—"

The psychic turns down the lights in the room with a dial at the center of the table next to a salt lamp that creates shadows on the wall.

Bruno stirs and says, "Cary—" But he is interrupted by Theo who says, "Don't need to talk to Cary, bud. You talk to me now—Now, tell me who you're working for and don't use acronyms either—"

After taking a moment to reflect upon his answer Bruno says nothing. Theo begins to torture him. He sits the empty sardine can in front of a fan, and he turns the fan on high speed. The smell blows into Bruno's face.

In the other room, Cynthia watches the interrogation on the video monitor.

Soon enough Bruno reveals his answer: "NYPD."

"I said no acronyms," Theo says as he stops the torture from proceeding. He picks up a hot poker from the fire place. It is bright red. He walks across to the other side of the room where he has prepared an ice bucket, and he says, "I'm not from your city in case you haven't noticed, so don't use anymore acronyms, alright?" He drops the poker next to Bruno's face. It melts through the fabric of the couch cushion immediately.

CARY is listening to chanting sounds coming from all around the room while the psychic extends his arms to summon spirits for guidance. He says, "We will be full with your mercy, oh holy ones!"

There is a curtain that leads out to the front of the psychic's cottage and into the main doorway that goes back out to the path. Behind the curtain a shadowy figure stands in complete obscurity. The figure raises a shotgun and puts the butt of the shotgun to their shoulder.

Back in the room of the inn, Bruno has a pile of ice on his head. He says, "That feels alright there—" To which Theo stops scooping and piling the cubes to say: "It's not supposed to feel alright—It's supposed to—" Theo clamps the ice pliers open and closed with menacing excitement.

"Cary!" yells Bruno. "Where is he?"

"He's safe next door. Don't worry," says Theo.

"What—No!" exclaims Bruno, and he tries but fails to get up, falling to the floor. Ice flies across the room. "The innkeeper— Don't trust the innkeeper!"

Theo goes to the window, where he spots the cottage. In the midst of the sounds of creaking floorboards and chimes blown by the wind, in the distance is a haze of light coming from the psychic reading room.

In the center of the room is a table covered in red velvet cloth that is attached to the tabletop by an epoxy, but it hangs loosely around the edges enough to touch the ground all the way around the circumference of the sturdy, round protuberance. One chair on either side of the table, each halfway around the room, they sit across from another. The psychic's turban slips enough to require him to adjust it in between shuffling a deck of cards and getting The Crystal Ball lit. He hits around the table's top a number of times to get the ball glowing.

A powder of smoke appears in the center of the ball. The cloud has a fluid, fine outline, where the smoke is dancing and suspended like an amoeba in the center of the ball.

"When I say . . . the three magic words," says the psychic, "your problems will presents . . . itself in the space inside . . . The Crystal Ball before your eyes . . . ."

"I say, I'll give it a shot, mate," says Cary to the psychic, as he leans forward with intrigue; he starts to draw closer to the ball with every inch of his being until he forgets the space around him.

It is just The Crystal Ball. It takes over his mind, and he can't see anything else around. It glows, and the psychic's eyes roll backwards and upwards towards the jewel below his silky hat. Cary closes his eyes to no longer see the table or the psychic. It is only the crystal ball because it has already seeded itself inside his head.

The psychic says the following, in a trance state:
"Oh holy,
Oh divine,
of wondrous wonders of whence shall be
unknown,
fill this ball before us with . . .
. . . what is not yet understood."

From all around the room . . . comes a trembling commotion. To which the psychic says, "Spirits, you have found us— This is not normal to happen so soon— You have flocked to us tonight with messages for this man?"

The commotion is heightened into a tumultuous racket. Cary's desires begin to manifest before his mind's eye, like smoke from a smoldering surprise. Somehow in his empirical wisdom the psychic has recognized this, and he instructs, "Ask for what you desire, now!"

Cary says, "Okay. I believe you! I thought this was hogwash, but I believe." The psychic hammers the table with his fists and says, "To yourself, now! The desire. Out with it!" The spirits are restless. And the pounding continues. Cary thinks to himself about Adeline, and he says to himself these words: "My one true love, if you're actually here with me, give me a sign."

The psychic pounds his fists and the room goes absolutely void of light, apart from a bead that travels into the space to poke and possess the grey smoke within the crystal ball. The psychic says, "When I say these three magic words . . . you will have your sign."

The ball glows bright, and the shadowy figure steps into the room with the shotgun loaded and ready to fire on Cary.

"I knew I had the gift—All these years I tell people: I speak to the dead," says the psychic before his voice shakes the windows of the building; he chants, "Squel-tuminuous, foretuitist, domingo—"

In a rush, Cary opens his eyes to find he is seated next to Adeline. She looks as wholesome as she did when they first met. As the gunman pulls the trigger Cary leans in just like he leaned in to see the ball before, but this time he kisses Adeline. It's the first kiss they've had since she fell into a coma over five years ago. But it's not the sudden motion leaning forward that saves Cary's life. No, for some odd reason the long barrel of the shotgun blows up, due to an obstruction. Much like the way a gun backfires, it lets out an explosive spark that badly burns the shooter's hand. The weapon drops to the ground and the perpetrator runs off.

Almost every cop in the district shows up to the scene, but Stegner calls off the majority of them onto patrolling the area because the inn is clean. They know it's clean because the cops had been staking out the place ever since Cynthia tipped them off about their operation. Sergeant Gerald Manus and Crime Scene Investigator Victoria Carteret scour the area around the inn for clues. They find one glove worn by the shooter is a thin black leather one, and it was smoothly polished. It comes back clean when Victoria takes a closer look for hair follicles, but Gerald discovers the other glove that received substantial damages when the shotgun produced the mild explosion. And Victoria does find it to contain some of the shooter's blood—enough to run their databases for a match but nothing in the system comes back with a high enough probability to take seriously, so forensics gives their notes to Stegner:

"The shooter may have left us enough to convict him if we ever find him—" says Victoria Carteret. "Or her," adds Gerald Manus.

"I think," says Captain Larry Stegner, "it's for the best,

given the particulars of this situation, to send everyone in your party away from the area. Pronto. Get packed, and get out. It's not safe here."

"No time for a safety detail, Captain?" asks Theo.

"You're the detail," says Stegner before returning to the investigation already in progress at the inn. "Get going." Theo takes to his room, and he and Cynthia pull the sedan up to load Bruno as discretely as possible. Cary is waiting in the car when they get back with their luggage. And they're gone from the inn.

"First that psycho in the cabin," says Stegner, "was slaughtered by a dirty cop——"

"Detective Peters is still on the run," says McKindley.

"Now, we have another incident with Cary nearby," says Stegner. "Do you think Bruno Peters is involved as the shooter?"

McKindley shrugs his shoulders, and they go around to question the locals. McKindley takes point. When he opens the innkeeper's door, the old man's body slumps out with a note attached to his chest.

"What does it say?" Stegner asks McKindley.

"I'm not sure how to put it," says McKindley, "but it's nonsense about taking a life to right the wrongs. What wrongs was this old innkeeper *schmutz* righting by offing himself?"

"I don't know," says Stegner, "but that paper . . . . It's printed, yellow tinted, homemade press quality." When they take a look around the property, they notice the similarities in the lettering on the psychic's sign. It's the place where the incident happened, so they proceed with caution. The psychic has no way of denying the note came from his press.

McKindley nearly has the psychic all the way in his squad car when the man takes off one of the detective's leather gloves to reveal a wound on his left hand. The psychic says to anyone who can hear him, "That mark is fresh. Oh so fresh. Where it came from, do you know?"

Stegner doesn't know what the psychic is talking about until he sees the wound and remembers picking up the shotgun, with its powder on the muzzle, when they were called to the scene after the incident.

Before Stegner has time to reach for his sidearm McKindley beats him at the draw of his own weapon. He takes Stegner down with a shot to the chest, a bullet that knocks him over but catches on his armor protection.

McKindley is off in the squad car with the psychic cuffed and in the back seat before Stegner even reaches his feet again. Stegner realizes at that moment . . . He thinks to himself, "It was McKindley who killed Rottingham . . . . He was there before I was . . . . Now he tried to kill Cary . . . ." And the captain's mind reels in wonder for who else McKindley has wronged in the past . . . .

"You're out of your mind," says Stegner over the radio, "if you think I won't call the US Feds. I've got a maniac cop on the loose, and now you and your wife think you can save the freaking world by yourselves? You've got to be kidding me."

"Larry," says Theo, "jurisdiction doesn't matter when you know something is right—"

"You haven't got jurisdiction anywhere," says Stegner.

"Give me twenty-four hours," says Theo, "before you go talking to the Feds. I'll do their job for them to make sure it gets done right."

"The Feds there know how to do their job already," says Stegner.

"Sure," Theo says, "they'll do their job because they have bills to pay, or else creditors will hunt them down."

"What are you saying?" asks Stegner.

"When I left here the first time," says Theo as he kicks in the door at the Anything Goose Saloon, "damn near everyone I knew had stacked up debts they couldn't pay." He looks down the line at a bar filled with cops on the Goose's payroll, and he says,

"Any chance one of you could afford to buy me a drink?"

The place is loud enough to cause Stegner to turn his radio down. The officer sitting at the bar closest to Theo hears him asking for a drink, so he says, "We drink for here free, but I guess I'm paying for it somehow."

"Are you on the clock?" asks Theo. But he doesn't get any response from the cop who turns back to his drink. Theo says into the radio: "Everyone here is trashed to the point that they won't know if I keep going."

"Just because the Goose has the cops on his payroll," says Stegner, "doesn't mean they're loyal. He lets up on his radio call button and realizes the message didn't go through to Theo. Theo left his radio on for him to hear what is going on in the bar, so Captain Stegner waits and listens before placing any calls to federal authorities. He closes his eyes and focuses in on the sounds at the bar; he's grateful for Theo finally showing his intentions and finally trusting Stegner.

Once Theo finds his way to the back of the bar he opens the outside gate to let Cynthia in to take a look at the strange machine they must operate, if they want to get to the rest of Cary's family. Cary enters through the gate as well; he's helping Bruno get around, but he lets go of the detective when they get in through the back lot, near the jetty of rocks that leads out into the open ocean. Bruno makes it to the jetty on his own, but he doesn't join for the entire walk along the jetty to the submersible vessel.

Bruno stops Valentico on her way onto the submersible elevator. He says, "I'm sorry . . . If I ever may have crossed a line with you, Gabby—" She interrupts to say, "It's not Gabby. I didn't give you my real name." He shakes his head and says, "It doesn't matter. Listen. Maybe in another life you and I would be something." Bruno is soaked in blood from the wound on his arm that has grown infected and red.

"Careful," says Theo.

"I mean to say to her and you," says Bruno, "I mean to say I'm sorry. That's all."

Cynthia nods and says, "Yah. You'll find what we have—"

"If he makes it," says Theo. "Eh . . . I'm sure you will—

No hard feelings, I suppose, because you didn't know, but now you know about us—so keep your eyes high and your hands off of her from here on out."

"Deal," says Bruno, and he nods and rests his body on top of a large rock jutting from the jetty. "I'm going to stick around up here. I'll make sure . . . nobody follows you down." With Bruno's permission, the others leave him to board the submersible elevator that takes them down into the depths of the ocean.

A few moments pass by and the bubbles from the submerg-evator stop rising to the surface. When a few loud voices in the distance appear Bruno takes cover behind the rock he has been resting upon. The voices are those of the sibling team of Bile and Sybil Deville.

"And you're off to go to the moon," says Bile, "and leave your big brother behind. That's fine. Fine by me. We're through."

"Don't make me choose," says Sybil. "Life with two strangers or death on this rock with you— Wait. Where's the thing that takes us down?"

"Maybe someone is using it," says Bile.

"Don't be stupid," says Sybil. "Not another soul knows it's here but us."

"You two aren't going anywhere," says Bruno, "unless it's back out the way you came. This here is a dead end. Better turn and run."

Bile lights his cigar. It takes a moment to catch on fire. He puts out the flame, blows smoke out his lungs and says, "What can you do to stop us?" He maneuvers has head to get a look at Bruno's arm, and Sybil points out the blood dripping from under Bruno's hat. The wound on his arm is swollen and Bruno isn't moving with great coordination.

"I'd like to give you some advice," says Bruno, "since I was once in the same situation you are when I was looking after my sis—"

"What are you saying?" asks Sybil. "The words just come dribbling from your popped-pill that once was your head."

"You're taking orders from this woman, eh?" the detective asks with a poke at Sybil. "I've finally stopped listening to my sister. Look at where that got me . . . ."

"Shut up—" interrupts Sybil.

But Bile interrupts her to say, "He's right, you know—All our lives I do what they tell me—and for what? Money? Drugs? Nice pool where I watch pretty women swim? Yeah, that was my fantasy. But I'd give it up if my dear baby sister was fit to leave it behind—"

"She can take care of herself, bro," says Bruno.

Bile takes his sister by the wrists and says, "I'm leaving, see? You're on your own, kid—" And he finally goes on his own to roam and find a seaside home to settle upon where he won't have to swindle to make it his own . . . .

Bruno grabs Sybil by the waist to hold her back from leaving toward the edge of the jetty, where he fears the submerg-evator will reappear any moment now. Sybil doesn't have to claw much at his face and neck to free herself. She rips apart the flesh on Bruno's neck like she has the claws of a jaguar, and she wipes the blood in her slick hair. As she steps over Bruno, she spits on him and says, "You're a traitor and coward, and I hope your brain hemorrhages but you live just long enough to see this planet fall apart." She leaves in the same direction as her brother, even if she might never find him.

Bruno closes his eyes; he is prepared to accept his fate when she's gone and he is alone with his own thoughts. He has lost too much blood to go on sleeping and living, so he holds back on sleep, until he can't help but dream a little of death, and his dreams begin to become his condition.

Jerry's long, wet sideburns stay plastered to his jaws, but his thin ponytail moves in the rush of air that fills the cave when the submerg-evator arrives. "Why do I bother saving electricity when you lazy scientists keep taking the elevator?" Jerry says before the doors open. He adds one more quip as the doors are opening: "Do you know your carbon footprint is getting bigger?"

When the doors open, Jerry draws his sidearm from the waterproof bag he carries, and he's on the radio saying, "Putting out an All Police Bulletin for those who are close enough to respond— You know who you are and you know . . . where we are," Jerry snorts in laughter before he drops the radio to the ground to free up both hands and steady the aim of his pistol. He is shifting back and forth between Theo, Valentico, and Cary when he says to Cary, "I can't believe you actually came here."

With the gunman's attention drawn to Cary, Theo and Valentico are able to move off from the stalemate to duck behind a stalagmite rock formation that points upward from the cave floor. Theo tries the radio, he says, "Captain? Stegner, can you hear me?" But it's no use.

"You came here for your family, right?" asks Jerry. He seems to have dismissed the other two occupants to focus on Cary, although he does keep an eye open for anyone moving toward the one and only door that goes further into the facility. "I thought you would have given up on them," says Jerry, "just like you gave up on your wife when she slipped away into a coma."

Cary knows Adeline is there. He can feel her. When she steps out from the submerg-evator she is glowing brighter than a person usually glows when in an underwater cave. Cary doesn't even have to look around to know she's there.

Theo shouts, "Eventually the wolves will come for you, mate. Organized crime has no place in the justice system."

It comes from all around, far more magnificent than the bright glare covering a snowy ridge on a clear, cloudless morning. But looking into it is impossible, so Theo and Valentico remain hidden. Meanwhile Jerry fights with what he is inside and refuses to cower or bend. His pupils dilate and grow small, dilate and grow small before they burst altogether, for the light is all he sees. It even fuses with his memory of sight.

When the blindness sets in, Jerry's eyes become grey. He swings his arms in the air with force enough to knock someone over, but he loses his footing. The punching becomes poorly placed blows and pummels intended for someone but reaching nobody at all. Cary leaves him batting his fists at the still air when he steps to the side.

To the ground goes Jerry who roars, "MY EYES!" He falls into the water and has trouble swimming. The splashing and thrashing help him get to rocks at the far end of the cave, where he drops his body onto a rock in a painful way. He says, "What happened to my eyes, god?"

Cary blocks the light some, but when he drops his arms it doesn't have the same affect on him. His eyes adjust to the pure white light, and she shows herself to him: Adeline's profile in the cave, filled with every piece of energy she could gather from the universe, glows to help Cary. She says in a vibratory way, "This is as far I can go."

Cary takes Cynthia and Theo from their hiding spot and he leads them from that cave, while the light remains close behind. Cary and company go into the first chamber beyond the door that Jerry had once guarded dearly.

"Give me a second," says Theo as he works with a tool to open a small control panel of a keycard accessible lock.

Cynthia takes Cary by one arm with both hands, affectionately, and they take a step back. Theo speaks for her when he says, "No matter what happens, we talked about it already, and we believe you. I want you to know we're doing everything in our power to get your family some place safe."

Theo springs around to say: "I've got it." Cary pushes the door open with his shoulder, and he says, "Thank you both." He passes by Theo to move on through the door.

The long white tubes lead to the young girl's arm. It's quite a sight for her grandfather to see the saline solution keeping her nourished some and counteracting that poison working against her young body. The relief comes to Oriel when Cary unplugs the IV from the wall.

"What did I tell you," says Oriel, "your father has arrived." Theo begins working to break the locks that bind the old man.

Cary brushes Emily's hair away from her face with his hands, and he takes her into his arms. He gently kisses her forehead and whispers into her ear, "You were right to believe in Mommy . . . . She's been helping me get you back."

Father and daughter wait by the door, while Theo and Valentico help Oriel regain his composure from having his body strictly bound to the wall for so long. Cynthia asks, "Are you okay?" Oriel responds, "My leg is numb, but I'll be fine if we can get out of here."

Out of that chamber and into the hall they go before they run into another keycard access only door. Theo breaks the panel to get to work.

"Let me hold her," says Oriel. He takes the young girl into his arms, and he says, "It's going to be okay now your papa has found us."

"I believe you now," says Cary. "All of your stories you were telling . . . ."

"Well," says Oriel, "maybe not all of them."

Cary slides through the door once he hears the electronic lock click open. He moves to shut the door behind him and says, "Thank you both for all of this—" Cynthia reaches for Cary, but he moves quickly by her and Theo.

Cynthia says, "Wait," as Cary shuts the door. "We'll come with you," she says. Theo tries to open the door again, but the lock is jammed. He begins working to get it open again.

"This isn't your fight—It's mine," Cary says as he takes a pipe propped up against the wall and jams it hard— down, way down —down into the floor board in front of the door. It holds in the cavernous clay, deep below the floorboards. When Theo gets the lock open again, it's no use. With all their might the door won't budge open.

Even with his allies and family behind him Cary confidently walks ahead, but he hasn't any idea what awaits him. He wonders if the Goose has a trap along the corridor, so he looks left and right into offshoots of the cavern that are lit even less than the main corridor that seems to go on for miles. He takes the main corridor and circles around the entire research facility.

After deciding to venture down a dark offshoot at the end of the main corridor, Cary finds himself standing on the long, raised platform. The platform once rose a couple feet all around the walls, which were once adorned with synthetic Elixiumbrium-filled test tubes but are now flush to the tubeless wall. For, limp bodies of the test subjects now take up the negative space between the platform and the walls.

"What have you done?" asks Cary. "All these people are

dead because of your greed."

"I did it in the same name of science that your family has fought to promote," says the Goose.

"You did it in the name of self-interest," says Cary.

"Those people were prisoners," says the Goose. "I got them out from behind bars . . . on work release. Now they're free—free from this planet, like the mice on a sinking ship."

"You're mad," says Cary.

"Perhaps," says the Goose, "working on a poultry farm exposed me to something that causes residual build up of certain chemicals found in fertilizers. It's had more of an effect on my body than the doctors expected. Perhaps the feathers that poke from my skin fail to compare to what boils beneath the surface." Cary is close enough now that he can tell the Goose is carrying a glass case with the synthetic Elixiumbrium formula inside. "I was doing these men a favor, for they were a part of history, and they don't have to be witness to the final stories of our planet. You, however, are not so lucky."

He boards another submerg-evator. However, the design of this vessel is different, for it is fit with a place to put the synthetic, magnetically charged Elixiumbrium formula. And it's designed to launch the contraption into space with the Goose as the single occupant.

When the elevator doors start closing Cary springs into action, moving quickly. Sounds of the bilge pumps warming up to flood the facility signal a final evacuation of the cave system.

Cary pries open the doors to reach an empty elevator chamber. He must use a great deal of force to jam his fingers and hands between the doors enough to gain leverage to push them entirely apart. Water rushes in through the door, as Cary spots the elevator rising in the chambers, and he's able to grasp a part of its metal undercarriage, but that sharp steel is hard on his hands and quickly mangles them.

The entire contraption within the elevator chamber starts moving at twice the speed of a typical elevator. It picks up speed again, and now it is rushing to the surface. But Cary holds on and braces his body accordingly.

Whey they reach the surface the submerg-evator bobs up

and down while the Goose loads the formula, and a robotic voice inside the elevator says, "Prepare for launch."

The inspector takes a pen from his pocket and jams it through the line of oxygen underneath the elevator. The pierced line bursts open in front of Cary, and like a drake dives for fish, he ducks down under the water before swimming out and away from the vessel.

The Goose opens the door when he discovers a lack of breathable air. He coughs and notices Cary swimming near the shore. Before he can make a move or say a single word a group of owls come from the sky and overtake the vessel.

When he reaches the shore Cary turns back to watch the contraption lose its buoyancy, and no signs of life escape its plunge into the abyss . . . until the owls emerge, one of which holds a corked test tube in its talons.

"Sometimes things are so frightening in life, we comp[illegible] uo.n to uoing what .e .now is stu lly the right thin[illegible] wrote Denzel.

Theo l[illegible] t the tr_p when he c me u.on a bloouied figur[illegible] to the bone an [illegible] at ripped to [illegible] shreds.

"We fin th[illegible] to simply save ourselves," w[illegible]

T.eo [illegible] .tood nonon.t[illegible] [illegible] ming. She moved into the ruin, [illegible] Theo. They na-rad their last [illegible]p before getting [illegible]r

"We have to do it or those we love," wrote [illegible]nz[illegible]l. "

Epilogue

"Now we have floods, great fires, fire burning up the landscapes. All those people," says Oriel to the Brood. "Nobody would be here if those tides had stopped."

The Brood hoots in unison, and Oriel is enveloped in a harmony among the birds. He says to the Brood, while speaking loud to compensate for the hooting, "We have each other to hold, and people do escape from natural disaster, but many do not—Only the strong survive when the lands become nothing more than mud. And tides rule the lands. Perhaps, if we spin the moon to some degree, it could be more catastrophic. What do you suppose?"

The Brood accepts the strange formula that has been proven lethal for ingestion. The owls accept what is necessary to right the tides on planet Earth.

"What the hell happened here?" asks a member of the SWAT team on a megaphone.

"At least you were good enough for something," says Theo as he picks up the badge from around Bruno's neck. Theo goes back to the submerg-evator and says to Cynthia, "Relax. They'll be easy on me as long as they think I'm with a cop—"

When he gets close enough to talk with the SWAT team, he says, "I'm working with Bruno Peters. He's NYPD. He's been shot—send help—"

When he becomes conscious in the ambulance, Bruno tells the whole story to the authorities. Cary has the living proof he didn't do anything to his family to go along with Bruno's testimony, which helps explain their unpleasant conditions.

Emily woke from her dream unharmed in every way. She brags and says that she remembers it all. Her and Henry Edwards have plenty to talk about.

"I mean you and I already stole it once," says Oriel to the Brood, who caws collectively. One owl moves toward Oriel to examine his injured leg. Oriel says, "Alright. I know when to give up—But I'll listen if you call." Oriel makes a hoot like the owls and they join together.

The Brood takes the formula with the plan for each individual owl to disperse on their own, flying along all the continents of the world. Going where the water meets the land, they fly the paths that Oriel had intended to travel with his ballooning.

Since the formula has been lethal for humans to ingest . . . it is likely lethal to owls as well. But something needs to be done, so the owls fly the coasts. Let's hope there's enough of them to recharge the tides before the poison takes its devastating effect. Oriel tracks them along the way and readies his balloon in the chance that one of the owls should fail. He and his balloon stay ready . . . to complete the Elixiumbrium's movement. The timing for this operation . . . is crucial.

Adeline opens her eyes and says to Cary, who is nearby, "I had a terrible dream . . . . I was a spy, I suppose. And you were . . . in trouble with the law . . . ?" Cary is by her side when she says, "You were so stupid to not realize I was a spy the entire time. It was dramatic and everything was unbelievable."

Cary laughs and says, "Sure is unbelievable. You were there. You were there for me . . . for them . . . more than anyone could ask of a mother."

Henry Edwards comes in to ask Cary to read a bedtime story when he sees his mother is awake. He goes from sleepily asking his father to read a story to rubbing his eyes and saying, "Mommy, you're awake."

She stands up and spins in the room, and Cary can't help but remember the woman in the snow who spun before his eyes. He asks her: "Do you remember any of it, dear? How you helped me . . . in your dream." His breath is rhythmic and his eyes water to the brink of letting himself weep.

But she touches his knee and says, "In another dream, I remember there was a man looking for something he lost . . . . Was it an ice skate?" He is surprised and says, "It was!" She goes on to say: "I don't know. I only remember that it was winter. Vinter," she says in a Swedish accent and giggles some at the thought.

She covers her floral tank-top with a dreadful black and slate-grey, striped turtle neck that looks like static on a television screen, and she moves to join her husband and son on the single bed. But suddenly she stops herself from getting comfortable . . . . She darts to the door, rushes back to give her husband and son each a kiss, and she goes into the next room over.

She kisses her daughter on the cheek for the first time. Emily is asleep. She smiles and brushes the girl's hair back.

"Mommy?" asks the child. "Hi, my Em," says the fond mother.

"What are we reading?" asks Cary loud enough for Emily to hear her father is close by. "Is this a new one that Mommy might like, too?" He picks up the book Henry Edwards is holding, he examines it closely enough to make Henry Edwards laugh. Cary picks up his glasses, puts them on, and opens to the first page.

"You're here," says Emily.
"I'll be here, baby," replies her mother.

the phone and controlle
the top drawer. The re
ent.

Cary gasped and sa
ever you are. If you hav
come foreward..."

All at once the line
turned off. Cary felt aro
crimson. evening sunlight
then he nudged the tape r
before reaching the phone

He took the book dow

BIOGRAPHY

for Writer/Creator of

The Procurements of Sonny Valentine: All Kinds of Stories

&

Asleep in the Skies

. . . .

SHAUN VAIN lives in America but travels and writes fiction throughout the world.

HE loves animals and cycling, and he's a naturalist.